Wick's breath hung in his throat . . .

Without breaking stride, the warder grabbed one of the fancy multicolored lanterns from the ship's railing. He turned to face the last Boneblight . . . when the Boneblight dove at him, the warder turned the flame up high and held it up before him.

When the flame touched the Boneblight, it caught fire at once. Screaming and squalling, wings burning quickly, the flaming creature fell into the harbor . . .

Hobnailed boots thundered across the docks, coming toward Wick at a hurried pace.

"There he is!"

A barge pole was quickly passed up to the dwarf. He shoved the end of it down to Wick.

"Now ye just grab onto that and we'll have ye outta them waters in a trice."

Teeth chattering from the cold water, Wick gladly reached for the pole. Even as his hand closed on the pole, the little librarian saw another dwarf bring out a cudgel. Before Wick could move, the dwarf rapped him on the head and everything went black.

The
Rover

Mel Odom

A TOM DOHERTY ASSOCIATES BOOK
NEW YORK

This is a work of fiction. All the characters and events portrayed in this book are either products of the author's imagination or are used fictitiously.

THE ROVER

Copyright © 2001 by Mel Odom

Edited by Brian Thomsen

A Tor Book
Published by Tom Doherty Associates, LLC
175 Fifth Avenue
New York, NY 10010

www.tor.com

Tor® is a registered trademark of Tom Doherty Associates, LLC.

ISBN 0-812-34194-8
Library of Congress Catalog Card Number: 2001027474

First edition: August 2001
First mass market edition: September 2002

Printed in the United States of America

0 9 8 7 6 5 4 3 2 1

This book is dedicated to those individuals who helped me step up to the task.

To my wife, Sherry, and my children, Matthew Lane, Matthew Dain, Montana, Shiloh, and Chandler. With all my love.

To my good friend and compatriot and editor, Brian Thomsen, without whose vision and insight this tale would never have graced these pages. (We matched Wick for tales of derring-do, and these stories alone should stand us to a pint in any alehouse in the country—whatever country!)

To my good friend and agent, Ethan Ellenberg, who has stood with me in the deepest trenches and always fought the good fight. Simply one of the very best in his chosen field.

And to Tom Doherty, who came on board as a believer in the magic of storytelling. Thank you for your trust.

1

A Meeting of Dreadful Portent

Shadows, Wick thought sourly as he studied the treacherous mass of darkness at the end of the long bookcase, *are foul and nasty things. They're mostly useless, only showing someone where he is when he already knows he's there. And what's the good of that?*

Of course, evil things that dwelt in darkness loved shadows because they allowed them to walk in the light of day—just before they pounced on an unsuspecting victim.

Holding tightly onto the glimmerworm candle he carried, Wick paused between two huge bookcases in Hralbomm's Wing of the Great Library and let out a long, quiet breath that whistled slightly between his teeth. The books at his back felt reassuring. At least the thick volumes bound in stone and leather on the split log shelves offered protection from that direction. There was no defense against what possibly hid in the shadows in front of him.

After the slight sound of his inadvertent whistling breath had died away, silence filled the room again. At this time of morning, slightly before eleven, the Great Library was always quiet. The thick stone walls and the cavernous rooms filled with bookcases never allowed the everyday noises of Greydawn Moors, the town farther down the foothills of the Knucklebones Mountains, to enter the library.

Gathering his failing courage, Wick lifted the glimmerworm candle high as he could. The shadows bent back as if afraid of the green-tinged candle flame. The candle was a good one, the delicate blown glass tubing fully two feet long and possessing a fluted reflector plate behind the flame. He'd refilled it only that morning with the dark green lummin juice milked from domestic glimmerworms raised on the island.

The candle had been a gift from his father, Mettarin Lamplighter, and Wick was proud of it. He'd gotten it on one of the last pleasant birthdays he had enjoyed before his father had developed a deep and lasting disappointment in him. It was his father's sighs, Wick often supposed, that were the hardest to bear. No one could sigh so disconsolately as his father could.

Steadying his trembling hand, taking a deep breath, Wick stepped forward on weak knees. "Be warned, large and putrid goblinkin," he said in a deep voice.

He was fairly certain only goblins would lie in wait so silently in the early hours—and it was still before noon!—because trolls and other things too horrible to mention wouldn't lurk about quite so early. Trolls, however, stayed on the alert for new victims to knock on the head and enslave . . . except, of course, for those dwellers that were baked into pies.

"And this is the only warning you shall be given," Wick bravely continued, struggling hard to keep his voice from cracking. "After this, no quarter will be asked, and none given. You face a warrior born this morn," he wanted desperately to rephrase that last, "for I am Edgewick Lamplighter, Master Librarian at the Vault of All Known Knowledge."

He drew himself to his full three feet four inches in

height and tried to look severe, much older than his seventy years which, actually, was quite young as dwellers went and more formidable than life as a librarian had made him. (Dwellers, in general, hardly ever reached four feet in height, so Wick was sometimes considered short even by their standards. Although about the same height as dwarves, dwellers were symmetrically built, not broad-shouldered and barrel chested. Nor were they as slender as elves. Dwellers were just little people, able to live meagerly and on the leavings and—*mostly*— abandoned things of others.)

Wick kept his red-gold hair neat and himself presentable most of the time. As usual, he wore the white-fringed light gray robes of a Third Level Librarian in the Vault of All Known Knowledge. However, he now saw, he hadn't noticed the dark purple chulotzberry stain on his sleeve from this morning.

The shadows twisted and fell back again, as if reluctantly giving ground before the glimmerworm candle.

For a moment, enjoying the power of the flame and the way the title "Master Librarian" rolled so easily from his tongue in the agonizing silence, Wick felt as brave and fierce as Taurak Bleiyz. Taurak had been a dweller as Wick was, but Taurak had been a mighty warrior who had ventured down into the Bleak Pits of Darkhearted Vormoral to save fair Gylesse, the woman he loved above life itself. At least, until the next story. Taurak, as it turned out, was a dweller of considerable appetites and was always about, rescuing one love or another. Of course, Taurak's bravery and mighty strength had also come from carrying his magical warclub, Toadthumper.

Claws skittered in the darkness ahead and the short hairs on Wick's neck stood up.

The little librarian forced himself to breathe. More than anything, he wished he could run from the room. But if someone saw him running, what then? Most of

the other librarians, even the ones at his own low rank-
ing, made it a point to stay away from him. A chance
to ridicule him for running from shadows would be too
much for many of them to resist.

Claws scratched at the stone floor again, but the shadows drew no closer.

Trolls don't have claws, Wick reminded himself, then
instantly remembered, *but they often let their toenails
grow long and curved so they can be used as weapons.*
He waited, pressed tightly against the bookshelves, fearful to make any move. Drawing in a deep breath, he
realized the rotten stench that usually accompanied trolls
wasn't present.

I am not afraid, Wick told himself, raising the candle.
The lummin juice burned steadily even with him jerking
it around and shaking on top of that, proof of his father's
craftsmanship. Panting, he stumbled forward on fear-
numbed feet. *I have slain poison-tongued Terror Toads
alongside Taurak Bleiyz in Donsidance the troll queen's
private chambers. I have climbed the Ogre Leper's Forgotten Maw with Carrad Muzzyl and found the Philos-
opher's Skull.*

The shadows continued to draw back, but the claws
skittered on the stone again. This time they sounded a
little frantic.

I have survived attacks by the undead pirate crew of
Purple Lament *in the Dagger Straits,* Wick went on,
growing a little more confident, *and dug up the treasure
of Captain Kallyn One-Eye.*

It didn't help that he knew all the adventures he
thought of were ones he'd encountered in books. Adventures, at least in real life, were much too dangerous.
He preferred the life of a librarian, even the life of a
Third Level Librarian . . . but still, he loved the excitement that he only borrowed from books.

As Wick neared the end of the bookcase, leaving the

shadows pressed up tight against the wall there, the claws froze and the noise they made faded.

"I'm only toying with you," Wick stated, trying to make his voice steely as he continued to advance. "If you run now, I'll spare your life. I'll—"

Without warning, the little librarian tripped over his own feet. He fell face forward, breaking his fall with one hand and managing to keep the glimmerworm candle whole with the other. He fearfully thrust the candle forward toward the sound of renewed claw skittering, afraid that the creature might attack in his moment of defenselessness.

"I warned you!" Wick shrieked, lying prone with the candle before him, wrapping his other arm around his head to protect his face. "I'm not in the mood for taking prisoners today!" When no attack followed, he spread his fingers and peered cautiously between them.

The candlelight spread its warm, green-tinted glow over the foul fiend that waited on him in the shadows. The creature, scarcely as big as the dweller's fist and covered in soft gray fur, looked up with black, beady eyes beneath pink, shell-like ears. It held a tiny morsel of hard yellow cheese between its front paws.

A mouse, Wick realized with relief, not even a *full-grown rat.* The little librarian breathed a sigh of relief as he watched the tiny pink nose twitching as the mouse continued to frantically nibble at the cheese.

"Aha!" Wick exclaimed, his mind seizing on a new game. He pushed away the fear that had filled him and shoved himself to his feet. The trembling left his knees and he dropped into a swordsman's stance. He'd never had any formal training, but the Vault of All Known Knowledge carried several good treatises on the art, and reading was his life. He let the glimmerworm candle dance at the end of his arm, and made swishing motions that caused the flame to burn brightly for a time. "So, a shape-changing wizard, are you? See how easily I see through your mouse disguise? I am a very experienced warrior. I recognize you for the base-hearted villain you truly are."

The mouse, evidently afraid of a full-grown dweller towering over him, stuffed the cheese crumb into its mouth and darted away.

Wick heaved himself to his feet and flicked his candle-sword through the air. "No evil wizard has ever escaped the righteous indignation of Sir Edgewick Lamplighter, champion swordsmaster and righter-of-wrongdoing." He launched himself in pursuit of the mouse, catching his empty hand on the bookcase and swinging himself about into the next aisle.

Quick as a wink, the mouse scampered on, running over the shoe of the man standing there.

"Ahem." The man cleared his throat disapprovingly.

Wick drew himself up short, narrowly avoiding a collision with the man. "Grandmagister Frollo!" the dweller gasped, suddenly noticing he still held the glimmerworm candle like a sword. He pulled his arm back and looked as innocent as he could. He quickly stepped back three feet, dropping his eyes. "I didn't know you were here."

"I gathered as much, Librarian." Grandmagister Frollo, dressed in the charcoal gray robes that represented his office, cinched by the thin black cord that held the keys to all the rooms of the library, headed the Vault of All Known Knowledge.

As humans went, he was tall and blade-thin, slightly stooped from all the years spent as a librarian hunkered over books. His features were pinched and severe, a step removed from harsh. A long, twisting gray-and-white beard hung to his chest. His hazel eyes held buttermilk yellow dots. Inks of several colors stained the ends of his fingers of both hands from handling quill and inkwell.

"So," Grandmagister Frollo said, putting his hands together behind his back, a sure indication that he was somewhat displeased and was on the verge of a stern lecture, "I see you have saved the library from yet another horrendous threat, Librarian Lamplighter. A shape-shifting wizard this time, no less." The fierce brows knitted together. "How very brave and adventurous of you."

"No, sir," Wick replied quickly, "that was purely in jest. Merely something to amuse myself. I was only chasing the mouse away before it could disturb the books."

The grandmagister nodded. "I suppose that would explain all the shrieking I heard only a moment ago."

"Well—" Wick's face burned fiercely in embarrassment as he sought for an excuse. Preferably, one that he hadn't used before, though there had to have been precious few of those. At the moment he couldn't think of a single one.

The mouse hesitated at the end of the bookcase, its cheeks puffy with cheese. The black eyes gleamed in the candlelight as if it found merriment in Wick's plight. Then it was gone, scuttling under the bookcase and vanishing from sight.

"Well," Grandmagister Frollo prompted.

"I didn't exactly know that it was a mouse at first," Wick admitted glumly.

"You didn't know? Why, it looked every bit the mouse to me."

"Mouses aren't always what they appear," Wick said weakly. "In Roltho's *Bestiary of Furry Friends* there is mention of at least fourteen—"

"Mouses?" Now a tinge of outrage rang in the grand-magister's voice.

"Mice," Wick replied quickly. "I meant *mice*." The

proper use of language was the grandmagister's pet peeve.

"I happen to be familiar with Roltho's work," Grandmagister Frollo stated. "None of the twenty-seven varieties of mouse-looking creatures he documents happen to be shape-changing wizards."

Wick pursed his lips. He lifted the candle. "It was very dark where I found the mouse, sir."

Grandmagister Frollo nodded. "Um-hum. Not being able to see the mouse clearly, then, you believed it to be a shape-changing wizard."

"That's not entirely correct, Grandmagister."

The grandmagister's gaze turned fiercely dark. He was never, *never,* NEVER told he was wrong.

"Begging your pardon, sir," Wick apologized, bowing deeply. "What I meant to say was that I at first believed the mouse to be a troll."

Grandmagister Frollo shook his head and *tsk*ed loudly. "Librarian Lamplighter, there never have and there will simply never be any trolls in this great library. I refuse to allow it."

"Of course, sir."

"It is your imagination that misleads you," the grandmagister said disgustedly. "If I have taught you anything in the years that you have worked here, surely you remember what I have said about imagination."

" 'Imagination, whether trifling or wild,' " Wick intoned guiltily, slumping his shoulders, "dulls or shackles an otherwise orderly and logical mind, and wastes thinking power that could surely be put to good use elsewhere.' "

"Precisely. Now you see again for yourself what harm can be caused by this—" Grandmagister Frollo hesitated at word choice, which Wick knew was a very bad thing, for the man never minced and never hesitated over words, despising those who did, "*aberration* you exhibit."

Wick winced, suddenly feeling as though his whole cherished career as a librarian—even a Third Level Librarian after all these years—teetered on the brink of disaster.

"This *imagination* of yours has been responsible for You giving yourself a good scare," the grandmagister continued, "and for your toppling Snerchal's *Adventures in the Writhing Snake Mountains*, Astomasq's *Once a Thergalian Thief*, Zeltam's two-volume discourse *Caravaning in the Great Whiskery Desert: Before and After*, Pohlist the One-Handed's *A More Cautious Guide to Roc Hunting: Beware the Really Big Snappa!*, and Iskar Shayl's *Magic Lantern Story-Telling* to the floor."

Wick didn't doubt the grandmagister's guesses. Two of the six at least were correct. The librarians in the Vault of All Known Knowledge firmly believed that Grandmagister Frollo knew where every book was, in what room it was stacked, and when it had first been brought in from the outside world. Since no books had been brought into the library in hundreds of years, it was considered quite an accomplishment.

"Yes, Grandmagister." Wick hurried around the bookcase and quickly picked the books up. He lovingly placed the tomes back on the shelf in the correct order.

"When I started looking for you this morning and didn't find you in your room, the kitchen or your assigned wing," the grandmagister said, "I knew I would find you here. You were returning a book, weren't you?"

Wick's face flushed with shame, which barely outweighed the sheer terror of having the grandmagister search for him. *What can he possibly want?*

"Yes," Wick admitted. "But it *was* only one book." Through a supreme effort of will the grandmagister wasn't aware of, the dweller had managed to curb his reading binge of the volumes in Hralbomm's Wing.

Grandmagister Frollo's eyes roved the shelves in obvious disdain. "What book was it?"

Wick only hesitated a moment. "Slanskirsk's *1007 Zenkariquian Nights*." It had been a truly wonderful book, a thousand and seven stories about wizards and warriors and dungeons and death traps. The dweller had been captivated, reading well into the morning hours.

"I suppose it had to be the annotated version by Vassely, the Mad Monk of Bethysar," Grandmagister Frollo stated with regret.

"Yes." Wick's shoulders slumped in dismay. The book had been a massive tome, all the book a single dweller could carry and still stealthily stumble up and down staircases without breaking his neck.

The grandmagister stalked down the bookcase, eyeing all the volumes distastefully. "You know how I feel about Hralbomm's Wing, Librarian Lamplighter."

"Yes, sir." Everyone at the Vault of All Known Knowledge knew the grandmagister's thinking on every room in the great library.

"This wing is filled with frivolity, something that has no place in a proper history of the world. And that is what we have here in the Vault of All Known Knowledge. We are the last bastion of hope, the final torch that will hold back that dreadful beast, Ignorance, father of the corrupting twins, Superstition and Irrationality."

Solemnly, feeling as though he had an anchor about his neck, Wick followed his master. After the Cataclysm had decimated populations and ravaged the world of whole races, when the very idea of civilization had hovered on the brink of disaster, the Old Gods had engineered a plan that had caused the construction of the Vault of All Known Knowledge.

Wick took pride in the fact that a dweller had been chosen to care for the First Book, the one the library designers had used to safeguard the island and start building. As those men had constructed the great stone edifice, others had searched out books lost in the world and brought them back. Now they had each and every one, and so it would be until a future grandmagister felt it safe to return them to the world. Until that time, dwellers would continue to serve the grandmagisters of the library.

"Imagination, as I have profusely illustrated upon more than one occasion," Grandmagister Frollo pontificated, "is simply a marriage of convenience between misinformation and an impatient passion to understand. A truly educated scholar *knows*, while an uneducated charlatan blends fact and fiction into a concoction gossip-mongers want to hear. A true student washes his hands, and his brain, of such things."

Wick trailed a hand over the book spines, struggling to keep from taking a tome from the shelf when he spied an interesting title. However, he did remember where they were located. He managed to snatch his hand way just before Grandmagister Frollo looked back at him to make sure he was paying attention.

"Were it within my power," the grandmagister declared, "I would rid the library of these particular books. They offer nothing educational, and only rob an impulsive librarian with an attention deficit of his already finite time in this place."

"Begging the grandmagister's pardon," Wick said, "but I wasn't reading that book during the time allotted to my duties here at the library. I never neglect those."

"I know you do not." Grandmagister Frollo stopped unexpectedly and turned to face the little dweller. The old man shook his head sadly. "I wasn't talking about your duty periods, Librarian Lamplighter. A librarian lives by the time that he spends between the covers of a book. You spend more than most. However, I hate to see that time go unrecognized by you as a precious commodity and squandered on volumes such as these." He swept a hand in irritation at the bookcases surrounding them.

"Forgive me, grandmagister," Wick apologized, "for I did not mean to anger you."

"You don't make me angry," the old man snapped. "In fact of the matter, you vex me, Librarian Lamplighter, you vex me like a good dose of chafing wartneedle pox. By the First Book, if most of my other librarians had the zeal and the passion, as well as the sheer grasp, you exhibit for the written word, the task of finally cataloguing all the volumes in this building would not seem so insurmountable."

Pride swelled within Wick. He'd labored hard at the library for years only to never progress past his current level. No one had ever been a Third Level Librarian for as long as he had. *The grandmagister* has *noticed!* Suddenly, the thought that Grandmagister Frollo had been searching for him seemed not so daunting. Perhaps his promotion, which Wick considered to be long overdue, was again up for review.

"Yet," the old man continued in a more strident, thundering tone, "you insist on cluttering that great pumpkin of a head of yours with the most trivial literature contained within these magnificent halls." The grandmagister exhaled deeply and continued a little more calmly, but the effort showed. "I have tried to understand it, tried even to believe that you will some day grow past these debilitating pursuits, but there are days like today when my doubts overpower my dedicated attempts to believe those things."

Just as quickly as the feeling of pride had come to Wick, it went away even faster. The little dweller gazed down at his unpolished shoes and his guilt suddenly seemed too much to bear. His father was disappointed in him, and so was the grandmagister. "I humbly apologize again, Grandmagister. I will try to devote myself more to the readings you suggest."

"Very well, Librarian Lamplighter." The grandmagister cleared his throat. "However, I didn't seek you out to remonstrate you over your reading habits. Despite your diversions and incessant ramblings through this great library, I've found you to be more dependable than many."

Now this was looking up. The air returned to Wick's lungs. "Thank you, Grandmagister."

"That was an observation," Grandmagister Frollo advised, "not a compliment."

"Of course, Grandmagister."

"I have a task for you."

"Gladly, Grandmagister."

"I need you to go down to the Yondering Docks and deliver this," Grandmagister Frollo pulled a thick package wrapped tightly in cheesecloth and twine from beneath his robes, "to the Customs House for shipping."

"Of course, Grandmagister. What is it?"

Grandmagister Frollo blinked irritably. "Librarian Lamplighter, I have taken obvious care that this package is wrapped securely." He popped one of the tight twine lines, making it thrum against the cheesecloth for a moment. "Were I to hire a town crier to go about announcing the package and what it contains, I think that would defeat the purpose of the wrapping."

"Of course, Grandmagister. I was only inquiring because I wanted to know how best to handle the package."

"With care, I would think, that would reflect somewhere between the concern one would show for an elven blown-glass figurine and a goblin hog's-head cheese."

Bile rose at the back of Wick's throat momentarily at the thought of a goblin hog's-head cheese. It was made, of course, from real hogs' heads. "I could take the package to the ship it's going out on. I really don't mind."

"Whether you mind is irrelevant," the grandmagister said. "If I'd wanted you to take the package to the ship, I'd have asked. What I want you to do is to deliver it to the Customs House."

"Will someone pick it up there?"

A frown turned the grandmagister's face sour. "No, Librarian Lamplighter, I'm sending the package to the Customs House to rot."

Wick's face flamed. He made himself be quiet.

"Are we quite clear on your duties now?"

"Yes, Grandmagister."

"Oh, and this letter as well." The old man produced a letter. There was no address on the letter. The insignia of the grandmagister's ring—an open book and quill— was pressed into the wax seal.

Wick took the letter. "Yes, Grandmagister." He looked at the package and the letter, and his curiosity gnawed at him from the back of his mind like spoor beetles, which were known to crawl for miles after only getting a fragrant hint of a fresh prize waiting to be claimed.

"Off with you, Librarian Lamplighter," the grandmagister ordered, shooing Wick with one ink-stained hand. "There are only so many daylight hours librarians are graced with, and many, many pages to turn."

"Of course, Grandmagister." Wick bowed and backed from the room, carrying the heavy package in one hand, the letter in the other. "You can count on me."

The old man glanced at him threateningly. "If I can't, Librarian Lamplighter, I know where you sleep."

2

Yondering Docks

Greydawn Moors bustled with activity. Normally, the city was early to bed and early to rise, making the most of the natural light. But any time the cargo ships put into the harbor, the dwellers and dwarves alike hastened to get their goods and wares down to the docks to sell or trade them. The island was mostly self-sufficient, but there were still a number of foods and textiles that had to be traded for, as well as creature comforts and new seed stock for the various planting seasons for the grain fields and corn fields that lay just outside the city.

Wick guided the cart through the main street that cut through the heart of the city. The cart's wheels clacked across the seashells scattered across the street with severe snapping noises. Dwarven road builders dredged up fresh seashells from the north coastline once a month, hauled them by cart into the city, and patched road sections damaged by constant use.

Turning onto Raysun Street, Wick glanced at the old wishing well on the corner where dweller graybeards sat on hardwood benches and spoke to each other of their problems, dreams, and memories. The little librarian remembered going there with his grandfather, sitting on the old man's knee and listening to the stories they told that had been handed down to them from generations past. Grandpa Deigeh always had a pocketful of cheeryberry licorice in those days, and the cheeryberry flavor had always left Wick with a smile on his face.

The dwarven houses and shops on either side of the street were most readily noticeable. Crafted with dwarven skill and a love for straight lines and permanency, the stone houses were slightly larger than dweller homes. Each house corner was perfectly squared off and each door frame and window was perfectly level. The chimneys were works of art. They used wood to accentuate the use of the carved stone blocks. The dwarves painted their homes in staid, solid colors taken from the hues of stone and woods they worked with. Their gardens were small and neatly organized, filled with small carvings of animals and people that moved and danced when the wind blew the small vanes that powered them.

Dweller homes, on the other hand, tended to be constructed in a much more haphazard fashion. Where the dwarves took time to clear away old buildings and homes that had fallen in disrepair, the dwellers simply tore out the worst of the areas and shored up the rest, leaving sagging walls and off-center, patched roofs. Dwellers were used to living in spaces between anything that had spaces between, including other buildings, in alleys, and rock formation. There was safety in numbers. Chimneys didn't go straight up from dwellers' homes; they staggered up through roofs, twisting and rambling, a hodgepodge of stones thick with mortar.

Dweller homes were painted in bright colors in outlandish combinations, and festooned with objects and ornamentation scavenged from everything that caught a dweller's wandering, acquisitive eye and fancy. Most of what caught dwellers' eyes glittered or gleamed or glistened. Shiny shapes dangled from under the sagging eaves and were hammered onto doors and walls. All of those reflective surfaces were polished mirror-bright.

Usually two or more dweller homes were built together, leaning against one another for support.
Sometimes as many as a dozen houses were clustered
together, as long as every house could maintain its own
entrance and exit. Sometimes those entrances and exits
included stairways and crosswalks that extended over
other houses. They reminded Wick of frog eggs to a
degree, all of them touching each other, independent yet
needing the support of the others.

All in all, dweller housing tended to seriously irk the
dwarven population. The dwarves took pains to see to it
that their houses stayed well away from nearby dweller
houses. If they didn't, the dwellers had a tendency to
build additions onto their houses, encroaching on dwarven territory.

The little librarian eyed the sun dropping quietly in
the western horizon and continued on to the docks.

Wick stared in wonderment at all the tall-masted ships
berthed in the harbor just beyond Yondering Docks.
Even after reading so many books about ships and sailors and sailing, he'd had no comprehension of how big
the vessels really were. He pulled the cart to a stop beside a sailcloth-maker's shop and stared at the ships in
total awe.

Fog clung to the harbor, thick, gray cottony clouds of
it scudding close to the bruised-purple water. Close in,
he could see through the fog and the shapes of men and
ships, but further out, the fog was impenetrable, leaving
the rest of the world to the imagination.

Some days, Wick had heard, the fog burned off and
a man standing on the shore had a clear view of the
Blood-Soaked Sea as it stretched north and east. The
south side of the island rarely experienced the fogs that

the harbor area was filled with most of the time. A few of the older dwellers liked to tell tales of the dark days after the Cataclysm and how the Builders had worked their sorcery, bringing in the clouds to hide the harbor from goblin and goblinkin eyes. The dwarves that lived in Greydawn Moors maintained that the weather was a natural occurrence, born of the land and sea.

The dwarves liked to take their magicks in small doses. Humans had always wielded the great magick of legend, though only a few of them. Still, those few who possessed such power seemed to know no bounds. Elves knew forest magicks, spells and wards that helped with the guardianship of the lands they had sworn to protect. And dwarves, with their canny knowledge of metals, gems, and stone, swore they knew no magick at all, only the trades their fathers had taught them. Occasional dwellers and other races knew only small magicks that went over well in taverns but offered no real power.

Wick wished he could have seen out into the Blood-Soaked Sea. He didn't know when he would get down to the docks again.

Seashells had been brought in from the oceans, cracked under the hammers of dwarves, then laid thickly over the mud that wound in between stone warehouses and businesses around the docks. As a result, the roads looked white and pearl gray with a few pinks thrown in. On those few clear days, shortly after a rain, Wick's oldest brother Moryhr had described the roads as gleaming iridescence.

Moryhr's recounting of the roads on those days had always reminded Wick of the tales of the Ceffalk Elves. The Ceffalk Elves had disappeared even before the Cataclysm, but they reportedly built magick roads that extended deeply into the past and sometimes into twisted worlds that might have been. These days, the Ceffalk

Elven roads were only tales, and no one knew if they had really ever existed.

Nearly all of the buildings around the docks showed dwarven skills. A few ambitious dwellers still maintained a presence in the Yondering Docks, but the harbor area was generally known as a dangerous place. There were far easier and safer ways to live in Greydawn Moors, and dwellers as a rule preferred those ways instead of the adventurous ones.

Out in the harbor, bells rang, echoing over the water and seeming to come from the fogs. Wick's skin goose-bumped as he heard them. When he was a child, his mother had told him stories of terrible monsters the dwarves had captured from the Blood-Soaked Sea and brought into the harbor to aid in its protection from the goblins. The monsters, his mother had told him, preferred the taste of goblin flesh, but had been wreathed in collars with great bells on them to warn friendly ships that the monsters had surfaced and could pose sailing hazards.

The bells were actually on the small longboats that carried cargo in from ships out in the harbor that couldn't reach a berth. The pilots clanged them continuously so other longboats and ships would look for them in the thick fog. The clangor of the bells mixed in with the shouted commands of captains and quartermasters to crew as well as conversations yelled between ships. The creak of the ships and the litany of pinging noises from the mast riggings added to the cacophony.

The Customs House sat on a spit of land thirty feet above the rest of the docks. The construction was definitely dwarven. Huge stone blocks had been hauled up to the area and cunningly crafted into large, interlocking puzzle pieces. The stones showed different striations, from wavy curves to ragged jags, and colors that ranged from blacks to blues to reds. No stone was colored or shaped like any other. Wick couldn't even begin to guess how long the construction had taken. The building stood four stories tall, with elegant balconies and a steep roof that centered around a lighthouse that went up another forty feet.

A well-traveled road covered in flagstones wound up a ridge that led to the Customs House doors. Two small stone bridges spanned wide ditches along the way. A handful of carts stood in the area before the building, though Wick noticed that a number of captains and quartermasters simply walked back and forth.

The little librarian urged the mule forward again, heading for the Customs House. He knew he had to finish grandmagister's assigned task and return to the Library quickly.

The waiting room in the Customs House was ornate. Wick gazed in wonder at the paintings that decorated the walls. He recognized some of them as works that had been done before the Cataclysm. Elegant dwarven furniture provided seating in small groups around low tables or at half a dozen desks. Most of those areas were taken already.

"So *you're* the one," the Customs House clerk announced when Wick finally reached him. The clerk was gray-haired and quite well advanced into his years. Ink gleamed wetly on his thumb and first two fingers, but Wick noted that none of the ink left smears on the papers he labored over.

"I'm the one?" the little librarian repeated, not sure at all what the clerk was referring to.

The clerk looked at the little librarian curiously, then frowned sternly. "Yes. A human has been here three times to pick up this package."

"I got here as quickly as I could," Wick said. "It is a long trip from the Library."

"So it is," the clerk replied, poking at the package experimentally with his quill. "The man waiting to pick this up will be quite relieved to see it."

"Of course," Wick said. *Is he here?* He glanced around the large room quickly, but no one stepped forward to claim the package. "May I tell the grandmagister it has been delivered?"

"Of course," the clerk said, handing Wick a receipt. "We're the best Customs House around."

Wick also knew they were the *only* Customs House. He took the receipt and carefully put it away. But questions he knew he shouldn't have been thinking about filled his mind.

Outside the Customs House, Wick wasn't able to let go of his curiosity. It was, he knew, a dweller's worst fault and greatest weakness. He waited, watching the people who entered the building.

Nearly ten minutes later, the arrival of a tall human pricked Wick's interest. At first glance the tall man's long stride was deceiving, not giving away how fast he covered the ground. He came on foot, a broad-shouldered man dressed in worn brown warder's leathers. A long sword hung at his left hip and he kept his hand on it as he hurried. He wore his dark brown hair cut short, mostly squared off, and his face was tanned and sharp-featured. He vanished inside the Customs House and reappeared almost instantly with Grandmagister Frollo's package. He walked down the long trail back toward the harbor area, glancing around him often.

Probably, Wick thought, *most people won't even notice him watching so carefully.* But the little librarian had. The man's behavior was certainly circumspect.

Wick took off after the long-legged warder. He stayed to the other side of the street, letting the human walk along the street nearest the docks, and tried to stay out of sight. As the little librarian dodged between the buildings, he tried to remember everything he'd read in *Maktorleq's Art of Shadowing, a Guide to Subterfuge for the Men Behind the Kings.*

The warder's behavior became more defensive as he stepped down into the shadows among the buildings fronting the docks. Dusk had thickened to the west, Wick knew, because the fog seemed darker back in that direction, and dark gloom had settled in over the city. It wouldn't be long before night covered the harbor.

Without warning, the warder turned and strode down an alley between two warehouses that had closed for the night. His reflection passed swiftly across the glass in the small windows, and his outline dimmed slightly in the thick fog.

Across the street, Wick hesitated, watching the man walk away. *You have to know what he is about,* he told himself, *or you won't have a decent night's sleep for a month.*

The little librarian hurried into the alley. The air between the two warehouses absolutely reeked of foul odors. Rotting vegetables as well as chicken and pig bones littered the area between the warehouses.

The stone warehouses were a hundred fifty feet long by Wick's estimation, and stood two stories tall. The eaves hung well out from the buildings, almost touching in the center.

Some primitive instinct made Wick freeze. A skittering noise sounded on the rooftop to his right. Dread filled him as he looked up.

What looked like a misshapen elf hung upside down from the eave of the building. The creature was long and thin the way elves were, but it had a squared-off head

and blunt features that included a massive, piggish snout
and two ivory fangs that curled up on either side. The
thing held onto the underside of the eave with curled
toes and one hand. The other hand held a short scythe.
The thing's shoulders were narrow but held great bumps
on them, and it was the color of old mahogany. Deep-
set ruby eyes gleamed as they focused on Wick. The
thing cocked its head like a dog listening to a flute
player. The puzzled expression it made showed primarily
through the thick brows, hardly touching the lipless
mouth.

A hissing snarl came from the warehouse on the other
side of the alley, and Wick suddenly knew the creature
above and in front of him wasn't the only one there. He
wished he could turn and run, but his legs seemed
locked. He turned his head slowly and spotted two more
of the creatures hanging from the eaves to the left. Another creature moved across the warehouse roof in a low
crawl. Claws scraped the slate tiles.

"Not thisss one, my brothersss. Thisss one isss nothing
to usss."

Fearfully, Wick turned to look at the first creature he'd
seen. It had turned its head back toward the human warder striding into the fog.

"Come, we mussst go!" the creature declared urgently.

Wick watched in astonishment as the creature released
its hold on the eaves and dropped like a rock. For a
moment he thought the thing would flatten against the
fog-dampened ground. Then it unfurled great leathery
wings that caught the air with a liquid *pop*. Only then
did Wick realize that the foulness that he'd smelled actually came from the creatures, and that odor—like the
trapped musk of a desecrated grave—told him that the
creatures were Boneblights.

Lord Kharrion had fashioned the first Boneblights toward the end of the Cataclysm, when the forces of good

repelled his attacks at last and started to drive him from the world. As each battle successfully won by the elves, dwarves and humans pushed the skirmish lines back, the Goblin Lord had used some of the oldest magicks of evil to raise a new army.

On moonless nights, Lord Kharrion's sorcery drew the bones of his conquered goblin troops from the earth of the battlefields where they'd been lost and left unmourned. Then the Goblin Lord had wedded the decayed flesh and bone to the raw pain and anger of innocents he had tortured to reave those emotions. There was nothing in the Boneblights of the individuals that had been killed so that they might live except the emotion of his or her death.

Boneblights did not truly live, yet they were not undead as some creatures were. They had been fierce warriors, truly dedicated to Lord Kharrion, and served as his personal guard at the end. After his defeat, all the Boneblights were believed destroyed. However, talespinners still told stories of the creatures.

Four other Boneblights joined the first, swooping low, then gliding to the end of the alley. They went quickly, cutting through the swirling fog easily.

Now run! Wick told himself. But for some reason he couldn't follow his own advice. His legs moved, but they carried him toward the end of the alley where the creatures had flown.

The human warder had reached the docks, still watching carefully. But he didn't hear the Boneblights gliding up behind him.

"Look out, warder!" Wick yelled. "Boneblights follow you!"

The warder turned, drawing his long sword in a twinkling. His face was grim as he surveyed the five Boneblights closing on him. He tucked Grandmagister Frollo's package inside his shirt and took up his sword in two hands. Instead of fleeing from the Boneblights, the warder stepped toward them.

The sword flashed, catching lantern light from a nearby cargo ship, then cleaved through the lead Boneblight's head down to its shoulders. Boneblights had no blood in them, but the wound was still gruesome. A Boneblight's head was its only weakness. Once the head was shorn from its shoulders or crushed, a Boneblight turned to dust and broken bones.

The warder dropped from the path of his second attacker, then pushed himself up on his free hand, sprinting quickly toward a nearby frame where a pair of dwarven sailors mended a net.

Wick still ran toward the warder, drawn by the mystery of Grandmagister Frollo's package and the inability to quit the scene. *Oh, curiosity is surely a dweller's most unkind doom!* he lamented as he rushed out onto the street.

Quick as a fox, the warder dropped and slithered under the net as the second Boneblight struck. The creature's claws raked the air where the warder had been only a moment ago, then it smashed into the net. The dwarven sailors that had been at the mending backed away at once, drawing the long daggers at their waists and swearing.

On the other side of the net, still prone on his chest, the warder slashed through the nearest support pole with a single sword stroke, allowing his attacker to become entangled in the folds of the net. Rising effortlessly to his feet, the warder grabbed the lummin juice lantern from the keg where the dwarven sailors had put it to work on the net. He smashed the lantern over the third Boneblight's skull, coating it in lummin juice and dodging out of the way. The foul creature screamed angrily.

"What goes on there?" a watchman from a nearby ship demanded in a hoarse voice.

"Boneblights!" one of the dwarven sailors who had been mending nets cried out. "We've been attacked by Boneblights!"

Confusion swiftly passed along the nearby ships. It wasn't unheard of for pirates to pillage plunder quietly from ships lying at anchorage. The sailors didn't leave their vessels, but they did batten down the hatches, shouting out orders and lighting more lummin lanterns. The eddying fog covering the harbor so thickly masked some of the action taking place on shore.

"Someone send for the harbor guard!" another sailor roared out. "Whoever them people are a-makin' all that noise, why the harbor guard will slap knots on their gourds right quick enough!"

The harbor guard, Wick thought to himself as he hid behind an empty wagon only forty or so feet from the netbound Boneblight, *would be helpful.* The harbor guard had a reputation for no-nonsense dealings, and oftentimes were the heroes of one tale and villains of the very next.

Before the warder could set himself for the fourth Boneblight, the creature raked long nails across the man's chest, ripping his blouse and scoring the skin beneath. The warder swung his long sword as he turned, avoiding most of the Boneblight's attack, but only buried the blade across the creature's back where it did no real harm.

Wick saw pain etch the warder's face as blood soaked his shirt. The warder stumbled against a stack of crates awaiting shipment, ducking under the remaining Boneblights' attack. Turning, the warder ducked through the stacks of the crates, using their closeness against his pursuers.

One of the Boneblights landed on the crates. From the way its arms and legs bent, Wick suddenly realized that they had more joints than a human's, elf's, or dwarf's.

Then the Boneblight sat back on its haunches, cocking its head to one side and then the other as it tried to follow its prey within the maze of crates. Seeing it like that reminded the little librarian very much of a praying mantis.

The wind gusted, picking up a small envelope near the net that still held one of the Boneblights captive.

Wick knew the envelope hadn't been there earlier. *There's only one place that could have come from,* he realized. *I wonder if I can get to it before one of the Boneblights spots me?* Then he realized what he'd thought and shook his head at himself. Only the most grisly fates awaited any dweller that started any thought with *I wonder.*

Still, he did wonder if he could get to the letter now gleefully hopping across the sandy shoreline. He was terribly quick, after all. He glanced back at the warder, seeing that the three surviving Boneblights had clustered around the crates.

Unable to bear his curiosity any more and wanting desperately to know why any package the grandmagister could have sent would have been of interest to Boneblights, Wick sipped a quick breath. Of course, it was possible that the Boneblights were simply looking for the warder and it had nothing to do with the package at all.

The warder's sword licked out, shearing the head from another Boneblight that collapsed into a heap of dust and bones.

Taking that as an omen, though dwellers were raised from an early age never to trust such things, Wick sprinted toward the letter. He glanced fearfully in the direction of the warder and the two Boneblights. Drawing on the great speed and dexterity that dwellers had and kept despite how round some of them got, the little librarian scooped the envelope up from the sand. It was still sealed, although the wax was cracked, and he could tell the fine writing had been done by Grandmagister Frollo's hand.

"Foul guttersssnipe," an evil voice rasped. "Dwellersss alwaysss take thingsss that do not belong to them. Ssso quick to run, ssso quick to hide. Mussst punisssh you!"

3

Boneblights

Renewed terror suddenly flooded Wick's heart as he glanced up at the Boneblight snugged up in the net and hanging from the remaining pole. The creature snapped its razored fangs through the net strands, making bigger the hole it had already started.

"Yaaahhh!" Wick screamed in wide-eyed panic. He was no hero to confront a creature as darkly evil or powerful as a Boneblight. He had absolutely *no* wish to do that, and not even a weapon to do it with. The little librarian turned and tried to run, but his feet slid out from under him in the loose sand. The crack of leathery wings behind him told him the Boneblight was in pursuit.

Glancing back over his shoulder, Wick saw the Boneblight fly into the air for a short distance, then come straight for him with a distended maw and reaching claws. Galvanized into action, Wick pushed himself back *toward* the Boneblight, knowing the creature couldn't turn in that direction in mid-flight. He remembered that from a warder work on the habits of flying predators.

After missing Wick, the Boneblight pulled up at the last moment, spreading the great wings and catching the wind so that it rose. Its claws trailed briefly through the sand.

Sailors hung over the edges of nearby ships with lanterns in their fists, striving to see. The pale light hardly made a dent in the gloomy fog that clouded the shore, but it was enough so that Wick could see the Boneblight better. And he knew if he could see the Boneblight, it could certainly see him.

The little librarian scrambled to his feet and fled back toward the wagon. It was the nearest cover available to him. He felt the Boneblight's merciless gaze on him, knowing it was coming around for another attempt. Clutching the envelope tightly in his fist, Wick dove under the wagon. The heavy *thump!* of the Boneblight slamming into the side of the wagon sounded almost immediately afterward.

Although he didn't want to, Wick turned to look. *Did it fly over the wagon, only bumping it in passing?* He needed to know that before he darted from the other side and tried to run back through the alley.

The Boneblight lay on the ground at the side of the wagon. It groaned in pain, something Wick would never have believed Boneblights could or would do, and put one hand to its head.

If only the Boneblight had hit the wagon harder, Wick lamented. But he seemed to be having a run of bad luck today. At the front of the wagon, the horses stamped in consternation, pulling at their load but halted by the chocks blocking the front wheels.

Beyond the horses, the warder broke free of the crates and the two Boneblights striving to get him. He dashed across the sandy beach, covering the ground quickly.

Wick suddenly felt as though his right ankle had been gripped in an iron band. He looked down and saw that the Boneblight had seized his ankle in its thin, bony hand. Malevolent red lights flickered in its eyes and it distended its jaws, intending to bite the little librarian's leg.

"Nooo!" Wick yelped hoarsely. He kicked his free foot into the Boneblight's forehead as it snapped its jaws tight. The sharp fangs missed him by a scant inch but shredded the lower hem of his robe. A desperate plan filled the little librarian's mind. Simply trying to escape the Boneblight by running under the other side of the wagon wasn't going to do. He recalled a daring escape attempt that Galadryn Carrolic had used to escape a pair of ferocious beasts in Deepmud Bogs.

He kicked his feet against the sandy shore, inadvertently breathing in some of the fine dust. Despite the fact that the Boneblight was there to very probably rend him limb from limb, Wick sneezed so hard his ears popped. *Oh, and wouldn't that make a fine epitaph,* he thought. *Brought unto death by a lowly sneeze.* He sneezed twice more, great blowing gusts that tossed more sand in all directions, and one of them that drove his head sharply up into the wagon bed.

The horses stamped in frustration and fear as they pulled at the wagon. The wheels rolled momentarily up on the big chocks, but didn't get up high enough to go over.

"Easy!" Wick called as he crawled rapidly under the wagon on elbows and knees. He glanced back and saw the Boneblight hissing angrily and swiping under the wagon with its claws. Hurriedly, he stuffed the grandmagister's letter into a pocket of his robes.

Flipping over onto his back, Wick kicked first one wooden chock from under the wagon's front wheels, then the other. He saw the Boneblight crawling under the wagon now, hissing as it clawed its way toward him. The horses stamped close to the little librarian's head, shaking the traces, no longer aware that the chocks had been moved.

"Haw, horses!" Wick yelled. "Haw, haw!" Then he reached up for the wagon tree. Before he could grab it, though, the horses took off. In frightened disbelief, the little librarian watched as the wagon shot by overhead, pulling the tree out of his reach. "No, horse! Whoa, horse!"

But the fear-maddened animals made no attempt to stop. Their hooves thudded close to Wick's head, throwing sand into his face. The little librarian forced himself to remain still to avoid the churning wheels. He heard a sickening crunch of bone and waited to feel the pain in his legs, thinking either the Boneblight had gotten him or the wagon had.

After the wagon passed, he sat up, expecting to see the Boneblight coming for his throat. Instead, the Boneblight lay in several pieces, smashed beneath the wagon wheels. Several of those pieces had once been the creature's skull. Wick surveyed the disassembled Boneblight in total awe.

"Are ye all right?" someone asked.

Rough hands helped Wick to his feet. He looked up into a dwarven face that showed concern. "Why, yes," the little librarian answered, truly astonished. "Though I didn't expect to be."

The dwarf kicked the pile of ash and broken bones in disgust, but a little trepidation as well. "Boneblights. Hmph! Thought we'd seen the last of them things." A crowd began to gather from a nearby tavern, pooling around different lummin juice lanterns as if to ward off the night. "I never thought I'd meet someone that had actually done for one of them blasted things."

"Actually, I—" Wick started to explain that the wagon had accidentally run the Boneblight down, but he heard the whispered conversations by the tavern's patrons and thought better of that. "Actually, that's the first Boneblight I've struck down."

"Oh, so ye're new at this Boneblight fightin', are ye?" the dwarf asked, eyeing Wick more boldly.

Wick thought quickly, not liking the idea of losing the sudden popularity he had gained. Being the center of attention, especially positive attention, felt quite good. And positive attention from others was something that dwellers enjoyed. He cleared his throat. "What I meant to say was that this is my first Boneblight *today*." *There,* the little librarian thought as he looked at all the surprised faces around him, *that sounded suitably impressive.*

"Well, ye're in luck this evening," one crusty old salt stated, " 'cause there was a mess of 'em a-headed thataway." He pointed in the direction the human warder had run.

The warder! In all the excitement, Wick had forgotten about the man and Grandmagister Frollo's package.

"An' if ye're in such an all-fired hurry to find them Boneblights," the old salt said, "ye can even borrow Dhaobin's horse."

The crowd cheered and a sorrel gelding was quickly brought out. The saddlebags were stamped with the official seal of the Customs House.

"Dhaobin might not like me taking his horse," Wick protested.

"Dhaobin delivers packages to them what can't get out after them," the old salt said. "He's in the tavern yonder gettin' a head start on sleepin' off what's gonna be a miserable bender. By the time he wakes up in the morning, ye'll have done for all them Boneblights an' that ol' nag will be none the worse for it." The old man turned to the others. "Get him up in that saddle, boys. Any man what wants to fight Boneblights and such surely deserves the loan of a good horse."

Before Wick could politely turn down such a generous offer, he found himself lifted and put astride the sorrel.

Someone slapped the reins into his hands, then slapped the horse on the rump, sending the animal careening wildly through the docks.

The little librarian held onto the saddle horn and yelled in fear. *Dwellers* aren't *men of action!* he screamed inside his mind. *We're peace lovers, book lovers!* He guessed that the men in the tavern had been too deeply into their cups to remember that. His feet didn't reach the stirrups and he bounced crazily, almost falling off. The horse had the bit in its teeth and Wick was unable to pull back on the reins sufficiently hard enough to halt the fleeing creature. He only hoped it had enough sense to turn away from a Boneblight when it met one.

Hoarse shouts echoed up and down the ships along the docks. Dwarven sailors stirred from theirs vessels carrying axes, swords, and belaying pins in their mighty fists. In seconds, an army had formed from the Yondering Docks. And Wick, on the wildly galloping gelding, led them all, yelling, "Stop! Stop!"

For a fleeting moment the little librarian almost enjoyed the sensation of leading and wished that he had something elegant to say instead of screaming in fear. But perhaps the onlookers would only think that he was in a berserker rage, unwilling to stop until the Boneblights were destroyed. Actually, he was all for the Boneblights being destroyed; he was just afraid of being killed himself in the process.

Although he hadn't thought it possible, Wick spotted the human warder ahead. Sailors of all races scattered before the warder when they discovered the manner of creatures pursuing him.

The horse drew abreast of the warder as the human darted under a cargo net hanging from a massive boom arm. The net contained crates of different sizes, as well as hogshead barrels and casks, suspended almost twenty feet in the air. The Boneblights dove, one flying slightly behind the other as they swooped after the human.

On the other side of the cargo netting, the warder lashed out with his sword, cleaving through the support hawser that held the net. The cargo net crashed down, narrowly missing both Boneblights and scattering sailors and goods in all directions. Vile oaths and vituperative language followed the warder and his attackers.

Wick didn't know how the man could still run, but his long legs churned the ground. The warder changed directions like a big cat, turning almost instantly. A desperate look was on his face as he caught sight of Wick on the rampaging horse. Without any kind of warning, the warder turned his steps toward Wick and the horse, closing fast.

Why is he coming at me? Wick asked himself. The little librarian kicked the horse in the sides, his legs much too short to reach down into its withers. Unfortunately, the horse couldn't go any faster. He watched helplessly as the warder ran up a short stack of crates just in time to intercept the horse.

The warder leaped from the crates, landing almost effortlessly on the horse's broad back behind Wick. The human reached around Wick and took the reins from the little librarian.

"I have serious need of your horse for a moment, dweller," the man said in a deep voice. "I beg your indulgence." He put his feet into the horse's sides. "Hee-yah!"

The gelding redoubled its efforts, stretching out into a longer stride.

Wick held onto the saddle horn, bouncing high with bone-jarring thumps, thinking he would be slung off at any moment. Fearfully, he turned and glanced behind himself and the warder. *No!* The Boneblights winged after them in pursuit. The malevolent red eyes gleamed.

Turning so much in the saddle left Wick unbalanced.

He slipped and would have fallen from the horse had the warder not grabbed him quickly by the nape of the neck.

"Go easy there, little warrior," the warder advised, clamping hold around the little librarian's neck with a grip like iron.

"They're chasing us," Wick said.

A faint smiled pulled at the warder's lips. "Yes."

"Will they kill us?"

"Only if they catch us."

And the sailors that just lost a net full of cargo aren't going to be any too happy either, Wick realized. Those men had fallen in behind the Boneblights and he really didn't think it was just for the joy of chasing Boneblights.

The warder tugged gently on the reins and laid a knee into the horse's side. Instantly the great animal turned and followed the lead, rounding a stack of wine casks and leaping over a double-stacked crate of chickens. The chickens squawked in alarm, trying to scatter inside their cages and sending feathers flying.

The horse came down on wood planking, then galloped down the dock. The iron shoes rang and thumped against the split logs that made up the docks.

And the dock they were on, Wick observed with some anxiety, ended only a short distance ahead. "We really should stop."

"The Boneblights will catch us."

"Why did we come this way?"

"I've a ship to catch, and already it leaves without me."

Looking out into the harbor, Wick spotted a three-masted caravel setting out into the Blood-Soaked Sea. "There's always another ship."

"Not one for a long time heading the way that one is."

The horse's hooves thundered against the dock. Wick tried in vain to spot the ship's name. The running lights were lummin juice lanterns with multicolored lenses. "You've missed your ship," Wick pointed out. "It's too far out to sea."

"Not yet."

The strident screams of the Boneblights split the air behind them. Wick didn't dare look, but he really didn't think he could have taken his attention from the end of the dock, which was rapidly approaching. *How do all the heroes in those stories live through such events as these?* the little librarian asked himself. *They fight monsters and evil men, and then they swagger around and drink ale all night.* He just wanted a warm bed to crawl into—*immediately.*

"Here," the warder commanded, handing Wick the reins.

"I really don't think that's a good idea," the little librarian protested. "You see, the horse doesn't listen when—"

"Make him," the warder suggested. He placed his hands on the back of the saddle and pressed down, getting his feet under him on the horse's rump. Then he leaped, throwing himself toward the nearest ship resting at anchor nearly ten feet away. "Good luck, little warrior."

Amazed, Wick watched as the warder caught a low-hanging yardarm and hauled himself up into the ship's rigging. The little librarian felt his mount's muscles bunch suspiciously, then release. By the time he turned around, Wick saw that they'd run out of dock. The horse went airborne for just a moment, then dropped toward the water.

Wick kicked free of the horse on the way down, thinking desperately of the grandmagister's letter in his pocket. He'd never gotten the chance to return it to the

warder, and now it was going to get all wet. Then the
little librarian dropped into the harbor and the ocean
closed over his head.

A fleeting moment of panic filled Wick before he remembered that he *did* know how to swim, though it
wasn't a skill he was often called upon to use as a librarian, nor did he often care to indulge in such behavior. He kicked upward, led by the lantern lights pooling
on the choppy surface.

He hacked and coughed for a moment, feeling water
tickle his ears, but he looked for the Boneblights immediately. Both creatures had chosen to speed after the
warder. One of them darted through the ship's rigging
after the warder while the other Boneblight flew around
the ship to head him off.

Wick treaded water and watched as the warder leaped
through the first ship's rigging then into the next, graceful as an acrobat. From the second ship, the warder
leaped into a third, crawling toward the crow's-nest. The
ship he'd indicated that he had passage on was the very
next one, and all but twenty feet of the caravel had
moved forward past the ship next to it.

The first Boneblight overtook the warder at the third
ship's crow's-nest. Anticipating an easy victory, the Boneblight flapped its wings and raced straight at the warder. Only the man wasn't there when the foul creature
arrived. The warder grabbed the crow's-nest mast with
one hand and spun around, drawing his sword with his
free hand.

As the Boneblight passed through the area where he
had been, the warder struck off the creature's head with
the sword. With what seemed still a part of the same
motion, the warder sheathed his sword again and jumped
out toward the departing vessel, arcing his body and
shoving both arms in front of him as he flew forward
and started to fall at the same time.

Wick's breath hung in his throat, and for a short time he felt certain the warder had leaped to his doom, or at the very least a cold swim in the sea. But the warder had timed his leap precisely, dropping inside the aft sail as it stretched out full-bellied from the wind. The warder slid down the canvas, stretching out right before sliding down toward the stern castle deck so that he landed on his feet.

Without breaking stride, the warder grabbed one of the fancy multicolored lanterns from the ship's railing. He turned to face the last Boneblight, raising the lantern's hurricane glass that protected the flame inside. When the Boneblight dove at him, the warder turned the flame up high and held it up before him.

When the flame touched the Boneblight, it caught fire at once. Wick remembered then that the warder had drenched one of the Boneblights earlier. Screaming and squalling, wings burning quickly, the flaming creature fell into the harbor. It continued to burn for a short time even after the dark water closed over it.

The warder turned from the last of his attackers and glanced into the harbor after Wick. The little librarian didn't know for sure, but he thought a broad, generous smile curved the man's mouth as he waved farewell. The ship's crew closed in on him.

He's insane! Wick thought. *That's the only explanation there can be!* The darkness of the fogbound shore quickly obscured his view of the warder and the ship, so the little librarian didn't know if the crew welcomed their drop-in guest or took him into custody.

Hobnailed boots thundered across the docks, coming toward Wick at a hurried pace. Crewmen aboard the nearby ship shone lanterns on the little librarian, shouting, "There he is!"

Abruptly, the bright glow of a lummin juice lantern broke over the end of the dock. Wick squinted in pain and held up one dripping hand to shield his eyes against the light. The water muddied in color around him as it reflected the light.

"Are ye all right, dweller?" The dwarven sailor peered down at Wick with one eye screwed up tight. He held a short-hafted, double-bitted axe in one hand.

"Yes," Wick replied. "But I'm afraid I lost Dhaobin's horse. It was just here." He looked around the water in vexation. He had thought the animal could surely swim. *Unless one of the monsters that inhabit the Blood-Soaked Sea slithered up and wolfed him down!* The thought had Wick treading water much more quickly, gazing around in consternation for a quick way out of the water.

"That horse ye rode into these waters so brave-like," the dwarf said, "has already seen himself fit to get to shore."

Following the man's pointing arm, Wick saw the horse clambering up from the shallows at the other end of the dock, the warder in tow with the letter in hand held high above the surf. Suddenly, he felt foolish in the water.

"That was a mighty brave thing ye did," the dwarf said, "a-rescuin' that feller what was in so much trouble."

"I—" Wick began.

"Never have seen anything like it." The dwarf glanced over his shoulder at the crowd that had filled the end of the dock. "Well, I'll be hornswaggled! All ye men are here, and ain't a-one of ye got a pole between ye to help this brave man from them cold waters."

"It's all right," Wick said. "I'll just swim to shore."

"It ain't fittin'!" the dwarf roared loudly. "The halfer done took on a warrior's responsibilities by a-killin' them Boneblights! Surely he ain't a-gonna have to save himself, too!" A barge pole was quickly passed up to the dwarf. He shoved the end of it down to Wick. "Now ye just grab onto that and we'll have ye outta them waters in a trice."

Teeth chattering from the cold water, Wick gladly reached for the pole. Even as his hand closed on the pole, the little librarian saw another dwarf bring out a cudgel. Before Wick could move, the dwarf rapped him on the head and everything went black.

4

Shanghaied!

Ooooh!" Wick groaned in pain. The effort only intensified the harsh, throbbing agony trapped within his skull. He started to open his eyes, but bright light lanced into them and he quickly thought better of that. Memory of the race along Yondering Docks haunted him, but he knew that had to be a dream inspired by too much wine and his recent reading selections from Hralbomm's Wing.

Still, he stretched out a tentative hand. Bedding covered him. *There,* he told himself almost happily. *See? Your brains aren't leaking out of your poor, bashed skull! You're in your room in the Library. Erkim is probably over in his bed wearing that ridiculous night mask.* However, Erkim's customary snoring and sleep-talk was missing. So was the weight of the book on Wick's chest that he normally went to sleep with. *It's nothing to be alarmed about.* He even tried to believe that, but the whispering doubt remained in his mind.

He extended his hand out further and found the edge of the bed. Still lying on his back, he reached out the other side of the bed. *Odd,* he thought. *The bed is much narrower than I remember. And it's a trifle harder as well.*

Suddenly, as he continued to waken, the rise and fall

that he felt throughout his body was more noticeable. At first he'd thought the sensation had been created by consuming too much razalistynberry wine or one of the occasional sick headaches he got from reading for too long in one position.

"Get up outta bed, ya goldbricker!" a shrill, arthritic voice screeched. "Get up outta bed! Ye're wasting daylight, ye no-good, bilge-blasted layabout!" Vile, graphic curses followed the screeched orders.

The language was so graphically foul that Wick could not believe it. He'd only occasionally found such obscenities in books he'd catalogued over the years at the Vault. He'd never met anyone that cursed with such intensity.

Despite the harsh glare, Wick opened his eyes. The details of the room didn't immediately register. The cramped space was far smaller than his room at the Library. And he was lying swaddled in a gently swinging hammock, not in his bed.

A sudden explosion of red, yellow, blue, and green feathers beat at the air at the foot of the hammock. The creature streaked straight at the little librarian. The frantic motion of its wings made the creature look incredibly huge. "Get up outta bed or I'll yank ye up by yer hair meself!" Long claws flashed toward Wick's face.

"Yaaahhhh!" Terrified, the little librarian twisted away from the dreadful creature. The hammock writhed beneath him and overturned, dumping him to the hardwood floor with a loud splat. The wind left his lungs and dizziness swam sickeningly through his head.

"Get up! Get up!"

Wings beat the air only inches above Wick. He wrapped his arms over his head protectively. His fingers found the large knot behind his left ear. In disbelief, he cupped the protruding swelling, thinking it was still the size of a hen's egg. His own touch pained him. *It wasn't a dream!* The cold realization sent sheets of panic cascading through him. *Where am I?* He forced his eyes open again and stared at the hardwood floor before him.

The oak planks had been sanded smooth in past years and had fit tightly. Long seasons of hard usage and the usual toll the sea had on things had left scars and a little warping that needed a patient hand to make right again. Evidently, no one had cared enough to straighten those things out. The brine smell of the sea filled Wick's nostrils as he struggled to fill his lungs again. *No! This can't be!*

"Lazy goldbricker!" the raucous voice continued screaming. "I'll have the flesh off yer bones, I will! I'll be feedin' ye to them monsters a-lyin' in our wake if'n I have to pack ye down their gullets a piece at a time meself!"

Cautiously, Wick looked up. He covered his face with one hand and peered through his splayed fingers.

The horned rhowdor stood little more than a foot tall, but the twin horns of twisting pastel pink made it appear taller. The wingspread reached nearly three feet and made the bird appear fiercer and larger than it was. The chest and most of the wing were the bright red of low-burning coals, but yellow patches mixed in there as well. The wingtips and tail held a green color so dark it looked blue and black in places. The hatchet face bore chiseled features made up of a heavy, curved beak and a single glowering emerald eye. The other eye was covered by a scarred black leather eyepatch with a skull outline embossed in metal studs. A gold hoop earring depended from one wild, bushy ear tuft. Besides having a fierce appearance, rhowdors were also extremely intelligent.

"Avast there, ye bite-sized little sardine!" the rhowdor blustered. The bird cocked his head and crowed more foul language. "What ye think ye be a-lookin' at? Ain't ye ever seen a proper pirate afore?" He puffed out his feathered chest.

Wick's pride was stung, and in spite of the fact that he knew he'd probably be better off simply keeping quiet, he said, "Actually, I have seen pirates." If pirates had taken him, it only stood to reason that some of them *had* been about the Yondering Docks and he'd seen them. "But I've never seen a popinjay proclaiming to be a pirate before."

"Ye'll walk the plank and sleep with the fishies, ye bilge-rat!" the rhowdor threatened. He leaped from his perch and flew to the other end of the hammock, scrabbling quickly to maintain his balance. The long claws clicked along the metal eyebolt screwed into the wall.

"You're a foul fowl," Wick remonstrated as he scooted under the hammock.

"We got no time for shirkers aboard this vessel," the rhowdor threatened. "We'll bone ye and boil yer flesh to use as grease to keep the oarlocks nimble. Yer filthy tripes will be used as fish bait. Ye won't go to waste on ol' *One-Eyed Peggie,* I'll warrant ye that." The bird moved threateningly back and forth along the eyebolt. His horned head cocked and twisted as feathers ruffled at the base of his neck.

The door opened suddenly and a dwarf strode into the room with the rolling gait of a sailor. He stood tall and broad for his kind, his shoulders nearly an axe handle across, making him look fully as wide across as he was tall. He wore sailor's pants with flared legs, a long-sleeved shirt with red and white horizontal striping, brown leather shoes, and a red kerchief around his hair. His beard was fierce and long, dark brown mixed with a light dusting of gray, and braided with bits of yellowed ivory bone carved in fish shapes. Gold hoops hung in his ears.

The dwarf took in the scene, then scowled at the rhowdor. "What ye be a-doin', Critter?"

"Wakin' up this worthless sardine," the rhowdor replied.

The dwarf *hmphed* out loud but kept looking at the bird doubtfully. "You ain't one for niceties. An' not much in the way of introductions, neither." He glanced at Wick. "Get up from underneath that bed. Hidin' from this crusty ol' bird like that just ain't—" He hesitated. "Well, it ain't dignified, is all I'm saying."

The sacrifice of dignity to make sure I keep my face intact isn't a bad trade-off, Wick thought. He cautiously clambered to his feet, keeping a watchful eye on the rhowdor. He also stayed on the other side of the hammock from the dwarf. The ship caught enough of a wave that the little librarian rocked back on his heels and bumped up against the wall.

"Can't even stand up on a deck when the sea's as smooth as glass," Critter observed. "What kind of pirate is this little halfer gonna make?"

Pirate? Wick glanced from rhowdor to dwarf and felt his stomach twist sickeningly.

The dwarf sighed heavily and faced the rhowdor with his ham-sized hands on his hips. The sea and seasons had marked the sailor, laying on a dark tan and scars grayed out with the passage of time. "Don't ye have somethin' ye're supposed to be doin'?"

"I—" Critter started to protest.

"Better be gettin' to it," the dwarf warned, "or I'm a-gonna find more for ye to do. Got a heap of barnacles could use some attention, and that sharp beak o' yers scrapes 'em off right nice."

Critter flapped his wings in acute dissatisfaction. "I ever mention there's a certain lack of appreciation in yer tone with me, Hallekk?"

"Every day since ye boarded, ye puffed-up feather-duster," Hallekk grumbled. "If'n Cap'n Farok hadn't of taken such a shine to ye, I'm thinking ye'd already have showed up in a pot pie or a stew. Now get on with ye."

Critter turned his emerald eye on Wick. "This one's gonna be trouble. Ye mark well me words. Got despair showing bone-deep in him. An' hidin' from a bird? What kind of pirate is that goin' to make, I ask you."

"Get on with yerself," Hallekk commanded gruffly.

Reluctantly, shooting Wick a truly venomous look, the rhowdor flapped his wings and took to the air. He zipped unerringly through the porthole above the little librarian's head.

Wick ducked quickly.

The rhowdor's raucous laughter echoed in the room for a moment before fading away.

But the sound of men's voices as well as the creaking of ship's rigging and the snap of sailcloth taking the wind came into the cabin from outside. Unable to stop himself, Wick turned and caught hold of the porthole. He had to pull himself up on tiptoes to see over the porthole's edge.

He stared out in disbelief at a brief expanse of deck below the porthole. Railing surrounded the deck, adorned with coils of rope and belaying pins. Beyond the deck and the railing was a rolling horizon filled only with blue sky and red-purplish waves of what could only be the Blood-Soaked Sea.

Heart beating rapidly, Wick turned to the dwarf. "There's been an awful mistake," he said in a voice dry with fear.

Hallekk folded his arms across his broad chest and shook his head. "Nope. No mistake."

Wick released his hold on the porthole. He swayed easily to the rise and fall of the ship's deck, but looked awkward when compared to the dwarf. "You don't understand. I'm no sailor, and I'm definitely no pirate."

"Don't fret none about that," Hallekk advised good-naturedly. "By the time we polish ye up fer awhile, ye'll be both. Whether or not ye'll be any good at it is up to how much of yer heart ye put into it."

"She's called *One-Eyed Peggie*," Hallekk said as he strode across the rolling ship's deck in a sure-footed stride. "On account of the captain what built her."

Wick followed the dwarf in a daze, still not believing he was truly aboard a ship cutting across the Blood-Soaked Sea. He stared in awe at the dwarves crewing the ship, listening to them talk and swear at one another with coarse humor. They didn't sound or look at all as disciplined as the pirates he'd read about in the books from Hralbomm's Wing. Captain Manklin of *Swift Lightning* would never have allowed such a raffish crew to gather in his sight without a fight.

All of them seemed ferocious. Many of them bore tattoos on their arms, shoulders, and backs. Some even had tattoos on their craggy cheeks above their beards and on their bald heads. All the tattoos appeared to be of fish or sea monsters. None of those inked images seemed especially welcoming.

"I suppose the captain named the ship after his wife or a woman he knew?" *Be pleasant*, Wick told himself. *If these pirates can see that you're a pleasant person, they'll soon see that you're not pirate material either. Once they see that, why, they'll put you right back at Greydawn Moors. Won't they?* He felt good about the plan; at least he was doing something. He pulled himself up the steep stairs leading to the stern castle.

"No," Hallekk said. "*One-Eyed Peggie* was named after the captain herself."

"The captain was a woman?" Wick had never heard of a woman being captain.

"Why sure," the dwarven pirate said. "Piratin's a good trade fer a woman if'n it's in her blood. And it were sure enough in One-Eyed Peggie's."

"It were? I mean, *was?* She's not still captain?" Wick asked.

"No. She passed on nigh two hundred years ago. But she left this fine sailing ship behind." Hallekk stepped to the top of the stern castle and waved Wick up after him.

The little librarian pulled himself up cautiously. Now that he was in the ship's stern, he felt the twisting motion of the sea more strongly. He held onto the railing, envying the way Hallekk apparently glided over the rocking deck. The cold wind, laced with salty sea spray, lashed over Wick, coating his exposed skin and wetting his robe.

Except for *One-Eyed Peggie* and a few white and brown birds, the sea was empty.

Wick stared out across the purple-red sea. The horizon was choppy and bleak in all directions. The sun hung almost straight above the ship, glaring down through a hoarfrost of wispy clouds. His eyes burned, and finally teared up, but it wasn't from the cold or the wind or the salt spray.

For the first time, the little librarian realized how very far away from home he was. As legendary as the height of the Knucklebones was, he couldn't see the mountain range anywhere. *How long did I sleep?* he wondered. *And how far did we sail?* He turned around again, staring at the unfamiliar sight of the Blood-Soaked Sea.

"Little man," Hallekk asked in a stern voice, "be ye sick or some such?"

"Yes," Wick replied softly. "I am sick." *Homesick for certain.*

"Faugh, an' don't worry yer knob about it none, matey," Hallekk said somewhat cheerily. He dropped a heavy hand on Wick's shoulder. "Them feelings what writhe around in yer guts, why they's just yer body's way o' acclimatin' itself with the sea is all. After all, a man is most nearly all water hisself. It's just the sea's way of sayin' ahoy and takin' ye back where ye come from."

No, Wick thought morosely. *I don't belong here. I'll never belong here.*

Hallekk slapped Wick on the shoulder, nearly driving the little librarian to his knees. "C'mon, little man, I'll stand ye to yer morning victuals if ye've got an able stomach. Cap'n Farok will want to see you after that."

"So they didn't call One-Eyed Peggie one-eyed because she was missing an eye?" Wick looked over at Hallekk in confusion.

"Naw." Hallekk shook his big head. "One-Eyed Peggie had two eyes like most everybody ye see." He sipped at his grog, which the pirate ship seemed to keep vast amounts of.

Grog was a thin, watery ale. From his reading at the Vault, Wick knew that ships kept the grog aboard for their crews. The little bit of ale laced in the water wasn't enough to fog a man's senses even if consumed in large amounts, but it did help counter the stale taste of the tepid water and help keep it from going rancid.

"Then why was she called One-Eyed Peggie?" Wick asked. They sat in the large galley belowdecks amidships.

At first, the little librarian had been horrified by the conditions of the galley. Dirty dishes as well as clean ones—at least Wick hoped some of the dishes were clean, since they were using some of them—were stacked all over. Remnants of other pirates' breakfasts still yet remained on the long tables bolted firmly to the decks. Pirates grumbled and cursed as they washed other dishes in huge tubs of steaming water. Soapy suds splashed to the deck.

"Because Peggie had the one eye, ye see."

"No," Wick said. "I'm afraid I don't see at all. I thought you said she had both eyes."

"She did. I'm talking about her own eyes, of course. She was only missing the leg." Hallekk leaned back and took out a pipe. He quickly stuffed the bowl and lit up.

"One-Eyed Peggie only had one leg? She was born that way?"

"No. She had two. Up until the time Ol' Torbhor up an' et her other one."

Thoughts of cannibalistic pirates sudden filled Wick's mind. He glanced down at the bones of the breakfast steak Hallekk had on his plate. The little librarian had only taken porridge and pieces of fruit for himself. "Torbhor?"

"Aye." Hallekk nodded, smoke wreathing his head. "Ol' Torbhor were a feisty sea monster. Until the day that he up and et One-Eyed Peggie's leg off. 'Course, she weren't known as One-Eyed Peggie in them days. Ol' Torbhor woulda et the rest of her, too, but her crew was too quick for the big beastie."

"Then why," Wick persisted although part of him didn't want to, "did they call her One-Eyed Peggie?"

" 'Cause after Ol' Torbhor bit off her leg, One-Eyed Peggie went a-fishin' after him. Spent three years trackin' after him through the Blood-Soaked Sea."

"Did she catch him?"

"Aye, that she did, and it were a powerful fight, I'll warrant ye that." Hallekk took a few more puffs on his pipe, knowing with the skill of natural-born raconteur that he had a captive audience in the little librarian. "One-Eyed Peggie harpooned that great beastie herself, she did. Ol' Torbhor dragged that whalin' boat around the ocean for six days. Even through a nasty waterspout what pulled 'em all up from the sea before ploppin' 'em back down and near bustin' the boat in half."

"But One-Eyed Peggie got Torbhor?"

Hallekk shook his head. "No. Ye see, she only got the one eye. That's why they call her One-Eyed Peggie. Ol' Torbhor got off with his other eye—but it was a close thing." The dwarven pirate hooked a thumb over his shoulder at the nearest porthole. "Some say Ol' Torbhor still swims these waters, but I couldn't rightly say either way."

"What happened to One-Eyed Peggie?"

"Why, she up and captured herself a good-looking man, she did. A blacksmith to the kings of Marzatlan to the far north, he was. He come down to the Blood-Soaked Sea a-lookin' for a star what fell into these waters. One-Eyed Peggie took the blacksmith's ship as a prize. She intended to ransom him back to the dwarven kings, you see. Only while she was a-waitin' on the ransom money, the blacksmith fashioned her a leg outta that fallen star. Like near to flesh, it were, from all accounts I've heard. An' One-Eyed Peggie fell in love with this great strappin' dwarf, and him with her."

"Then what happened?" Wick asked as a bell sounded from outside.

"Why, she up and sold the ship and moved off to Marzatlan with the blacksmith." Hallekk tamped his pipe out with regret. "Guess we best be a-gettin' ye up to see the captain. He'll want to look ye over with the other new crew." The big dwarf pushed up from the table.

"The other new crew?" Wick couldn't help but ask.

As it turned out, One-Eyed Peggie's crew had shanghaied three other crewmen while at Greydawn Moors.

Captain Farok sat on the edge of his bed, perched

behind a small desk that folded out of the wall. He scowled at the recruits. Charts and maps covered the tiny desktop in front of him. Fishing weights and seashells held down the papers at the corners. Age stained the captain's hair, turning it a silvery gray with the buttery luster of old bone. His face sagged and clung to his eye sockets and mouth, looking like it was going to cave it at any moment.

Wick thought Captain Farok was the oldest dwarf he'd ever seen.

Farok moved his head ponderously in Hallekk's direction, then waved a gnarled hand. "Well, don't just stand there, Quartermaster Hallekk," he ordered in a wheezing voice.

"The new crewmen." Hallekk stood at rigid attention, his hands clasped behind his back and his chin lifted proudly. "We mustered them in at Greydawn Moors, and they're all ready to give themselves to piratin'." The quartermaster nodded at the first dwarf. "Able-bodied seaman, Cyaratin, Cap'n Farok."

"Experienced?" The captain sized the young dwarven man up with a steely glare.

"Aye, sir," Hallekk replied. "Five years. I got ship's names here if'n ye need 'em, Cap'n."

Farok waved the offer away. "Let me see yer hands, Seaman Cyaratin."

Reluctantly, the dwarf offered his hands.

The captain took both of them in his own hands for a moment. "You know ropes?" he asked.

"Aye, sir," Cyaratin replied. "An' plenty of 'em. Ain't a knot been tied that I ain't seen."

"You work in riggings or nets?"

"Both, Cap'n, but I find me callin' in the yardarms and ratlines of a ship. I been a spotter, too."

Farok grunted in pleasant surprise and looked back at

the man with new regard. "Do ye have good eyes in yer head, then, Seaman Cyaratin?"

"Aye, sir."

The captain glanced at Hallekk. "Get this man with the rigging crew. And put him with Zeddar. I want him able to identify neutral ships in these waters by sundown."

"Aye, sir."

Farok moved on to the next dwarf, felt his hands, and pronounced him fit for the gunnery crews. The third new recruit was another dweller wearing faded and patched sea clothes, pants tarred as proof against the elements and a wide-necked shirt. The captain scowled at the dweller, who took care not to lock eyes with Farok. "Ye brought me a halfer, Hallekk."

"Aye, sir."

"Ye know how I feel about halfers."

"Aye, sir, but Seaman Trosper has some shipwright abilities. I thought he might be valuable."

"Very well, Hallekk," Farok said. "I'll leave his fate to yer judgment, but see to it that this creature don't go a-gettin' underfoot. An' I want none of our gear nor tackle to go a-missin'. I got a ship here to run." He glared at the dweller. "I take the hands offa men what steals from *One-Eyed Peggie*."

Trosper bristled at the captain's veiled threat, but wisely kept his mouth shut.

"No sir," Hallekk agreed. "This halfer here won't be no problem a-tall. He's a good 'un, he is; a halfer what knows his place."

"Mayhap." Farok's brow furrowed over his eyes. "But I always found that halfers were the first to shirk their workload. I won't abide no slackers on *One-Eyed Peggie*. We'll trawl 'em and use 'em for fish bait, we will." He dismissed Trosper with a negligent wave, moving his fierce gaze on to Wick.

The little librarian returned the captain's unrelenting eye contact and felt like he was going to throw up. Even the grandmagisters hadn't invoked such naked fear within him.

"*Two* halfers, Hallekk?" Disgusted wrinkles deepened the deep pits of Captain Farok's eye sockets. "Ye have the nerve to bring me a *pair* of 'em?"

"Ah but, Cap'n," Hallekk said, "this here's the halfer what fought them Boneblights along Greydawn Moors' docks last night."

Farok gazed at Wick. "Is that right, halfer?"

Wick hesitated only for a moment, then shook his head. "No." The scowl deepened in the dwarven pirate captain's face. "No, Captain. Sir."

"Ye're not the one?"

"Well, I'm probably the one all the talk was about," Wick admitted. "The Boneblights were trying to kill me."

"An' ye fought 'em?"

Wick hesitated only a moment, then shook his head. "No, sir. I ran from them. The warder was the one who fought the Boneblights."

"Well now," Hallekk said, "an' that's not how it looked last night."

Captain Farok burst out laughing, but it wasn't an expression of good humor. "Do ye know what ye got fer yer troubles, Hallekk? Do ye really know?"

The big dwarf hung his head.

"Give me yer hands, halfer," the pirate captain commanded.

Wick's belly quivered as he stuck his hands out. The captain's own hands felt like they were covered in barnacles. They shook a little with age, but there was no denying the great strength they contained.

Farok pushed Wick's hands away. "Why, these are the hands of a man what ain't never known much in the way of honest work, Hallekk! No, what ye've taken on here, Hallekk, is an unproductive mouth to feed. A leech, a tripes worm what'll only suck up the food ye've managed to put in yer own belly."

Wick wanted to protest. Even his father had never made him feel so low about becoming a librarian.

"What is it ye been a-doin' with yerself, halfer?" the pirate captain demanded.

"I'm a . . . a . . . librarian," Wick whispered.

"A *librarian,* was ye?" Captain Farok rolled his eyes. "A wastrel by any other name, I tell ye. Readin' and writin' and such—*faugh!* An' when has them skills been for naught but misfortune, I ask ye?"

"Those skills can be very important," Wick replied, then wilted before Farok's fierce gaze.

"Oh, really?" the pirate captain responded, leaning closer and driving Wick back a half-step. "An' was I to put ye over the side of ol' *One-Eyed Peggie* now, would ye be a-knowin' yer way home?"

"There are constellations in the sky," Wick said, remembering some of the books he'd read in the Vault.

"Constellations?" Captain Farok shook his head. "Ye expect to be a-seein' constellations while ye're out in the Blood-Soaked Sea? Out here in all this fog? Why, ye can't hardly see the bloomin' hand in front of yer face some nights because of the fogbanks, an' ye're expectin' to see stars?"

Oh. Wick had to admit that he hadn't thought about that.

"An' ye spend half of yer time in the water while the sun's up," the pirate captain said. "What are ye a-gonna do so's ye don't lose yer position durin' them daylight hours? Bob up and down in the sea a-waitin' for nightfall? An' ye think some sea serpent or other monster from the depths ain't a-gonna think ye're a tasty little treat an' come and snatch ye up to keep its gullet from retreatin' to its backbone?"

"Perhaps," Wick suggested in a soft, trembling voice, "it would be better for all concerned if you simply returned me to Greydawn Moors."

"Return ye to *Greydawn Moors?*" Captain Farok looked fit to explode. He pushed up from his bed and walked around the desk, falling into a short pacing route up and down the length of his quarters. His boots thumped against the hardwood deck. "Why ye great ninny! An' here I was a-thinkin' that the grandmagisters took only the bright halfers up to the Vault!"

Wick's face burned.

"Them sailors at Greydawn Moors," Captain Farok said, "why they'll know what we was about by now. They'll know *One-Eyed Peggie* is a pirate ship. Maybe they won't rightly recall her name, but they'll know the cut an' draw of her, an' know her again if'n they see her. Men what live on the salt, ye lummox-brained little halfer, they know ships and the men what sail them. It'll be years afore we can throw down an anchor in Greydawn Moors again."

Years! The word flew through Wick's thoughts and thudded with the grim finality of a headsman's axe.

Farok stopped pacing and glared over at Hallekk. "Warrior, bah! Ye know what ye got here, Hallekk?"

The big dwarf looked embarrassed. He looked away and scratched behind one freckled ear. "No sir."

"Why then, I'll tell ye, I will. Ye got an overqualified potato peeler, Hallekk. That's what ye got for yer troubles." Captain Farok turned his harsh gaze on Wick and shook his head. "Put him in the kitchen with Slops. Let's find out if'n the halfer can wash dishes."

"Aye, Cap'n."

———

I—who have studied at the Vault of All Known Knowl-edge—I'm going to be a . . . a . . . a dishwasher? On a pirate ship? Wick shook his head in stunned disbelief as he followed Hallekk from Captain Farok's quarters. The little librarian gazed around at the ship, watching the pirates as they worked in the rigging and on the decks.

"Avast there, ye dirty swabs!" Critter roared from a lanyard amidships. The fierce rhowdor flailed his wings with a noise like distant thunder. "Make sure ye change out that water in them buckets! Otherwise ye're just a-changin' out the dirt a-coverin' them decks!"

The pirates growled curses back at the obnoxious bird.

Critter cursed back at them, then spied Wick. "Ahoy, mateys, yonder comes the new cook's helper." The rhowdor sprang from the lanyard, wings beating the air. Sunlight glinted from the metal studs forming the skull on the bird's eyepatch.

Some of the pirates paused in their work and studied Wick. "Thought he was a warrior," one pirate said. "Not no cook's helper. Supposed to have killed a half-dozen Boneblights last night."

"Come to find out," Critter crowed, "he's just a Vault *librarian!*"

Derisive laughter suddenly rung out from the pirates.

Wick wanted nothing more than to turn invisible or somehow shrink down through the deck into the hold below.

Without warning, *One-Eyed Peggie* listed hard to port, rolling against the natural motion of the sea. The pirates scrambled to grab hold of the railing.

Wick bent at the knees instinctively and rolled with the sudden twisting lunge of the ship. He only skidded a few inches across the deck before he came to a stop, leaning into the deck's steep incline as it crested the next wave.

Pirates cursed in strained voices. They looked over the ship's sides.

Standing near Wick, Hallekk held his ground with ease. The big dwarf cupped his callused hands around his mouth. "Zeddar! Do ye see anythin' out there?"

Wick glanced up into the rigging and spotted the crow's-nest built at the top of the main mast high above. A dwarf held onto the crow's-nest sides with clenched fists as the topmast swung wildly from port to starboard several times.

"It's not out there!" the dwarf in the crow's-nest bellowed down through his own cupped hands. "The cursed beastie is beneath us!"

"It's gonna try to roll us into the sea and gobble us up!" another pirate shouted.

Hallekk made his way to the starboard railing, stumbling with the awkward sway of the ship's deck.

Terrified, Wick followed. The little librarian's mind conjured up a thousand images of monsters he'd read about in texts and seen painted in books. In those books, heroes had managed to vanquish some of those fierce beasts, but he wasn't on a ship of heroes now.

"Grab pole arms!" Hallekk roared, reaching down beside the railing and freeing a twenty-foot-long harpoon. A cruel, triangular blade nearly a foot long capped the harpoon. "Stand by to repel the beastie if'n we hafta!"

One-Eyed Peggie rolled again as the unseen monster slammed against the keel. Timbers groaned as the ship fought the sea and the monster and the wind.

"It's gonna tear us apart!" a pirate yelled.

Wick closed his fists on the railing and stared down into the dark water. Surely if there were really a monster of some sort down there it would be visible. But even though he strained his eyes, he couldn't see anything.

Pirates squalled in horror as a huge, lumpy snout suddenly pushed above the waterline. The monster's head

was nearly ten feet across, but looked even bigger when
the jaws gaped. Seaweed and small fish tumbled through
the long, serrated teeth, winding through the three rows
to spill back into the ocean. Mottled gray-green scales
covered the creature. Bulbous black eyes raked the pirate
ship and crew with animal cunning.

Wick had never seen a creature larger than the monster before him. He wanted to run, but he wanted to
absorb every detail he could about the monster. He'd
never seen anything like it in any of the books at the
Vault.

"Harpoon it, ye swabs!" Critter screamed in his loud,
raucous voice.

Wick caught the rhowdor's fluttering movements from
the corner of his eye. Critter scrambled through the rigging, taking care to keep sail and rope between himself
and the fierce sea denizen.

"Ease off there, mateys," a strong, thunderous voice
called out.

Glancing above, Wick spotted Captain Farok standing
at the bow castle railing. Wind churned the tails of the
pirate captain's greatcloak.

"Have a care how ye're a-treatin' that ol' codger,"
Captain Farok ordered. "Could be he's just a-nosin' us
over and ain't meanin' no harm. Ye go a-pokin' about
on him, ye're only gonna get him all stirred up."

Critter fell silent but didn't cease scrambling up the
rigging.

Crouching to make himself smaller behind the railing,
Wick stared at the sea monster in rapt fascination. *What
is it and where does it come from? Is it a creature that
has simply outlived its time, or one that was magicked
from some other place?*

The monster cocked its head to one side and rolled its
baleful eye as if carefully surveying the deck. Whiskers
as long as oars suddenly flared out from the sides of its

face. Barbs covered the ends of the silvery white strands. Small green bloated parasites bulged from between the creature's scales in several places.

"Hold steady," Captain Farok ordered. "First man what stabs yonder beastie without my command is a-gonna end up in the drink with it. We'll make our escape while it's a-feastin' on yer bones, we will."

"Feed it the halfer," one of the pirates suggested. "We'll get away while the monster's a-feedin' on his bones."

Wick swallowed hard. He didn't doubt for a moment that the crew would throw him in if the order were given.

"Hallekk, have a few of yer men run up some more sailcloth. I'd rather fight the war between the wind and the sea than with the likes o' that thing. Let's see if'n we can put some distance betwixt ourselves and our admirer."

"Aye, Cap'n." Hallekk called out names and set the men to work. "An' I'll have ye a-movin' slowly so's ye don't disturb the beastie by drawin' attention to yerselves."

Dwarven pirates moved carefully across the deck and unfurled more sailcloth. The canvas billowed out as they swung the rigging around to a new tack. *One-Eyed Peggie* reacted at once, coming around to the new heading and pulling slightly away from the monster.

The sea serpent immediately twisted its head and set out in pursuit. It glided effortlessly through the high waves.

"Steady, steady," Captain Farok called out. He remained at the bow castle railing, looking out over his ship at the big monster that threatened it. "Ye move an' ye have a care, maybe the beastie will get bored of us and seek its distraction somewheres else."

One-Eyed Peggie gathered speed, fleeing with the wind now instead of trying to tack against it. Still, the waves stood at least twenty feet tall and they rode against those. When the pirate ship rose up a wave, it slowed, but it gained headlong speed on the other side.

"Water's almost as fast as the wind today," Hallekk groaned. "An' that beastie don't have a care about neither."

Wick knew it was true. Even as he held fast to the railing and tried not to be sick, he watched the sea monster duck below a wave then crash through on the other side as if it were nothing. "Will it continue to follow us?" the little librarian asked, raising his voice to be heard above the groaning timbers and cracking sailcloth.

"Don't know," Hallekk answered. "These bloomin' beasties got nothing better to do than follow a ship around. Even if they ain't hungry."

"Maybe it could be distracted," Wick suggested. *One-Eyed Peggie* reached the apex of another wave, then tilted sharply forward as her bow sank down. She rushed pell-mell down the other side of the wave, deep into the trough of the oncoming one.

"Ain't nothin' gonna distract that thing," Hallekk said. "Less'n it's another beastie about as big or bigger. An' that ain't good, because sometimes they just decide to share what they find instead of fightin' over it." He shifted the harpoon in his hands.

The pirate ship continued gaining speed, creeping up the side of an oncoming wave, then crashing down almost out of control on the other side.

Wick watched Captain Farok, seeing the huge wall of water swell behind the man as the ship's bow dropped again. The next wave crashed into the bow, drenching the sails and sending water cascading across the deck. Water spilled over the edge of the bow castle, coming across in a solid sheet for a moment before *One-Eyed Peggie*'s bow lifted above the oncoming wave.

The dwarven pirates cursed and shouted, but none of them raised their voice at the captain.

Although the ship traveled across and through the sea in stomach-spinning lurches, Wick knew that the monster following them couldn't maintain the pace. The ponderous coils might pass through the water beneath the ocean's surface more easily, but the serpent's energy wasn't as boundless as the wind. For a time, the gigantic creature continued to pace *One-Eyed Peggie*. Then it disappeared beneath the waves.

Wick hung onto the railing, scouring the violent water. The pirate ship hurtled through the water, dipping lower into each new wave till the decks from bow to stern ran with water. The little librarian felt certain that they were going to hit the bottom of the next trough much too hard and break the ship in half.

A harsh ripping noise filled Wick's ears. He glanced up toward the sound and saw that one of the topsails had broken free of the rigging. The splintered yardarm banged against the mast and the loose sailcloth fluttered in jerky spasms.

"Look out!" Critter called as he hung upside down from the rigging.

Even as Wick turned, he saw the sea monster's gigantic maw sweeping down at him, propelled by the twisted coils of its scaled neck like an arrow released from a bow.

5

Secret of the Pirates

Instinctively, Wick moved at once, but even as he did, the ship's deck dove again. His effort only tripped him up as his legs got tangled, throwing him off balance. Water drenched him as the sea monster tried to snap him up.

Before the gaping maw could close over him, though the stink of the creature's fetid breath filled Wick's nose, Hallekk ran forward and scooped the little librarian up in one great arm. "Move, little man!" the pirate growled. "Ye will make nary a bite for that great lummox, an' mayhap only whet his appetite for more!"

Slammed against the wet deck by the dwarf's much greater bulk, Wick skidded for a few feet. The sea monster's teeth thudded against the wooden planking, shattering at least a half-dozen of them into splinters.

"Stick that blasted thing!" Hallekk roared. The dwarven pirate shoved himself to his feet, one fist still curled around the harpoon's haft.

Partially dazed from the back of his head striking the deck so hard and without warning, Wick caught the nearby railing and watched as a dozen pirates rallied across the treacherous deck to answer Hallekk's call. Hallekk beat them all, though, rearing back and driving his harpoon deep into the sea monster's throat at the base of the long jaw. Others ripped into the scaled flesh only a heartbeat later.

Blood streamed down the sea monster's throat as it lifted its head in painful surprise. The wind caught *One-Eyed Peggie*'s sails again full-on at the top of the next wave and drove her away from the sea monster.

Wick pulled himself up as the enraged sea monster continued trumpeting. It shook itself angrily, twisting high above the sea, then *One-Eyed Peggie* shot down the other side of the wave. When they crested the next wave, the sea monster was nowhere in sight. A huge grin twisted the little librarian's lips. "We beat it!" he yelled, surprised to still be alive. And surprised, too, at the sudden camaraderie he felt with the pirate crew. "We beat it!" He glanced at the pirates, expecting them to join him in the victory celebration.

The dwarven pirates all looked at him, panting and barely managing to stand.

"All right," Wick corrected himself, "*you* beat the sea monster, and—" *And what?* he asked himself. *I'm very proud of you?* He really didn't think they would care. The victorious feeling died a quiet, quick death inside him.

"Hallekk!" Captain Farok roared from the bow castle railing. "Ye've got a sail a-flappin' about aboard my ship."

"Aye, Cap'n. I was just on my way after seein' it mended." Hallekk turned and assigned four men into the rigging.

Wick stood by the railing and watched the crew ascend the rigging, moving as gracefully as monkeys as they went up and up and up. If any of them fell to the deck, the little librarian had no doubt that they wouldn't survive the impact. And that was only if they hit the deck. In the ocean swells they'd be lost instantly with no hope of survival.

The pirates worked quickly to secure the loose sail-cloth and broken yardarm. As Hallekk called out further orders, other men stripped some of the canvas from the yardarms and slowed *One-Eyed Peggie*'s headlong rush through the sea.

"Hallekk," Captain Farok called only a couple of minutes later. "Get yer new potato peeler belowdecks. Topside is meant only for sailin' men. Them's been my orders since ye walked onto *One-Eyed Peggie,* and they'll stand." He turned his back and started down the stairs toward his quarters.

"Aye." Hallekk looked at Wick and jerked his head. "Let's go, little man." The big dwarf took the lead, leaving the first mate in control of the ship.

"Thanks," Wick said, "for saving me back there."

Hallekk shrugged and smiled good-naturedly. "Sea monsters don't always see too good topside. It mighta missed ye."

Wick gazed at the cracked planking where he'd been standing. "I don't think it would have missed."

"Bad luck," Critter squawked high overhead. "Ye're a halfer what's carryin' bad luck. That there sea beastie come to ol' *One-Eyed Peggie* a-lookin' for ye, drawn by the smell of bad luck what clings to ye. We'd be better off a-drownin' ye in the hold like a bilge rat."

A handful of the nearby pirates looked at Wick as the little librarian passed. Pirates, Wick knew, were a superstitious lot, and some of them might even believe the rhowdor's words.

"Bad luck," Critter accused again. "Some warrior ye got there, Hallekk. Gonna bring us nothin' but trouble and death, he is."

"Ain't ye done with them dishes yet, halfer?"

Weary and aching from the backbreaking labor of the

last eight days, Wick didn't bother looking up. Nor did he bother pointing out the obvious fact that he wouldn't still be elbow-deep in the harsh soapy water if he'd been finished with the dishes. During these last eight days, he'd gotten to know Slops' face pretty well and he knew how the man would look now. The dwarven ship's cook only had the one expression: flinty-eyed anger mixed liberally with pure mean.

Wick took the last wooden bowl from the scouring bucket, passed it through the rinsing bucket, then wiped it dry with the towel that he kept draped over one shoulder. He started every morning before breakfast with a towel and kept it changed out during the day.

"That's the last of it," Wick admitted.

The galley was darkened now, lit only by the one whale-oil lantern Slops allowed during the nightly cleanup. The foul smoke given off by the burning whale oil stung the little librarian's nose. Whale oil didn't burn as cleanly as glimmerworm juice while traveling the Blood-Soaked Sea.

When Wick had objected to the foul-smelling whale-oil lanterns and suggested they use the glimmerworm juice kept down in *One-Eyed Peggie*'s hold, Slops had laughed at him. So had several other pirates and Critter. Outside of Greydawn Moors, as it turned out, not much glimmerworm juice and candles were gathered or made. As a result, there was no casual use of the glimmerworm juice. On the three mainlands along which the pirate ship sometimes traded, glimmerworm juice was only used by the wealthy to light their homes.

"Then hurry up and empty them buckets," Slops complained. "I gotta get me some sleep soon. Breakfast comes early of a morning on this ship."

Wick put the wooden bowl away in the stacks at the side of the kitchen area and made sure the stacks were secure. He knelt and grabbed the soap bucket by the handle, then lugged it up the steps, moving automatically now to *One-Eyed Peggie*'s pitch and yaw. Even though it had seemed like forever to him, Hallekk had told Wick that he'd gotten his sea legs much quicker than most new pirates.

Slops sat at one of the tables, pipe smoke wreathing his head. He yawned and scratched his homely face irritably. "I've definitely seen faster dishwashers than you, halfer."

Maybe, Wick thought to himself, *but at least I know for a fact that the dishes start out clean the next morning.* He bit his tongue. "I'm working on it."

"Gonna have to do better," Slops grumbled. "I can't stay up all night watchin' ye do them dishes, then still be expected to get up in the mornin' and lay out a proper feed for this crew."

You could help with the dishes. But Wick didn't say that either. Slops had big-knuckled, rough hands that were surprisingly quick, and he didn't hesitate about smacking anyone that he thought was sassing him in the kitchen.

Wick stumbled on up the steps. Carrying the heavy bucket of soapy water in both hands made the going awkward, but he lacked the strength to carry the bucket in one hand. It was thirty-seven stair steps till he reached the main deck. He glanced at the black sky, noting that the habitual fog that plagued the Blood-Soaked Sea had parted somewhat during the evening. For the last three days and nights, it had rained. A wet sheen still clung to the decks.

The two moons lent a silvery hue to the curlers rolling across the ocean. Jhurjan the Bold and Swift gleamed crimson in the sky. Gesa the Fair only winked shyly further to the north. The gentle wind brought in the chill from the sea that prickled Wick's skin.

The first night aboard ship—that he remembered—

had been horrible. Not since his early days as a novice at the Vault of All Known Knowledge had he been crowded into such a small space with so many others.

Most of all, though, Wick missed reading. Though Slops took care to see that there were no idle moments in the little librarian's day and actually well into the night, Wick desperately needed the comfort of a book. All of the crew aboard *One-Eyed Peggie* were illiterate and had no interest in books. Most of them didn't believe Wick could really read, or that he was even a Librarian.

Wick took a fresh grip on the bucket of soapy water and hesitated only a moment before stepping to the railing. Though they hadn't seen another sea monster since the one that first day, the fact remained that there were plenty of them in the ocean. Some of them were nocturnal feeders that were known to snatch crewmen from ships' decks. Or so Wick had been told.

He lifted the bucket of soured, soapy water and dumped it over the side. Chunks of food and pools of grease mixed with the soap plunged down into the sea in a long splash that was barely audible above the constant slap of the waves and the creaking rigging and straining sailcloth above.

The sea was slightly lit up around *One-Eyed Peggie.* Captain Farok kept a half-dozen whale-oil lanterns burning aboardship as running lights, so other ships that might be in the area would be warned that *One-Eyed Peggie* was in the area.

Wick stared hard out at the blackness and gray fog mixing above the sea. He didn't know how far *One-Eyed Peggie* could have come in eight days' sailing time, but he knew the distance had to be considerable. And nearly all of it had taken him far from Greydawn Moors.

"Thinkin' of throwin' yerself over?"

Startled by the nearness of Hallekk's voice, Wick

turned around. The metal bucket he carried clanged against the railing.

"What's goin' on down there?" one of the watchmen posted in the stern demanded.

"Nothin' to worry yer knob about," Hallekk replied. "Go on about yer business."

Wick looked up at the big dwarf and felt guilty. "I didn't hear you come up."

Hallekk grinned a little. "Way ye was a-thinkin' so hard, I'm not surprised. Never seen a man had a way of thinkin' so hard as ye." He leaned on the railing and looked out to sea. He took out a pipe, then glanced at Wick. "Ye smoke?"

"Occasionally." Wick wondered if the question was a trick. Still, while the rest of the crew and Critter treated him rather shabbily, Hallekk had never gone out of his way to be unkind to him.

"I've an extra pipe." Hallekk dug in his jacket and brought out two pipes and a pouch. He filled both and passed one to Wick, then offered a light from the nearby whale oil lantern.

"Thank you," Wick said, still feeling slightly wary.

"Do ye know why ye didn't throw yerself overboard?"

Wick shook his head. He'd been too scared to do much more than think about it. Swimming for shore wasn't an answer.

"Why, it was because ye knew a-throwin' yerself over the side wasn't a-gonna get ye home, little man." Hallekk blew smoke out and it was quickly stripped away by the wind. "A man sets himself a goal, he kinda knows when he's a-workin' toward it an' when he ain't. Drownin' or gettin' et by some ugly sea monster, now that ain't a-gonna get ye home, is it?"

Wick waited a moment, then asked, "And what will it take to get me home?"

Hallekk shrugged. "Why I don't know. Just know that doin' that won't."

"I shouldn't be here," Wick said.

"I know, little man, I know." Hallekk looked away. "An' partly that's my fault, an' I'm sorry as I can be for it. Figured we could conk ye on the knob, make use of ye for a little while, and ye'd escape and make yer own way back to home with a slew of new tales for the tellin'." He puffed on the pipe. "If'n that was what ye wanted. Of course, there was always the possibility that ye would come to like *One-Eyed Peggie* and decide to stay aboard her. There's worse things a man can do with his life, I'm a-tellin' ye."

"I'm not cut out to be a pirate."

"Nope," Hallekk agreed. "But ye could be a sailin' man. If'n ye put yer mind to it. Ye got the makin's for it. In my years, I've seen a lotta men walk a ship's deck. Most of them could do it after awhile. But ye're comin' up on the trade natural like, learnin' in days what it took some months to master."

"It's not a trade I'd wanted."

"Nope, an' me neither. Me da was a stonecutter, an' he trained me to be a stonecutter, too."

"Then why are you a pirate?"

"Same as you," Hallekk said. "Went into town and got whonked on me knob when I wasn't lookin'. Next thing I knew, I was at sea for seven years. By the time I finally made it back to Cuttersville where I'd come from, I found out me da had died in the quarry. An' the sea had laid her mark upon me; I couldn't wait to get back to a deck beneath me feet and sails a-poppin' over me knob."

"I'm sorry about your da." Even though Wick could barely keep his eyes open, Hallekk's story moved him.

"It's okay. Me da and me wasn't all that close. See,

he was trainin' me to be a stonecutter like him, but that
wasn't the path I wanted to follow."

"What did you want to be?"

Hallekk grinned and shook his head. "Back then, I
didn't know. I just didn't want to be like me da."

"I wanted to be like my father," Wick said.

"Oh? He a librarian, too?"

Wick smiled sadly. "No. He doesn't exactly approve
of me being a librarian."

"Then why wasn't ye what he was?"

"Because I wanted to be a librarian more than I
wanted to be a lamplighter."

"Betwixt ye and me," Hallekk said more quietly, "I'd
keep it to meself about what ye was if'n ye talk to crews
of other ships. Librarians don't really got good names
away from Greydawn Moors."

Wick couldn't believe his ears. "How could anyone
say such a thing? Why, the Vault of All Known Knowledge is the only thing standing between the world and
the darkness of ignorant savagery. If we didn't keep the
world's learning safe, we would lose everything. Lord
Kharrion and the goblin hordes almost took the world's
knowledge from us once. Don't they know that?"

"Aye." Hallekk nodded and puffed on his pipe. "I've
heard them legends."

"Legends!" Real anger touched Wick, for the first
time overriding the fear that he'd lived with for the last
eight days. "Kharrion's threat was not a legend! It's the
truth!"

"Mayhap," the big dwarven pirate said, "mayhap it
was the truth then. But it's not the truth now, little man.
At least, it's gettin' so's it ain't the truth. See, most folk
have a way about them, of rewritin' the past to work
into what they see now. Then that becomes the truth.
An' what they're sayin' now is that the librarians are a-
feedin' themselves off other people's fears. Fears—some

say, mind you—that are put there by the librarians in the first place so's to make themselves out to be heroes and wise men and puff up their own importance." He rolled an eye over at Wick. "And to keep eatin' without doing any real work."

"That would never happen!" Wick declared.

"An' ye know this to be true yerself? Did ye ever see Lord Kharrion or all them goblins what he was supposed to have stirred up?"

"Of course not. But I've read hundreds of books about the wars that took place against Lord Kharrion. Many of the battlefields where those encounters took place still remain, and so do the scars of battle upon them."

"So ye say," Hallekk agreed. "An' so may ye believe. But not everybody's got that belief." He waved out across the water. "Why, ye get out far enough, them stories change. There's them what believe the Vault ain't named the Vault of All Known Knowledge for all them books on them shelves. There's some what think fabulous treasures are hidden there."

"What kinds of treasures?" Wick asked.

Hallekk's gaze took on more interest. "There's them that talk of gold an' gembobs an' suchlike that are kept in the Vault. A few of 'em even talk of wizard's trinkets an' charms."

Wick didn't say anything. Images of the rooms in the Library that contained things like the quartermaster had described flashed through his mind. But each one of those items was a very important piece of the world's history as well. Their worth couldn't just be counted in gold.

Hallekk continued leaning on the railing. He pulled at the pipe casually, attention seemingly on the gray smoke that slipped away from him.

"It's not like that," Wick said.

"Oh? An' there's not them things there?"

"A few. But they're vases from past kingdoms. Heirlooms left by great families of elves and humans and dwarves. Many of them are histories."

"An' they're not worth anything, eh?"

"They're worth more than the gold and gems in them."

"Some folks, they don't care much for history. It's today that they care about. History don't fill yer belly when it's a-pressin' against yer backbone."

"People like that," Wick whispered, "would only tear the Vault apart, loot what they immediately recognized as valuable, and leave the rest to fall into ruination."

"Aye. An' probably spend their ill-gotten gain as quick as a man could. But it would be a high time while they had them coins a-jinglin' in their coin purses, wouldn't it?"

"Men like that couldn't rob the Library." Wick desperately wanted to believe that.

Hallekk scratched his chin, then glanced at the little librarian. "What I'm seein' of Greydawn Moors, little man, ye folk aren't exactly well protected. Oh aye, the Knucklebones Mountains might afford a terror or two for them what might be the least bit fainthearted, but they's climbable."

"There are the dwarven warriors and the eleven warders who have sworn to protect the Library."

"An' not near enough of 'em if more'n a few ships dropped anchor at Yonderin' Docks an' decided to crack open the Vault."

The thought filled Wick with fear. He'd always thought the goblinkin had been the greatest enemy the Library would ever have to worry about. But if legends were spreading about unguessable wealth held within the Vault of All Known Knowledge, what would keep human, elven, and dwarven brigands from tearing down the walls and looting the Library?

"Now an' don't be all grim-faced," Hallekk said. "I didn't intent to scuttle yer boat none."

"You don't know how important the Library is."

"I know some people think the Vault is important. That's part of why I keep on bein' a pirate."

"I don't understand," Wick said.

Hallekk grinned. "Well, a pirate's life is excitin' enough for me, but there's more to piratin' than just a-takin' other people's treasures. At least, it is here in the Blood-Soaked Sea. Us dwarven pirates, why we're the first line of defense against them what come a-lookin' for Greydawn Moors and the Library."

The little librarian glanced at the big dwarf doubtfully. "I've never heard anything like that."

"Mayhap ye hasn't, but it don't make it any less true, little man. I don't think it's anythin' all them grandmagisters of late would be prideful of admittin'. I've heard tell they kind of throw their noses in the air when it comes to the likes of me."

"I'm afraid I don't understand." Wick felt terribly bewildered.

"Ye bein' a librarian an' all, that's just one of the reasons ol' Cap'n Farok didn't take to ye so kindly upon first blush of meetin' ye. Us dwarven pirates in this part of the world is bound to the Library, an' grandmagisters of late don't seem to want to remember that. The grandmagisters kind of lord it over us, an' the pirate cap'ns, why they's ready to mutiny, they is. But they can't. Just let one of them pirate cap'ns decide to sail out of the Blood-Soaked Sea an' see what happens to him an' his crew."

Just one of the reasons Captain Farok didn't take kindly to me, Wick thought ruefully, but his curiosity was raised. "What happens?"

"Why their ships fall apart on 'em," Hallekk replied. "Drags 'em right down to the bottom of the sea an' tucks 'em to be with the fishes in Torloc's Locker."

"Why?" Wick was fascinated, and the empty bucket was almost forgotten at the end of his arm.

" 'Cause the pirate ships in these waters has got wizards' spells on them is why. Most of the pirate ships out a-sailin' on the Blood-Soaked Sea were first financed by the grandmagisters from the old days."

"But why would the grandmagisters finance pirate ships?"

Hallekk relit his pipe from the whale oil lantern. He puffed to get it going again. "When ye think of the Blood-Soaked Sea, what do ye think of first?"

"Why—sea monsters," Wick admitted.

A scowl fitted itself to Hallekk's broad face. "Okay, well what do ye think of after that?"

Wick considered. "The storms that are said to wrack this sea."

The scowled furrowed deeper lines into Hallekk's features. "An' then what?"

Wick really didn't want to earn the wrath of the sour-faced big dwarf, so he didn't mention the eternal fogs that seemed in place over the sea. "Well, then the pirates."

Hallekk snorted. "Ye only hear of pirates third 'cause ye ain't a-faced pirates what's screamin' at ye an' a-comin' at yer throat with a bared cutlass."

"No," Wick said. "I never have." *Nor would I ever want to.* Yet, here he was on a pirate ship where that very thing might happen. He shuddered.

Hallekk *hmph*ed in disgust. "Not a-thinkin' of pirates first thing. Why, ye oughta be ashamed of yerself."

"I've never heard that the grandmagisters conscripted pirates."

"Me," Hallekk said, "I'm a-guessin' they ain't none too proud of their hand in it. An' pirate cap'ns don't talk about the arrangement neither, but that's what happens."

"Why?" Wick's curiosity got the better of him.

"Because Greydawn Moors needed protectin', of course. Do ye really think them dwarven guards an' the elven warders on the island are enough to properly defend the Vault?"

"It helps that no one in the outside world knows where Greydawn Moors is."

"Aye, an' that's the main part of the Vault's defense," Hallekk said agreeably, "all them people a-thinkin' the Vault is a myth. But most seafarin' folk is mighty curious. Always a-wonderin' what lies over the next horizon, ye see. The Builders chose Greydawn Moors with care, just so's most of them curious sea folk would stay away. The Builders picked one of the most inhospitable places in all the world to place the Library. They took into account the monsters an' the weather, an' were glad of them an' it. An' some say the old wizards specially spelled up the algae that fills these waters."

"Algae?" Wick asked.

"Why sure," Hallekk said. "That algae is red, like fresh-spilled blood. It thrives in these waters, an' it's what gives the Blood-Soaked Sea its name. Ain't 'cause them sea monsters is constantly a-gnawin' on each other." He glanced at Wick. "A learned man like ye, why ye didn't believe them old tales, did ye?"

Wick only blinked at the big dwarf, not wanting to lie and not wanting to admit the truth either.

"If'n that was true, why there'd be a shortage of monsters in these here waters, there would. It'd take an awful lot of blood to turn these deep waters this red." Hallekk relit his pipe. "The wizards put the algae in the water an' put spells on it so it would never die. Then they arranged for the building of the pirate ships. Poured a lot of gold into the hands of a lot of shipwrights, I'm here to tell you. Then they magicked 'em."

"Magicked them?" Wick repeated.

Hallekk nodded. "Put wizards' wards on 'em what kept them ships bound to these waters. See, the grand-magisters gave the ships to them dwarves what was willin' to be pirates. An' then they made sure them dwarves wasn't a-gonna abscond with the ships by magickin' 'em to fall apart if they sail too far from Greydawn Moors. I've heard tell of whole crews a-goin' down with ships what tried to sail beyond the reaches of the Blood-Soaked Sea."

"The dwarves didn't want to be pirates?"

"No. Generally speakin', dwarves is happier on land. On top of mountains or livin' under 'em, ye see. An' they like workin' with their hands." Hallekk paused, studying the clouds scudding across the face of Jhurjan the Bold. In heartbeats, the clouds obscured the fierce moon. "No, them dwarves what signed on as the original pirates didn't come to the work natural-like. But they knew it was necessary 'cause the Builders told 'em so."

"So you aren't real pirates?" Wick asked.

Hallekk bristled. "Of course we are, and I'll keelhaul the first man what makes the mistake of a-thinkin' we ain't."

"Oh," Wick said quickly, "I would never say anything like that."

"That's good. 'Cause I won't stand for it." Hallekk gazed out to sea and sniffed. "Gonna rain soon. Ye can smell it in the air."

Wick started to agree, having realized that agreeing with Hallekk was a plan to follow, but an angry shout interrupted him.

"Lazy halfer! I mighta known ye'd be up here a-jackin' yer jaws an' me sufferin' an' not gettin' enough sleep as it is!" Slops stood in the doorway leading down belowdecks to the galley. His big-knuckled fists rested at his hips. "Well, ye done an' signed on for a world of hurt tomorrow, I'll warrant ye that."

"Leave him alone," Hallekk ordered, turning to face the other man. "I been a-watchin' how you been a-treatin' the little man here, an' I know ye been a-tryin' to break him. Only he's tougher than ye think. He's handled everythin' ye've dished out to him since he's been in the galley."

Slops crossed his meaty arms and puffed out his chest. "An' who do ye think ye are to be a-tellin' me my business?"

Wick took a step back instinctively.

Hallekk seemed to swell to twice his size. "Why, ye daft lummox, I'm quartermaster of this ship is who *I* am! An' don't ye ever think about forgettin' that! If'n ye forget again, I'll wallop ye and put a swellin' on yer crusty ol' knob what'll make ye twicet yer size!"

Wick's knees trembled. *Even if Hallekk spares me from Slops' wrath tonight, he'll make up for it tomorrow!* He started to take a step toward Slops.

"Ye just stand yer ground there, little man," Hallekk said without looking at him. "I ain't dismissed ye yet."

Wick's heart sank as he looked at the evil glare Slops shot him, but he stopped dead in his tracks. Of the two, he'd rather have Slops mad at him.

Slops cursed colorfully, then turned and marched belowdecks.

Hallekk dumped the ashes from his pipe over ship's side, then thumped the railing to fully clear the bowl. "Don't ye worry none about ol' Slops, little man. I'll have a word or two with the cap'n come morning. As quartermaster, managin' manpower is one of me duties."

Wick wasn't at all sure that course of action would help, but he wasn't about to try to talk Hallekk out of it either. Tomorrow, he was certain, would be a very bad day to be in the galley. He yawned tiredly in spite of his fears, barely managing to cover his mouth.

The big dwarven quartermaster smiled at Wick gently.

"I know ye're tired, little man. Ye should see yerself off to bed. But I wanted to talk to ye tonight, kinda put the thought in yer knob that maybe ye can still serve the Vault whilst servin' aboard *One-Eyed Peggie*." He shrugged. "Pirates an' librarians, we all serve to protect the Vault's interests."

"If you don't mind my saying so," Wick said, "but you don't really sound like you believe that."

"Oh, I believe these ships what was give to the dwarven pirates all them years ago will fall apart if'n we don't carry out our orders," Hallekk said. "Look around at ol' *One-Eyed Peggie*. However long it's been since them troubles with Lord Kharrion an' his goblin army, ol' *Peggie* don't really look none the worse for wear of it. Takes a little tendin' now an' again to keep her afloat, I'll warrant ye that, but not as much as other ships I've seen. Why, if'n ye get over to the mainland an' any of them ports what the goblinkin run, ye'll see some ships in true sorry shape. An' ain't none of them more'n fifty years old." The big dwarf slapped the solid railing in front of him. "No, ol' *Peggie*'s some magicked up, an' I know that. It's enough for me. The rest of it about the Vault an' how important it really is, I don't really know. But then, I don't really care either. My home is out here on the salt, not in Greydawn Moors. I don't have to believe in them legends."

"But it's all true. The librarians shelter the knowledge that will keep the Darkness from the lands."

"Seems to me," Hallekk said, "that a man a-wantin' to keep back a heap of darkness would pass around the light to others so it'd be bigger. Instead, the grandmagisters seem intent on holding all that knowledge—and light—at the Vault for themselves."

"Because releasing the knowledge unsupervised into the world again can be catastrophic," Wick said. Even as his words died away, he knew that his argument was

weak in the eyes of anyone brought up outside Greydawn Moors.

"Get yerself abed, little man," Hallekk said. "Time an'
tide await no man."

Wick knocked the ashes from the borrowed pipe and
handed it back to Hallekk, thanking the man profusely
for his generosity. The big dwarven quartermaster only
waved the thanks away as if the gift of the pipe were
nothing, then went on about his rounds checking with
the night men aboard the pirate ship.

Wearily, the little librarian returned to the galley to
leave the bucket. He glanced around fearfully before
stepping into the galley proper to make sure Slops
wasn't waiting up for him to start on the abuse that
would certainly start on the morrow. Wick breathed a
sigh of relief when he discovered the galley was empty.

After he'd put the bucket away, Wick retreated to the
crew quarters. He stared in dismay at the bodies filling
the large room. The pirates slept in shifts, dividing up
the watches, but most of them slept at night. Even the
small corner of the room he'd claimed seemed filled with
cast-off clothing from earlier work chores.

His nose wrinkled in disgust. He'd read about the
closeness of sailor's quarters in books, but the experience didn't compare. A book talked about the sometimes
rancid odor, but actually being there was awful.

Carefully, he threaded through the sleeping bodies and
the hammocks until he reached the corner of the room
he'd been left with for the past seven nights. Thankfully,
his hammock was still on the floor. It was twisted, but
it remained whole if unattached. He had no idea where
the borrowed bedding he'd been given was, but he
hadn't been using it anyway because it was so dirty.

After rolling the hammock up and tucking it under his
arm, Wick returned to the ship's main deck. He'd seen
men tie hammocks to the rigging before, and there were

a few there now, but he'd never dared sleep out in the open. Besides the sea monsters, there was the pirate crew that seemed to hate him.

He had to struggle with the knots and the length of the hammock cords, but he finally got them right. Carefully, he eased his weight onto the treacherous hammock. The cords rolled up tight against him, following the contours of his body. He sighed in near content.

Sleep didn't come easily. The little librarian's mind was filled with all that Hallekk had told him. Wick continued to struggle with the idea that the Builders of the Vault of All Known Knowledge had established the Blood-Soaked Sea pirates. But the reasoning behind that seemed clear enough. And Hallekk had no reason to lie.

Wick listened to the sound of the wind through the sails above him, listened to the creak of the rigging and the yardarms. Despite his best efforts to relax and the fatigue that ached within him, sleep evaded him. His mind raced, dredging up the hardships Slops would undoubtedly be inspired to put him through starting early the next morning. He burrowed into the hammock, pulling the bedding around him. His eyes closed only for a moment.

"Fire!" a man yelled suddenly. "Fire's a-comin'!"

Wick's eyes snapped open as he sat up and he immediately spotted the ball of fire arcing across the sable heavens. Other pirates took up the hue and cry of warning, filling the ship with anxious noise.

Against the night as it was, Wick couldn't properly judge how big the fireball was. For a moment it looked as though the fiery missile would miss the ship, then it turned and veered straight for *One-Eyed Peggie*.

As he watched the fireball, Wick knew it wasn't of natural origin. Should it land aboard, the thing could very well be the death of them all. He roused himself from the hammock, twisting and spilling out in his fear and fatigue, as the ship quickened around him.

The fireball slowed in its headlong descent as Wick pushed himself to his feet, and then it neatly landed on the yardarm near the crow's-nest.

6

Embyr

Wick ran across *One-Eyed Peggie*'s yawing deck, drawn to the flaming figure standing atop the yardarm. Even as his curiosity pushed him on, fear twisted his stomach with ragged claws when he realized what the flame-being might be. *They've been gone for hundreds of years! They disappeared at the end of the Cataclysm! One of them can't be here now!*

The figure stood wreathed in the night's gloom, appearing and disappearing behind the billowing sails. Flames created a nimbus of twisting orange and yellow lights around the figure's head.

The pirate in the crow's-nest yelled and drew his cutlass, but cowered at the other end of his weapon. Quick as a striking deathadder, the flaming figure swept the dwarven pirate's sword aside and slapped the man with the same hand on the return blow. The two impacts resounded over the ship's deck. The pirate pinwheeled from the crow's-nest, arcing high out over the ship, then fell. The pirate flailed his limbs and screamed until he vanished beneath the water.

"Aldy!" Hallekk's voice rang out. "Get a line out to that man afore he drowns!"

"Aye, sir!"

With Hallekk on deck, the pirates formed a skirmish

line, obviously taking comfort in the burly quartermaster's presence. Wick paused at the railing and glanced back as Hallekk strode out on deck.

Hallekk gazed upward at the flaming invader, one scarred fist wrapped around the hilt of his cutlass. "Chaury, go and wake the cap'n."

"Aye, sir." A man scrambled from the motley group forming on the deck.

"Belay that order, quartermaster," Captain Farok bellowed from behind.

The pirate crew glanced up at the forecastle. Shifting lantern light fell across Captain Farok, twisting the shadows and spinning them in all directions.

"I'm among ye," the old captain went on in a commanding voice. He gazed bravely into the top rigging of his ship. "Only a dead man could sleep through the likes of this."

Wick swallowed with difficulty, wondering if the captain truly knew what he faced. Hundreds of men, dwarves, and elves had faced creatures like the one on the yardarm during the Cataclysm, and they had fallen without ever defeating one.

"Who's come aboard my ship without my leave, quartermaster?" Farok demanded.

"I don't know, sir," Hallekk answered, waving to a handful of dwarves that had armed themselves with bows. "But I means to find out." He turned to the archers. "You men ready arrows."

Wick couldn't believe it. *Surely they're not going to try to shoot her!* He watched in frozen amazement as the archers nocked their arrows and pulled the fletchings back to their ears.

One-Eyed Peggie gently rode the waves. Breakers crashed against her bow and port side, the drumming sound echoing up over the ship. Sailcloth popped overhead.

Hallekk cupped his hands around his mouth. "Get out of that ship's riggin' or we'll feather you."

The flaming figure's head barely bent down for a moment, as if deciding that the pirates gathered below were hardly worth the effort. Fiery wings spread out behind her for a moment, then quickly folded in again.

Hallekk picked three men standing close to him. "You three clamber up them ropes an' put a sword 'twixt that thing's wind and water if ye hafta."

The three pirates sprang into action at once, quickly swarming up the rigging. Fingers and toes hooked into the rope as they climbed.

Near-panicked, Wick walked from the railing to the big dwarven quartermaster's side. "Hallekk," he called softly.

Hallekk never looked in the little librarian's direction, his eyes intent on the three pirates nearly halfway up the rigging. "Not now, little man. I got business to tend to."

"You can't send those men up there," Wick said.

"Already been done."

"It's a mistake."

That got Hallekk's attention. He lowered his gaze and glowered at the little librarian. "Mistake that was made was that thing's choice of landin' spots."

Wick gazed back up at the flaming figure as it surveyed the three climbing pirates approaching the crow's-nest. The figure remained at ease, as if the climbing men represented no threat. "She didn't have to land here."

"She?" Hallekk repeated.

Without warning, Critter glided out of the shadows and perched on Hallekk's broad shoulder. "The halfer knows who's up there," the rhowdor shrilled. "Done come up with a new way to bring more ill luck on us, he has."

All the pirates nearby gave Wick harsh stares. Although there had been no more instances of attacks by sea monsters, almost all of the crew blamed Wick for the appearance of the sea serpent eight days ago.

The little librarian shrank into himself. He wanted to do nothing more than remain lost in the background. But that would never do—not if he wanted to live long enough to see the next morning. "If you get her angry, she'll burn the ship," Wick said, "and us with it."

"Who is she?" Hallekk demanded. "I've never seen the like as someone such as her—if'n it is a her."

"An Embyr. One of Lord Kharrion's Embyrs."

"I never heard of no Embyrs."

"They're creatures Lord Kharrion made near the end of the Cataclysm. They're dangerous."

Hallekk shook his head in fierce pride. "Ain't no way whatever it is can be more dangerous than a ship full of Blood-Soaked Sea pirates."

"An Embyr is." Wick watched as the three pirates closed on the flaming woman. They climbed more slowly now, warily spreading out to attack her from three sides. Drawing their swords, they closed on her, making their way up now with one hand. "She'll burn the ship, Hallekk, and us with it."

Hallekk shook his head stubbornly. "Ain't no way she can destroy a whole ship."

"*She* can," Wick replied. "Several accounts exist concerning whole cities the Embyrs laid waste to during the Cataclysm." He watched almost breathlessly as the three pirates drew back to menace the fiery woman with their cutlasses.

Imperiously, she gestured at the three men. Flames darted from her fingers and coiled briefly around the rigging the men clung to. A wisp of smoke fluttered from the rope strands and they parted as though a fast blade had cleaved them.

The three pirates tumbled back through the rigging, squalling fearfully and crying out for help. Luckily, they maintained holds on the rigging and when the ropes got caught up in the sails and yardarms below, they managed to hang on long enough to grab back into the rigging and start down.

"Cut the halfer's throat," Critter urged. "It's him what's drawn the fire-lady to us. He's served as her scout."

"Archers," Captain Farok called.

"Aye, sir," the men armed with bows shouted in unison.

"No!" Wick glanced at the dwarven pirate captain, knowing the man wouldn't hesitate to give the order. "You've got to stop him."

"See?" Critter crowed. "Even now the halfer's a-seekin' to protect his co-conspirator. Why, if'n you listen to him, we'll all be—"

Hallekk brushed the rhowdor from his shoulder. Critter protested in a vile curse, then flapped his wings and glided to the railing where two men helped aboard the pirate who'd been knocked from the crow's-nest. "Not my job to be a-tellin' Cap'n Farok his business."

"Fire!" Captain Farok roared.

Bowstrings thrummed as the archers released their deadly missiles. Of the five arrows, only four came close to the fiery-headed woman. She folded her arms across her chest, flared her wings threateningly, and glared at the arrows as they burst into fire, turning to small, ashen clouds before they reached her.

Hallekk clenched Wick's shoulder in a massive fist. Worry tightened his voice. "Is she a wizard, little man?"

"No," Wick answered. Hallekk pushed him toward the forecastle so fast that Wick had to run in order to keep from being dumped face-first onto the deck. Fearful pirates made way for them, but the little librarian noted that they all gazed at him with hatred in their eyes. *They're blaming me!* He couldn't believe it.

Suddenly, the fire-headed woman's mocking laughter rang out over the ship. It was cold and calculated, a hollow sound that had never known mirth. The sound gave Wick goosebumps. The Embyr's voice pealed through the night above the dull growl of the ocean. "Who commands this vessel?"

"I do," Captain Farok called without hesitation. No one else spoke, and the pirates standing around the captain took small steps that carried them away from the old man. If Farok noticed the attrition in the ranks, he gave no sign of it. "I'm Cap'n Farok Roguar of the good ship *One-Eyed Peggie,* an' I've given ye fair warnin' to step clear of me vessel."

Hallekk pushed Wick to the top of the stairs and toward the dwarven pirate captain. "If ye know she's an Embyr, as ye called her, then ye got to have some idea of what-all she's about."

"Revenge," Wick gasped, almost out of breath from the rapid pace Hallekk kept, "Embyrs burn for revenge."

The big dwarf shook his head. "I know we ain't done nothing to her. Have ye ever—"

"Not me," Wick replied hurriedly.

The flames around the Embyr's head blazed brighter and stood taller, no longer bowing before the wind filling *One-Eyed Peggie*'s sails. She threw a hand forward and a fireball took shape in an instant, launching from her palm.

The fireball sped across the distance in the blink of an eye, but most of the pirates moved faster. Wick dove for the forecastle deck and wrapped his hands over his head. Only a few feet away, Captain Farok dropped behind the railing.

With a thunderous *WHOOSH!,* the fireball slammed into the railing and reduced a three-foot section into flaming splinters. Pirates cursed and cried out, but they stayed hunkered down where they were, fearing another such attack.

Cautiously, Wick peered through his spread fingers. Heat from the flames clinging to the wreckage of the railing pressed against him like the doughy bread from an oven. Steam rose from the water-dampened decks. The explosion echoed in the little librarian's ears.

Hallekk grabbed Wick by the elbow and helped him to his feet. The big dwarf thumped at the cinders clinging to his jacket as he pushed Wick toward Captain Farok.

"Do not," the Embyr shouted, "presume again to tell me what to do, dwarf."

Frightened, Wick glanced across the ruin of the forecastle railing and saw that the woman remained near the crow's-nest. He squatted down beside Captain Farok at Hallekk's heavy-handed insistence.

"Why did ye bring this halfer over to me?" Captain Farok demanded. His rage and fear drew harsh lines around his mouth.

"Because, Cap'n," Hallekk said, clapping Wick on the back, "this little man knows what that thing is. I mean, what *she* is."

Captain Farok scowled and spat. "She's sudden death is what she is, Hallekk. Any fool what's got an eye in his head can see that." He glanced at the flames leeching at the forecastle deck only a short distance away. He pointed at one of the cowering pirates around him. "Get that fire put out this instant or I'll see that ye get the lash if'n we survive this."

After only a momentary hesitation, the pirate crawled on hands and knees across the deck. He retrieved a bucket of wet sand from the forward railing kept there for emergencies, then poured it over the flames. The wet sand extinguished the fire with an audible hiss.

Farok studied Wick suspiciously. Then he raised his

voice and glanced at the flame-being. "All right, woman, ye got me attention. What is it ye'll be a-wantin'?" Then he lowered his voice to a whisper as he returned his attention to Wick. "What is she?"

"An Embyr," Hallekk replied.

"An *Embyr?*" Still seated, Farok turned carefully and stared up into the rigging, weighing his words carefully. "One of them foul creatures Kharrion made at the end of the Cataclysm? Supposed to sit in judgment on the races of men, elves, dwellers and dwarves?"

Hallekk looked at Wick.

"Yes," the little librarian said, surprised at the captain's knowledge. "You know about the Embyrs?"

Farok grunted. "Somewhat. Me ol' granny was a tale-teller what liked them old stories. I've heard of the Embyrs. Supposed to be seven of 'em, right?"

"Nine," Wick corrected automatically, then quickly added, "sir."

Farok nodded and gazed carefully over the railing. "I stand corrected, halfer. But it don't matter a whit to me how many of 'em survived the final battles of the Cataclysm. I'm a-thinkin' I already got one too many Embyrs on me ship now." His direct gaze narrowed. "Is she here for you, halfer?"

"No," Wick said. "I've never seen an Embyr before tonight. Most scholars had believed they'd passed from this world with the defeat of Lord Kharrion."

"I came," the Embyr stated calmly in her chilling voice, "to burn you and your ship, Captain Farok."

"Why?" Farok asked irritably. "Me an' mine ain't ever done nothin' to you."

"Because I wish to," the Embyr taunted. "And because I can."

"An' that remains to be seen," Farok roared.

"I'll burn you," the Embyr promised, "because it will satisfy me to do so." She held her hands out at her sides at shoulder height. Flames exploded in sheets from her fingertips, cascading into the white-capped waves for the space of a drawn breath. Billowing white steam shot up, bleeding into the gray fog. At the same moment, all the lanterns aboardship suddenly blazed, the flames momentarily breaking free of their confines.

"What brought you to me?" Farok asked.

The Embyr drew her arms into herself and began to sing. The magic inherent in her words drained the moisture from the air surrounding *One-Eyed Peggie.*

"She can't answer your question," Wick said, watching the fiery-headed woman. "Even she doesn't know what brought her here. Embyrs are vindictive creatures, created from hate by Lord Kharrion to do harm to everyone. Taldour had a saying about Embyrs in his *Collected Works of Omens and Portents from the Cataclysm.* 'No man may know the whim or will of the Embyrs, and although a man can see where an Embyr has been, it is hard to know when one is coming.' "

"Did Taldour happen to mention any ways of gettin' rid of an unwanted Embyr?" Farok asked.

Hesitantly, not wanting to get the captain's ire directed at him for however long they had left to live, Wick said, "No." He glanced over at the Embyr.

The Embyr stood with her arms spread in front of her, while high over her head melon-sized fireballs appeared in the sky and began orbiting each other. As she sang, the fireballs grew greater in size and glowed more brightly, changing from a deep red to orange and yellow.

"What's she doing?" Farok demanded.

Wick listened to the beautiful music. "She's singing her death song."

"She's gonna die now?" the pirate captain asked.

"No," Wick replied. "We are."

Farok gave a soured *harumph.* "Ye have the nerve to call yerself a learned man, an' ye sit here a-cowerin' an' not a thought in that great melon of a head of yers how we're a-gonna get out of this."

"There's no denying an Embyr's moment of vengeance." Wick knew it was true. In all the tales of the Cataclysm, the Embyrs had never been defeated.

The fireballs spun faster above the Embyr's head.

"C'mon, little man," Hallekk said, his voice tight with desperation. "Think. Everything has a weakness. We got a whole ocean here to drown her in if'n we can figure out how."

Wick shook his head, searching through his memories of the creatures. "You can't drown Embyrs. They pursued Malnichik through the Floating Cities on the Dragonwing Sea. Even when they had to go underground in the islands and one of the sisters was trapped in a flooded chamber she didn't die. She still burned her way through the wall. Malnichik died only moments after that."

"Ye really know how to make a man feel hopeful, don't ye?"

Wick thought frantically as he watched the fireballs spin faster and faster, till they blurred into a solid ring of flame. *Everyone wants something. That's the cornerstone of Lhomror's* Edicts of Bartering in the Non-Feudal Community. *But what would an Embyr want?* Although the little librarian thought fiercely, nothing came to mind. He thought of his family, knowing that if things ended here and now, none of them would ever know what happened to him. They would only forever wonder. It would be a truly sad thing, and even that would be mourned for—

A glimmering of an idea rocked his mind. His breath caught as he turned the idea over. It might fail, might turn into a last-minute burst of wasted breath—but it might save them, too. Or at least give the Embyr pause.

Knowing they were almost out of time before the Embyr struck, Wick forced himself to stand on trembling legs. Due to his short height, he only raised his head and shoulders above the railing. He held his empty hands high and addressed the Embyr. "Wait." His voice cracked. "Please—wait."

Her fiery head turned toward him. Her cruel lips turned up in a cold smile despite the flames surrounding her. "No." She drew her arm back, preparing to cast the spell. The heat from the spinning fireballs had already warmed the pirate ship and driven the fog into retreat.

No? Wick was shocked. In the books he'd read from Hralbomm's Wing, heroes and villains and foul creatures always granted each other some temporary respite. That was the time when all the great speeches were made. In the real life histories he'd read, great leaders took those moments to work out treaty details that often saved the lives of hundreds of men. At least during those times a warrior had proper time to make peace with his maker.

"Goodbye, halfer," the Embyr said. She drew her arm back and threw the whirling fireballs at the little librarian.

The light of the flames blazed, filling Wick's vision. *"I know who you are!"* he shouted as loudly as he could manage. He watched, paralyzed, as the fireballs soared toward him. *"I KNOW WHO YOU ARE!"*

Then the fireballs retreated, pulling back to the Embyr in the blink of an eye. They orbited over her head. "What did you say?" the Embyr demanded.

"I said," Wick told her in his quavering voice, "that I know who you are." From the Embyr's body stance, he realized that she had heard and was interested in what he had to say. "I knew who you were—from *before* the time you were changed."

"I was not changed," the Embyr replied. "I have always been what I am."

But you hesitated, Wick thought, *you hesitated be-*

*cause somewhere deep inside yourself, you know that you were something—some*one—*else.* "Do you remember King Amalryn?"

"I know no one by that name," the Embyr replied.

"You know him," Wick insisted. "Lord Kharrion took him from you and made you into the thing that you have become." He hoped that all the old texts he'd read concerning the Embyrs were correct. "I've been taught that you will know a lie that has been told to you."

She nodded slightly but kept her hand up to control the whirling fireballs. "No man may lie to an Embyr."

"Am I lying to you?" Wick remained standing with effort, forcing his legs to hold him upright. He shook all over and his voice continued to crack.

The Embyr waited, and the hiss of the flames burning in the air sounded all over the ship, drowning out the waves lapping against *One-Eyed Peggie*'s starboard side. "You believe the words you are saying," she said after a moment.

"Do you remember King Amalryn?" Wick asked.

"The name means nothing to me."

Wick's hope began to sink. If the Embyr couldn't remember King Amalryn because of Lord Kharrion's spell-weaving, *One-Eyed Peggie* and her crew had no chance. "Amalryn ruled the elven city of Cloud Heights. Once, the kingdom was thought to be the most beautiful of all the arboreal communities the elves built. Even the dwarves were jealous of the city's flawless design."

"Not likely," Captain Farok breathed. "But keep talkin', halfer. At least she ain't a-blastin' us yet."

Wick swayed on the ship's deck as *One-Eyed Peggie* ran with a port wind. He tried to ignore the captain's words. The little librarian's throat was dryer than he could ever remember it. "King Amalryn lived within Cloud Heights, in a castle crafted completely of amber. When the sun hit the castle, it shone like a jewel clutched

in the branches of the tallest tree in Silverleaves Glen."
Pictures of the elven kingdom had been rendered in several of the books Wick had read. The amber castle sat amid thick branches, glinting yellow-gold against the riot of green and silver leaves.

"You are wasting my time," the Embyr accused.

"No," Wick said, "I'm not. It's said that the Embyrs burn brightest because time stands still for them. They can't remember the past; all that holds true for them is the present."

"Not true," the Embyr declared.

"Then tell me," Wick said, trembling terribly because he knew he might only raise the creature's wrath, "where you were before you arrived on this ship."

The Embyr shifted uncomfortably on the yardarm, maintaining her stance without apparent effort. "You vex me, halfer."

"You can't remember," Wick said gently, "because Lord Kharrion made you so you couldn't. He took many things from you to make you as you are."

"They were worthless things," the Embyr stated. "I did not need them. Who needs to remember yesterday when it is today that is meant for the living?"

"King Amalryn," Wick went on, mastering the quavering in his voice with effort, "was blessed with children. He and his queen, N'riya, had twelve children—three sons and nine daughters. By all accounts, the elven king loved his children with a father's proud fierceness. His children, he told all his friends and those who had business dealings with him, were his treasure, his life, and his legacy. Everyone who knew him knew this was true."

The Embyr held out a hand. "Come more closely to me, halfer, that your words will not be whipped about by the wind. I would hear more of this king and his children."

Wick glanced into the rigging, seeing how high she was above the unforgiving deck and the treacherous water. One misstep would surely mean the death of him. "Lady, climbing into the ship's rigging is not—"

"Come," the Embyr declared, and this time it was not an invitation, but an order.

Reluctantly, Wick went back down the forecastle stairs on trembling legs. He stopped amidships and looked up into the rigging. The ship yawed at least six or eight feet each way with the pitch of the ocean. The Embyr stood easily on the yardarm, but the little librarian knew it would not be the same for him. He'd gazed down from heights before, the Knucklebones were filled with spectacular views, but he'd been anchored the whole time to the earth.

At the foot of the main mast, he reached for the bottom of the rigging and found it inches out of his grasp. He sighed with relief. *I can't reach it. Surely she will understand—*

Two powerful hands caught Wick up under the arms and hoisted him up toward the rigging. "I got ye, little man," Hallekk said from behind him. The big dwarf lifted the little librarian easily within reach of the rigging. "Grab ahold an' start climbing."

Numbly, Wick seized the rigging with his hands and hooked his toes into it as well. He clung to the rope strands for a moment, feeling his body pull away from the rigging as *One-Eyed Peggie* surged forward, then press against the rigging as the ship bottomed out between swells. Climbing rigging definitely wasn't like climbing a ladder in one of the big rooms back in the Library.

"Don't freeze up, little man," Hallekk coaxed. "Ye can do this."

Wick remained plastered against the rigging. He gazed upward at the fiery figure waiting for him. Even now, he knew, Lord Kharrion's spell of forgetfulness would be working against him. How long would the Embyr remember what he'd told her without him continuing his tale? Five minutes? Perhaps ten? Struggling against the cold, fearful doubt concerning his own climbing abilities as well as the course he'd taken to face the Embyr, the little librarian freed a hand and reached upward.

"That's it," Hallekk encouraged. "Keep a-goin'. Ye got it now."

The little librarian kept climbing, losing himself in the mass of billowed sails. He felt the increased sway of the ship rocking his body lazily. Before he could stop himself, he glanced down. The deck tilted nearly sixty feet below him, and suddenly—with the black ocean spread all around *One-Eyed Peggie*—that height seemed greater than any other he'd known.

Wick froze. His stomach turned flip-flops, like a hare trying in vain to escape a hunter's trap.

Hallekk looked up at him. "Keep climbing, little man."

Carefully, fearing the slightest move might tear him free of his precarious perch, Wick shook his head.

"Halfer," the Embyr called down.

Wick pulled himself against the rigging tightly and squeezed his eyes shut. He willed himself to reach up again. But he couldn't. He was too afraid.

"Lady," Hallekk called from below. "He's seized up, scared. He's never been in a ship's riggin' before. It ain't his fault he can't make it."

"You try my patience, halfer," the Embyr said.

"I apologize," Wick mumbled. He closed his eyes again, but the vision of the ship's deck dancing below him wouldn't leave his mind.

"Lady," Hallekk called up again, "if'n ye will allow it, I'll climb up there with the little man. I can help get him a-goin' again."

"Do it."

The rigging suddenly jerked in Wick's grip, causing him to tighten up even more. He slitted his eyes and saw Hallekk scrambling up through the rigging as if the feat were nothing. In seconds, the big dwarven pirate clung nonchalantly to the rigging beside Wick.

"I can't let go," the little librarian said.

"Sure ye can," Hallekk said with a good-natured grin. "I'm here. I ain't a-gonna let nothin' happen to ye. Climbing this here riggin', why there ain't nothin' to it."

"I can't move my hands, Hallekk." Wick couldn't believe the pirate didn't understand him.

"Listen, little man," Hallekk said gruffly, "maybe ye're a librarian an' ye know a whole slew of words more than I do, but I know men an' I know the sea. An' I'm a-tellin' ye now ye can do this thing."

"I can't," Wick insisted.

Hallekk leaned in close to him, whispering into his ear. "If'n ye can't, little man, we're all dead. Now ye relax, an' ye listen to me because I'm good at what I do. I ain't never lost a man outta this riggin' that I come up to get."

Wick squeezed his eyes shut and tried to will away the vertigo that gripped him. He nodded and swallowed hard. "I don't know if I can convince her to leave us alone."

"I know." Hallekk clapped him on the shoulder. "But ye've kept us alive this far. I've got some faith in ye, I do. Now ye put some faith in ol' Hallekk."

"Okay." Wick breathed out with difficulty, then forced his head upward before opening his eyes. The Embyr remained standing above him. He reached up with a shaking hand.

" 'At's the boy," Hallekk congratulated. "Just keep climbin'."

Slowly and with great fear, Wick made the rest of the

climb to the crow's-nest. The whirling fireballs gener-
ated enough heat to make him sweat and feel uncomfortable in his clothing. He clambered into the crow's-
nest, hoping that he would feel more secure. But with
the way the ship pitched on the ocean that wasn't possible. He studied the Embyr.

Her build was elven, thin and petite. Her pointed ears
showed against the sides of her head through holes cut
into the hooded garment she wore that covered everything but her face like another skin. The garment hugged
her body, making her look even more slender and totally
smooth. Upon closer inspection, Wick was surprised to
see that the garment appeared to be crafted from lizard
skin. The scales were so darkly red they were almost
black. Flames curled around her head like a mane caught
by the wind. Her gloves and boots were the same dark
red as the body garment. The fiery wings were at least
twenty feet across and had an abbreviated skeleton structure buried in the flames.

Her face was pale white, resembling snow on a moun-
taintop, but her lips were blood red. Deeply set eyes
burned like obscenely glowing coals under blond eyebrows. Occasional sparks drifted up from those eyes and
faded away into the night. She regarded him with glacial
intensity despite the flickering fires showing within.

"Tell me of this elven king," she ordered.

Wick gathered his wits and tried to figure out where
to begin. He was a Third Level Librarian at the Vault
of All Known Knowledge. He might not be a pirate, or
even a sailor, but he was better than a potato-peeler and
dishwasher. Wisdom, Grandmagister Ludaan had always
said, was strength in all things that only grew stronger
with time.

Hallekk clambered into the the crow's-nest with the
little librarian and hunkered down so the Embyr
wouldn't perceive him as a threat. The big dwarf whis-

pered, "Ye're not alone, little man. Come what will of this, ye won't face it by yerself. Ye got me word on that. Ol' Hallekk will never let a man with some spunk in him die by himself."

"Thank you," Wick whispered, feeling pride and uncertainty all at once. If he were wrong about the Embyr, Hallekk would probably have had a better chance of surviving by staying below. The little librarian looked at the Embyr and began in his best voice.

7

A Dark Tale

Long and long ago," Wick began, "when the world was still young and ripe and full of promise, and the blight that became known as Lord Kharrion was unknown, there lived an elven king named Amalryn deep within the bountiful forest called Silverleaves Glen."

The Embyr stood resolutely, but the little librarian knew from her body posture that his words claimed all her attention.

"King Amalryn was a warrior," Wick continued. "He fought the goblinkin that lived within Silverleaves Glen as his father and his father's father before him. It was during his reign that the Dhirtpur goblins were finally driven from the forest. But Amalryn was a man of peace as well. Once the war had been won, he sheathed his mighty blade and turned his attention to building Cloud Heights into the most majestic elven city that had ever been."

"And this city was made of amber?" The Embyr's voice softened.

"Yes," Wick replied. "Each building, each home, was made from the purest amber that could be mined by the Krupperdell dwarves, who lived along the Wandering Mere and were renowned for their mining skills. The

Cloud Heights elves traded herbs and spices that could only be taken from the tops of trees, as well as the best sculptures and paintings their artisans could create. As you know, dwarves like things that are bright and shiny and unique."

Hallekk grunted in agreement.

"Some of the elven goods," Wick said, "were traded to humans. Wizards in those days always needed specially crafted things for the holding of spells or wards, even occasional thoughts. Or so I am told. In return, the Krupperdell dwarves got mining contracts from the humans that other dwarves might have gotten. It was a very profitable arrangement for all concerned."

"The city was very beautiful," the Embyr whispered. Lights flared in her eyes that looked like burning coals.

"Yes," Wick agreed. "The houses shone the color of spun honey, and even carried a glow about them for a few moments after sunset."

"The city was destroyed." The words turned harsh, and pain creased the Embyr's smooth face.

"Yes, in time." Wick hurried on, not wanting to leave the Embyr thinking dark thoughts of destruction. "But before then, King Amalryn ruled and his people knew nothing but peace and prosperity. The city was built and gleamed like crusted jewels in the sun. Elven children played among the leafy boughs."

"There were rope ladders strung between the buildings and trees," the Embyr said quietly. "Tell me of King Amalryn. What was he like?"

"King Amalryn was a handsome elven man," Wick said. "He had thick red hair—"

"Like yours?" the Embyr asked.

Wick felt embarrassed, and the feeling was most irritating intruding as it did while he was scared for his very life. "The king's hair was striking. Some said that it looked like hammered fire. He wore a small beard—"

"That just covered his chin," the Embyr interrupted. "And his eyes were the cool dark green of perfect emeralds." Excitement flared within the Embyr and her features softened. A small smile touched her lips.

As Wick watched the Embyr's transformation, he realized it was hard to keep in mind that she was singularly the most deadly person—*thing,* he forcibly reminded himself—that he had ever encountered. But for the moment he could see the child that still lurked within. "The king, it is said, had an easy way about him, a willingness to laugh and share his life that the other kings before him had not. The historians say that he was king by blood, but ruler by the will of his people."

The Embyr focused on Wick again. "Tell me of the queen. Was she pretty?"

"She was very pretty," Wick assured her. "Her hair was blond, so pale that it only remained a whisker short of white. Her features were likewise fair and as pure as milk, for the Rainbow Falls elves preferred the shady expanse of the Carthig Forests, and the moonlit nights to time spent out under the sun." The love between King Amalryn and Queen N'riya was the subject of several books and long poems.

"How did they meet?" The fireballs pulsed occasionally in their mad flight over the Embyr's head.

"The elven clans shared the Belling River," Wick answered. "Though they were more than a hundred miles apart, the roots of the trees that housed the Cloud Heights elves fed from the same waters that the Rainbow Falls elves used first. The two elven clans were aware of each other, but seldom did more than a little trading. Each remained fiercely independent of the other. The arboreal elves couldn't understand why the Rainbow Falls elves chose to live on the ground like men and dwarves, and the Rainbow Falls elves begrudged the Cloud Heights elves their arrogance of the choice of living in the trees."

"But they never fought," the Embyr said.

"Not each other," Wick agreed. "But there were others. Besides the Belling River, they also shared a common enemy. When the goblinkin left Silverleaves Glen, driven out by the swords and spears of King Amalryn's fierce warriors, some of those creatures invaded the lush valleys of Rainbow Falls, thinking to rout the elven clan and take up residence there. Lady N'riya was the oldest of her father's children. As such, she'd insisted upon becoming trained as a warrior. Most elven women are trained to fight, but not as warriors on a battlefield. Lady N'riya, however, wore armor and rode at her father's side."

Sparks blazed from the Embyr's eyes. "Her father had trouble saying no to her."

"Exactly. Princess N'riya's stubbornness was legend among the Rainbow Falls clan. However, the goblinkin had a plan. They worked hard and created rock falls along the narrowest part of the Belling River, at a juncture where it plunged through the foothills of the Hunkered Mountains. Within hours, the river was dammed. The river began to rise, swelling up onto its banks, and less than a week later—as the goblinkin had known it would—the rainy season hit."

Pain crossed the Embyr's beautiful face. She shook her head. "Please hurry with the story. I'm afraid I will forget."

Wick studied the Embyr and saw the flickering knowledge that had dawned in the burning eyes. *She does remember part of it.* A chill skittered down the little librarian's spine despite the heat the Embyr gave off because he knew there was so much more he would have to tell her. "As the Belling River swelled during the rainy season, it flooded the upriver lands of the Rainbow Falls elves, spilling over onto the banks and creating great swamplands where their homes had once been. And further downriver, a great drought like no one had ever before seen threatened the Cloud Heights elves."

The creak of *One-Eyed Peggie's* rigging sounded mournful. Hallekk sat on his haunches in the crow's-nest, totally immersed in Wick's story and seemingly no longer aware that they sat looking death in the eye.

"Incredibly," Wick went on, "Silverleaves Glen began to wither. Leaves fell from the trees and littered the ground. For a time, there was talk that Kireek, the elven goddess, had turned away from the Cloud Heights clan. But King Amalryn raised his army and marched upriver. In the meantime, news of the goblins' success reached still more goblins who were all too willing to fight the elves."

"Goblins have always been jealous of the elves," the Embyr said. "They envy the beauty of the elves."

"By this time, Lord Kharrion had begun his war against the world. He'd gathered magic items from far and wide, and built army after army. Still, not all of the goblins believed in him, but they were aware of the foulness that became known as the Goblin Lord. So they gathered there in the Hunkered Mountains to war against the Cloud Heights elves and the Rainbow Falls elves. And that is where King Amalryn met the Princess N'riya. The battle for the Belling River in the Hunkered Mountains lasted for months. The goblinkin had dug into the mountains, using caves and tunnels that were already there, and they'd dug still others, knowing the elves would come to them."

The Embyr's eyes blazed again, sending sparks streaking. "But the goblinkin didn't defeat the elves."

"No. The elves loved their lands, and during the prolonged battle, King Amalryn came to love the Princess

N'riya, and she came to love him." Wick paused. "Their love for each other was the strength their people needed to win that battle. At the end of it, the goblinkin were driven from the Hunkered Mountains and the Belling River was freed once more."

"Then the king and princess were married."

"From all accounts," Wick said, feeling sorrow at what lay ahead in the story, "they were the happiest family anyone had ever seen. Not only did the king and queen's love for each other and their children unite their clan lands, but it drew other elven clan lands under their banner. For thirty years, the king and queen guided the Western Empire, and they watched the growing threat of the goblinkin under Lord Kharrion in the southeastern lands."

"They feared Lord Kharrion," the Embyr said in a small voice.

"And Lord Kharrion feared the king and queen. As the Goblin Lord advanced his armies across the world, destroying everything in their path, King Amalryn and Queen N'riya sent forces and gold to help those cities in need. People who no longer had homes to live in found new homes in the Western Empire. The army there grew, and the king and queen were able to send more warriors out to combat Lord Kharrion's goblinkin troops. Then the day came that the Goblin Lord could no longer ignore the growing Western Empire."

One-Eyed Peggie rode the sea roughly, twisting and turning slightly. Glancing down, Wick saw that Captain Farok had taken the great wheel himself. The ship's crew clustered in knots, talking among themselves as they gazed fearfully up into the rigging.

"Lord Kharrion struck without warning," the little librarian went on. "Before King Amalryn and Queen N'riya would have thought it possible, a bloodthirsty goblin horde materialized within Cloud Heights, and it was led by Lord Kharrion himself. For thirteen days, the Battle for Cloud Heights raged. The warriors of the Western Empire fought valiantly, but their forces had been spread too widely as they sought to salvage what they could of the ransacked cities. They couldn't be re-called in time. At the end of those thirteen days, Lord Kharrion entered the amber keep of Cloud Heights as its new master."

The Embyr shuddered and hugged herself tightly. She drew her fiery wings in close around her slender body.

A pang of regret passed through Wick. For the first time, he thought the Embyr looked small, a pale flicker bravely lit against all the darkness of night around her.

"What of the king and queen?" the Embyr asked in the thinnest of whispers.

"Lord Kharrion," Wick said softly, "wished to make examples of them. The Goblin Lord bound the king and queen and made them watch as his warriors executed their three sons."

"Please," the Embyr said hoarsely. Liquid fire trailed down her inhumanly beautiful face.

Hesitation stilled Wick's tongue for a moment. "I can stop, lady, if you wish." *And if I do, will you still want to burn us all?* He could hardly breathe.

"No," she said, "you can't stop. I must hear it. *All of it.* I can almost remember."

But you don't want to, do you? Wick wished there was some other way, but he knew there wasn't. "After King Amalryn's and Queen N'riya's sons were dead, the Goblin Lord turned his malicious attentions to the nine princesses. For a month, the Goblin Lord prepared his spells, then he summoned the king and queen and their daughters from the dark caves in the riverbanks of the Belling River where they'd been kept as prisoners. None of the family had seen each other during that month, and each of them had feared for the others."

The fog pulled in toward *One-Eyed Peggie* again, no longer held at bay by the Embyr's blazing heat.

Wick steeled himself against the memory of the pictures he'd seen rendered in the texts he'd read. "King Amalryn and Queen N'riya were bound by iron spikes and their chains to the floor of the great amber palace. They could not touch each other. Nor could they touch their daughters. Then the nine princesses were secured to the floor in a like manner in a circle around Lord Kharrion. The oldest of the daughters was twenty-five. The youngest was named Jessalyn. She was eight."

"Jessalyn," the Embyr repeated in a hoarse half-whisper. *"Jessalyn."* She gazed at Wick with her burning eyes. "I had forgotten. I had forgotten so much."

"I know," Wick said, and was surprised at how thick his own voice was. It cracked, betraying him for a moment when he started again, and he felt hot tears cooling on his cheeks as the wind passed around him. He didn't want to go on, but he knew he had no choice. "Using those evil spells and cantrips he'd learned, Lord Kharrion stripped the princesses' humanity from them, and he stripped their memories of who they were and what had happened to them. Despite the pain and agony of the changes that wracked them, the princesses lived."

"No," the Embyr said fiercely. "They didn't live. They only survived." Her fiery eyes locked onto Wick's. "Why do you think that they did that?"

Heart near bursting with fear and the unexpected pain of the loss that had happened all those years ago, Wick held her gaze, aware that she had the power to turn him into a cinder with an eyeblink. He couldn't turn away from her, couldn't turn away from the honesty and misery that she showed him. "Some say that hope still dwelt in the princesses," he stated softly.

"It can't be," the Embyr argued. "Not after everything they had lost."

"The king and queen," the little librarian said, "gave each of their children the greatest gift of all when they were born."

"It is a curse."

"Each of their children," Wick stated, "was given a longing for what might be. As each child in turn was born, except for the twins—and they were gifted at the same time—King Amalryn and Queen N'riya blessed their sons and daughters with a magic spell from the Old Ones. Legend has it that each child would someday have a great destiny to fulfill, a moment in time that would mark history with their passage for ever and ever."

The Embyr lifted her head, revealing her flame-stained cheeks and her otherworldly eyes. "You are not evil."

Wick shook his head slowly. "No."

"And you don't deserve my anger," the Embyr said.

"I truly don't believe so," Wick replied, feeling only slightly relieved. In the next moment, the Embyr could forget she'd ever come to that decision.

The Embyr unfurled her wings slightly. The wind caught them, spreading the fiery membrane out a little more. "What became of Lord Kharrion?"

"He was destroyed," Wick said.

"If Lord Kharrion is dead, shouldn't I be freed from his curse?" the Embyr asked.

"I don't know," Wick answered. "The spells the Goblin Lord used were very old and powerful. You and your sisters were ensorcelled to be his heralds. He'd hoped that you would rain down destruction upon those who opposed him."

"And did we?"

Wick swallowed hard; he really didn't want to answer the question because it would only burden her. "Yes."

"We must have done terrible things."

Hundreds, Wick remembered from his reading, but he didn't have the heart to mention any details.

She gazed down at the deck. "Those men fear me." Her fiery gaze rested on him. "And you fear me."

The little librarian nodded wordlessly, knowing there was nothing he could say to soften the truth.

"It is an awful thing to be feared." The Embyr let out a long breath, and flames charged out with it. "If we meet again, I won't know you, will I?"

"No."

Her chin came up defiantly. She locked eyes with Hallekk for a moment, then returned her attention to Wick. "I could have destroyed this entire ship."

"Yes," Wick said. "You could have."

"I could have slain you before you told your tale."

A shiver passed through the little librarian. "I'm very glad you didn't."

The Embyr spread her wings. The wind hammered through the thin membrane between the bony ridges and threw doughy heat over the little dweller. "I have to go, before I forget everything. And I want to remember long enough to get far enough away that I won't come back. Along with everything else that I forget, I need to forget that you and this ship are here."

"That," Wick agreed, "would probably be for the best."

The Embyr turned and walked without apparent effort to the end of the yardarm away from the little librarian. There she stopped, and when she turned back to Wick, her fiery gaze was troubled. "You spoke of nine princesses."

Wick nodded, dreading what he was certain would be asked.

"Do you know," the Embyr asked softly, "which one of the nine princesses I am?"

"No, Princess, I don't. I'm sorry." Wick looked at her sorrowfully. *How much pain can one so young endure?*

"No one remembers?"

"I don't know."

The Embyr looked away. "What is your name? I forget if you told me, and if you did, I apologize."

"I am Edgewick Lamplighter, Third Level Librarian at the Vault of All Known Knowledge. My friends call me Wick."

"May I call you Wick? I mean, for the time that I remember you?"

"Of course."

"Would you do me a favor, Wick?"

"If I can."

The Embyr recrossed the yardarm toward him. Fiery tears streamed down her face. "Remember me, Wick. Remember that despite the evil things that the enchantment on me makes me do that I wasn't always evil."

"I will," Wick promised. Tears filled his own eyes as he looked upon her fierce, bright beauty and saw the pain and confusion in her.

She reached for him with her hands, the flames dying away from them.

Hesitantly, Wick took the Embyr's hands in his. Her hands were surprisingly cool and small within his.

The Embyr withdrew her hands from his and the flames rushed back down over them. "Goodbye, Wick." She turned and ran back along the yardarm. Without breaking stride, she launched herself from the end of the yardarm. Her fiery wings ignited in a sudden inferno and swept out. She hurtled through the darkness from *One-Eyed Peggie* like a flaming load from a catapult.

"Goodbye, Princess," Wick called around the thick lump that had filled his throat. He stood in the crow's-nest, no longer bothered by the heights or the pitching sea. He watched as her light grew dimmer and dimmer. And he felt suddenly guilty for his own homesick pangs. The Embyrs had no homes; they did not even have each other or themselves.

Hallekk dropped a heavy hand onto the little librarian's shoulder. "C'mon, little man, there's naught ye can do here."

"I hurt her," Wick whispered. "I told her what she was. I reminded her of her lost family."

"She will forget, little man. Give her five minutes an' she won't even remember yer name. We get really lucky, she won't remember we was here."

"When I last saw my father," Wick said, "before I unwillingly began this voyage, we argued. I was working on a set of lanterns that I always helped him with. We never knew where they came from, nor did their owner. But I got the idea that I could check resource books and figure out where the lanterns came from." The little librarian halted, unable to go on.

"An' why would yer da have trouble with that?"

Wick watched the flickering light disappearing over the distant horizon and felt suddenly cold and lonely and uncertain. "He told me not everything had to be known in this life, that not even Librarians could know everything—or even should." He glanced at Hallekk. "I think my father was right. She didn't need to know everything that I told her."

Hallekk scratched under his chin and thought for a moment. "Little man, if'n ye hadn't have known what she was—bein' an Embyr an' all, I mean—an' if ye hadn't a-told her about, I'm thinkin' everybody what's aboard *One-Eyed Peggie* would be dead now. It was the Goblin Lord what made the greatest wrong. Ye was just a-tryin' to make the best of what we done got handed tonight."

Wick stared at the horizon and was barely able to make it out through the thick swaths of fog that swirled in around the pirate ship.

"Now let's ye and me climb on back down this riggin' an' see if'n there's anything the cap'n might need done."

Hurting and confused, afraid that his trembling arms and legs wouldn't support his weight, Wick threw a leg over the crow's-nest and followed the dwarven quartermaster down the rigging.

A creaking door woke Wick the next morning. The little librarian hung heavily in a hammock and stared up at the wooden deck above him. The sunlight threading through the porthole was almost blinding.

Sunlight? Panic filled him. He flailed at the bedding, trying desperately to heave it out of his way. The hammock tilted crazily before he could stop it, and he hit the deck with a mighty thump.

"Little man!" Hallekk growled in consternation. "Are ye all right, or have ye managed to knock yerself daft?" He came from the doorway and helped Wick to his feet.

"I overslept," Wick explained hurriedly. He glanced at the sunshine splashing on the wall beside the twin hammocks. After Captain Farok had calmed the men last night and it became apparent that the Embyr would not be returning, Hallekk had offered the use of his room to Wick, saying the men on watch would be too excited and talk too much for the little librarian to sleep. *Slops is going to kill me!* He pulled frantically at his clothing. "Slops will slap knots on my head for being late to the galley."

"Slops ain't a-gonna be slapping no knots on yer knob." Hallekk laughed and leaned against the wall, folding his thick arms across his chest.

Wick blinked at the big dwarf in confusion. "Slops has enjoyed bullying me."

"Maybe so," Hallekk agreed. "But them days are over."

"Why are they over?"

"Them's cap'n's orders. When I told Cap'n Farok

how ye saved the neck of every man jack aboard *One-Eyed Peggie* last night, why he thought ye needed re-wardin'."

"No more galley work?" Wick asked, hardly daring to believe it.

Hallekk held up a hand. "I swear, little man, ye will never peel another potato nor scrub another pot for Slops aboard this ship." He shrugged. "Well, that is, unless ye do something stupid an' make the cap'n mad at ye. Now get yerself together an' let's shake a leg. Cap'n wants to see ye in his quarters."

Doubt mingled with Wick's joy. "He wants to see me?"

"Aye. An' he was bein' generous about it, too. Told me to let ye sleep in, he did. But I knowed he'd get tired of waitin' too, so I thought I'd come on in here an' see if ye'd awakened yet."

"Why would the captain want to see me?" Wick asked.

"To give ye a proper thanks for a-savin' ol' *One-Eyed Peggie,* of course. An' to let ye sign yer articles."

"My articles?"

Hallekk nodded happily. "After a bit of persuadin' on me part, Cap'n saw fit to make ye a part of this ship's crew. Ye get yer oath given ye an' ye'll be a proper pirate!"

8

A Proper Pirate

A *proper pirate!* The words spun in Wick's mind as he stumbled out of Hallekk's quarters and onto *One-Eyed Peggie*'s deck. *Every promotion I achieved in the Vault of All Known Knowledge took years of hard work. But I'm promoted from potato-peeler to proper pirate in eight days?*

The other pirates working the deck paused in their chores to stare at the little librarian.

"Ye bilge-rats quit yer starin' an' get back to them chores," Hallekk roared at the pirates. "If'n what ye got ahead of ye today ain't enough to keep ye occupied, why I'll just be around in a minute an' oblige ye with another list."

The pirates turned back to their chores with increased alacrity, and Wick followed Hallekk's lead to the captain's quarters. The quartermaster rapped his knuckles against the door.

"Come in," Farok ordered.

Hallekk led the way inside and Wick followed.

The captain sat at his desk and gazed at Wick without humor. "Ye had yerself quite a night last night, halfer."

"Yes, sir," Wick responded.

"*Aye,* sir," Hallekk whispered quickly.

"Aye, sir," Wick said.

Farok *harumph*ed perhaps a tad unhappily. "Were ye scared when ye climbed up there to talk to that foul creature?"

For a moment, Wick wanted to object that the Embyr wasn't a foul creature at all, but he knew there was no use arguing with the captain's point of perspective. "Aye, sir. I was very much afraid."

Farok nodded but he looked far from pleased. " 'Twas an uncommon brave thing ye did, halfer."

"Aye, sir."

The captain leaned forward. "Personally, I likes me pirates what has a little modesty when they're a-talkin' to their cap'n. Otherwise, I get to thinkin' maybe they ain't scared of me enough."

"Oh, Captain Farok," Wick said, "I don't think there's a man in this crew that's more afraid of you than I am."

The captain *harumph*ed again and reached down under the edge of his bed and pulled out a large glass jar. Something red and purple swirled slowly inside the clear liquid filling the jar. A large cork covered in melted yellow wax sealed the neck of the jar. The jar thumped heavily when the captain placed it on the desk. "Quartermaster Hallekk has recommended ye for a full pirate's wages aboard this ship."

Hypnotized, Wick watched the red and purple object stop swirling inside the jar. Abruptly, the object turned toward him, and the little librarian found himself looking into a large, dark green eye over a foot wide. Without warning, the eye blinked and Wick backed up into the closed door behind him with his arms raised defensively. His voice was so tight he only squeaked when he tried to yell.

Captain Farok laughed loudly and slapped the desk, causing the sea monster's eye in the jar to blink again. "There's yer hero what ye're asking a pirate's wages for,

Hallekk. Scared of a little eyeball in a bottle what can't do him no harm."

"I didn't tell him about the sea monster's eye, Cap'n," Hallekk said. "I think we caught him unawares."

"Well, we're pirates," Captain Farok roared, slamming a fist against the desk. "An' we're the roughest, toughest pirates in the Blood-Soaked Sea, by thunder. A pirate's gotta have something to swear his loyalty to, and aboard *One-Eyed Peggie,* it's the sea monster's eye she took all them years ago." He switched his attention to Wick. "Do ye understand that, halfer?"

"Aye, sir."

"Now give me yer hand, halfer, and let's be done with this afore I change me mind." Captain Farok stuck a withered claw of a hand out, capturing the little librarian's hand and dragging it to the wax-covered cord that sealed the jar with the sea monster's eye. "I'm gonna have ye give yer solemn oath now, at least, as solemn as any halfer can be trusted to give it."

Wick nodded, staring deeply into the sea monster's eye.

"From this moment forward," the captain said, "ye shall be treated as one of the crew aboard *One-Eyed Peggie.* Ye'll follow the orders of yer commanding officers though the Blood-Soaked Sea may be a-boilin' around ye. So says ye?"

Wick glanced at Hallekk, who nodded. A similar scene from *Taurak Bleiyz and the Forty Pirates,* when the mighty dweller warrior had gone sailing to recover a vast treasure, played through the little librarian's mind. He recalled how Taurak had responded. "So says I." However, Taurak's voice probably hadn't cracked when he'd answered.

"Nor shall ye steal from another pirate aboard *One-Eyed Peggie* on penalty of being marooned, or having yer gullet slit," Captain Farok said. "Other ships is fair game. So says ye?"

"So says I," Wick replied, and he felt like he was sinking deeper and deeper. Thoughts of returning to Greydawn Moors dimmed.

"Nor shall ye try to run away from yer responsibilities to this ship. Otherwise, ye will be marooned on an island with only a bottle of drinking water and a knife. So says ye?"

Wick hesitated a little over that one, but the fierce gaze in Captain Farok's eyes and the deep stare from the sea monster's eye prompted him to answer quickly enough. "So says I."

"An' if ye should carry an unprotected flame down into the ship's hold, ye know that ye will be flogged. So says ye?"

"So says I." Wick continued the pirate's promises, swearing never to strike another pirate or to fail to care for his weapons. He also promised to be brave in battle against chosen prizes or engagements with other pirates if it came to that. He didn't know how he was going to do the latter, but he couldn't *not* promise the old captain.

Captain Farok released Wick's hand. "I welcomes ye as a new pirate aboard *One-Eyed Peggie,* halfer. Hallekk will see to yer trainin' an' such."

"Aye, sir," Wick replied. "Thank you, captain." *And what would Grandmagister Ludaan think about me becoming a pirate? Grandmagister Ludaan had first appointed Wick as Librarian. To say nothing of my father and mother and siblings! Will they look upon having a son and brother who is a pirate as something greater than a Librarian?*

Captain Farok slapped his hand against the top of the jar. Inside, the sea monster's eye blinked in response. "Something ye might not have heard about this here eye, halfer."

"Sir?"

"When ol' Peggie gouged it from that there sea monster what took off her leg, she had a hex put on this eye by a sorceress. Legend has it that the sea monster can see whatever this eye sees, an' he knows what passes inside this ship. If a man—even a halfer—makes a promise on this here eye then breaks it, why the sea monster will come after that man as long as he remains within the Blood-Soaked Sea. In all the years that I've captained *One-Eyed Peggie,* ain't no pirate ever run away from this ship. Although, I've heard tell a few years back before that two men did try to escape this ship. Ain't no one ever heard of them since."

Wick blinked at the sea monster's eye, which blinked back at him. *Maybe the two men never came back to the Blood-Soaked Sea. Hallekk says he doesn't know if that sea monster is actually still alive after all these years.* But as he gazed into the jar, the little librarian found he didn't like the idea of testing the theory. And if he couldn't abandon *One-Eyed Peggie* when the chance presented itself, how was he ever going to go back home?

"Ye're dismissed, halfer," Captain Farok replied. "I got work to do." He turned his attention to the map charts in front of him. "Whatever ye do, don't make me regret givin' ye this appointment."

"No, sir," Wick said.

"Hallekk tells me he told ye of how it's our sacred and bounden duty to keep the Blood-Soaked Sea clear of any that would harm yer precious Vault."

"Aye, sir."

"Well, just so's ye know it, we'll be a-doin' that, too."

"Aye, sir." At least, Wick thought, that was an honorable aspiration.

Hallekk cleared his throat. "Sir? The other thing?"

Farok looked annoyed as he shifted his glance from

the big dwarven quartermaster to Wick. "Aye, there is the other thing. For a-savin' *One-Eyed Peggie* from the Embyr last night, I'm a-givin' ye a little token of me appreciation."

Wick waited, but the captain didn't move.

"Well don't just stand there, ye bilge-blasted barnacle," the captain said sourly. "Name something ye'd like to have as a token of me appreciation."

"Oh no, sir," Wick said. "I couldn't do that."

" 'Course ye can," the captain stated. "An' if'n ye don't let me discharge this debt what Hallekk feels I owe ye, I'll have ye back down belowdecks a-peelin' potatoes before ye can blink."

And suffer under Slops' unmerciful hands? Wick cringed inside. He thought swiftly. "I'd like a book, Captain."

"A book, says ye," Captain Farok said. "Ye stand there and ask me for that, all the while a-knowin' that there ain't any books left outside Greydawn Moors. And precious few of them what could read them anyway."

"No, sir," Wick replied. "What I meant was, I'd like some paper. I've seen crates in the hold below that have sheets of packing paper in them. If you'd give me permission, I can make my own book." The thought had crossed the little librarian's mind nearly a week ago after seeing the crates in the cargo hold, but he hadn't acted on his impulse out of fear.

"Will ye be a-takin' much paper then, halfer? Them packin' papers don't grow on trees, ye know. An' it comes in handy preservin' glasswares and candles and suchlike."

"No sir. Not much at all."

Farok glanced back at the chart before him and waved a hand. "As long as ye don't go a-gettin' greedy, I'll allow it."

"Thank you, sir." Exultation swelled within Wick. He

felt nearly a foot taller as he followed Hallekk back
through the captain's door. And, for the first time in
eight days, he felt more like a Librarian than he did a
pirate.

"Can I see what ye got there, halfer?"

Startled, Wick glanced up and saw Zeddar, the pirate
ship's main lookout, clambering over the side of the
crow's-nest to join him. Self-consciously, the little librarian closed the book he held.

Zeddar was a young dwarf with an angular face instead of a round one. His hazel-green eyes were quick
and bright and alive with interest. He hadn't yet gotten
old enough to put on a dwarf's full beard growth. But
as a pirate who virtually lived in the high rigging and
constantly scanned the sea for predators as well as prey,
Zeddar had no peer. He wore a thick woolen shirt and
woolen pants.

"C'mon, Wick," Zeddar pleaded good-naturedly, "ye
know ye want to show it to me."

Wick smiled a little. In the last two weeks since he'd
been officially named one of the pirate crew, he'd
worked hard to learn the rigging and day-to-day cleaning
that was part of the vessel maintenance.

During that time, in the few hours that he had to himself, the little librarian had also crafted a journal for himself. True, the finished product had nowhere near the
craftsmanship of a book assembled in the Vault, but it
served his purposes and occupied his mind and hands.
The book measured some six inches by nine inches, and
fit perfectly inside his shirt when he had to climb the
rigging or tend to other chores. The pages weren't even,
and weren't even all the same color of white, but they
held ink and charcoal well, and he was in the process of
experimenting with dried algae and resins as a medium

for adding color to the illustrations he was doing.

"Maybe just a peek." Wick gave in to the pride that filled him. He thumbed the shaved wooden cover he'd fashioned, tracing the letters of the title he'd burned into the unfinished oak. *SHANGHAIED!* the title read. And underneath was the subtitle, *Being the Narrative Journal of the Adventures of Third Level Librarian Edgewick Lamplighter Among the Ferocious Pirates of the Blood-Soaked Sea.* The subtitle might have been a little long and time-consuming to burn in, but he rather liked the way it looked on the top cover.

In the last two weeks, he'd added three hundred pages to his book. He'd included the confrontation with the sea monster, and even mentioned the tedium of working for Slops in the galley, including the meals that had been served each and every day. From there, he'd started adding observations about the weather and the sea and sailing in general. He'd even added sections concerning the fish and fowl of the sea, surprising himself by branching out into such areas. The stories and songs of the pirates had also found their way onto his pages.

Once the pirates had discovered what he was doing, they'd been amazed and fascinated. It wasn't long before each pirate told Wick a tale that they felt he should be obliged to include in his book.

Reverently, Zeddar reached for the book as Wick handed it to him. He stared with rapt attention at the illustration Wick had been working on.

"Ye've got the hands and fingers of an artist, ye do," Zeddar said.

"It's nothing," the little librarian said, acting modest but feeling terribly proud. "What you're calling art is merely rendering—a skill that anyone can learn." All of the Librarians had to have some skill at rendering, and every dweller that Wick knew of could draw.

"But this is beautiful," Zeddar insisted.

Wick smiled as he peered over the dwarf's shoulder. In fact, he did consider the rendering one of his better efforts. It showed the view from the crow's-nest, peering down onto *One-Eyed Peggie*'s main deck. The sails billowed from the masts, and individual pirates were shown working at everyday tasks. The hard lines were laid down in ink, carefully drawn despite *One-Eyed Peggie*'s present rolling gait. He'd captured waves beside the pirate vessel with smudged charcoal rubbed deeply into the paper.

"I mean it, Wick," Zeddar went on. "If ye did this piece bigger an' in color, why I bet ye could sell it to some alehouse keeper for hangin' in back of the bar."

Actually, that was probably the *last* place Wick thought he would want to see anything hang that he had done. "I don't think so."

"No," Zeddar insisted, "ye're good at this, ye are. Never have I seen the like." He flipped carefully through the pages, revealing the drawings of Hallekk and Captain Farok, pausing for a moment to linger at the rendering of the Embyr.

Caught in a halo of flames that somehow seemed to leap off the page—even Wick had to admit that particular drawing had come out in truly satisfying detail—the Embyr stood stark and beautiful and deadly—and somehow she had come out as lonely as well. All of the renderings occupied pages between pages and pages of his monographs and essays. Other pages held notes and fragments that he hoped to turn into still more material, and rough drafts of articles he'd already written that awaited polishing.

"Thank ye for a-sharin' yer work with me," Zeddar said, handing the book back.

"You're welcome," Wick said. "Thank you for being so interested."

"I've brought a bite to eat. If'n ye're of a mind to

share an' ain't gotta rush off." Zeddar pulled free the large scarf knotted over his shoulder. The blue and purple material strained under the weight of its burden.

"I'm in no hurry." Wick gazed out at the Blood-Soaked Sea. The sun still remained hidden by the thick, rolling fog, but at least it was wet today. Usually the fog carried just enough condensation to prevent him from working on his book during his watch.

Zeddar untied the knotted scarf and revealed the selection of tartberries, mushapple—whose dimpled marmalade skin showed how ripe the sweet meat inside was—three different kinds of cheese, dill bread and sourdough bread, baked raisin chips, and thick wedges of spicy, jalapeño-nut mushpie. He even had a bottle of mulled ardyl-grape wine spiced with nutmeg.

"After standing watch all morning," Zeddar said, digging into the repast, "I thought ye might be hungry."

"I am." Wick shoved his book inside his shirt so he wouldn't forget it, then proceeded to make a cheese sandwich.

They ate in silence, and it didn't bother the little librarian much. Despite being somewhat accepted into the pirate crew and the efforts they all made to tell him stories or educate him in the mysteries of the sea, he didn't have much in common with the dwarves. The dweller shipwright, Trosper, continued to avoid Wick, which was more curious than annoying.

Wick turned his thoughts to that evening's entertainment. Of late, once the sun had settled down over the Blood-Soaked Sea and it wasn't too wet to be on deck—which was actually most of the time—the pirate crew hung a few lanterns amidships and settled in for one of the stories that Wick would tell them. After they'd discovered his book and the pictures that he'd drawn inside, they'd asked questions. Those questions hadn't taken long to ferret out whole stories, which the little librarian was only too happy to share with his new comrades. Sometimes the dwarven pirates took turns telling stories afterward, or they danced or sang sea shanties.

"Ship!" Zeddar said suddenly.

Startled, Wick took a moment and tried to figure out what the dwarf referred to. He offered the small handful of baked raisin chips to Zeddar.

The dwarven lookout quickly stashed his food back into the large scarf, staring out over the edge of the crow's-nest. "Not chips!" He flung out an arm, pointing. "A *ship!*"

Wick tracked the direction and barely made out the triangular sails budding against the distant curve of the horizon. "What is it?"

"A merchanter by the looks of her," Zeddar answered eagerly. "Keep an eye on her while I go below and notify the crew. They're a-gonna have to keep quiet if we're a-gonna sneak up on her." He threw a leg over the side of the crow's-nest and tossed a long coil of rope over as well. Before the rope could nearly have had the chance to finish uncoiling, the young dwarf slid over the side.

"Sneak up on her?" Wick repeated, glancing down over the crow's-nest's side.

Zeddar slid down the plunging rope attached to the yardarm below. "Of course we're a-gonna sneak up on her. How else do ye expect us to overtake her for whatever treasure might be aboard her?" A grin split the dwarven lookout's face nearly from ear to ear. "Ol' *Peggie*'s a-gonna give ye a chance to earn yer keep today, Pirate Wick!"

"Wick!"

Glancing up from the ship's deck, watching the flurry of action as the pirates ran to their stations, the little librarian spied Hallekk leaning over the forecastle railing. "Aye, sir."

"Get up here and get out of the way, little man," Hallekk advised. "One of them pirates down there is like to run over ye in all the excitement."

At the top of the stairs, Hallekk met him with a grin and thrust a cutlass into his hand.

"There ye go, little man, now ye look the part of a proper pirate," the big dwarf said. "Only ye might want to grit yer teeth a little more. An' work on yer scowl. For the life of me, ye look like ye're more ready to throw up than anything. Just think fierce thoughts." He grabbed the little librarian by the shoulder and hauled him up to the ship's prow.

Wick stood at the prow railing and breathed deeply. The salty air cleared his head, but filled as it was with the ocean spray, it chilled him to the core. All the fabulous stories he'd read of pirates and brave captains battling through one sea or the other suddenly didn't seem so fabulous.

"Stand by, spinnaker!" Hallekk bellowed.

Wick gazed at the other ship. It was less than two hundred yards away now and he could make out the men standing alongside the starboard railing. The dim sunlight sparked from metal surfaces. *Probably cutlasses, knives, and arrowheads!* The little librarian discovered that his throat had gone dry.

"Spinnaker crew standing by," someone called back.

Hallekk spun around, facing the stern castle, which was slightly higher than the forecastle. "By yer leave, Cap'n."

"Thank ye, Hallekk." Captain Farok looked grim at the stern castle railing. He kept his hands folded neatly behind his back.

Wick glanced around at the fierce dwarves lining up at the prow railing around him. They carried shields, cutlasses, and bows and fairly bristled with greed. Incredibly, thcy started singing sea shanties.

"We are the crew of One-Eyed Peggie," they sang, loudly and badly.

"We've sacked ships and taken treasure,

Battled sea monsters—hey, heggie, heggie. And badly rhymed.

We're a-gonna catch you at our leisure!"

Captain Farok called out a course correction in his thunderous voice. *One-Eyed Peggie* came about smartly.

Hallekk nodded at the other ship. "That ship is from Zohophir, far to the south, an' they ain't never traded with Greydawn Moors before. An' they ain't a-gonna start now."

"Why?"

"It's in our Pirate's Code," Hallekk responded. "Them what's traded occasionally still will be permitted to. But them's only small nations an' cities what knows about the Vault and its importance. We can't have no newcomers stumblin' across the island. Why, there's no tellin' who all they might up and tell."

"So we have to rob them?"

"Mostly, we're just gonna scare them good, little man. We gotta keep the Vault secret, right?"

Wick considered the implication of Hallekk's nonchalant question. *Is protecting the Vault of All Known Knowledge worth the lives of innocent people?* It was one thing to think of defending the location of the Library from goblinkin, but quite another to be willing to harm people whose only fault was in growing brave enough to sail uncharted waters. Little more than a hundred yards remained between the ships.

"Loose the spinnaker!" Captain Farok bellowed.

Lines ran through shrieking pulleys so fast that Wick felt certain the hemp rope would catch on fire. The crew kept buckets of water on hand for just such an emergency, which didn't happen very often.

The spinnaker was an additional sail that came up from the prow of the ship. It was designed solely for use when running with the wind, when speed was of the essence. The massive sail was made of sailcloth stained coal black and poured out into the wind like a raging storm cloud. As the sail filled with air till it belled like a robin's proud breast, the grinning skull and crossbones limned in white stood out starkly.

"Well now," Hallekk said dryly, "that oughta answer any questions they might have been a-havin'." He smiled, then lifted his voice and joined in the pirate sea shanty. He looked absolutely fearless.

Pulled by the additional sail, *One-Eyed Peggie* lunged across the ocean.

Upon closer inspection, Wick saw that most of the people aboard the merchanter were a mixture of humans and dwarves. That stood to reason, though, because survivors of the human and dwarven nations from Eastern Krumass had primarily settled Zohophir. Eastern Krumass had been very civilized, a blend of Old World manners and coffers filled by trade ships, before the Cataclysm consumed it.

Wick had never seen so many humans in his life outside of a book. Due to his Library training, Wick tended to think of most humans as wizards and scholars. He knew from his reading that his perception of them was incorrect, but still it stuck with him after the example Grandmagister Ludaan had first instilled in him. Many humans were no more skilled in magic or books than the dwarves, elves, or dwellers.

Without warning, arrows leapt from bows aboard the fleeing merchanter. The feathered shafts flew through the air between the two ships like flocks of deadly birds.

"Cover!" Hallekk growled. "Take cover!" He lifted

the heavy shield at his side and held it up as he ducked beneath it.

Wick took shelter beneath Hallekk's great shield as well. Above them, Critter screamed in alarm. Then the rhowdor ran through the rigging, wings beating furiously, cursing the archers aboard the merchanter. Terrified, the little librarian peered through the slats of the prow railing and watched as another volley of arrows leaped across the distance.

Wick felt the vibrations of the arrows striking the deck, and he heard the clangor of the arrows that struck the shields as well. Incredibly, throughout the din of near-death, none of the pirates were harmed. And they still sang in loud, boisterous, off-key voices!

"All right then," Hallekk cried, "let's up an' at them, me hearties! Archers, bend those bows, but I want not a single casualty amongst that other ship!"

"Aye sir!" the archers cried back as they took up their places. They nocked their arrows and fired three volleys on Hallekk's marks.

Hunkered against the railing as much as he could, Wick struggled to keep control of the panic that threatened to overwhelm him. *If Grandmagister Frollo ever hears of this, I'll never be allowed to set foot inside the Library again!*

"Are we going to take the ship?" Wick asked Hallekk.

The big dwarf grinned and shook his head. "No. We've plenty of supplies from our layover in Greydawn Moors, though I would like to complement our supply of fresh fruits. Apples and raisins keep for a very long time, but a man can definitely get his fill of them. We're just here to give them a good scare so they stay well clear of the Blood-Soaked Sea and Greydawn Moors in the future."

"*Catapults!*" Captain Farok bellowed, his voice rising above the din on the pirate ship.

"Aye, sir!" a pirate responded.

"Make ready," the captain ordered.

"Makin' ready, Cap'n."

Standing at Hallekk's side, Wick glanced up at the old captain. With the wind whipping around the man and the fierce gaze in his rheumy eyes, Farok looked like a force of nature that would never bend or break. *The stories that man must know,* the little librarian suddenly realized. During the evening storytelling events, the captain had sometimes listened in covertly without displaying any interest at all, and had never relayed the stories he had to have known. *Battles and sea monsters and treasures,* Wick thought, *why, there may be any number of books inside him!*

"Loads ready!" the catapult crew chiefs called out as they thrust lit torches onto the rough, oil-soaked pitch and tar loads that weighed at least two hundred pounds. The flames caught gradually and spread across the loads.

Wick took his homemade book from inside his shirt and seized a small bit of charcoal. Turning so his back would block the ocean spray breaking across Onc-Eyed Peggie's prow, the little librarian quickly blocked out the scene of the captain and the catapults onto a blank page. His effort was very rough, but it captured the placement and lines of tension in the machines as well as the crews. And it captured Captain Farok, steady and in control.

"Hallekk," Captain Farok called.

"Aye, Cap'n," Hallekk responded.

"After we fire these two loads," the captain said, "we'll want to spring our final surprise."

Hallekk grinned. "Aye, sir, that we will."

"What surprise?" Wick asked nervously.

"Don't you go a-frettin', little man," the big dwarf told him. "This'll be fun. C'mon."

Reluctantly, Wick followed Hallekk across the deck

to the portside of the prow. The big dwarf grabbed a thick rope that led up into the rigging. Wick followed the line of the rope and saw it thread over a block-and-tackle assembly high above. It was attached to a heavy sandbag and another rope. Following the second rope back down again, the little librarian was surprised to see it disappear over the side into the waterline.

Hallekk gripped the knot tying the rope to the railing. He watched the merchanter with savage glee. "We ain't done this one in awhile, little man. Ye're in for a treat."

"Fire!" Captain Farok roared.

Both catapults cut loose with a resounding *SPROING!* As the flaming pitchloads vaulted into the air, *One-Eyed Peggie* rolled over just a bit in reaction.

Wick put his book away inside his shirt again as he watched the flaming pitchloads fly high. They looked like comets as they trailed smoke and fire behind them. When they reached the apex of their climb, they plummeted. For a moment, Wick felt certain the crew chiefs had accidentally hit the merchanter.

Instead, both flaming pitchloads landed only a few feet short of the merchanter. The round missiles threw up huge waves of water over the abandoned starboard railing and disappeared for a moment. Before the water had finished swamping the merchanter's deck, the pitchloads floated to the surface. Amazingly, the flames had fed on the oil for the brief time they were beneath the water and stayed lit as they bobbed on the waves.

The pirate crew started singing again. *"We are the crew of* One-Eyed Peggie!*"*

The crew aboard the merchanter, realizing they hadn't been struck after all, returned to the starboard railing. Their archers readied another volley.

"Hallekk!" Captain Farok growlcd.

"Aye, Cap'n!" Hallekk yanked on the knot and loosened the line. Immediately, the huge sandbag hanging high in the rigging above plunged toward the deck.

As he watched, heart in his throat, Wick saw that at least a dozen other sandbags dropped from the rigging as well as from concealed places behind the main sails. The pulleys shrilled as they spun.

Almost immediately, *One-Eyed Peggie* slowed in the water like she'd dropped anchor. *Or like something has grabbed hold of her*, Wick thought unhappily. He glanced over the side just in time to see thick, black tentacles exploding up from the ocean with frightening speed.

9

Ill Wind

Yaaaaahhhhh!" Stumbling and crying out, the little librarian tripped over his own feet in his haste to spring back from the groping tentacles.

The tentacles rose high into *One-Eyed Peggie*'s rigging, wriggling and writhing in anticipation. They hugged the sails and masts jealously. All the pirates dove for the deck in unison, moving like they'd been trained for the moment, screaming and bleating in fear. And *One-Eyed Peggie* lurched like she'd gone aground, spilling pirates forward.

"Yaaaaahhhhh!" Wick yelled again as he rolled helplessly for a moment and peered at the tentacle within arm's reach above him. He pushed his feet against the deck and scooted back. *One-Eyed Peggie* bucked against the sea now instead of cutting clean through it.

Hallekk lay only a few feet away, roaring with laughter.

He's insane! Wick thought desperately. *His mind has snapped!* Thick water droplets splashed the deck around him as it fell from the tentacle above.

Suddenly, above the noise of the straining rigging and protesting wood and the clamor of the sea, laughter rang out.

Still shuddering in fear, certain he'd been trapped on a ship of madmen, Wick glanced around at the pirates. They all still lay on the decks where they'd thrown themselves, but they were laughing out loud now instead of crying out. Their huge guffaws filled the ship.

"Stow that bilge, ye reprehensible loons," Captain Farok commanded. He still stood at the stern castle railing, implacable as ever. "Ye get outta hand like this, them crewmen is gonna know something ain't right."

Something isn't *right!* Wick stared up at the still-quivering tentacle above him. If he wanted to—which he *definitely* did not want to—he could have touched it. The black tentacle was easily bigger around than he was, and it continued to quiver as it held onto the mast. *One-Eyed Peggie* bobbed wildly on the water.

"Hey, little man," Hallekk called gently, "are ye okay over there?"

"No," Wick whispered, "I'm not okay. We're about to be dragged to the bottom of the sea by this . . . this *thing!*"

"Ye're a-talkin' about this thing?" Hallekk reached up and gave the tentacle a good-natured slap, like a warder showing affection to a favorite wolf pup. "This thing ain't a-gonna do ye any harm. This here's Gretchen the Sea Monster."

Looking more closely at the tentacle, Wick was chagrined to realize that it wasn't made up of bristly flesh and knobby hide as he'd imagined. Instead, it was made up of sailcloth that had been strategically ripped and tattered.

"It's a fake?" the little librarian asked, getting up cautiously. He gazed up into the rigging. Now that he was looking he could see the ropes that held up "Gretchen's" tentacles.

"Hallekk," Captain Farok called from the stern. "Fetch ol' Gretchen down outta me riggin', would ye? Leave her up there like that an' she's a-gonna dry out and likely tear herself in the wind."

"At once, Cap'n." Hallekk quickly assembled a work group. The big dwarf ordered some of the sails lowered first, and *One-Eyed Peggie* stopped fighting the sea as hard.

Wick followed Hallekk to the port railing and gazed out at the sea while the big dwarf started hauling the sandbag up. The merchanter changed course and steered clear of the pirate ship.

"Oh, we won't be a-seein' them again any time too soon," Hallekk observed. "Can ye imagine the way them sailors will be a-tellin' the tale tonight, an' in every tavern they bend an elbow in for the rest of their days? Why they was a-fightin' the bloodthirsty pirates of the Blood-Soaked Sea, just a-barely survivin'—or maybe a-givin' us pirates the thrashin' of our very lives—when up comes this fierce sea beastie from the depths an' drags them evil pirates below the waves."

Wick knew it was true. He'd thought the encounter was going to end that way. His hands still trembled a little as he coiled the sopping rope on the deck at his feet. "You've done this before?"

"Aye," Hallekk grunted as he hauled the sandbag up. Once it was clear of the water, the weight was much greater. The sodden sandbag thumped heavily against the ship's side. "An' it's never failed to work yet."

Considering the way the tentacles had sprung from the water like a tripped hunter's trap, Wick didn't doubt that. Despite the fact that he knew the tentacles were made from sailcloth, in his mind's eye he kept seeing a dreaded kraken lashing onto the ship. *That probably comes from reading Erghiller's* Beneath the Deep, Deep Waves.

"How long has 'Gretchen' been in service?" the little librarian asked.

Hallekk shrugged. "Don't know. Haven't asked. Gretchen's been aboard *One-Eyed Peggie* longer than I have." He took up the line that Zeddar threw down, tied it to the sandbag, and began hoisting the sandbag back up into the rigging.

Wick took hold of the rope and pulled in unison with Hallekk. As the sandbag rose, the tentacles descended again into the ocean and the series of hoops sewn inside the sailcloth stood out like ribs. A lot of thought had gone into the tentacles' design, and he found himself curious about whomever had first fashioned them. "Do all the Blood-Soaked Sea pirate ships have tentacles?"

"Can't say," Hallekk said. "So far, *Peggie*'s the only Blood-Soaked Sea pirate ship I've seen. We all got routes we run. Keeps us spread out."

"Where do the tentacles stay below?" Wick asked.

"There's furrows cut along *Peggie*'s sides," Hallekk explained. "Once we get them tentacles back underwater, I'll send swimmers down to tuck 'em up nice an' neat. They'll stay there until we need 'em again."

"Was it just pulling the tentacles out that slowed the ship so much?" Wick asked.

Hallekk shook his head. "Naw. Besides a-havin' tentacles, Gretchen's got an apron she drops out along the keel line. It's really just a big net what's been pretty much sewn together. When it cuts loose, it starts an almighty drag on ol' *Peggie*."

Wick remembered. He hauled on the rope with all his strength, feeling the soreness in his hands from working the rigging the last two weeks. At least the blisters had started to fade, giving over to unaccustomed calluses that he had to admit he took some pride in. His mind turned over the events of the last several minutes and he wanted badly to get a chance to work in his journal. There was so much to add, so much to comment on and catalogue and—

"*Cap'n Farok!*" a man yelled.

Startled out of his reverie by the naked fear in the man's hoarse voice, Wick turned toward the pirate.

Captain Farok remained upon the stern castle. "What is it?"

A group of pirates gathered around the ropes that manipulated the stern starboard tentacle. They gazed at the tentacle above in disbelief.

"Tentacle's stuck in the riggin', Cap'n," one of the men declared. "An' there's a goblin stuck with it, too!"

The announcement quickly drew the other pirates and the buzz of excited conversation filled the deck. Wick hurried over to join them, staring up into the rigging, often frustrated by the billowing sails.

"There it is!" someone else shouted.

The fog cover over the ship broke, revealing the body high in the rigging. The tentacle had borne it up and lodged it firmly against a supporting yardarm. With the bright sun behind it, only marred now and again by drifting masses of thin fog, Wick could only see the outline of the body. He wasn't even able to make out if it was indeed a goblin.

"Is it dead?" Critter demanded, landing in the rigging on the other side of the trapped tentacle. "Ye don't want to go near no goblin what ain't properly dead. They'll claw ye and bite ye, and generally just smell bad."

Hallekk gripped the rigging and called out to Zeddar, who was still in the crow's-nest. Together, they approached the body and cut it free of the rigging. Released, the tentacle flopped out into the ocean.

When the body was free of the rigging, Hallekk held onto it by one ankle. "Get yerselves clear away," the big dwarf warned. The pirates quickly fled the area directly under the body. Then Hallekk released it.

Wick knew from the way the body hit the deck that no life remained.

It was the first goblin and murdered humanoid Wick had ever seen. For a moment, the sick nausea that suddenly formed in the pit of the little librarian's stomach almost erupted.

The splotchy gray-green skin of the goblin gave its heritage away immediately. Nothing else in the world vaguely humanoid was that color, Wick knew. In life, the little librarian guessed that the goblin might have been a little greener than the gray pallor its death had visited upon it.

The goblin's head was shaped like a triangle, with a flat, broad skull that led down to a narrow, pointed chin sprouting a tuft of black whiskers. Stone beads and bits of bone worked into the foot-long whiskers declared the goblin's tribe and personal history. The misshapen ears were the size of a human's hand, and curled over like wilted leaves, coming to points. Brass earrings lined both ears, and coarse black hairs thrust out of them. The forehead was a thick shelf of bone hanging over deep eye sockets.

"Is it dead?" a young pirate asked.

"Well," Hallekk growled as he clambered down, "I didn't hear him a-complainin' about the fall, nor that wallopin' sudden stop at the end."

Usually, Wick remembered from his reading and the tales he'd learned growing up in Greydawn Moors, a goblin's eyes burned orange or red. However, Wick chose not to peer too closely into the dead goblin's eyes. Beneath the cavernous eyes, the high cheekbones stuck out like they'd been chipped from granite, standing out nearly as far as the flat, upturned nose. The lipless mouth hung partially open to reveal scraggly yellow canine fangs. Long black hair hung over the goblin's shoulder in a twisted braid threaded with more stone beads and bone bits. If the goblin had been standing, the hair would have hung down to his thighs. Metal glinted at the end

of the braid, and upon closer inspection the little librarian saw the cunning weapon wrapped within the hair.

Hallekk dropped to the deck and pushed his way
through the crowd of pirates. "Those of ye what ain't
seen goblinkin before take heed of that spiked blade
what's wound up in its hair." He knelt and lifted the
braid so the blade could be better seen. The blade was
shaped like a feather, but only a dozen spikes stuck out
from it. "Ye can bet them sharp tines on that blade is
poisoned. Goblinkin what wear them hidden blades always daub 'em in poison."

The pirates drew back as Hallekk freed the blade from
the thick braid by slashing the last few inches of hair.
He threw the braid section and blade over the ship's side.

Goblins were taller than dwarves and elves, but
shorter than humans. They were built broad across the
chest and shoulders like wolves and other predators that
depended on speed and endurance. Their arms hung
longer than their legs, but both hands and feet looked
two sizes too large for their bodies. Hard black talons
covered the ends of the fingers and toes. Coarse black
hair shadowed bodies that looked like those of famine
victims. Despite their ravenous natures, most goblinkin
never seemed able to put on too much weight and remained feral in appearance.

"Hallekk," Captain Farok asked as the pirates stepped
aside to allow him passage, "what do we have here?"

"A mystery," Hallekk growled, "an' one's that totally
unwelcome."

"The body looks fresh," the captain observed.

It surely doesn't smell fresh, Wick thought. The little
librarian's nose wrinkled in disgust at the gamy odor.
Combined with the queasiness already rolling through
his stomach from looking at the dead creature, it was
almost too much.

"We're too far out to sea," the captain continued, "for

a body to have come from the mainland, an' there are no islands in these waters."

"No, sir," Hallekk agreed, kneeling near the body. "Judging from the leathers this'n is a-wearin', an' these calluses on his hands, I'd say he was a sailor. Maybe a pirate."

Surprise pushed Captain Farok's bushy brows up a little. "That's not good news. So far, there have been no reports of goblin ships this far west. They've stayed much closer to the mainland."

Hallekk nodded.

Wick swallowed hard. Even if they had sailed in a straight line from Greydawn Moors, twenty-two or-three days wasn't enough distance for him to feel comfortable about goblinkin so close to his home. Even if he wasn't there at the moment, his family was. And so was the Vault of All Known Knowledge.

The goblinkin hadn't sailed too freely on any of the seas before Lord Kharrion brought about the Cataclysm. Humans had primarily ruled the seaways, while dwarves and elves remained content to be held by territorial boundaries. It had been humans that had built the great ships that had conquered the oceans and united the continents, and they were doomed forever by that wanderlust that fired so many of their kind.

"His leathers are also covered with tar to keep the sea out an' the warm in," Hallekk went on. He pointed at the beaded moisture trickling across the goblin's garments. The foul creature was dressed in a leather vest over a homespun shirt and leather pants. Dirty cloth straps wrapped his feet. No cobblers existed among the goblinkin, and no dwarven tradesman would make shoes for them. "Then there's this." The big dwarf pointed to a terrible wound in the goblin's side.

Captain Farok peered more closely. "A sword wound?"

"Aye, sir. Made with something straight thrust into him. Weren't no cutlass blow what did that."

"From someone who was trained in the art of the blade."

Hallekk nodded. "That's what I'm a-thinkin', and that leads to even more curious thoughts."

The goblin's presence and his death were mysteries that pulled at Wick's attention. Puzzles concerning thefts and murders were some of his favorite reading from Hralbomm's Wing as well as the more adventurous stories. There was something about pitting oneself against the puzzle solver in the stories that intrigued him. Often, the little librarian figured out who had managed the crime or foul deed—it was always a dead giveaway, mostly, if there were goblins involved—before he reached the end. But this present set of mysteries didn't guarantee a solution.

"He has a ship somewhere nearby then," the captain said in a quiet voice.

"Aye, sir," Hallekk said, gazing out over the prow. "An' one close by, too, I'd say."

"Double the night watch, then," Captain Farok said, "an' keep the crew sharp."

"Aye, sir."

The captain pulled his robes tighter against the chill breeze sweeping *One-Eyed Peggie*'s deck. "Get us under way as soon as possible, Hallekk. If there's a goblin ship out there, we've got to find it."

Personally, Wick thought that was the last thing they needed to do, and hoped the Blood-Soaked Sea proved too big and too foggy for them to do that. And if there was a goblin ship out in the Blood-Soaked Sea, what did that mean for them—and for Greydawn Moors?

Within three days, shipboard life returned to normal aboard *One-Eyed Peggie,* and talk no longer centered on the dead goblin that had been found in Gretchen's tentacles. Wick continued working on his watches and his book, constantly filling the pages with images and words. At noon on the third day, the pirates hoisted a net full of bluefin up from the Blood-Soaked Sea.

Wick sat on the steps leading up to the stern castle and watched. Even Captain Farok had come out on deck to watch.

The pulleys shrilled and the lines creaked as the heavy net was lifted and swung over to *One-Eyed Peggie's* hold. Seawater cascaded down, splattering the deck. The pirate ship rocked as the huge weight teetered in the net.

Without warning, Zeddar's urgent voice cut through the air from the crow's-nest. "Sails! Sails off the starboard bow!"

Wick put his book away. During the past hour he'd sketched four different pictures that depicted the fishing efforts. The little librarian's stomach turned cold.

The sails faded in and out of the roiling fogbank to *One-Eyed Peggie*'s starboard. The belled canvas looked dirty against the white fog.

"She's got the wind!" Zeddar yelled down from the crow's-nest. "She's behind us, an' she's got the wind!"

"Man yer stations," Captain Farok ordered. "Can ye see who they are, Zeddar?"

Wick rushed to the railing and peered through the swirling fog. The ships seemed thinner than the pirate vessel, like they were on edge and cut through the water rather than gathering speed and breaking across the top of it the way *One-Eyed Peggie* did.

"It's goblins, Cap'n!" Zeddar cried back over the whip and crack of the sails.

"Stand an' face 'em, Cap'n?" Hallekk asked. "Or do we let 'em try to overtake us, then pick 'em off?"

"They've got the wind, Hallekk," Captain Farok replied. "If we turn an' face 'em an' they have an inexperienced crew, we could find 'em broadsides of us an' us all a-goin' down into the briny deep. Ye can't trust goblins to run a ship the way she should be run."

"Aye, Cap'n."

"Give ol' *Peggie* her head and let's see what kind of seafarin' goblins they be," Farok ordered. "An' run up our true colors."

"Aye, Cap'n." Hallekk gave the order and the black flag ran up the main mast. It furled in the air. The fishing crew let go the net and the load of fish dropped into the hold for later duty.

Even though he was prepared for it, Wick was still almost tossed from his feet when *One-Eyed Peggie*'s spread sails reached out and caught up the wind. The pirate ship rose up in the water and ran. Still, for all of *One-Eyed Peggie*'s speed and her crew's skill, the goblin ship came on.

The long minutes stretched as the chase played out, but Wick knew how it would end. The goblin ship had already built up too much speed.

"She's going to overtake us," the little librarian said to Hallekk, who stood beside him.

"Aye. That she is. But we'll run her a bonny little chase before she does."

Wick wiped the brine spray from his face, trying to ignore the sting in his eyes. "What do we do when she catches us?"

"We fight," Hallekk answered simply. "Ain't no two ways about it. Killin' them goblins what's got brave enough to invade the Blood-Soaked Sea is what we was put here to do. Every one of them we kill is a message to the rest that they ought not come out here. Elsewise, the Vault ain't gonna be safe like we promised."

Wick studied the ship, noting its clean lines. "Do gob-

ins usually have a ship so neat-looking?" From the way
he knew the goblinkin to live, he didn't expect such a
ship.

"No." Hallekk squinted and stared at the goblin ship.
"Mayhap that's one they stole, but they sail it like they
know it."

"So what has drawn them out here?"

"I don't know, little man. But if'n we get our hands
on a couple of them, mayhap we'll get the chance to
ask."

Less than a half hour later, the goblin ship came
alongside *One-Eyed Peggie* but stayed out of bowshot
range.

Wick held onto the railing as the pirate ship sped
across the waves. He was drenched with sea spray. Fear
kept his belly tight. Other than the dead goblin, he'd
never seen goblins before. But they gathered along the
railing of the other ship.

"Steady as she goes," Farok called out from the stern
castle.

Dwarven archers stood alongside the railing.

Surprisingly, a white flag ran up the goblin ship's
main mast where a red flag with a black fist clutching a
sword already rode.

"They're surrendering?" Wick asked Hallekk in surprise.

"They want to talk," the big dwarf replied. "An' that's
passin' strange, 'cause goblinkin always want to fight."

"How many have you fought aboard ships?"

"A couple," Hallekk admitted.

"But they were never in ships like these?"

Hallekk glanced at the little librarian. "Never. What
are ye a-thinkin', little man?"

Wick shrugged, still turning the ideas over in his head.
"I was just thinking that if they weren't concerned about
themselves, then it must be the ship they were concerned

about. And why would they be concerned about the ship?"

"Well," Hallekk said, "goblinkin ain't well known for their swimmin'. Ye seen the drownt one the other day."

"Hallekk," Farok called.

"Aye, Cap'n."

The old captain shifted up by the railing, never taking his eyes from the goblin vessel. "What are ye a-thinkin' about their white flag?"

"I'm a-thinkin' how goblinkin always turn things to their advantage if'n they can."

"They can overtake us now if'n they care to," Farok pointed out. "They've proved that."

"Aye, sir."

"An' if'n we were to stop an' offer to listen to what they had to say?"

"We'd be within bowshot of each other as well as hailing distance."

A sour smile twisted Farok's haggard face. "An' I'm a-willin' to believe we got better archers."

"Aye, sir. That'd be right."

"Then, mayhap, a bit of parley will benefit us. Run up the white flag, Hallekk."

Hallekk turned and shouted the commands.

Wick watched the fluttering white flag snake up the main mast to join the black one that flew so proudly. A sense of foreboding stole over the little librarian. Grimly, he turned and surveyed the goblin ship as it pulled closer.

The goblins crossed the ship's deck, taking up positions. They crowded the prow and stern castles, and many of them even hung in the rigging. They looked, Wick couldn't help thinking, like a clutch of locusts clinging to cornstalks.

It only took the goblin ship a few moments to match *One-Eyed Peggie*'s speed. A crowd of goblins wearing chainmail and loose red shirts marked with the black fist holding the sword pushed through the goblinkin on the deck. They surrounded a huge warrior festooned with knives and two swords, one carried at his hip and the other carried sheathed down his back.

"I am Arghant Dhane," the big goblin declared in his guttural speech. He thumped a fist against his breastplate. "I'm captain of *Ill Wind*. Who's yer captain?"

"I am Captain Farok, master of *One-Eyed Peggie*," Farok replied.

"I've heard of ye," Arghant said. "There's some in these waters what fear ye."

"They've got reason," Farok stated evenly.

"Faugh!" Arghant struck his breastplate again. "Ye've never crossed blades with me, Cap'n Farok. Mayhap ye've got a reason to fear me."

"I've never met goblinkin I had any reason to fear."

Sensing that things were going to remain peaceable at least for a few minutes, Wick quietly stole his book from his blouse and opened it to a blank page. He licked the end of his charcoal and quickly blocked out the goblin ship. He took brief pauses, catching bits of dialogue and phrases from the goblin and the pirate captain as they continued their discussions, and wrote on still other pages.

"Then ye should learn to fear me, Cap'n Farok," Arghant said. "I've sent seven ships an' seven crews to the bottom of the Blood-Soaked Sea theses past two months, an' I'm prepared to send even more. I got no mercy in me heart for the likes of ye and yers."

"I wasn't the one who suggested we talk," Captain Farok said sternly.

And in that moment, Wick realized how proud he was of the old man. The way Farok disciplined the crew, and the way he was able to put steel in his spine when he was facing his enemies was nothing less than heroic.

Despite his pirate calling, the little librarian couldn't help thinking, *Grandmagister Ludaan would have liked Captain Farok.*

"I didn't come to just talk," Arghant said. "I come to negotiate the terms of yer surrender."

"*Surrender,* is it?" Farok roared.

The crew of *One-Eyed Peggie* cheered him on, stamping their feet against the deck and rattling their weapons against the railing.

The goblin crew roared insults and spat over the side of their ship. Vile and crude oaths filled the air on both sides.

Anxiety filled Wick, but while his stomach churned, his hand somehow remained steady enough to capture pictures and words.

"Why," Farok went on, "I'd never surrender to the likes of ye if'n ye had to come rouse me from me death-bed."

"If ye value yer crew, ye'd think twice—"

"Ye loathsome creature," Farok roared. "Ye're not makin' any sense a-tall. First ye're a-braggin' about how ye sent seven ships' crews down into the brine and their ship with 'em, and then ye're offerin' me terms? Why, I ain't a-gonna believe ye."

"Fine!" Arghant yelled. "Ye don't have to believe me. But I didn't come here alone."

The words rolled over *One-Eyed Peggie*'s deck. For a moment, the hoarse shouts the pirate crew offered the goblinkin came to a halt.

"Ship!" Zeddar suddenly squalled. "Ship's a-comin' hard aft!"

Wick turned, as did most of the crew, to peer through the fog into the distance. Nearly three hundred yards back, looking like a pale ghost, another ship like the one Arghant commanded shifted in and out of the fog layers.

The sound of beating drums, faint at first, began to grow in intensity as the new ship sailed closer.

Hallekk swore. "Blasted goblinkin foxed us." He ran across the deck and pulled himself up into the railing. "An' I never seen two goblin ships at one time anymore. There's more a-goin' on than what we're a-seein' here, little man."

"Put on sail!" Farok commanded.

Hallekk quickly took up the order, bellowing it across the deck till it seemed his voice rolled like thunder. In short order, the crew put on more sheets, and *One-Eyed Peggie* once more leaned into the wind. But drums sounded aboard both goblin vessels now as they sailed in pursuit. The savage beat pulsed, almost loud enough to drown out the shouted conversations aboard the pirate ship. The little librarian had read about such tactics in books that discussed battles with goblins, but even his great imagination had never come close to how frightening the sound actually was.

Wick followed Hallekk up into the rigging, but he knew at once that the pirate ship was no match for either of the two goblin ships. The new vessel lined up directly behind *One-Eyed Peggie*. At almost the same time, the belled canvas sails relaxed, drooping on the lanyards and yardarms.

"She's stolen our wind," Hallekk declared hoarsely. "If the captain can match us, we're dead in the water."

Farok called out orders to the helmsman, but the goblin ship behind them, blocking the wind off so that *One-Eyed Peggie* slowed, mirrored every move the dwarf made.

The first goblin ship sailed up on the port side of the pirate vessel. For the first time, Wick became aware of the stench that clung to the goblin ship. The vessel smelled of death and decay and old blood. The little librarian sneezed at the strength of the stink even in the wind.

"Yonder ship is a slaver," one of the pirates commented. "Ye can tell by the foul stench a-clingin' to her. Once ye get that smell in yer nose, why ye never forgets it."

Arghant stood at the railing and yelled across the splashing waves between the two ships. "Yer choice, Cap'n Farok. Ye can surrender to me, or ye can die."

"One's pretty much the same as the other," Farok yelled back. "But if'n ye try taking me ship, me crew will slit yer gizzard for ye, they will."

Arghant turned to his men and screamed orders. In the next instant, the goblin archers fired arrows. The projectiles streaked across the sea, snapping in half or bouncing off dwarven shields. Other arrows struck the side of the ship or tangled in the drooping sails.

"Get up, ye scurvy seadogs!" Hallekk yelled. "If'n they want a taste of steel, why we'll be after givin' it to them! Ready bows!"

Wick watched as the dwarven pirates lifted their bows and nocked arrows, pulling the strings back to their bearded chins. The little librarian put his journal away, but he knew he could trust those images to stay fresh in his mind. He took cover behind the railing. *One-Eyed Peggie* rolled awkwardly to the top of the next wave, waddling like a plump duck without the wind under her wings.

"Fire!" Hallekk ordered.

The dwarven archers let fly, and the arrows rained down on the goblin ship. Goblins fell back, pierced by the arrows. Blood spread across the ship's deck, becoming treacherous to those standing beside a fallen shipmate.

"Ready bows," Hallekk cried out almost immediately.

On board the goblin ship, Arghant screamed orders, but most of his crew was in disorder.

"Fire!" Hallekk commanded.

The dwarven arrows flew again, and again they raked victims from the goblinkin. Still, the goblins readily took up their positions as Arghant urged them on.

There are simply too many of them, Wick thought as he watched the battle. The dwarven archers were much better than the goblinkin, but the goblinkin carried a larger ship's crew on one vessel, much less the two of them. *Hallekk has to realize that, too.*

"Aft ship is comin' around!" Zeddar called from the crow's-nest.

"Lay on sail!" Farok commanded.

As soon as the goblinship following the pirate ship pulled away from the stern, *One-Eyed Peggie* dug her canvas claws into the wind and yanked. The ship cleaved through the sea again, gaining speed immediately.

How do the goblins know to work their ships in tandem? Wick wondered. *And how did Arghant manage to get two nearly new ships?* The questions plagued him even during the time he feared for his very life.

Without warning, Arghant's ship steered into *One-Eyed Peggie*. A crash of thunder mixed with the crack of splintering wood, and part of the pirate ship's port railing broke free. Goblins hurled boarding lines, striving to lash the two ships together.

Pulling the skinning knife Hallekk had given him from his boot, Wick took a quick breath and ran along the railing. He reached between the rails and sawed at the lines. As each line was cut, it dropped back into the sea. An arrow thudded into his boot, piercing the toe but miraculously missing his foot. Still, the arrow nailed his boot to the deck and tripped him, sending him sprawling. Even as he looked up, Hallekk severed the last boarding line with his axe.

"Archers, fire!" the big dwarf bellowed.

The hum of bowstrings, like the buzz of dragonfly wings, rang out over Wick's head. He glanced through the railing as he reached down and snapped the arrow shaft in two. He yanked his boot free of the stub as he saw the forward line of attacking goblinkin go down like a wave crashing onto a beach.

A huge cheer went up from the pirate crew, and it drew increased vile oaths from the goblinkin.

Then the wind died again as the goblin ship coming up on the starboard side settled back into the stern position, stealing the breeze.

"Ready bows!" Hallekk growled.

The archers nocked more arrows.

"Cap'n Farok!" Arghant bellowed from his ship, now eighty yards away.

Farok held a hand out to Hallekk. The big quartermaster signaled his crew of archers to stand down. The pirates quickly spread out to aid their fallen comrades. Wick knew that a few of them were already dead. Although the goblin archers weren't as good as their pirate counterparts, some of the arrows had still struck home.

"Cap'n Farok!" Arghant called again.

"What is it ye're a-wantin'?" Farok demanded.

"If'n I want, I can take yer ship," the goblin captain shouted.

"We got a lot of pride in *One-Eyed Peggie*," Farok countered. "If'n ye do take her by some chance, she ain't a-gonna come cheap."

Arghant stood in the stern castle. Two goblins holding full shields stood on either side of him, ready to defend him. "I don't have to kill ye. I'd settle for robbin' ye."

"If'n I say no?" Farok argued.

"I got more warriors than ye do. I'll worry at ye for days, and I'll take bites outta ye an' yer crew every chance I get. An' there'll be plenty of chances."

"Ye come all this way for me cargo?"

Wick glanced at Hallekk, who shook his head.

"That don't make no sense," the big dwarf muttered. "Goblinkin ain't all that interested in trade. They've only been interested in gettin' what they needed to get by."

"I said I'd *settle* for the cargo," Arghant replied.

Farok paused. "Might be worth it to me to see ye work for it."

"If I do," Arghant said, "I swear to ye that not a one of yer crew will escape. I won't rest till I see 'em all dead."

Farok remained silent.

Wick knew the old captain had to weigh his decision carefully. Arghant wasn't idly boasting; the goblin captain would stay at his chosen task. When goblinkin got the scent of someone else's blood, they were loath to give it up. Some legends had it that goblins had been born in the shadows, raised from carrion feeders and given an intelligence, then driven to kill or enslave every other creature in the world. Lord Kharrion had reached that dark spark inside the goblin race and fanned it into a consuming flame.

"Captain Farok," Arghant thundered, "I await yer decision impatiently."

Farok swept his gaze over the crew spread across *One-Eyed Peggie*'s deck. "Ye men would fight, an' I know ye would die for me an' this ship an' our flag. But me, I'm a-thinkin' that today ain't our day. There'll be another day. An' there's others that need to know the goblins are a-gettin' ships from somewheres." He cleared his throat and gripped the stern castle railing. "Those of ye that have been with me know I don't run from fights. More often than not, I start 'em."

Nervous laughter echoed through the crew, but it only lasted for a moment.

"I ain't a-gonna ask ye to vote on this," Farok contin-

ued. "I'm a-gonna make the decision. That way, if'n
there are any stories about this later, people can say ol'
Cap'n Farok was the one what crawfished on the fight."

"Cap'n," Hallekk started.

The old captain held up a hand. "I'll not hear of it,
Hallekk, I swear I won't. I count seven men a-lyin' dead
there at yer feet, an' I'm not a-gonna count any more
if'n I have a choice. An' I do as long as I'm cap'n of
this vessel."

"Aye, sir," the big dwarf grumbled.

It's the only thing to do, Wick thought desperately. *If
we fight, we're going to die.* He looked around at the
crew, surprised at how many of them he comfortably
called friend these days.

"Cap'n Farok," Arghant called, his tone bordering on
mocking.

"Get yer knickers out of the twist ye're a-puttin' 'em
in," Farok yelled back. "I'm willin' to part with half me
cargo."

"That's not goin' to be—"

"Half!" the old captain growled. "An' any more ain't
open for discussion."

For a time, the only sound over the sea was the wind
through the sails and rigging. Wick stood nervously,
wondering what the outcome might be. He didn't want
to die, and he didn't want to see the men around him
die either. But he knew the only way the goblinkin
would give in would be to believe *One-Eyed Peggie*'s
crew would be willing to die for anything less.

Finally, Arghant yelled, "Agreed."

10

The Bargain

Wick lurched across the pirate ship's deck as he carried a small crate that was incredibly heavy. Since there were no markings on the crate, he had no clue what was inside, but it seemed to gurgle quite happily. Somehow, even without markings of any sort, Hallekk seemed to know what was in every box, bundle, and bag that the hold held. *One-Eyed Peggie* sat silent and still on the sea.

The dwarven pirates worked quickly to unpack the hold and load it into longboats Arghant had sent over from his ship. Still, the job took hours, even longer than unpacking the monthly supplies carried up the Knucklebones Mountains to the Library.

Pirates filled the longboats and carefully tied down all the crates and bags. As soon as one of them was full, the goblin crew pulled on the rope they had attached to the longboats, reeling the boats in like fish. Sifting through all the cargo took hours, and Captain Farok wouldn't stint on the bargain.

Finally, the last load was fitted onto one of the two longboats and pushed out away from *One-Eyed Peggie*. Wick watched glumly with the rest of the pirate crew, aware that they were now at a rather precipitous moment. The stench coming off the goblin ship was intense

enough that Wick's stomach turned and churned threateningly.

When the goblinkin pulled the last longboat next to
their own ship and began unpacking it, cackling with
gleeful greed, Arghant stepped up onto the stern castle
with his two guards again.

"An' how do I know this is half yer cargo, Cap'n
Farok?" the goblin captain demanded.

"Because I give ye me word," Farok responded. "An'
whatever else I may be, I'm a man of me word." A sour
smile carved his haggard face. "Then again, ye're welcome to pipe aboard an' have a look about for yerself."

"With a small party of warriors?"

"No." Farok shook his head.

"No," Arghant replied. "I'd rather trust ye on the
amount than on me safety."

"I'll take that as a compliment, then." Captain Farok
faced his foe across the open expanse of the Blood-
Soaked Sea. The fog was dense enough now that the
two ships blurred occasionally, almost but not quite
swept from view. "An' I'll be a-prayin' we get the
chance to do this again someday."

"There will be another day," Arghant promised.
"There's a lot of us goblin pirates a-turnin' eyes toward
the Blood-Soaked Sea. An' we're all a-thinkin' mayhap
ye dwarves have been a-runnin' these waters for far too
long."

"Then we're done with this business," Farok said.

"No," Arghant said. "We'll also have the halfer ye got
aboard yer ship."

Wick took an involuntary step back as the goblin captain's eyes lit on him. A change in the breeze brought
the stench of the goblin ship rolling over him. The little
librarian swallowed bile.

Immediately, the pirate crew rose up in arms. "Ye'll

not get the little man without a fight," Hallekk declared, leading the hoarse shouting.

"The dweller," Captain Farok proclaimed, "is part of this crew. Ye'll not be taking a crewman as long as I live."

"Ye may not live for much longer." Arghant waved and goblin pirates stepped to the railing again. They raised their shields and showed their readiness. "An' I can't believe ye'd be a-willin' to sacrifice yer whole crew for a halfer that can't be worth much as a pirate."

Wick was surprised, too. Very few people had ever stood up for him, and none of them had ever had to risk their lives to do it. His eyes burned.

"Don't ye worry none, little man," Hallekk said, clapping him on the shoulder. "Them goblins won't take ye from this ship without a-bleedin' for ye."

Fearfully, Wick glanced back at the goblin crew. Blood lust showed on their fierce faces. He knew the goblinkin wouldn't turn away from the battle once they started it.

"He is crew," Captain Farok insisted. "An' not one crewman aboard my ship would be a-willin' to see another crewman off to yer untender mercies."

Hallekk and the crew roared their approval of Captain Farok's decision. They stamped their feet and slapped their weapons against the ship's railing, creating a furor.

Immediately, the goblinkin began beating their drums again, filling the air with savage thunder. The beats seemed somehow predatory.

More frightened than he'd ever been in his life, even after the frightful things he'd been through before leaving Greydawn Moors and since, Wick glanced at the men around him. The thought of them dying on his behalf nearly broke the little librarian's heart. Most of the crew, though of ill-mannered disposition many days, he'd come to know as good-hearted men. They hadn't asked for their lot to be cast upon the sea, but they'd seen the worthiness of the cause they championed. The Builders had established the Blood-Soaked Sea pirates as a defense against goblin encroachment, and to hide the true secret of the Vault of All Known Knowledge.

Wick knew no matter how much the thought scared him that he could do no less. He touched Hallekk's arm. "Hallekk," he said hoarsely, his voice breaking.

The big dwarf glanced down at Wick with a fierce grin. "Don't ye worry, Wick. We'll not be a-lettin' them have ye. Ye'll not know the weight of a slaver's collar as long as there's a breath in me."

Wick tried to speak, but couldn't. His voice betrayed him, staying locked up tight in his throat. He shook his head slowly.

Understanding hit Hallekk. The fighting smile dropped from the big dwarf's face, leaving only concern. "No, little man. Ye can't mean what I think ye're a-meanin'."

Wick swallowed hard, hoping he didn't pass out from fear. His legs trembled and he could scarcely stand. "It . . . it's the only way, Hallekk."

"We can fight them, little man."

"We didn't fight them for the cargo," Wick said.

"But it's only cargo. Not a man's life."

Their conversation drew the attention of the nearby pirates. Many of them weren't so quick to agree with Hallekk and the little librarian couldn't blame them.

"I need to speak to Captain Farok," Wick said.

Hallekk hesitated.

"Please, Hallekk," Wick pleaded. "Before I lose my nerve and find myself unable to do what I know needs to be done."

"By the Old Ones," Hallckk breathed in resignation, "but it ain't fair, little man. Ye didn't ask for none of this."

Wick couldn't say anything. He turned his attention from the big dwarf to the stern castle where Captain Farok stood. The old captain looked down at him, and Wick guessed the man somehow knew what he planned. Was approval in those old eyes? The little librarian didn't know, but the captain's gaze allowed him to straighten his spine and walk on legs that threatened to go out from under him at any moment.

Captain Farok exchanged glances with Wick as the little librarian climbed the stairs with Hallekk at his side. Every pirate on the ship had gotten quiet, and even the goblins had stopped beating their drums.

Wick stopped before the old captain. "Captain Farok," the little librarian said in a quavering voice.

"Aye, Wick."

"I can't let you fight these goblins for me."

The captain put fire in his voice, speaking loudly enough that every pirate aboardship could hear him. "An' I can't let them take ye."

"Sir, I respect your feelings," Wick said, "but if you fight them, you're going to die."

Anger flamed the old captain's face. "Have ye no faith in this crew, then?"

Wick's knees trembled and nearly buckled. He wished he could just let the captain give the order to fight. It wasn't his decision, after all. He could—but he knew in his heart that he couldn't. "Captain Farok, I have all the faith a person could have in this crew. I know what they would do. If you give the order, they would die to protect me."

"Not ye," Captain Farok replied. "They'd be a-dyin' to protect the sanctity of this ship. We're pirates of the Blood-Soaked Sea, an' there's not fiercer fightin' men to be found."

"If they would die to protect the sanctity of this ship,"

Wick said, wishing his voice didn't break so, "then how can I expect myself to do any less?"

"Wick," the old man argued, "ye're not captain of this ship."

"No, but perhaps if I surrender myself to the goblinkin, they will let the rest of you go free."

"An' they may not. We've already had the taste of their treachery, an' it's as foul as the odor a-comin' from that ship. They might start out askin' for you, then ask for another an' another."

"If they do, then you'll know."

Captain Farok shook his head. "They only want ye out of spite, Wick. Just one more concession to embarrass me an' take the pride from this ship."

Wick had to work to make his words come out of his tight throat. "Sir, with all respect, if we fight them, many of this crew will die. I can't be responsible for that."

Captain Farok was silent for a moment, then, "It's a brave thing ye're a-doin', Wick."

Wick shook his head. "It's not brave. It's the only sensible thing to do." His voice broke. "If I was brave, I wouldn't be so afraid now."

"Fear an' bravery," Captain Farok said, "ye're a-gonna find, always live under the same sails an' share the same breezes. An' oftentimes they seem to chart a man's course no matter what he thinks he'd do if given his choice."

The old captain's voice broke then, and the sound surprised Wick.

"Something for ye to know, Wick," Captain Farok said, "I've always found a man a-layin' out his course by wits alone often ends up in reef-filled waters than one who's a-layin' out his course by followin' his heart. Ye've got a good heart. I've seen that in ye. An' ye'll never find a truer compass."

Wick wiped his face, hoping no one noticed the tears

on his face. "We have to hurry. If we wait much longer, I don't know if I'm going to be strong enough to do this."

Tenderly, Captain Farok laid his hand on Wick's shoulder. "Ye're stronger than ye realize, Third Level Librarian Wick, an' I've met few men as brave as ye are."

Despite the old captain's shaking hand, Wick felt the strength in his grip. The little librarian drew strength from the touch. He straightened a little more and squared his shoulders. "You'll have to give the order," Wick said. "I don't think I can."

Captain Farok nodded. "As ye will. But know ye this: If'n ye ever find yer way clear back to the Blood-Soaked Sea, there's a berth a-waitin for ye aboard *One-Eyed Peggie* should ye want it."

"Thank you," Wick said.

"Hallekk," Captain Farok said.

"Aye, Cap'n." Hallekk snuffled.

"Get this sailor a boat. I'll not have him sent over to them blasted goblins a-ferried by their crew. An' if ye can't find enough brave men to pull them oars, ye come get me an' I'll pull one with ye."

"Aye, Cap'n."

"Thank you, Captain," Wick said.

Hallekk dropped his hand onto Wick's shoulder. "C'mon, little man, afore I don't have the guts what ye do."

The little librarian walked with Hallekk at his side. They returned to portside amidships. Hallekk helped him into the longboat, then clambered in himself, yelling that he needed a rowing crew.

Wick was surprised how many pirates volunteered, even though they knew they'd be rowing to their deaths if the goblinkin chose to be treacherous. The goblin archers could easily kill everyone aboard the longboat before it could get back to the temporary safety of *One-Eyed Peggie*.

Hallekk picked five other men from among the crew, then the longboat was lowered into the water. All of the pirates called their goodbyes, and they were all stern-faced and sad.

Wick sat in the longboat's prow, his stomach rolling with the rise and fall of the choppy waves between the two ships.

"Are ye okay, little man?" Hallekk asked as he pulled his oar in front of Wick.

"No," Wick admitted truthfully. He glanced over his shoulder at the goblin ship. "You may have to pry me out of this boat when we get there, Hallekk." He was embarrassed to admit that it was possible. "But if it comes to that, I need you to do it."

The big dwarf shook his head. "I don't know that I can do that."

When they reached the midway point between the two ships, Wick could no longer control his stomach. The stench from the goblin vessel was stronger than ever. Unable to hold back, he leaned over the longboat's side and threw up, fully expecting a sea monster to rise from below and gobble him down whole. It wouldn't have surprised him.

Instead, he rose again to hear the jeering laughter of the goblins. His ears burned and he felt miserable, which triggered another bout of nausea. Only this time there was nothing to come up and the dry heaves wracked him, sapping what little strength he had left. The goblins continued to jeer him.

"Steady on, little man," Hallekk encouraged.

Wick wiped at his mouth but couldn't escape the sour taste that somehow mirrored the stink clinging to the goblin ship. He wanted so badly to be brave about what he was doing. So many of the heroes he'd read about in

Hralbomm's Wing could face insurmountable danger and terror and never even bat an eye. And he was throwing up.

When the longboat reached the goblin ship, a goblin kicked a rope ladder down. "Climb up, halfer."

Wick stood on trembling knees that refused to hold him. He would have fallen if it hadn't been for Hallekk steadying him with a hand.

"I just want ye to know," Hallekk said, gazing into Wick's eyes, "that I've never met a braver man." He hugged the little librarian in a fierce embrace, and tears stained his face.

"I have a favor to ask," Wick said.

"Aye."

"If you should return to Greydawn Moors, look up the Mettarin Lamplighter family. Let my ma and da know what's become of me, that I wasn't exiled by the Library or left of my own choice."

"I will, little man."

Wick set his hands upon the rough rope ladder. The goblins jeered him, calling at him to hurry. "And tell my da," the little librarian went on, "that I love him and I'm sorry I didn't try to understand him more." Then he pushed himself up the rope ladder, hoping his arms and legs didn't betray him and cause him to slip and fall into the sea.

He went up three steps, but found himself lacking the strength to go any further. He pulled at the ropes but couldn't manage the next step.

"Haul the halfer up," someone ordered above.

Wick hung on resolutely as the ladder was hauled up. He bumped against the ship's hull with bruising force as the ladder twisted. Then rough hands seized him and yanked him aboard. Black talons cut into his flesh and grinning, gruesome faces filled his vision.

A goblin seized him on either side, pinning his arms

as they dragged him across the deck to Arghant.

"Do you want us to kill the men aboard the longboat?" a goblin asked eagerly.

"No," the goblin pirate said. His eyes raked Wick in cruel disdain. "Let 'em live. If'n we push that old cap'n any harder, he's liable to attack us. Farok's one of the ones we were warned about."

One of the ones we were warned about? Despite his fear, Wick's mind raced. Who had warned the goblins? And why?

Arghant leaned in against Wick, his brutish face only inches from the little librarian's. The stench clung to the goblin as well, leaving him smelling like a dead thing that had gone sour and moldy. "An' what about ye, halfer?" the goblin captain demanded. "Do ye feel all high and noble for sacrificin' yerself for all yer shipmates? Ye saved their lives, ye know."

Wick tried to make his voice hard and cold, but it came out stuttering and weak. "You sh-should b-be g-glad that I c-came. My only re-regret is th-that I prob-probably sa-saved your life, t-too." Still, the little librarian took some measure of pride in the anger that blanched the goblin captain's face.

"Stupid halfer!" Arghant backhanded Wick, knocking him free of the two goblins that held him.

Wick hit the deck and barely held back a moan of pain. His stomach rebelled on him again, drawing him up as the heaves took him.

"Yer arrogance is gonna be the death of ye," Arghant declared. He reached down and hauled Wick up with one fist. He slid his cutlass up under the little librarian's throat. "Yer life is mine to do with what I will."

Wick hung from the great fist. He seized the goblin's wrist, but he could not even wrap both of his hands around it. He was too frightened to say anything.

"Ye hear me, halfer?" Arghant demanded.

Wick tried to answer, but his voice was stuck in his throat.

Arghant shook him. "Speak when ye're spoken to, halfer. I get more money for ye in Hanged Elf's Point if ye're whole, it's true, but I got a cargo hold full of halfers. One more or less ain't a-gonna matter to me."

"I h-hear you," Wick stuttered. His heart hammered in his chest. Although he'd never hated anyone in his life, he knew hatred now, and he was surprised to understand how much hatred came all wrapped up in fear.

Arghant threw him to the deck. "Take the halfer below with the others."

Wick lay on the deck weakly for only a moment, then someone yanked him up by the back of his shirt. A goblin stepped forward and clapped manacles to the little librarian's wrists. They pulled him to his knees, then brought out a blacksmith's hammer and drove steel pins into the manacles to lock them.

Wick yanked at his hands, nauseous again when he realized he was going to be bound. He hadn't thought about that when he'd offered to surrender himself. Panic filled him and took his breath away. The short chain held him and the manacles bit into his flesh. Before he knew it, a steel collar snapped closed around his neck as well. The goblin yanked him roughly, bending him over so his back was bent, then snapped a chain from the steel collar to the manacles. Another set of manacles was attached to his ankles.

"In case ye decide to take yer chances in the water some night," a goblin snarled. He grinned, showing gapped fangs. "Even bound up so, there's a few of yer kind that choose that over slavery. Ain't a-gonna stand for that neither."

They yanked him to his feet.

Sick with fear and nausea, Wick could hardly stand on his own. His chain links clinked against each other as the goblin ship rolled on the waves. The stink filled his nose, overloading his senses. Everything had a nightmare quality about it, feeling unreal though he knew it was truly happening. He desperately wanted to wake up and find himself in bed at the Library.

But that wasn't going to be true.

That was never going to be true again.

Arghant grabbed Wick's wrist manacles and pulled him to the railing. The goblin captain pointed out *One-Eyed Peggie* as she sailed away. "They must not care too much about ye, halfer. There they go."

Wick didn't argue. He didn't have the strength. Everything seemed dead inside him, bound up by the weight of his chains. Instead, not knowing what else to do, he lifted his hands and waved goodbye.

Without warning, Arghant struck him, knocking him senseless.

11

Enslaved

Wick fought against the darkness that lay over him like a heavy quilt. He reached up, listening to the clinking links of the chains that bound him. The stench let him know immediately where he was.

"Take it easy," a calm voice told him.

"Who's there?" Wick demanded. He turned toward the voice, trying to peer through the gloom.

"Harran. I'm a dweller like yourself."

Wick tried to sit up, but the effort set off another dry heave spell.

"Just sit back and relax," Harran advised. "You're chained down anyway, and there's no place to go."

Wick laid back down, breathing shallowly so his stomach would stop turning. He patted his blouse and found to his great relief that he still had his journal. "Where are we?"

"Bottom of the ship's hold."

"Arghant's ship?"

"Yes." Harran laughed without humor. "The goblinkin call her *Ill Wind*. Arghant heard a phrase somewhere about how death was an ill wind. Still, you have to admit after smelling her that she's aptly named."

Other chains clinked in the darkness. Someone labored through a hoarse, racking cough, and for a moment Wick had thought the person had died. Then another rasping breath came. More chains clinked.

"You're chained, too?" Wick asked.

"All of us are."

" 'All of us?' " the little librarian echoed.

"There are dozens of us down here," another man said. "But none of us were picked up from a Blood-Soaked Sea pirate ship."

"Some of the others are suspicious of you for that," Harran pointed out. "They've never heard of a dweller pirate before."

Wick remembered Trosper, still aboard *One-Eyed Peggie*. "There are a few."

"Not where I'm from."

"Where is that?" Wick asked.

"I'm from Moroneld's Harbor."

The name struck a chord in Wick's mind. "Along the Shattered Coast?"

"Yes. You've been there?"

"No, but I've heard of it." One of the most destructive battles in the Cataclysm was fought along the Shattered Coast. Human mages had warred against the dark forces Lord Kharrion had controlled. Goblinkin armies had swept down from the remnants of the Western Empire after King Amalryn and his family had been murdered and changed. It was the first time the human mages had faced the Embyrs.

"Where are you from?" Harran asked.

"Further north."

"Lottar's Crossing?"

Wick thought for a moment, trying to place Lottar's Crossing. He didn't want to mention Greydawn Moors, and he didn't want to make himself more suspicious to the other dwellers held captive in *Ill Wind*'s hold.

Lottar's Crossing was nearly three hundred miles

north of the Shattered Coast. It had been primarily a dwarven city that had sprung up from seven mining villages that quickly grew together. Upon occasion, there were minor battles between dwarven clans over mining rights when the long tunnels started to intermingle. Lottar's Crossing referred to the common ground the seven villages eventually came to share, named for the dwarven clan leader who had managed to negotiate the usage of the land.

"Yes," Wick said. "I'm from Orsin's Saucer." The village was real, a small hollow along the Rolling Jewel River.

"I've never heard of it," Harren admitted.

"I have," an older man said weakly. "They make glass there. Window panes and bottles, mostly."

"Right," Wick said, struggling to remember what he could of Orsin's Saucer. "Greengloss glass. The finest glassware anyone could ever want."

"Hrumph," the old man said in the darkness. "At least, that's what a man from Orsin's Saucer will tell you if you ask him. I've seen glass just as fine made in other places. And they made a lot more of it. The place should be named Orsin's Wallow, if you ask me."

"How did you come to be on a pirate's ship?" Harran asked.

"My da sent me down to the docks in Wexlertown," Wick said, improvising, remembering the terrain clearly now from Harferd's *Treatise on Stained Glass-Makers and Blowers*. "While I was there making arrangements for the shipment, I went down to a tavern for a drink. Somebody hit me over the head. Next thing I knew, I was on the pirate ship." *There. That's close enough to the truth.*

"They told the goblinkin that you were one of the crew," still another voice said.

Wick thought quickly, hating the way the lie kept

threatening to get all tangled up. "They only told the goblinkin that because they wanted to keep me to ransom back to my family."

"A glassblower's family? Where would they get the idea that a glassblower's family would have enough money for ransom?"

"I told them my father was very well known," Wick said. "And around our village, he is." Everyone in Greydawn Moors knew Mettarin Lamplighter. "The pirates just didn't know how small Orsin's Saucer is. It's not a port, you know, and they have never had cause to go there."

"The pirates sounded like they were going to fight for you."

"I know," Wick said. And he knew he would always remember that. "But in the end, they didn't." *Only I have to know the real reason they didn't.*

"That was a clever ruse on your part," Harran commented. "You think quickly on your feet."

"I try to," Wick said.

"Pity all that thinking hasn't taken you elsewheres than here," someone said. "From here, it's a short trip to Hanged Elf's Point."

"What's Hanged Elf's Point?" Wick asked.

"A goblin city along the southern tip of the Shattered Coast," Harran answered. "Once, the city was called something else. It was an elven town, I think. But that was years ago, and even that might be myth. But the goblinkin live there now and operate their slave markets. They keep their ships there as well."

"I wasn't aware that the goblinkin had many ships," Wick said.

"They do now," Harran replied. "A regular navy of them."

"All ships like this one?"

"All the ones I've seen."

"But this one is new," Wick said incredulously.

"I know."

"Where are they getting them?"

"None of the dwellers along the Shattered Coast know. And none of them are going down to Hanged Elf's Point to ask."

"A dweller in Hanged Elf's Point," another said, "would be better off slitting his own throat. Otherwise, it's life imprisonment in the gold and silver mines, or working on the buildings in the city, or fighting in the arena."

"What arena?" Wick asked.

"You say you lived in Orsin's Saucer?" a man asked. "Why I thought even in Orsin's Saucer folks would have heard about the arenas the goblinkin have set up for their own amusement. They pit dwellers against ferocious beasts other dwellers have spent their life's blood to capture out in the Forest of Fangs and Shadows."

Wick had never heard of such a forest along the Shattered Coast, nor did he know of a town called Hanged Elf's Point. But the books he'd read concerning goblinkin and Lord Kharrion had definitely mentioned the evil arenas where the goblinkin slaked their blood-thirst. Before the Goblin Lord's rise to power, the goblinkin had often conducted such contests with captured prisoners, but Lord Kharrion had ordered such edifices built in each territory his army conquered.

"I've spent a lot of time in my father's shops lately," Wick said. "And I've never been one to get out much."

"Well, you're definitely getting out now," someone said sarcastically.

Wick lay in the darkness, feeling the weight of his chains on him. He'd read about such things in Hralbomm's Wing, and often thought that a hero getting captured was exciting because it only precluded wondrous escapes and amazing feats of derring-do. But that was only in the fanciful tales. Real people didn't manage such things. More often than not, the little librarian recalled from the histories he'd read, real people died in chains and dungeons and on torture racks.

He was no hero. He was only a Librarian who'd strayed too far from home one night. Maybe he wouldn't even be remembered as being important enough to remember. No future Librarians would sit down to read about him and wonder, *Whatever happened to Edgewick Lamplighter?*

After a time, he drifted off to sleep and didn't even know it.

"Wake, ye halfer wretches! Wake and get yer breakfast afore I just throws it over the side!" Someone beat on what sounded like a milk pail and the ringing concussions echoed throughout the hold.

Bright sunlight stung Wick's eyes as he roused. He blinked against the light, hoping his eyes would adjust quickly because the pain made his temples throb. He raised a hand over his eyes, feeling the heaviness of the manacle and chains. His body ached from sleeping on the hard floor of the wooden hull. His clothing was wet in places from the water that pooled and spilled across the floor. For all its newness, *Ill Wind,* as Wick had discovered, leaked from time to time. As a result, his sleep had been haunted by nightmares of sinking into the Blood-Soaked Sea while chained to the goblin ship.

The little librarian sat up with difficulty. He peered through spread fingers. The dark, shadowy forms that walked among the dozens of dwellers chained to the bottom of the ship gradually became goblinkin. Guards took up positions among the slaves, standing with bared axes while other goblins walked along the ragged lines doling thick gruel and water from five-gallon buckets.

Not having seen *Ill Wind*'s lowest deck earlier, Wick was appalled to see it now. Dwellers of all sizes and shapes were chained to long metal poles bolted down to the deck. None of them could do more than sit, and even if they had been able, even dwellers couldn't have stood under the low floor of the deck above.

Most of the sour, decaying odor Wick had been smelling he now realized came from the slaves themselves, not the goblinkin. His heart felt like it was going to burst as he looked at the people around him. Thankfully, there were no children, and only a few dweller women. Evidently the goblinkin slavers aimed to sell strong backs for harsh labor. The brine air that flushed through the slave's quarters from the open hatch smelled fresh and clean, but was quickly overcome by the lingering stink.

"You've never seen anything like this, have you?" a familiar voice asked in a hoarse whisper.

Startled, Wick peered over his shoulder, recognizing the voice as Harran's.

Harran was thin and sallow looking. Gray wisps showed in his unkempt brown hair and beard. His eyes lacked luster and were red-rimmed. His clothing hung in tatters. He held out his hand. "I'm Harran Fieldtiller. You never mentioned your name yesterday."

Wick took the man's hand and found that it shook slightly. "Yesterday?"

Harran nodded, glancing back at the goblinkin walking through the rows of chained dwellers. "You slept through the night."

Wick's head spun. How had so much time passed without him knowing it? "What time is it?"

"Morning," Harran replied. "They always feed us in the morning. Never early, though."

"What about noon and evening?"

Harran shook his head slowly. "Feeding slaves takes away from profits. Captain Arghant is a firm believer in pinching coppers. All that matters to him is that the slaves he's bought for trade make it into the port alive. At least, that most of them make it into the port alive. We've already lost a dozen or more."

Wick watched in horror as the goblinkin let the slaves drink from a dipper from the water bucket. The goblinkin with the gruel dipped out a portion into each dweller's cupped hands.

"As you've noticed, they don't give us any silverware or bowls either," Harran went on. "There would be far too many bowls to wash and spoons could be shaped into weapons or perhaps picklocks for someone skilled enough."

The goblinkin rounded the end of the line and started down the one Wick was in.

"Quickly, my friend," Harran advised. "Put your hands out or they will skip you. It's a long time till tomorrow morning."

Wick cupped his hands, waiting.

The goblin stopped and grinned at him cruelly. "Ah, so ye're the new one." He placed the dipper back into the bucket of gruel then reached out and pinched Wick's cheek. "Still got some fat on ye, don'tcha? Well, we can't have that. Folks what's buyin' a halfer, they already know they're a-gettin' purebred laziness. But a fat halfer, now they're a-gonna think they're a-biddin' on a halfer what's figured out how to get away with bein' lazy."

Wick's face flamed. He felt guilty of being better fed and in better condition than the poor dwellers around him. His hands trembled, and for a moment he thought of putting them down. Then he realized that he had to keep his strength up if he was going to have any chance at all.

"Can't have a fat halfer on the slaver's block," the goblin said. "Cap'n Arghant will have the hide off me back." He brought the dipper out and barely half filled Wick's hands. "So's until ye lose some of that fat, ye're on half rations."

Wick looked at the pasty white gruel sitting in his hands. It was cold and greasy and dirty white as if the pot it had been boiled in hadn't been clean. The appearance and texture made his stomach rumble threateningly.

The goblin moved on and the next one in line offered a dipper of water. "Open yer gullet, halfer," the goblin snarled.

Wick did as he was ordered. The goblin poured water into his mouth. The water gagged him.

"Don't spit it out," Harran warned from behind Wick. "Open your throat and let it pour down. You won't be given another dipper."

"Shut yer face," the gruel goblin ordered. "Or I'll be a-cuttin' ye to half rations as well."

The sound of flesh striking flesh reached Wick's ears as he managed to catch most of the tepid water in his mouth and swallow it down. After having slept all night without having anything to eat or drink, he had a powerful thirst. The dipper was empty long before he was ready for it to be. He looked at the gruel in his hands, squeezing it and watching it change shapes like an artist's clay or butternut cake batter that had set up.

"Looking at it too closely isn't a good idea," Harran said. "That will kill whatever appetite you have from just being hungry. You haven't gone enough days to truly appreciate that kind of hunger."

Shivering, Wick took his first bite. He was grimly aware of the attention of the nearby dwellers. Their wan faces haunted him. Seeing thin dwellers wasn't normal. He almost retched at the pasty taste of the gruel, and only the thought that the others watched him allowed him to keep it down. He glanced at the other dwellers still waiting for their gruel and saw the hunger on their faces. *How could anyone ever come to like this?* He couldn't help thinking about the meals he'd taken for granted at the Library. He took another bite and coughed to cover his gagging when it hung in the back of his throat.

"Small bites," Harran cautioned quietly. "The gruel is too dry and has no seasonings. It's hard to get down at first." He paused. "And you're in no hurry, Wick. You have all day to eat it, but if you don't eat it soon, your mouth will dry from lack of water and the gruel will be even harder to get down."

Wick rolled the greasy ball in his cupped hands and tried another bite. It wasn't any better. He ate his first breakfast as a slave slowly and without hope.

"Everyone along the Shattered Coast knows that the goblinkin are starting to unite," Harran was saying.

Wick lay on his back and stared up at the ceiling above him, listening fearfully to the news that Harran told him. There was nothing else to do. Most of the other dwellers slept, leaving only a few of them awake. Thin sunlight that barely turned the darkness gray slipped in through the hatch.

The sea slapped against the hull somewhere high over his head, reminding him that the compartment the dwellers occupied was well below sea level. *If a reef tears the bottom out, if a harbor isn't as deep as the captain thinks it is, if we accidentally hit another ship in the night, we'll all drown.* The little librarian believed that.

He continued to work at the manacles on his wrists, hoping to slip his hands free. So far, all he'd managed to do was chafe his skin. Still, he couldn't quit. The tinkling chain links echoed inside the hold.

"You're going to make sores on your wrists and ankles if you keep that up," Harran warned.

"I can't just lay here and do nothing." Wick didn't
mean to, but he heard some of the frustration in his
voice.

"You are doing something," Harran said. "You're surviving."

"Surviving to be a slave," someone said bitterly. "If
you want to do a real service to yourself, you'd die and
be done with it."

"I've heard tell," someone else said, "that there are
elven warders in the Forest of Fangs and Shadows that
raid Hanged Elf's Point and free enslaved dwellers."

"Ha," the first man said. "That's just a fairy tale, Que-
ben. Graybeards tell those stories to young men so
they'll have hopes of escape once the goblinkin have
captured them. I think it's cruel. How many people have
you seen that have ever escaped from Hanged Elf's
Point?"

There was no answer.

"Not many people have hopes of surviving slavery
after they're caught," Harran said quietly.

"What do you believe?" Wick asked.

"I believe there has to be a way, and that it is my
hope to stay alive long enough to find it."

"Why are the goblinkin uniting along the Shattered
Coast?" Wick asked.

"They follow a new pirate king who has managed to
convince them that unity would make them strong
enough to take even more than they already had. He's
making believers out of them. From what I hear, more
goblinkin are drawn to the Shattered Coast every day.
They sign up with the goblinkin navy and with the
army."

"Who is the pirate king?"

"A goblin named Orpho Kadar."

"What do you know about him?" Wick asked, thinking that if there were elven warders in the Forest of Fangs and Shadows and he got the chance to get away it would be good if he had as much information to carry back to the Vault of All Known Knowledge. He wished he dared write in his journal, afraid that he might forget some of what he was being told.

"Nothing," Harran replied. "Unless someone else knows of him."

One of the other dwellers spoke up hesitantly after a moment. "I was told that Orpho Kadar was a descendant of Lord Kharrion."

"Nonsense," an old man said. "Lord Kharrion is only a myth. A superstition used to scare small children."

"Lord Kharrion lived," Wick said, "and he died." *He has to be dead by now!* "It was the Goblin Lord that caused the Shattered Coast to be formed."

"More hogwash," the old man argued. "The Shattered Coast has always been shattered. The stories about Teldane's Bounty are myths as well. Can you even imagine those harsh, blasted islands infested by misshapen monsters and foul creatures that live in the sea as well as the land as being some kind of paradise?"

"No," someone said, and a number of other voices agreed.

How can they not believe? Wick wondered. *They live in the center of what had been one of the greatest magical battles of the Cataclysm.* It was beyond him, but he knew from their voices that they were serious.

Nine days later, Wick knew because he kept careful tabulation in his journal during those few times when everyone else was asleep, the little librarian woke in the middle of the night. He was weak with hunger, and this early in the morning, his tongue was thick from the chronic dehydration that set into him.

But even as fatigued and ill-used as he was, he knew from the way the ship moved that something was different. As usual at this time of morning, there was no light in the hold. Snoring filled the hold with noise, but he heard the quiet of the sea as well. The waves didn't strike *Ill Wind* as forcefully now, nor did the ship move quite so sprightly. She'd settled on an even keel, riding smooth as glass.

Wick knew it could only mean they were in shallow water. He sat up, his arms and legs shaking with effort from being underfed so many days in a row. His clothes, worn for days without washing, hung loosely on him. The journal remained a solid weight against his chest.

Over the last nine days, he'd trained himself to wake just before dawn. The goblins were never early to feed the slaves and he always managed to get just a few minutes to himself and the journal before anyone else woke. Making up for the missed sleep was easy. In the last nine days, he'd never left the hold.

He listened intently as goblin voices cried out to each other above. Although he couldn't quite hear the words, he knew the cadence and timber from his days aboard *One-Eyed Peggie*. Sails above dropped and the slave ship slowed. Excitement and dread filled the little librarian. There was no reason to stop unless they'd reached port.

He reached above him and found Harran's foot. He shook the foot vigorously. "Harran."

"Humph?" Harran pulled his foot from Wick's grasp.

"Harran."

"What?" Harran asked in the thick, phlegmy voice so many of the slaves had when they first woke. "What is it, Wick?"

"The ship has slowed. I think we're coming into port."

A moment of silence followed. The creaking timbers echoed around them, then Wick felt the ship tilt and heard the clank of the great anchor chain being windlassed out. *Ill Wind* shivered just a moment as her anchor dragged along the sea bottom then held. The ship swung around, bobbing in the crosscurrents as the anchor held it.

"You're right," Harran whispered. "We are coming into port."

Wick waited tensely in the dark, unwilling to speak any more. There was no reason to be excited about reaching portage—since he was only going to be a slave at heavy manual labor till he died—but he was. It was almost the same kind of excitement that used to fill him when Grandmagister Ludaan opened one of the sealed rooms in the Library and gave it over to him for sorting. He'd found so many treasures in those rooms, so many stories.

A long time passed, perhaps even hours. Finally, just as Wick's chin kept dropping against his chest, lantern light flared against the hatch.

The locking bolt slid back with a long rasp. Then the hatch flipped up and light invaded the hold. Goblinkin climbed down the narrow stairs and moved among the slaves. They carried small stiff whips and lashed out at the dwellers without mercy.

"Get up!" they roared. "Get up, halfers, afore we feeds ye to the hungry sharks what patrols the harbor waters."

Wick wrapped his arms over his head, protecting his eyes from the bright lantern light. Even though he was sitting up and obviously awake, he'd learned that the goblinkin didn't miss a chance to strike a confined slave.

"Wake up, halfers, or we're a-gonna spit ye, roast ye, an' eat ye ourselves."

Plaintive cries and protests punctuated the goblinkin's threats and heartless blows.

Wick felt the stinging slash of a whip across his neck and shoulders. He cried out in pain. Over the last few days he'd learned that the goblins expected their victims to cry out. If they didn't, the goblins struck again.

A large goblin that had run mostly to fat used the big key ring he carried to unlatch the metal poles that held the ankle chains secure. Other goblins slid the poles free, then walked among the dwellers and yanked them to their feet.

Yelling curses and flailing with the whips, the goblinkin started the dwellers up the stairs. Wick fell into line with them, receiving two more blows before he could get away.

The dwellers, in spite of their fear, shambled along, exhausted by the cruel conditions they'd been kept under and starvation. Some of the slaves had been kept aboard over a month without seeing the light of day.

By the time he reached *Ill Wind*'s main deck, Wick was trembling and winded. A city stood on the starboard side of the ship. It had been built among craggy mountains, placed on plateaus that looked as though they'd been chiseled there. There were nine such levels, all of them marked by lanterns and torches. The first six levels, staggered what appeared to be thirty or forty feet apart, held a handful of buildings each. Most of those, Wick felt certain, had at one time been military outposts or guardhouses. The last three levels were larger and were almost vacant except for a few crumbling ruins. They were *marketplaces,* the little librarian realized.

Above the nine ledges, at least eight hundred feet above sea level, stood the city. The homes and buildings spread out across the steep hills that pushed toward the sea coast far below like the puckered scar of an old puncture wound. The city was far larger than Greydawn Moors, yet—sheathed in darkness as much of it was—

appeared unoccupied. *Or maybe it's only because it is so near early morning.*

Still the design of the city seemed familiar.

I know this place, Wick realized. He racked his mind, trying to remember where he knew the city from, but couldn't. *The arrangement smacks of something elven, but they would have never named a place Hanged Elf's Point.*

Quickly, *Ill Wind*'s crew secured a rope bridge to the lowest of the nine levels. Cursing and swinging their whips, the goblins drove the dweller slaves across the swaying rope bridge suspended twenty feet above the white-capped surf pounding the rocky shore below.

Without warning, one of the men ahead of Wick stumbled and fell over the side of the rope bridge. The little librarian reached for the man, barely touched his shirt, then watched helplessly as the man plummeted into the ocean below. He searched the water for the man, certain that he wouldn't surface again with the manacles on his wrists and ankles.

"There he is!" someone shouted.

Wick spotted the man floating on his back, barely staying above water.

"Get a rope down to him!" a dweller man shouted. "He still has a chance!"

"No, he doesn't," a goblin snarled at the front of the line. "Nobody what falls into Hanged Elf Harbor has a chance in them waters."

Hardly had the words sped from the goblin's lips than the man below gave a painful shout then vanished, drawn deep into the harbor by something that Wick judged was very large. Light from the torches the goblinkin slavers carried played over the dark water for a moment. A large shark leapt from the water then, arching for the rope bridge stretched high above it—and the dwellers that stood there, frozen with fear.

The shark fell short of the rope bridge, missing the feet of the dwellers standing upon it only by inches, and disappeared back into the depths. But not before eliciting screaming fear and renewed efforts to get across the fragile structure that set it to wobbling.

Wick hurried across with the first of the crowd. His wrist and ankle chains rattled in his haste. He stood on the ledge and waited as the rest of the slaves were forced across the rope bridge at sword point.

"Keep movin'," the goblins ordered. "Them sharks can't get ye up here. Why, if'n they could, do ye suppose we'd a-tied a bridge across here?" He laughed at them, then cursed them coarsely as they slowly made their way to the other side.

Is the sea at high tide or low tide? Wick wondered. The water level wouldn't have to come up much to put the rope bridge in striking distance of the sharks. *Perhaps there's a loading time, or maybe this is high tide and the water just doesn't get any higher.*

Glancing out into the harbor, he spotted a dozen other ships lying at anchorage. Two more vessels slid gracefully across the water, either looking for harbor anchorage or leaving the city. Nearly two dozen small fishing boats were putting out to sea. Wick thought the fishermen were being overly ambitious until he spotted the first reddish rays of dawn breaking over the ocean to the east. Although it looked like the rising sun was coming from the ocean, the little librarian knew that it had to be rising over land somewhere nearby for the red color to show up.

The *Ill Wind* goblinkin led them to a garrison house that took up half the ledge. The guards carried the torches high, lighting the way across the stone.

Taking short steps so the ankle chains wouldn't trip him, Wick gazed at the stone beneath him. *It has been carved into this shape!* The hint of memory niggled at his mind, vanishing like the fog on the Blood-Soaked Sea before he could quite grasp it. Hunger pangs clenched his stomach. *Maybe if I could think about this without being crazed by hunger, I could remember what it is I've forgotten.*

A garrison house blocked the way ahead. The stone wall on both sides of it stretched out to bisect the ledge. Figures moved atop it.

Gazing through the gloom, Wick was barely able to make out the archers that held positions at the top of the stone wall, well protected from hostile foes.

"Halt!" a stern voice rang out. "Who goes there?"

"The crew of *Ill Wind,*" the goblin leading the slaves replied. "Serving under Cap'n Arghant. We've got trading rights here."

"Let's see them." A sturdy door built into the middle of the garrison opened tentatively. A web of iron bars closed off all entry.

The goblin crewmen stepped forward and held out his hand. A gem glowing with cold blue fire nestled in the crewman's hand. "If'n I weren't who I said I was an' had what I said I had, this gem wouldn't glow."

"A blue," the garrison guard replied, obviously surprised. "Ye don't see many blues. Yer captain must be a favorite of the king's."

"Cap'n Arghant is a favorite at many ports," the crewman said.

"What are you a-carryin' on the ship? I see slaves, but is that all?"

"No. We got some cargo we're intendin' to sell at the marketplaces, too."

The garrison goblin grinned. "It's a good time to be a-bringin' trade goods into the harbor. It's been a few weeks between markets of late." He lifted a lantern, shoved it through the bars, and waved it.

Almost immediately, stone grated and a wide door

opened on the right. Hoists lifted a massive stone block out of the way to reveal the door.

A brief conversation took place overhead that Wick couldn't make out. He glanced up and saw that the next ledge's garrison already had someone waving another lantern to the garrison on the staggered ledge above it.

The goblinkin herded the slaves through the open door at the end of the garrison and up a set of winding stone steps cut into the wall. Wick's attention was drawn to the stone walls on either side of the steps. Pictographs of great battles and mighty warriors showed in flickering glimpses revealed by the twisting torchlight. Most of them showed goblins victorious over humans, elves, and dwarves. But here and there, always marred in some way by the crude etchings of goblins, were elegant reliefs showing elves, humans, and dwarves at work or in battle.

The goblins rewrote what was on these walls, Wick realized. *They attempted to erase the history of this place.* So rapt was his attention on the artwork that managed to stay out of his sight so well that he didn't notice the missing step in front of him. His foot went down, found only emptiness below where he thought a step should be, and he tripped, falling forward into the dwellers in front of him. They went down in a tumble.

"I'm sorry," Wick cried, pushing himself up weakly, hampered by his chains. "I wasn't watching where I was going. I apologize."

The dwellers groaned and tried to get up. Two goblins stepped among them, cursing and lashing out with their whips.

Wick covered his head and shoulders, hunkering down to protect himself. Yet his eyes remained drawn to the images on the stone walls. While the goblins beat him, he could see the images on the walls more clearly. That view lasted only a moment because the goblins quickly beat them into movement again.

Each new level required passing through the garrison there. The *Ill Wind* crew showed their gleaming blue gem to each garrison chief, then went through the huge stone doors that were winched up by the crews above.

"I'd heard that Hanged Elf's Point was a fortress," Harran said quietly to Wick, "but I hadn't expected this."

"Goblinkin didn't make this," Wick said. "Have you noticed the carvings on the walls underneath the goblin carvings?"

"Yes."

"This town belonged to someone else."

"Maybe, but in all the time I've heard of it, this town has always been called Hanged Elf's Point."

That can't be the original name, Wick thought. In his fatigue, he leaned against the outside wall of the curving stairway. The stone had been worn smooth over the years. *Has it always looked this way? Or did the coastline get reshaped when Lord Kharrion cast the spell that created the Shattered Coast?*

By nature, few elves were seafarers. Their homes remained in the wooded glens and along mighty rivers. But there had been a few that had lived next to the sea. The little librarian knew them all, and he felt certain he would know this place if he could but remember where he'd read about it.

Thankfully, the air was much cleaner now that they had left the slaver ship behind. Wick breathed deeply, grateful of at least that respite. His legs burned from the continued effort of climbing the steps, and his back ached from being hunched over. "Why is this place called Hanged Elf's Point?" he asked Harran. Somehow, his curiosity still insisted on outweighing his fear at what was going to happen to him next.

"Because of the hanged elf," Harran replied.

"What hanged elf?"

"That one." Harran pointed.

Following the line indicated by Harran's finger, Wick gazed forward as they topped the sixth and final garrison stairway. From his new vantage point, the little librarian could easily see the final ledge on which the main city sat. Amid the shadows of the buildings rising from the steep hills was what appeared to be a gossamer spider web stretched out over the top market ledge. The web stood forty feet tall and was nearly that wide, and the strands glinted blood-kissed silver from the rising sun to the east. At its center was a lean figure, and even from the distance Wick could see the hangman's noose around the dead man's neck.

12

Hanged Elf's Point

How did the hanged elf get, well, *hanged?*" Wick asked, his eyes never leaving the strange sight. He almost fell when a goblin roughly shoved him from behind.

"Keep movin'," the goblin warned. "Ain't too late too throw ye over the ledges and let ye make yer way back up again, halfer."

Wick trudged forward, taking short, quick steps that made his ankle chain rattle across the stone ground. The goblin passed him by, walking forward with his twisting torch to harangue others.

"I don't know," Harran admitted. "I heard Orpho Kadar brought it with him when he arrived forty years ago. Before that, this city was just ruins with only a few goblins living in it."

"The elf was already hanged then?" Wick asked.

"Yes."

The goblins guided them up more steps. The slave party moved much more slowly now. Wick went to the aid of an old man ahead of him.

"Thank you, kind sir," the old man whispered, his breath wheezing against the back of his throat. "If those goblinkin knew I couldn't climb these steps, they'd like as not just throw me into the harbor for the sharks to feed on."

The idea left Wick appalled.

The old man gazed into Wick's face and looked puzzled. "You're not from around here, are you?"

"No, sir. I'm from Orsin's Saucer."

The old man nodded and leaned more heavily on Wick. "I heard of it. They make fine bottles there." He wheezed again, and the little librarian nearly stumbled while guiding them both up to the next step. "I make razalistynberry wine myself."

Razalistynberry wine! Oh, to have a glassful now, and a nice cheese and cucumber sandwich seasoned with tartberry spread! Wick's tongue felt swollen in his mouth from dehydration. The snack would be made even better if Nayghal, who was a janitor at the Vault and his closest friend, was there to share a good book with. The little librarian quickly retreated from such thoughts because they were more painful and heartbreaking than he'd expected. "I love razalistynberry wine."

"Of course you do," the old man said. "No one could resist such a fine wine, and I have been told that my wines are the finest of all. I'm Wine Master Minniger." He glanced at Wick. "Goblinkin, of course, have no appreciation for fine things. They are pigs that will drink any swill set before them."

Wick nodded in agreement, but worried that the goblin passing them on the stairway at the time might overhear the old man's comment and decide to punish him. The old man didn't look like he could handle much physical abuse.

"You must not have gotten out of Orsin's Saucer much if you haven't realized how cruel goblinkin can be," the old man went on.

"I'd always been told stories," Wick admitted, "but

I'd never seen a goblin before until ten days ago." *At least, not a living goblin.*

"And you've not heard the story of the hanged elf either?" Minniger asked.

"No," Wick replied.

"Back home in Currelburg where I'm from," the old man said, "I've got a tavern that my wife and three granddaughters manage." He glanced at Wick. "You've heard of Currelburg?"

Wick nodded. "It's north of Lottar's Crossing." It was also one of the original seven mining towns that had gone dry.

"Have you ever been there?"

"No."

"A pity," the old man said. "It's really a pretty town, full of history when so many towns you see these days have nothing in them that hasn't been ripped out and replaced."

Wick glanced around at the first of the market areas on the three ledges just below Hanged Elf's Point proper. Tents strewn across the flat stone competed for space with more permanent structures made of stone and timber. Goblinkin and dwellers were already hard at work laying out goods. The aroma of fresh vegetables made the little librarian's mouth water. Bleating sheep, cackling chickens, quacking ducks, and grunting pigs filled pens and cages at different stalls.

The *Ill Wind* crew kept their charges from the small crowds that had already settled into the familiar banter of haggling and trading for goods. The morning sky was lighter now and the red sun painted scarlet hues across the stone ground. A crew of dwellers wearing slave collars labored at one of the six windlasses mounted atop the second marketing ledge. They cranked the huge wheel and lowered a platform cage containing four big hogs that pushed at the side nets.

"I was in the tavern one night when an old human entered," Minniger went on. "You could tell he'd been long on the trail, and not getting much sleep either. He was on the run, you know, and not certain how far away those who pursued him were."

At the bottom of the windlass trip, more dwellers wearing slave collars opened the nets and used switches to urge the hogs out. The huge brutes were in ill humor and stridently protested being chased from the cage. One of them turned suddenly and bit one of the dwellers attempting to herd it. The dweller went down, crying out in pain as blood streamed from his wounded arm. Several of the nearby goblinkin only jeered and laughed uproariously while the other dwellers barely managed to turn the hogs from their intended victim.

Life, Wick thought in saddened horror, *is so cheap here.* Then a turn leading up the next stone staircase took the savage scene from him.

"So, being curious as I am," Minniger said, "I started a conversation with the old man, aiding it with an occasional glass of wine on the house. I didn't really expect him to talk much, but he had a way about him, a loneliness that overcame his fear. And, as I've said, I make the best razalistynberry wine. Perhaps that loosened his tongue as well."

Wick helped the old man up the next flight of steps. The effort left him dizzy and weak.

"As we talked, he told me of the hanged elf," Minniger went on breathlessly. He kept his attention focused on the step in front of him, moving on to the next step only after the last one had been conquered.

"Did the man have a name?" Wick couldn't help trying to get all the details. His work at the Vault of All Known Knowledge hinged on a researcher's ability to collect every available fact.

"This man never gave it to me," Minniger answered.

"And I'm intelligent enough to know when not to ask, if you know what I'm talking about. Lottar's Crossing still has several that pass through it with trouble on their tails. This man was no different than them, except that I think he was a mage."

"What makes you think that?" Harran asked, staying close to them as they rounded the staircase. He came up on the other side of the old man and lent his strength to Wick's.

"Have you ever talked to a mage?"

Wick remained silent, not wanting to mention his own experiences because they definitely weren't those of a glassblower from Orsin's Saucer.

"No," Harran answered.

"They've got ways about them that let you know. A certain way of thinking. And most of them never quite look at you. I mean, not as if you really mattered anyway."

"You're sure this man was a mage?" Wick asked.

"Without him actually casting a spell on me, yes, I was." Minniger struggled up the next step and took a long gasp. Thankfully, the caravan of slaves had reached another checkpoint. "And then there was the matter of the men who came a few days afterward."

"You knew them?" Wick asked. He glanced ahead, watching as Arghant talked with a group of garrison guards.

The goblin captain at this garrison caught the little librarian's eye. Where most of his companions were brutish and slovenly, this goblin appeared sleek and smooth. He wore a jeweled sword belted at his waist. Runes tattooed both his upper arms. As Arghant talked with him, the garrison captain moved along the line of dwellers, inspecting them.

"I didn't know the men who followed the other human," Minniger said. "But I knew what they were. They were Purple Cloaks, agents who do vicious and foul deeds for Fomhyn Mhout."

"I don't know who that is," Wick admitted.

With the sun edged up over the mountain and hanging on the eastern horizon, the livestock in the market areas below started to come more fully awake and protested their treatment with loud mooing, bleating, cackling, and grunting. Over all of that was the growing level of voices locked in verbal confrontations.

"Fomhyn Mhout," Harran said, "is the most powerful wizard of the Shattered Coast. He's been here more than sixty years." Suspicion showed on his face as he regarded Wick.

"Oh," the little librarian said. "I thought perhaps you were referring to some other Fomhyn Mhout. One I *didn't* know." *Please don't ask any more! I—and you— have more problems now than we need to be worried about why I don't know all of these things!*

"The Purple Cloaks are Fomhyn Mhout's emissaries," Harran continued.

"Exactly," Minniger said. "Most folk around the Shattered Coast are in disagreement of what Fomhyn Mhout's real reason for being among us is."

Wick dropped his eyes before the garrison captain reached him, praying that he didn't attract any attention from the goblin. Whatever the garrison commander was looking for, the little librarian was certain that he didn't want to be involved with it.

"Some say the old wizard lives on the Shattered Coast and searches for magic weapons lost here during the Cataclysm," Minniger said. "Provided, of course, that the Cataclysm ever happened."

Wick stilled his quick tongue before he could say anything. Lord Kharrion and the Cataclysm weren't stories to be told to frighten children. A cold wind gusted in from the ocean and prickled his skin. He glanced back at the harbor and saw more than a dozen sails coming over the distant southern horizon. Evidently a number of traders came to Hanged Elf's Point.

"But I do know that Fomhyn Mhout was interested in the old man that visited my tavern that day," Minniger went on. "They asked me about him, and described him very well."

"What did you do?" Wick asked.

The old man pressed a hand to his chest. "Me? What could I do? I told them that he had been in my shop only three days before, and I told them in what direction he'd traveled when he left."

"And what did they do?" Harran asked.

Minniger touched a small pink scar at his neck. "One of them put a blade to my throat and told me that if I'd lied to them in any way that they would return to kill me and my family. I believed him. They left following the trail I'd put them on. I don't know if they ever found the old mage."

The garrison captain finished his inspection of the assembled dwellers in slave collars.

"He's looking for any signs of disease," Harran said. "Diseased slaves aren't allowed into the city, I've been told. It cuts down on profits and the labor forces in the mines when diseases run rampant. Orpho Kadar, so I'm told, puts to death any slaver captains found guilty of selling spoiled goods."

Spoiled goods? Wick couldn't believe he'd just heard that. He gazed around at the men and women in the group from *Ill Wind,* then at all the slaves busy working the market areas. The whole idea was insane. Yet he couldn't deny that he existed because he was trapped in the middle of it.

A moment later, the goblinkin from the slaver ship got the group moving again. Below, Wick could already see another ship off-loading more dwellers in chains. He turned his attention away from the new arrivals, hoping he wouldn't remember the emaciated and cowering bodies, but knowing he would all the same. The tales of adventure he'd read from Hralbomm's Wing had never spoken of the true weight of the manacles that a slave carried. He clenched his fists in frustration. *Even had we died fighting. Arghant and the crew of* Ill Wind, he thought angrily, *at least not all of the goblinkin would have survived to keep enslaving others. I would have given my life for that.* And the certainty with which he thought that surprised him.

Oh, how you've changed, Third Level Librarian Edgewick Lamplighter, the little dweller thought. *But how could you not change after every misfortune you've been through?*

"I was told of a ship that came into Hanged Elf's Point a few years ago," Harran said as they filed through the narrow corridor leading into the city proper. "Orpho Kadar's people found sickness in the dweller slaves. Before they'd put foot inside the city, the garrison guards lowered their shields and drove them over the ledges to fall into the waters below."

Wick closed his eyes, images filling his mind of the senseless slaughter. Those poor people hadn't asked to be brought to the goblinkin city, and he was certain the sickness they'd carried hadn't been their fault either. Even those that lived to be slaves didn't have easy or safe lives.

"All the goblins aboard the ship were executed as well," Harran continued. "Orpho Kadar also ordered their ship burned, and it was. All of that served as an example for the other slavers. Another sick cargo of slaves has never reached the harbor."

Wick pushed his breath out, trying to concentrate. He glanced up at the body of the hanged elf in the gossamer web hanging over the harbor. Now that he was closer, he saw that the elf's body was wrapped in cloths, looking very much like a sinister tatterdemalion. The hanged elf held its arms out wide in supplication, but the face was masked.

"Was this one of Orpho Kadar's examples then, too?" the little librarian asked bitterly.

"No," Minniger answered. "According to the old mage I talked with, the hanged elf there is magical in nature."

"How so?" Wick asked.

"With it hanging there over the city," the old winemaker said, "I'm told that mages can't enter Hanged Elf's Point."

Wick studied the figure hanging in the gossamer web, wondering who he or she had been in life and if he or she had a family that still thought of him or her. That line of thinking all too quickly steered him into thinking about his own family. They still didn't know what had become of him after he'd disappeared from Greydawn Moors. The little librarian wondered if Grandmagister Frollo had kept his position open for long before he'd filled it. And Wick had no illusions about whether the grandmagister would fill a Third Level Librarian position. It was too important to be left vacant for long, and all too easily filled.

"Is that only a legend?" Wick asked. "Or do you suppose there's some truth in it?"

"All I know," Minniger said, "is that Fomhyn Mhout and his dread Purple Cloaks have never set foot in Hanged Elf's Point."

"Silence!" a goblin roared, coming back down the line of weak and staggering dwellers. "Be ye respectful during city hours or I'll have the tongues cut from yer heads! No halfer noise is allowed!" He whipped the slaves viciously.

Wick got his hands up just in time to keep his face

from being lashed, but the whip raised red welts on his arms.

Without a word, the dwellers moved through the heart of Hanged Elf's Point.

In wonderment and disbelief, Wick stared out over the city as they passed through. In decades, perhaps even centuries past, the city had been ornate and elegant. Tall buildings had stood five and six stories tall when the city had first been built. Most of them lay in sprawled ruins now.

Many of the streets had been cleared of rubble, but many of them still lay choked in broken rock and mortar and timbers. With the way the land rolled over the steep hills the city had been built on, some of the rubble piles spilled for a hundred yards and more.

Goblinkin had moved in and made the buildings and large houses their own. Other houses had dweller crews hard at work clearing debris and rebuilding broken walls and caved-in roofs.

The sheer number of goblins living within the city surprised Wick. Not since Lord Kharrion had the goblinkin lived together in such great numbers.

Their course took them by a row of blacksmith's forges. Inside the shops, sweat- and soot-covered goblinkin labored over anvils, hammering out swords and knives, spear points and arrowheads.

They make weapons? Wick saw a thick-bodied goblin blacksmith in a leather frock lift a red-hot sword blade in a pair of tongs, then thrust it into a vat of water. White steam rolled back off the sword blade. According to Marclan's *Treatise on Goblinkin and Their Lost Arts of War,* the goblins had largely lost the skills necessary to make weapons of steel. Until Lord Kharrion, though, the goblinkin had never known the secrets of forging hard metals.

Maybe some of them retained the knowledge from those days, Wick thought. But for so many of them to be here now meant that Orpho Kadar had purposefully sought them out and brought them to Hanged Elf's Point. That likelihood left Wick frightened. The goblin pirate king was raising an army and a navy perhaps only a month's sailing distance from Greydawn Moors.

The little librarian wanted to believe that was only ill luck, but he realized he couldn't afford to hope that was true. Arghant had told Captain Farok that the goblinkin were intentionally sailing more deeply into the Blood-Soaked Sea. *Do they know the Vault of All Known Knowledge lies in that direction?* Wick worried. The possibility started his stomach churning, reminding him that he hadn't even gotten his half ration of pasty gruel that morning.

He turned away from the clangor of the goblinkin forges. The hiss of heated metal in water behind him sounded like gigantic snakes.

By the time they reached the stockades, Wick and Harran were practically carrying Minniger, and they weren't doing very well at it. Both of them staggered even under the old man's slight weight.

High stone walls ringed the stockades, which were, for all intents and purposes, holding pens. Goblin guards patrolled the walls, all of them armed with swords and crossbows. Broken glass and pieces of sharp-edged metal embedded in the walls offered proof against any would-be climbers.

On two of the walls, narrow slats had been cut that offered viewing inside the pens. Wick quickly realized that the slats offered hand- and footholds, but the ex-

panse of wall above the slatted area was still too much
to climb up even if the guards hadn't been on patrol.

When they reached the double doors in the front of
the stockades, the goblin crewman who'd overseen thcir
transportation to the area halted them. He pulled his
sword from his hip. "Down on yer knees with ye, then,
and quicklike. I got me a powerful thirst on an' ain't the
likes of ye a-gonna kept betwixt me an a schooner or
two of ale real soon."

Some of the dwellers in the front row hesitated. Goblin crewmen quickly stepped in and beat them down with
cudgels, leaving bloody heads and faces in their wake.
Keening and moaning echoed around Wick as he
dropped to his knees. Grit covering the hard stone bed-
rock of the area ground into his flesh. During the harsh
journey on *Ill Wind,* the rot and mold that infested the
lower cargo hold of the slave ship had infested his clothing. It hung in tatters about him, offering scant protection and only a modicum of modesty.

"If ye want to go into this bloody," the crewman
roared, "because ye ain't a-willin' to listen to reason,
that's fine." He grinned cruelly. "Them what buys ye
ain't a-lookin' for sightly slaves. I puts a few knots on
yer head for ye before I leaves ye here, why they'll just
think ye've had a little sense beat into ye."

Wick felt his blouse for the journal, shifting it so that
it was less likely to show in case they had to submit to
some kind of inspection. *I should have thrown it into
the harbor when we were being brought ashore.* The
little librarian felt certain that if the book somehow made
its way into Orpho Kadar's hands that the goblinkin pirate king would understand what it was soon enough.

And if it is found with me, Wick suddenly realized, *it
will mark me. They would torture me to find out everything I know about Greydawn Moors and the Vault of
All Known Knowledge.* He felt beaten and helpless. His

family, the Vault, the city where he'd been born and
loved all his life, all of it lay vulnerable now because of
his selfishness. The book he had once been so proud of
was an object to despise and fear—ashes to the taste.
He was so smart he'd outsmarted himself.

A group of goblinkin marched from the front of the
stockades. They quickly set up tables on either side of
the entrance. Peering at them, Wick saw they had pliers
with powerful jaws. Each table had a crate of glistening
metal bits.

"Ye're gonna be marked before ye're turned loose inside the holding pens," the crewman said. "Ye'll get an
earring that carries the seal of *Ill Wind* cargo, showing
who owns ye before ye're put up on the slave block.
That's ye. If'n ye resist, I'm a-gonna beat ye bloody an'
senseless. Mayhap I'll even kill a couple or three of ye
to show ye I mean business. Have it yer own way, 'cause
I'll be a-havin' mine after that."

The slaves were quickly divided into two lines, and
the rest of the group was herded into one or the other.
Wick tried not to listen to the cries of pain that came
from the front of the line. He waited his turn, knowing
anything he could try to do would be futile. Crossbow-
men waited eagerly at the top of the wall, and everyone
there knew what would happen if they tried to run.

When it was Wick's turn, one of the goblinkin
grabbed him by the chain between his wrist manacles,
pulled him forward, and tripped him. The little librarian
couldn't help struggling when the man fell on top of him
as he had every other person that had been marked. The
goblin smelled sour and foul, and he giggled as he
punched Wick in the back of the head.

Sharp metal bit into Wick's left ear. He tried to struggle, but the goblin holding him down wrapped an arm
over his head and jammed his face into the ground with
bruising force. The little librarian's senses spun for a

moment and he almost hoped he would pass out. Then he heard the pliers ratchet as they closed, curling the metal marker thought the top of his ear. He cried out in pain, unable to stop himself. Warm blood flowed into his ear canal, making him temporarily deaf.

Before he could recover, two goblins swiftly yanked him to his feet. He stood woozily between them, trying to comprehend everything that was happening to him. Blood dripped from his split lip as well, and he tasted the coppery flavor against his teeth.

Another goblin sloshed liquid over Wick, drenching the whole side of his head. His ear burned terribly, and the acrid scent was definitely alcohol, perhaps some cheaply made homegrown vintage the goblins made.

"Keep that ear clean, halfer," the goblin warned, sounding strange since Wick could only hear him with one ear and that one was on the other side of his head. "If'n ye let it get infected and go rotten, I'll take the ear offa yer head and mark ye through the other one."

Wick looked at the goblin, working to comprehend everything he was being told.

"Ye run outta ears," the goblin warned, "then we start putting markers in the side of yer face." He grabbed Wick's shirt and yanked him toward the entrance to the stockades. "Keep movin' or they're gonna bury ye where ye stand."

Barely able to keep upright, Wick staggered to the next goblin. He was forced to his knees again. Senses swimming, feeling as though he were in some kind of nightmare that he couldn't wake from, he saw motion from the corner of his eye. He turned just in time to watch a hammer swish down. He closed his eyes, not wanting to see it hit him. Instead, the hammer struck the collar around his neck. The steel collar drove hard against his flesh, promising deep bruising. Then it burst open, freed from the pin that held it together. Two more swift strokes freed him from the wrist manacles as well, but they left him in the ankle manacles.

He was yanked to his feet once more, then thrown through a door he barely had time to see. He smashed against the crudely made iron bars, curling his hands around them just in time to keep from falling.

"Come on, Wick," Harran whispered. "You can do this. Don't let them see you weak."

Wick remained against the bars. "They know I'm weak, and if I move, they'll know that I'm only trying to fool them."

"Then do it for yourself," Harran said. "Do it for those dwellers who are going to have to walk around you when they're barely making it themselves."

Feeling ashamed, Wick pushed himself from the bars. He stood, swaying, and glanced at Harran.

Harran looked horrible. Blood dripped from his mangled ear and stained his shoulder. Dark shadows hung under his eyes. "Let's go."

Wordlessly, Wick nodded and followed the other man. The entrance turned out to be a long corridor that followed the inside walls of the stockades, curling three-fourths of the way around the holding pens. By his count, there were twenty lots inside the stockade, and each of them had its own entrance from the corridor. Goblin guards walked across the close-set bars overhead and opened the succession of gates by unlocking them and pulling them up, allowing entrance into lot eighteen.

Sullen and dispirited faces of dwellers peered at them from the other pens they passed. All of them were bedraggled and filthy.

Lot eighteen was an open barren space with worn stone as a floor. Nasty pallets lay scattered over the ground. Waste buckets sat in all four corners. The dwellers that had been processed early already started lining the walls, sitting or lying where they fell. And over it

all was the same stench that had filled the cargo hold
and given *Ill Wind* her name.

People have died here, Wick suddenly thought as he
entered the holding pen. He went numb inside, chilled
to the bone though he could now feel the sun's embrace
streaming from above. Angry throbbing filled the whole
side of his head, threatening to make him sick. *If I had
known this was what was going to happen to me when
I surrendered myself from* One-Eyed Peggie, *could I
have done it?* He seriously doubted it at the moment,
and that made him feel sad. *A hero would,* he told himself. *Was that what you were thinking you were when
you volunteered to go with the goblinkin?*

Hurting, Wick eased himself down beside a section
of the wall with the slats that peered outside over Hanged Elf's Point. The breeze helped wash away some of
the stench, carrying the sharp tang of the ocean. Then
the breeze shifted, drawing the stench from the inside
of the stockades, burying the little librarian in miasma.

Minniger staggered into the pen and crumpled only a
few feet from the entrance.

Wick looked at the old man, unable to see if he was
breathing, not knowing if Minniger was alive or dead.
He tried to push himself up, thinking that he should go
check, but he couldn't get up.

He thought of his father then, of how Metterin Lamplighter had picked him up after he'd fallen. He didn't
know how many times his father had come to him in the
dead hours of the night to comfort him when he had a
bad dream induced by the stories he'd read while studying at the Conservatoire of Literature. His father had
shown him how to tend to the glimmerworms, how to
milk them for the lummin juice. And when Wick's interest in lanterns had dawned, his father had trained him
then.

Now, when an ocean separated them and he was

bound in a slave pen, the little librarian suddenly realized how much his father had really been there to help him become everything that he had. *And the best that I have ever been able to do*, Wick thought, *was become a Third Level Librarian. The worst thing I ever did was accept that and tell myself it was enough.*

What would he do different if he had the chance, he asked himself. *Everything.* He'd been selfish in some ways, and he'd been arrogant thinking that he might contribute in any way to the Vault's real work. That was why Grandmagister Ludaan had never moved him up, and why Grandmagister Frollo found so much fault with him.

Memory of the Embyr and how he had hurt her by revealing the murder of her parents and brothers and her own enchantment by Lord Kharrion's foulness stirred Wick's mind. He grieved for her and remembered the child's beautiful face etched with the pain he'd caused.

There were so many, many things he'd done wrong.

Desperately, he tried to think back to the last happy moment he'd spent with someone.

Other slaves kept filing into the pen, filling up the space around them, but he fell into a deep slumber long before the last of them made it through.

Night lay over Hanged Elf's Point. Jhurjan the Swift and Bold raced in his scarlet glory across the dark, starry heavens while Gesa the Fair hid her lovely smile.

Wick stood at the slats and peered out at the city from within the holding pen. Despite the lateness of the hour, the city remained awake and alert. Goblins and humans walked the streets or rode horses beneath huge braziers that served as street lamps.

Wick's father had told him about such braziers that had burned in Greydawn Moors during the earliest days of the Building Time. They were the size of bushel baskets and held firewood that had been presoaked in oil. At the time, the glimmerworm production was small due to the few worms the first dwellers had brought with them. It was years before lanterns had been built and the glimmerworms were in satisfactory numbers to fill them.

A cart drawn by two donkeys made its way slowly down the side of the street. A goblin drove the cart and three dwellers in the back pitched firewood from the back of the vehicle into the braziers. Bright orange sparks climbed into the air from each brazier they fed.

Wick looked up involuntarily, drawn by the footsteps of a guard on the wall overhead. Braziers marked the stockades as well, stripping away most of the shadows in the pens. Still, nearly all of the people in Wick's pen were asleep, curled up and sleeping against each other for mutual warmth as the cold night air blew over them. Neither bedding nor new clothes had been offered, and Wick knew that provisioning those would have come from someone's profits.

He wished he could sleep. He knew he was tired enough, but his mind—as it so often did—wouldn't cooperate. He'd woken, roused by thoughts running through his head that he couldn't turn off. At first, he'd hoped everything he'd been through these past several days was just a dream, but one glance at the stone walls around him shattered that hope immediately.

"Can't sleep?" Harran asked.

"No," Wick replied quietly, not wanting to disturb those around them who'd found that healing balm.

"It would be better if you could."

"I know. I've tried." Once he'd woken, Wick's thoughts had turned immediately to the threat Hanging Elf's Point presented to everything he held dear. How long would it be before a goblin ship inadvertently discovered the island that had been so long lost in the fogs of the Blood-Soaked Sea, guarded by monsters and the dwarven pirates? He didn't know, and that uncertainty worried at him constantly. "I can't believe I'm seeing humans walking down the street with goblinkin."

"They do here," Harran commented.

"Before the Cataclysm, the goblins stood alone from all the other races."

"That was a long time ago," Harran said, "if those stories are even true."

"They're true."

Harran leaned back against the wall and stared up at Wick. He looked like he might have wanted to say something further but he kept his own counsel. "Things are different here, Wick. Different than I guess they must be from wherever you're from—Orsin's Saucer."

"Yes," Wick said, regretting that the lie was between them. Harran seemed intelligent enough, too intelligent to believe what he was being told.

"Here in Hanged Elf's Point, I've been told," Harran said, "anything goes. There are human, dwarven, and elven villages on the outskirts of this city as well as those of the goblinkin, and all of them want the free labor provided by owning dweller slaves."

The thought horrified Wick. "Humans, dwarves, and elves around here keep dwellers as slaves?"

"Yes. Even the people in Lottar's Crossing know that."

"I didn't," Wick said contritely. He examined the thought, finding it appalling. "The humans, dwarves, elves, and dwellers united to eradicate Lord Kharrion during the Cataclysm. How could they condone enslavement of our people?"

"Along the Shattered Coast," Harran said, "most people believe the dwellers are no more than pests that need to be controlled. Enslaving them is one way to accomplish that."

"So the humans, elves, and dwarves in town at the moment are here to buy dweller slaves?"

"Yes. Hanged Elf's Point is still restricted to goblinkin settlement. Orpho Kadar is very rigid about that. However, he'll take gold from whomever has it."

Raucous laughter came up the street outside the holding pen. Humans and goblins and dwarves stumbled out onto the street, hollering and shouting at each other. The elves that came from the tavern tended to stay among themselves.

"That's not what the Old Ones made the dwellers to do," Wick protested.

"You're referring to the legend of Daghuan the Survivor," Harran said.

Wick nodded, repeating the legend his father had first told him that had become one of the founding edicts in the Vault of All Known Knowledge. "The Old Ones created the dweller races to live in the small places of the world. In their wisdom, they had known that the dwellers would be necessary to prevent the loss of knowledge during the Cataclysm and the battles against Lord Kharrion. And in dwellers, the Old Ones knew they had a race who could survive any hardship and yet remain humble enough not to reach for the power they were given custody of."

"They can't survive any hardship," Harran stated softly. "They die in the mines around here and elsewhere easily enough." There was a trace of bitterness in his voice.

"It's because of the goblinkin," Wick said.

Harran shook his head. "It's not just the goblinkin who enslave us these days, Wick. There are humans and dwarves and elves that have fallen into selfish ways. They conquer each other occasionally, but they conquer us all the time."

Unable to continue making eye contact with Harran,

Wick looked away. He knew the man was telling the truth as he knew it, but that couldn't be true, could it? Human, dwarf, elf, and dweller had always stood against the goblinkin. That was one of the things that Lord Kharrion had underestimated. He glanced back out at the street, watching people who should be enemies strolling casually by each other.

These people have forgotten more than the evil of Lord Kharrion, the little librarian thought. *They've forgotten how close this world came to extinction even though they're living in one of the greatest graveyards left by the Cataclysm.*

He sat, wide awake for a long time, talking to Harran though his throat was parched. Their conversation drifted, not holding much to any one subject. After a bit Harran drifted off to sleep. And when the man did, Wick took his journal from under his shirt and used the bit of charcoal he had left to write. He sat in the shadows of the wall, the moonlight barely enough to let him see the words on the page as he wrote them. Mindful of the guards patrolling the stockades, he made sure he stayed out of sight as they passed.

Thought of destroying the journal was gone now. It was an important record. He wrote down everything he'd learned since arriving in Hanged Elf's Point about Orpho Kadar, the goblin ships, and the massing army. Grand-magister Frollo and others needed to know the news.

When he finished, he closed the journal. Tomorrow, if possible, he needed to find more charcoal to continue his work. Even if he never made it out of the goblin city, he had to find a way to get his journal out.

A whispered voice leaked through the slatted wall. It sound cold and cultured, the voice of someone used to speaking, and used to command as well. "What are you doing?"

13

The Man in Black

Surprised, Wick started to back away from the wall. Through the slats, he saw a midsized human dressed all in black standing in the shadows beside the wall. "N-n-nothing," the little librarian stammered. His heart felt like it was going to hammer a hole through his chest.

"You were," the man in black accused. Gloved fingers slid through the slats. In the opening of his hooded cloak, his face was narrow, patrician. Dark bangs hung over close-set black eyes on either side of a narrow, pinched nose. A thin, neatly trimmed beard and mustache colored his upper lip and traced his chin. "You were drawing. I saw you."

Wick said nothing, but took another step backward.

Goblin footsteps rang on the iron bars overhead.

"Stop, you fool!" the man in black hissed.

Spurred by the commanding tone in the man's voice, Wick froze.

"Keep moving like that," the man in black said, "and you're going to draw the attention of those ugly brutes patrolling the wall."

Unconsciously, the little librarian struggled to place the man's accent. Although learning accents was part of

any Librarian's acumen, Wick couldn't place the tall hu
man's at all.

The man smiled, showing very white teeth. "I'm sur
neither of us would want that."

"No," Wick agreed nervously.

"The goblins don't know you have your drawing pad
do they?" the man in black asked.

Wick didn't answer, but he held the journal tightly.

"Of course they don't." The man in black looked
pleased. "You have a secret, don't you?"

Wick remained silent. He watched a firewood wago
rumbling across the street behind the man. A flaming
torch mounted by the wagon's seat chased away som
of the shadows in the street.

The man in black moved quickly with smooth grace
somehow appearing even more fluid than a khelcat
Though the eroding shadows were chased past the slat
ted wall as the firewood wagon clattered past them, the
man in black appeared to melt into the darkness and wa
never revealed. When it had gone, the man in black
curled his gloved fingers back through the slats.

"I love secrets," the strange man said, eyes glittering
with black fire. "Especially those of other people." He
glanced at the book in Wick's hand. "Do you want t
tell me yours?"

"I have no secrets," Wick answered.

The man in black smiled again. "I like lies, too, my
small friend. They're like secrets that come in puzzl
boxes. Listen to someone lie carefully and often, and
you will learn to strip their secrets from them no matter
how hard they try to keep them."

Wick felt terrified. "Where did you come from?"

The man waved a black-gloved hand. "From the city
I was helping myself to someone else's secrets only mo
ments ago." He shrugged and grimaced a little, as if he'd

bitten into a sour apple. "And a little of their gold. Too little, actually, for my efforts."

They were both silent as one of the goblins crossed the wall above them.

Wick glanced around quickly, wondering if anyone else was awake.

"Do any of them know your secret?" the man in black asked.

"Yes," Wick answered.

The man in black raised his eyebrows, obviously pleased. "You lied!"

"No," Wick assured him. "I didn't. I—"

"Yes you did," the man crowed in delight. He clapped his black-gloved hands almost silently. Only the rough rasp of leather reached Wick's ears. "You lied, and now I know two things." He ticked them off on his hands. "One, you do have a secret, because—after all—you just told me that some of your companions know your secret. And two, I know how you look, how you sound, and how you stand when you lie."

Wick thought quickly, realizing he had made a mistake. He'd thought to take away the possibility of a secret by saying there was no secret. He was so tired from being held in the goblin ship for all those days, plus the long climb up to Hanged Elf's Point that he could scarcely think.

"Do you want to tell me now?" the man in black asked.

"Who are you?" Wick asked.

"That, my little friend, is one of my secrets. Perhaps you'd care to trade. A secret for a secret."

"You would lie to me."

The man in black grinned and shook his head. "Of course I would. That's one of the best ways to keep a secret. Now do you see why I so enjoy learning the secrets of others? It's one of the grandest games. Everyone knows how to play. It's just that some of us are better at it than others."

Another goblin guard passed overhead again. Wick remained silent, watching the black-garbed man draw again into the shadows.

"Are you an artist?" the man asked.

"Yes," Wick answered instantly.

"Hmmm." The man in black tapped his gloved fingers against his bearded chin. "That's, perhaps at best, a half-truth. So you draw, but you're not an artist. And tired as you are, you feel it important to both do the work you were engaged in—out of the sight of the others in this pen as well as the guards—and yet hide it as well."

Wick remained silent, wondering if the man in black was some kind of test that the goblinkin engineered. But he instantly dismissed that idea. The goblinkin were not that crafty even on their best days. "Why would you want to know the secrets of a slave?"

"How is it that a slave comes to have a secret that his jailers don't know about?" the man in black countered. Then he shrugged again and sighed in expansive contempt. "Of course, we are talking about these infernal goblinkin who don't have the sense the Old Ones gave geese when it comes to slyness." He focused on the little librarian again. "Whom do you show your drawings to?"

"No one."

"Then you draw them for yourself?"

Wick said nothing, wishing for nothing more than the man in black to disappear with the same speed he'd appeared.

"An artist who admires his own drawings," the man in black mused. He appeared to think that over for a moment, then shook his head. "No, I don't think that's true either. You would be a desperate fellow. Possibly even desirous of having someone else look at your art. But no, you choose to remain mysterious." He suddenly pressed his face against the slats, cocking his head to one side and fixing the little librarian with his left eye. "Are you a spy, little dweller?"

"A spy for who?" Wick asked.

"Exactly," the man in black agreed. "For *whom* indeed. Orpho Kadar has his enemies and jealous constituents. Uneasy lies the crown, they always say of kings. Has someone inserted you into the slave quarters to find out more about Hanged Elf's Point?"

"Would a spy subject himself to this?" Wick demanded, stepping closer to the slatted wall. He felt more at risk standing out from under the shielding embrace of the walkway overhead than he did closer to the man in black. "That's stupid."

"Stupid, you say?" The man in black smiled. "Have you ever considered the span between stupidity and genius?" He held out his black-gloved hand, forefinger and middle finger held tightly together. "They are as close as the seam between those two fingers, my friend. The only deciding factor is that one doesn't work and is called—unfairly, I sometimes think—stupidity. And if the other works, though it is just as foolhardy on the surface, why it's called brilliance."

"I want you to go away," Wick said.

"Whatever for?" the man in black asked. "Why, we're only now getting to know each other."

"I don't even know your name."

"Nor do I know yours. But you're interested in knowing my name, aren't you?"

Wick started to say no, wanted to say no, but he was afraid that the man in black would catch him in another lie. Then his hesitation dragged on too long to make any kind of response at all.

The man in black flashed his white teeth again. "See? Already we have a common bond. You would like to know my name as badly as I would like to know yours."

He hesitated. "At least, I think I would like to know your name. Perhaps the only thing of interest about you is what you consider important enough to draw in your sketchbook."

Wick made himself stand taller, no longer wanting to be afraid of the man in black. "I could call out to the guards and tell them you are here."

"Maybe I'm supposed to be here," the man said. "Have you considered that?"

"Yes," Wick answered. "But my secret gives away yours."

"Does it? And how does that happen?"

Wick leaned closer, looking up at the tall man, hoping that no fear showed in his eyes or in his posture. "If you were supposed to be here, you would order the goblinkin to hold me down and take my . . . my *sketchbook* from me."

"Where would the fun be in that, though?" the man in black asked. "Secrets are much more enjoyable when they're stolen from someone rather than beaten out of them. By the time you beat a secret out of someone, they don't care if you have it or not."

Without warning, the man in black lunged forward, throwing himself against the slatted wall. His gloved hand darted in, grabbing for Wick's journal.

Dodging back, the little librarian slapped the man in black's gloved hand away. His heart thundered in his chest and hammered at the side of his head where his ear had become infected from the marker.

A savage mixture of joy and rage twisted the man in black's bearded face. "You're very quick, my friend. Very few people are even as quick." He took his arm back through the slats. "Of course, I am working at something of a disadvantage."

"I'm going to call for the guard," Wick warned.

Unbothered, the man in black pulled himself to the

wall again, a dark silhouette standing in the darkness. "Why do you not call out now? Is it because you fear that I am so quick the guards will not see me and so beat you for disturbing them?" He cocked his head to one side. "Or is it *me* and concern for my well-being that keeps you from calling out to them?"

Wick said nothing. Time was on his side now. If the man in black continued to stay around, the chances were good that the goblinkin would discover him.

"Oh, you do fascinate me, little artist," the man in black said. "You are a puzzle I'm going to enjoy investigating." He glanced over his shoulder. "However, at the moment I'm afraid I do have a rather pressing engagement elsewhere." He turned back and smiled at Wick. "We'll continue this stimulating little chat at another time."

Wick watched in wonderment. The man in black never seemed to move, just evaporate like smoke, as if he'd never been there. Though the little librarian moved to the wall and peered through the slats, he never saw the man in black cross either of the streets.

Worn and worried, Wick sat on the ground and remained watchful. Somehow, the measured tread of the goblinkin patrolling overhead seemed reassuring now. Though he tried to remain awake, sleep claimed him, pulling him down deeply.

Rattling iron bars woke Wick early the next morning. He'd slept against the slatted wall, curled up into a ball as tightly as he could for warmth. His limbs moved stiffly and ached as he sat up. There was no sign of his mysterious late-night visitor and his journal was still hidden within his shirt.

Overhead, goblin guardsmen marched out onto the corridor that allowed egress into the slave pens. Their long, prehensile toes wrapped around the iron bars and held them with surefooted ease as they carried a steaming cauldron to the edge. Without preamble, they used ropes to lower the cauldron.

Wick sniffed, testing the air, and discovered that the cauldron contained more of the gruel they'd been fed aboard *Ill Wind*. However from the scent he felt certain there were pieces of apples mixed in with the gruel.

No bowls or silverware were provided, so the dwellers had no choice but to dig into the thick gruel with their bare hands. Another cauldron, this one containing tepid water and a single dipper, was lowered into the pen next.

Wick woke Harran, who'd slept through the arrival of breakfast. Then the little librarian's eyes located Minniger lying on the ground in the same place he'd gone to sleep yesterday morning. Trepidation filled Wick as he stared at the old man.

Slowly, the little librarian forced himself to his feet. His head throbbed from the effort and he could feel heat all over the side of his face where they'd put the marker through his ear. He ignored it as he hobbled over to Minniger's side. Respectfully, the little librarian knelt, barely able to restrain a scream as his knees threatened to come apart after all the stair-climbing the previous day. He touched the old man's shoulder and shook him gently.

"Minniger," he called. Then he noticed how stiff the old man's arm was. *No!* Gently, he pulled Minniger over so that the man lay on his back.

The old man stared sightlessly up at the clear blue morning sky.

The scream ripped through Wick's mind as he realized what had happened. Tears blurred his vision as sadness for the old man and hopelessness at his own plight filled him.

"Wick?" Harran called, stumbling over. "What is it? What's wrong?"

"Minniger," Wick whispered. "He's dead."

Harran knelt beside the little librarian and stared at the old man's body. "He went in his sleep, Wick. It was a gentle death, one almost anyone here would have hoped for."

"I know," Wick replied. "But he wasn't wishing for death. He only wanted to go back to his family, to serve the best razalistynberry wine anyone could ever hope to make."

The dwellers nearby pulled back from the dead man fearfully. That hurt Wick, too. In Greydawn Moors, death wasn't something to be afraid of. True, no one wanted to die, but the old and infirm were allowed to die peaceably in their own beds surrounded by people who loved them. Those sitting up with him or her would talk to the dying person, and keep talking even after that person could no longer talk.

Wick reached out for Minniger's hand, remembering how he and his father had held his grandfather's hand as the strength had drained from him. The little librarian clasped the winemaker's cold, callused hand and blinked away his tears. He wondered what it would have been like to sit across a table from Minniger and talk of stories and people the old man had met in his years. So much had been lost, Wick felt certain even from the short time he had known Minniger. "I wish I had known," he whispered. "If I had, I swear to you that you would not have died alone on cold, hard ground surrounded by enemies."

"Wick," Harran called softly.

Wick shook his head, memorizing the old man's face. Tonight, when no one was awake, he would draw Minniger's likeness into his journal. *I will not allow you to be forgotten,* he silently promised the old man. *If I live*

through this somehow, I swear to you that I will find out
about you and remind the world that you lived and that
you were important.

The promise felt cold and hollow, but it was all the
little librarian had to give. The cool wind sweeping up
the mountains from the harbor below burned his wet
cheeks with an icy touch.

"Wick," Harran said again. "There's nothing you can
do for him."

Wick nodded, unable to speak because of the swelling
caught in his throat. He looked up from Minniger's body
and at the faces of the other slaves. Most of them only
spared furtive glances or cowered in their own arms.

Harran pulled at his arm. "Come away. You're doing
no good here."

Wick glanced at Harran. "Don't you understand?" His
voice broke and he thought he sounded like a frog croak-
ing.

"The old man has passed on. What else is there to
understand?"

"This," Wick said, "this is all we have to look forward
to as long as we stay here."

Harran stared at him in silence.

Guilt almost held Wick's tongue, but his anger and
fear made him speak anyway. "We can't stay here."

Harran's mouth worked, as if he was trying to think
of something to say.

A shadow fell over them from above, and a raucous
voice demanded, "What are ye halfers a-doin' down
there?"

Legs trembling, Wick forced himself to his feet. He
wiped at his face, not ashamed of his tears, but knowing
that the goblinkin guards would only see that as weakness in him. "This old man has passed on."

The goblin wrapped his prehensile toes around the

iron bars near the wall and peered down suspiciously. "Is he diseased?"

"No!" Wick answered furiously. "He was old. Just old and ill-treated. The climb up the mountains to this place killed him."

"That's too bad," the guard said, shaking his head. "Some slaver captain somewhere has lost a few silvers."

Lost a few silvers? Wick blinked and shook with anger. He tried to find words to express the pain and rage that he felt, but even his vast command of the language failed him. There was nothing he could say that would ever make goblinkin care about one old dweller that hadn't survived long enough to become a productive slave.

"Ye stand there with yer fists a-clenched like that," the guard said, "an' ye're a-gonna make some taskmaster happy in a mine somewheres." He grinned cruelly. "Ye see, taskmasters hate it when all their slaves do what they're supposed to do all the time. I have half a mind to give ye a taste of the lash meself this morning. An' I would, except that ye're to be sold in a few days an' I don't want to pay the price for a-breakin' yer skin. But I'm a-gonna hope that all that bile ye're a-holdin' inside yerself comes loose one day and ye make a mistake."

Despite the anger that fed him, Wick's stomach turned cold at the goblinkin's threat. To survive and have any chance at all, he had to remain innocuous. This wasn't the way to do it. But at the same time, he had to ask himself, what chance did he really have?

He lowered his eyes from the goblin's. That, according to Esteff's *Rules of Aggressive Engagement,* was the first step to take when faced with a hostile confrontation that promised only failure. *Or death,* Wick thought bitterly. The little librarian stood with slumped shoulders and felt the aches and pains that thrived within him. He watched the goblin's shadow move suddenly on the ground and prepared himself for the coming blow.

Instead, a length of rope slapped against the stone ground, sprawling like a striking serpent for just a moment before going still.

"Tie that around the dead man's feet," the goblin ordered.

Wick stood still, unable to move, frozen by the horror of the suggestion.

Harran started forward after a moment.

"Not ye," the goblin thundered from above. "The little halfer there what's got such a mouth on 'im."

Wick glanced up at the goblin.

A cold smile twisted the goblin's lips. "Aye, ye're the one I want. Tie the rope to yer friend an' we'll fetch him out of there afore he starts to rot."

Sick dread rolled in Wick's stomach, but he couldn't make himself take the rope.

"Do it, halfer," the goblin growled, "or I'm a-gonna stick me a feather in yer head."

When Wick looked up, the guard held a crossbow in his hands. The little librarian had no doubt that the goblinkin would use it. He only thought for a moment of standing his ground, but he liked the idea of dying less.

"Do it, Wick," Harran whispered hoarsely. "He'll kill you if you don't."

Wick pushed his anger and pain aside, and with it—surprisingly—went much of his fear. He viewed what he had to do as a task. Kneeling, he picked up the rope and wrapped it around Minniger's ankles. He took care to make sure the rope was secure and tightly knotted. Then he placed his hands on his thighs and waited.

"Have ye got it then, halfer?" the goblin called down.

"Yes," Wick said. He watched silently as the rope was drawn up and the old man's body with it. Minniger's arms fell away from his body, sticking out like broken bird's wings. The image, backed by the red early morning sun, burned into the little librarian's mind.

The goblins hauled the body to the patrol walk, then lowered it into a wagon waiting by the slatted wall. Wick watched as the dweller driving the wagon started his team forward. The donkeys' hooves rang against the stone as it started down the debris-strewn street leading back to the harbor. The little librarian leaned against the wall in exhaustion, watching helplessly till the wagon wound through the whole and broken buildings of the city till it finally disappeared over a hill.

"Wick," Harran called.

The little librarian turned around slowly.

"You did all that you could do," Harran said. "Minniger was gone before morning even came." He held out his hand, holding a ball of gruel. "You need to eat to keep your strength up."

"Why?" Wick asked bitterly. "So I can be a slave better and longer?"

"Do you want to die?"

"No," Wick answered. "I want to live, and I want to go back home."

Harran placed the gruel ball in Wick's hand. "We all do, my friend. So let's eat and pray that it happens. But it will not happen on its own and we will need our strength."

Wick looked at the gruel in his hand. He swallowed hard, his throat parched and hurting. "Thank you, Harran." Slowly, his knees almost buckling under him, the little librarian sat on his haunches by the wall. He adjusted his journal under his shirt so that it remained hidden.

Harran sat beside him and slowly pinched bites from his own gruel ball.

As he ate, Wick became aware of the other dwellers in the pen covertly watching him. Whenever he looked at them, they looked away, as if afraid to meet his gaze.

He felt immediately self-conscious. He whispered to
Harran. "Why are they looking at me?"

"Because they're afraid of you," Harran answered quietly.

The answer puzzled Wick. "There's no reason for
them to be afraid of me."

"You stood up to the goblins," Harran said. "It's not
a wise thing to do. Those people think you're a troublemaker. The guards will remember you, and they will
notice anybody with you. If you ever fight them, the
goblinkin will kill you as a lesson to all the other slaves.
And there's every chance that they will kill anyone
around you as well."

Staggered by the improbable concept, Wick shook his
head. His sore ear throbbed in response as the heavy
marker pulled at the tender flesh. "But I'm no troublemaker," the little librarian protested.

"They believe you are."

Wick glanced at the other people in the pen, suddenly
ashamed of the way they looked away from him. How
could anyone ever think he was a troublemaker? Why,
they could ask anyone in Greydawn Moors. He was the
meekest, mildest dweller ever born. All his life, until the
night he'd been shanghaied from his home, he'd never
even been in a fight. Dweller children, as a general rule,
weren't overly aggressive. Running and hiding was what
they were best at.

But since that time, he'd fought Boneblights (more or
less), faced an Embyr, and been part of a shipboard battle as a pirate. It was a far cry from the Third Level
Librarian that he had been.

"I've been through some things lately," Wick admitted. "More than I like to realize, I think. And perhaps
I've changed a little in some ways, but I'm not a danger
to them."

"They see the courage in you," Harran said.

Wick shook his head and protested quickly. "I have no courage. When that goblin threatened me, did I dare him to shoot me? That's something a brave man would have done." He let out his breath. "If it had been Galadryn Carrolic who'd faced that goblin, why he would have plucked the crossbow arrow from the air and sent it winging back at him. And if I had been Taurak Bleiyz, armed with the mighty warclub, Toadthumper, I would have leapt up and laid waste to all those goblinkin about me."

Harran looked aghast at the suggestions.

"But I didn't do that," Wick quickly pointed out.

"You're a dweller," the other man cried. "Those thoughts should not even be in your head."

"They're not," Wick assured him.

"But you just thought them."

"No," the little librarian said. "I remembered them. Those are just men in stories. Not even men, really. They're more like ideas."

Harran shook his head. "Ideas are the worst of all, Wick. The most dangerous, thoughtless, and selfish thing a man can do is to have an idea like that. A man who thinks he can do something is more than just a danger to himself. He's a danger to a whole community if he convinces them to believe in him. You should never remember things like those stories."

Grandmagister Frollo would never have put it like that, Wick thought, *but he would have agreed with the sentiment.* He felt guilty and scared. What if he had such ideas on his own and no one was there to stop him? Could he trick himself into believing he was some kind of hero like the ones in the books in Hralbomm's Wing? He didn't think so. *And if I did somehow come to believe that here in this stronghold of goblinkin, I would be killed instantly, made an example for any others who might make the mistake of thinking such thoughts.*

The little librarian shivered. Thinking back on it now, he realized that the incident with the goblin had been a very near thing. *Surviving near-death once, facing it in the eye as I did the Embyr, can be very self-deluding.* He didn't recall thinking himself invincible at the moment. Had he? Or had he just not cared at the moment? Either, he knew, was dangerous.

Wick turned his attention back to Harran. "Why do you sit with me?"

"Because," Harran said, looking him squarely in the eye, "if you do something like that again that endangers all of us, I'll brain you myself."

The next three days went by in a blur for Wick. As it turned out, slaves waiting to be sold at auction were hired out as temporary labor for cleaning up Hanged Elf's Point. The work started at dawn, when gruel was doled out at the gates leading into the pens, and finished when sunset colored the western skies. The work was hard and dangerous. There wasn't a day that went by that Wick didn't return to the stockades tired and hurting. Three people from their pen were killed when a wall gave way suddenly and crushed the life from them before the fatigued work force could rescue them.

On the morning of the fourth day, they were fed one last time and herded over to the slave market in full slave collars and wrist manacles.

The slave market was only two streets over from the stockades. Wick walked in single file behind the other slaves and worried about where he would end up. The other slaves in his pen still didn't talk to him much, and even Harran's camaraderie had waned. And for the last three nights, though he had waited up and slept fitfully, Wick hadn't seen the man in black again.

The little librarian trudged through the broken alley

between two shattered buildings that weren't worth restoration. In their day, they had been beautiful works of architecture. Now they were only crumbled remains.

He stepped around a snarling gargoyle head that had a jagged neck stump, surprised that one of the goblinkin hadn't seized the once ornate piece as a trophy to keep in its den. Most of the slaves ended up in the mines. He'd learned that from listening to the members in the work force. But a great number of them were used in the arena, too, as gladiators. Dwellers who had physical infirmities were often used as gravediggers for the casualties of the battles that drew so many people from outlying villages. Orpho Kadar's vicious entertainment drew a blood-lusting crowd that lined the money purses of the pirate king.

Then there were the fields and orchards, Wick supposed, which wouldn't be as bad as being enclosed in a mine. They'd heard about the terrible accidents that happened in the mines as well.

What was really surprising about the possibility of being sold today, he'd realized, was that he'd started looking to the stockades for safety and security. While working on the cleanup crews, goblinkin roving the streets of Hanged Elf's Point felt compelled to heap verbal and physical abuse on every dweller they saw. However, they had to stop short of permanent physical damage. Of course, a lot of pain could be inflicted that wasn't permanent. So, would he be better off wherever he ended up? He didn't know, but he was convinced that leaving the stockades was bad.

The little librarian was so engrossed in his thoughts that he didn't hear the footsteps coming up on his side until the passerby was even with him. Black boots splashed through the puddles left from last night's rain, covering Wick's already-drenched pants. He ignored the soaking, chalking it up as one more miserable event in an otherwise horrible day.

Then a mocking voice that he recognized whispered so low that only he could hear. "So, my little friend, you're off to the sale today. And do you still have your secret in your possession?"

Startled, Wick glanced up at the man beside him, not surprised to find him dressed in a black cloak that nearly hid all his features. Only his bearded chin below an amused smile showed.

"And the one who buys you," the man in black said, "will have your precious secret as well. Of course, that's only if that person knows that you have such a thing." Without another word, the man lengthened his stride, leaving Wick far behind.

The little librarian watched the man in black go, not at all amazed at how quickly the tall human was able to disappear into the thronging crowd moving toward the slave auction. Before he was able to calm down from the man's mocking threat, Wick saw the huge fountain in the courtyard before him. Shock twisted his stomach threateningly.

The fountain was one of a kind, mentioned in dozens of books Wick had read at the Library. He knew where he was. And the knowledge, the realization of what the place had become, turned his stomach with sour sickness.

14

Sold!

The fountain stood three stories tall and filled the center of the huge courtyard in front of Wick. Crumbling hulks of tall buildings encircled the courtyard on all sides, dwarfing even the fountain.

Mountains stood tall and elegant on the fountain, ringed by a verdant forest of trees that had been painstakingly chipped from emerald-veined quartz that created hundreds of tiny rainbows in the spray that filtered through the fountain from the artesian well. On the right side of the fountain as Wick faced it, the quartz trees held small elven houses. Once, the little librarian knew from the books he'd read at the Library, gossamer strands of silver and horses' hair had joined those little houses, creating arboreal walkways.

The line of trees led the eye naturally down the mountains to a series of mines cut into the foothills. The broken-toothed ruins of dwarven houses stood there, crafted of small, individually made bricks. Here and there, remnants still remained of forges. *Perhaps*, Wick thought, *one of the small iron forges made for the fountain still remained in the rubble of what had been the dwarven village.*

Tears blurred Wick's vision as he saw what was left

of what he had seen in the books at the Vault of All Known Knowledge. The Shattered Coast, he knew, ran much further south than any of the Librarians and even Grandmagisters guessed.

Trails led from the dwarven village to a seacoast that had been chipped from a piece of dark gray granite longer than a wagon and the team that pulled it. The shelf of rock thrust out into the sea, which was represented by a huge, moon-shaped bowl that held only brackish water and broken rock now. In the beginning, though, it had represented the Silver Sea, one of the smallest ocean bodies in the area. In those days, huge reefs and a sickle-shape of mountains created by underwater volcanoes had ringed the sea, keeping it protected and easily defended. Those mountains had been called the Black Shields, named for the hard black rock that had risen from the sea when the volcanoes erupted.

The seafaring humans had settled the Silver Sea, and from that safe port they had established trade routes that had connected the world. *If water touches it, then a Silver Sea merchantman has been there,* Wick remembered. The saying was ancient, and had remained true until the Cataclysm. The little librarian stared at the brackish water and saw a few miniature broken ships floating in the sargasso created by algae and rocks. In one place, a section of mast stuck up that held broken, paper-thin sails of flaked alabaster.

The three races had lived harmoniously in the area but they hadn't ever been truly united until the Changelings—*or whatever their true names had been in those times,* Wick amended—had stretched forth their hands in friendship. The little librarian didn't know much about the Changelings' history even though he had spent countless hours in pursuit of the knowledge. He had wanted to learn what he could of the race as a gift to Nayghal. The library janitor was also a Changeling. The

the concer... the books that Wick ...re by a few scholars who had But most of the accounts ha... the Changelings. Often ...dicted each other. formation of the city where Wick st...one thing: the chains waiting to be sold—this evil place that wa...slave's called Hanged Elf's Point.

The little librarian raised his eyes, following the trails that led up from the miniature Silver Sea and the harbor where only crushed buildings remained that had been the human city. In the drawings he had seen, the human city was huge. Reports that had survived the Cataclysm indicated that it was the largest site of human habitation. Despite the restless energy and zeal for things new and different that drove them, thousands of humans had settled along the Silver Sea.

High above the Silver Sea, though, stood yet another city. The fountain representation of the city included many tall buildings that Wick saw were achingly familiar. He had passed by the buildings the fountain models had been based on when he'd arrived in the city. The Changelings never revealed their home in the area, and there were some historians who ventured the opinion that the Changelings lived somewhere inside or outside time and space as the rest of the world knew it. But all agreed that for the Changelings, this place held great importance. Or, perhaps, was a source of the magic they wielded so easily.

Wick stared at the city on the fountain, seeing the nine ledges that led up to it. Ringed as it was in mountainous terrain, the city wasn't easily accessible. Its location had been chosen with deliberation. The high ledges made it easily possible to keep out those who weren't wanted. And there, a congress of human, elf, dwarf, and Changeling representatives had gathered to tie together the needs and wants of all their races.

because that was

Mel Ohted. *Dream,* Wick re-

They had named there feeling the weight of his
what it was and *membered as a testament to the world that anything
chains, one dared could be achieved.*
that

Goblinkin hated the city because the combined armies of humans, elves, and dwarves had driven them from all the nearby areas. The caravan trade routes that wound through the mountains taking goods to and from the Silver Sea merchantmen rapidly became dangerous places for the goblinkin rather than the tradesmen.

No one had ever known what had happened to the city at the time of the Cataclysm, Wick knew. The great libraries that had been stored there had been shipped to Greydawn Moors, it was said, but the ships never made it to the Vault of All Known Knowledge. Some librarians thought that the ships had gone down in a violent storm at sea. Others believed that Dream had perhaps never existed. There was nothing left of the city except for bits and pieces of information that couldn't be verified, and hand-me-down stories told by humans claiming to be Silver Sea sailors.

The city had existed, Wick thought as tears ran down his face. He thought about everything that had been lost there. The thought of all the fine libraries of books that had probably been burned by torches carried by vengeful goblinkin under the orders of Lord Kharrion tortured the little librarian. But far, far more had been lost as well, he knew. With so many buildings in evidence, he was certain that not even the fine ships of the Silver Sea sailors had been able to get all of the populace to safety. He couldn't guess at the number of families that had died in their homes here, or in the streets fighting for their city.

This was also the place, Wick remembered, that the Changelings were said to have made their final sacrifice,

ment for ___
Goblin Lord's des_ intelligence and their wings as pay-
Is that true? Wick look_ vanity, in order to halt the
take everything in. He longed to be a__tain, trying to
journal and capture the image of the fountain. It w___
be a terrible thing to reveal it as it was now, but it would
also be a confirmation of all those legends, one more
linchpin in the chain of truth the Librarians of Greydawn
Moors labored to find amid their cataloguing efforts.

And *he* was the only one who knew.

A cold, mournful wind swept up from nowhere, rushing pell-mell over the slaves awaiting auction. Wick
shivered, listening to the sound of the wind fade away
as those gathered to buy slaves pulled at their cloaks and
outerwear to stay warm.

A rough hand pushed Wick's shoulder, breaking him
from the melancholy that gripped him. He tore his gaze
away from the great fountain with difficulty and glanced
at the grim visage of the goblin that had shoved him.

"Move along," the goblin growled gutturally. "It ain't
like we got all morning to get ye sold."

Wick moved forward, suddenly aware of the space
that separated him from the other slaves. They looked
back at him curiously, and a little angrily.

Maybe they're afraid that I'm going to cause trouble.
Wick looked away from them, not even glancing at Harran. If the goblinkin guards got the idea from his fellow
slaves that he might do something foolish, they might
deal harshly with him. And he might end up in the mines
for certain. That was how the goblinkin dealt with rebellious slaves, after all. Slaves that caused problems
were shackled to the floor by one leg in a mineshaft and
given no tools to cut through the chain that bound them.
They had to fill the ore cars with rock and rubble, and
in the event of a cave-in, there was no escape.

Wick shivered at the th... ...ach trying to turn inside out. Plea... ...n't let me be sent to the mines, he pl...

"...and what am I bid for these fine specimens?"

Hours later, hungry and more fearful than ever, Wick stood with the young members of his group from the blockades. The little librarian had quickly discovered that the groups were organized into lots by their ear tags first, then physical well-being and age. He had wound up with Harran and the other younger dwellers that remained in good shape despite the imprisonment and the cleaning labor of the last three days.

"They have strong backs for halfers," the auctioneer stated enthusiastically. He was a tall human with a long chestnut-colored beard, and his booming voice echoed across the expansive courtyard. He wore green and white robes, and a folded hat with a rolled brim. "And all of them are guaranteed to be in reasonably good health."

The crowd laughed appreciatively. The "guaranteed to be in reasonably good health" line never failed to draw a laugh.

As he stood on the raised auctioneering block, the little librarian gazed out at the crowd of prospective buyers seated on wooden bleachers. The wealthiest buyers occupied private booths that rose above the bleachers and were even served meals by scantily dressed human females. Vendors sold snacks from the backs of their wheeled carts and the spicy aromas made Wick's stomach grumble.

"This lot would be good candidates for the mines," the auctioneer suggested, glancing at the dozen booths that flew the banners of the various large mines that Orpho Kadar operated around the city.

The thought of the mines hurt Wick even more now

that he knew for certain where he was. Dream had never allowed mining anywhere within the city or even nearby regions. There had been a few mining towns even in dwarven history that owed their demise to overzealous digging that caused the whole town to collapse. Budhifer Tongalas had penned an amusing satire about a goblinkin mining town that had been devastated by a huge boar captured for the arena, called *The Boar, the Boors, and the Boring*.

The mine bidders waved their flags in lackluster enthusiasm. The bidding was sporadic and not very competitive at all. None of the orchard farms seemed interested at all, and Wick's hopes began to sink. He was going to die in the mines, and there surely wasn't a worse fate for a Third Level Librarian to—

"I'll take the lot of them," a harsh voice grated.

Wick turned, following the voice. He spotted a fierce-looking goblin with a leather eyepatch leaning out of a booth on the right.

"That's Boolian Toadas," one of the dwellers next to Wick gasped.

The little librarian recognized the name at once. Boolian Toadas bought slaves for the arena. The goblin was also a respected buyer because the arena constantly needed more slaves.

The auctioneer smiled broadly. "Welcome, Boolian Toadas. Well, this is the first time we've heard from you this fine morning. But better late than never, says I."

"It's the first time ye've offered slaves what's looked like they had legs under 'em," Boolian Toadas grunted. He tore a leg from a roasted chicken and chewed the meat from the bone noisily. "An' I was disappointed in the last sad lot ye sold me."

"Well, sir," the auctioneer said without missing a beat, "you could have returned them and asked for your money back—had they not been in so many *pieces*."

The crowd roared with laughter, enjoying the grisly joke made at the slaves' expense.

Two of the dweller men standing in Wick's lot threw up, and that amused the auction crowd even further. In truth, Wick felt certain that if his own stomach were not empty, he probably would have thrown up as well. According to the stories the slaves told each other in the pens, the Hanged Elf's Point arena housed all manner of vicious beasts and men. The human gladiators were the most prized—*and dangerous!*—of them all.

"Yes," Boolian Toadas replied, "but they served just fine as food for them wild pigs we brung in just last week. Was just as well, 'cause the sharks was a-gettin' fat down in the harbor, I'm told. Sailors new to these waters say we got the biggest and fattest sharks they've ever seen."

The crowd laughed again, applauding in appreciation.

"Ah, but my friend Boolian Toadas," the auctioneer said unctuously, "Captain Arghant himself brought these fine specimens from up around Lottar's Crossing. And were the raiders who capture our merchandise from those areas not so quick and skilled, we wouldn't have these to sell you now. As everyone knows, Lottar's Crossing breeds only the fleetest of foot halfers. Captains of slaver ships brave those treacherous waters and the navies that would prevent them from carrying on their trade because they know such merchandise is well respected here in our humble city."

No one bid against Boolian Toadas. It was accepted that once the arena supplier saw a lot that he wanted, he wouldn't let anyone outbid him. The arena was an important draw to the thriving goblinkin city. For a while, some of the mining labor buyers had bid against the goblinkin out of spite, driving the price up. Stories had it that Orpho Kadar had sent out assassins, had the men killed, and put their heads on pikes as an example. That had been years ago; no one had bid against Boolian Toadas since.

"Sold!" the auctioneer cried when no one offered a counter bid.

Wick was numb inside with fear as the auction guards led his group away. They stopped at one of the temporary holding pens in one of the courtyard's corners. Goblinkin quickly kicked their feet out from under them, forcing them to their knees. A fat goblin with broken teeth took a pair of pliers from a scarred box, then fetched out a bag of ear tags that bore the arena's mark.

Several of the dwellers broke down and wept. Wick didn't blame them in the slightest. The ear tags bearing *Ill Wind*'s mark hadn't completely healed yet, and with the way they were being fed and kept, the healing process remained a long time off.

The goblinkin worked relentlessly, and the pliers *snap, snap, snapped!* as they bit down through tender flesh.

Wick tried not to be sick as he waited his turn. *If I were stronger, braver,* he told himself, *I would fight these men.* He really wanted to, because once he entered the arena, his death was assured. But he kept his head lowered, walking forward on his knees as the goblinkin bade him. The courtyard's cracked cobblestones chafed at his knees.

Boolian Toadas stepped out of his booth long enough to come over to the holding pens to inspect his purchase. None of the dwellers dared look at the goblin.

"Ye do look like a fast bunch of halfers," Boolian Toadas commented. "Have any of ye got experience with fightin'?"

No one answered.

Boolian Toadas rubbed his palms together. "Well, I hopes some of ye are a-lyin' to me. I know there's halfers of around Lottar's Crossing what's tortured a goblinkin or three. Why, I've even heard tell of some what's turned cannibal and learned to enjoy goblin stew made from their victims."

Images of a stew with floating goblin parts filled Wick's mind, adding to his nausea. *Those are stories. They have to be. Dwellers are not warriors—or culinary barbarians.*

"Excuse me," a smooth, cultured voice interrupted.

Recognizing the voice, though not believing it possible, Wick looked up.

As confidently as a lord, the man in black stepped up to Boolian Toadas. "I wonder if I might have a word with you, good sir."

The arena procurement master looked over both his shoulders, then—when no one stepped forward to speak with the man in black—back at the individual who'd addressed him. The big goblin placed his hand meaningfully on the big broadsword at his side. "Ye're wantin' a word with me?"

The man in black smiled, then held his forefinger and thumb only a fraction of an inch apart. "Hardly any time at all, good sir, I assure you."

Boolian Toadas' face tightened and looked more fierce. "An' why should I be willin' to talk to ye?"

Although the human was dressed in black, Wick realized that the black clothing was not the same dress he'd been in the night they'd spoken. The little librarian slowly brought his hands to his midriff and closed them over his journal. The cold gray skies overhead felt like they were closing in on him. There was no escape from the man in black.

"I would consider it a favor, good sir," the man in black said brightly.

Why is he pursuing me so? Wick wondered. He studied the man's dress, trying to fathom something that would give him an indication as to what the man might want. *The journal is the only thing I can think of. But why would he want the journal?*

"I don't do no favors," Boolian Toadas responded unkindly. "Favors tend to be bothersome things, always a-breedin' thoughts in some person's head that ye might owe them yet another one."

"Perhaps then," the man in black went on smoothly, "I might be able to do you a favor."

"Don't need no favors."

"Really?" The man in black stretched out his hand, holding one above the other, holding them palm out. Then he clenched his hands into fists, gestured, and silver coins dropped from his top hand to the bottom one. They tinkled as they struck each other and he let them lie in a pile in his palm. The man in black leaned forward confidentially. When he spoke again, he whispered. "I know that Orpho Kadar probably doesn't pay his arena procuring manager *everything* that one in such an office is worth."

Boolian Toadas took a step forward so that the silver in the man in black's hand might be hidden from view. "Ye would be right about that."

"I thought we might make a little transaction," the man in black said. Then he glanced at Wick and winked while Boolian Toadas glanced around nervously. Before the arena master looked back, the man in black swung his attention to him.

"What *kind* of transaction?" Boolian Toadas asked.

"The profitable kind," the man in black answered. "The only worthwhile kind to be had."

"Profitable for who?"

"Why for both of us. Otherwise there'd be no profit to speak of at all."

"What do ye want?" Boolian Toadas asked gruffly.

"A slave."

Boolian Toadas narrowed his remaining eye and

scratched at his eyepatch. "There's plenty of slaves to be had on the auction block this mornin'."

"I want one of your slaves," the man in black said.

"Which slaves?"

"These." The man in black gestured toward the slaves.

Wick tried to concentrate on the conversation, but it only made the *snap-snap-snapping* of the pliers more sharp. He cringed and glanced ahead. Only seven slaves remained before he would acquire yet another ear tag.

"These slaves?" Boolian Toadas asked.

"Yes."

Snap! Another dweller ahead of Wick yelped in pain.

"So ye'd be a-wantin' a fleet-footed halfer, then?" Boolian Toadas asked.

"If we could come to an agreement on the terms, why then I would very much like one of these fleet-footed halfers."

Boolian Toadas leaned in more closely. "Ye'd be a-knowin' that these here fleet-footed halfers don't come cheap."

"I know."

"The only reason that I got them this cheap is because I buy in bulk."

"Of course. And because Orpho Kadar would have anyone who outbid you assassinated."

Boolian Toadas hesitated just a moment, as if he might take offense at the statement. Then he laughed and slapped his knee. "That is true, but Orpho Kadar also pays a fair price."

"Then I shall seek to emulate Orpho Kadar's generous example," the man in black said. He spread his palm, flashing the silver coins.

"Which slave do ye want?"

"It doesn't matter."

That's a lie, Wick thought. He still clutched his journal, trying to make sure it stayed out of view.

Snap! Another dweller yelped in pain.

"That's not enough," Boolian Toadas said.

"And what would be a fair price?"

The arena master hesitated only a moment. "Five more silvers."

"Done." Five more silvers trickled from the man in black's upper hand, tinkling against those in his lower hand. "And if it's all the same to you, I'll take the halfer here." He dropped a black-gloved hand to Wick's shoulder.

The little librarian cringed. I'm not going, he told himself angrily. *I'll tell Boolian Toadas that—that—* He sighed in defeat. If he told the big arena master that the man in black wanted his journal, then the goblinkin would want to see it as well. *I should have buried it. Or burned it.* There had been plenty of chances to do both during the last three days. But he had stubbornly hung onto it. *My conceit is going to lose the Vault of All Known Knowledge's greatest defense—its location!* Panic sped his heart in his chest.

"Is this halfer special to ye?" Boolian Toadas asked suspiciously. His single eye studied Wick closely for the first time.

Snap! "My poor ear!"

The man looked at Wick more closely as well, the showed a puzzled expression to the big goblin. "I don't know, good sir. Does he look any more special than any of the other halfers you've bought this morning?"

Boolian Toadas didn't speak and stared at the man in black.

Snap! "Ow!"

"No," the arena master replied. "This one doesn't look any more special than the others."

"Good." The man in black patted Wick on the shoulder. "Then we'll both be happy."

Snap! A dweller cried out.

Wick nervously looked at the line ahead of him. Only two dwellers remained between him and the pliers.

"But ye must see him as special," Boolian Toadas said. "Otherwise ye'd have reached for another."

"Really?" The man in black took his hand from Wick's shoulder.

Remembering how quickly the man in black has produced the silver coins with sleight-of-hand, Wick made certain his journal was still at hand. He sighed with relief when he discovered it was still there.

"You think I would choose another halfer?" the man in black asked. He made a production of glancing along the line of dwellers. "Do you think I've mistakenly selected a defective one?" He glanced back at Boolian Toadas. "I'd be frightfully cross with you if you sold me a defective halfer."

"Oh," the arena master said quickly, "this one isn't defective."

"And how do you know?" the man in black asked testily. "Have you seen this one run for yourself?"

"Why no. But I'm perfectly sure there's nothing wrong with this one."

"Yet you lead me to believe—after we have our bargain, mind you, and not before I paid you which would have only been decent of you—that there's something wrong with this halfer."

"That's not what I said," Boolian Toadas replied. "I was only curious as to why ye wanted this one."

The man in black shook his head. "You've got the reputation of a reputable man, good sir. I'd hate to think that the halfer I've selected is damaged goods." He glanced at Wick. "Open your mouth, halfer. Let me see your teeth. Is there some disease lurking in there, then?"

Wick stubbornly kept his mouth closed.

"There's no disease," Boolian Toadas assured him.

"Orpho Kadar allows no diseased halfers inside in the city. Surely ye've heard that."

"I have," the man in black agreed. "That's why I thought if I purchased a halfer from one of Orpho Kadar's own agents that I would be safe in spending the money I was given by the man who wanted a halfer. And now I find that this halfer hasn't even been properly beaten. Did you see the way he refused to let me look at his teeth?"

"I've hardly had him in me possession. Ye can't hold this halfer's obedience against me."

The man in black considered that, touching his beard lightly. "Perhaps not. Do we have a deal then?"

Boolian Toadas silently regarded Wick with deep suspicion.

Snap! "Ow!"

"Why," the man in black said, "if you're nervous about selling this halfer to me, perhaps I shouldn't purchase a halfer from you at all. Would it be a problem to ask for my money back?"

Boolian Toadas' hand clenched around the silvers. "Ye can't go about welshing on the payment. We have a deal."

"I thought we did, too. Until it became apparent that there was some problem."

"There's no problem."

"Then why haven't I left here with my halfer yet?" the man in black asked.

"I was only curious about why ye wanted this particular halfer," the arena master said.

"It isn't this particular halfer," the man in black said. "I would take *any* halfer you've got."

"Ye would, would ye?"

"Yes, in delight, good sir. I tell you that in all honesty. I'll gladly take any halfer ye have with red-gold hair."

Boolian Toadas glanced along the line of dwellers.

Wick knew he was the only one among them that had red-gold hair. "I only have the one."

The man in black glanced back down the line. "Ah, so you do. Pity. Perhaps I should try somewhere else. I do hate doing business at a place that doesn't boast a selection."

"No," the arena manager said quickly.

Wick looked around, noting that there weren't very many other dwellers with red-gold hair in the slave market.

Snap! "Ow!" the dweller in front of Wick yelped.

"We have a deal," Boolian Toadas reminded.

"Perhaps," the man in black said, "you wouldn't think ill of me for asking the return of some of those silvers I gave you."

"I think not." The big goblin raised his voice and made it stern.

The goblin holding the pliers grabbed Wick and pulled him forward.

Lightning fast, Boolian Toadas yanked the little librarian away from the jaws of the pliers and stood him in front of the man in black. The man in black never even looked at him. "Ye'll take this halfer, ye will. Or else I'll think ye're a-questionin' me ability at a-pickin' halfer flesh. An' in that, ye're a-questionin' Orpho Kadar's ability as well, ye are."

The man in black straightened his cloak and dusted the sleeves. "Well, I'd hardly relish the thought that any injurious action I might take on Orpho Kadar's name should reach his delicate ears."

"Ye're darn right ye don't want that to happen," Boolian Toadas remarked. "Ye'd probably have yer head on a pike before mornin'."

"Not likely a very joyous happenstance." The man in black grimaced and nodded. "Very well. I'll take this halfer and be glad, good sir, that you were gentleman enough to sell him to me."

"Do ye want him marked?" the arena manager asked. "If ye don't have a tag, we can notch his ear or nose for ye."

"If you would be so kind." The man in black extended a tag.

Boolian Toadas glanced at the tag and pulled at his eyepatch. "Ye got a picture of a toad on yer marker?"

"That's not a toad," the man in black said, "though I can easily see how the mistake could be made. However, that is a Callavarian bullfrog—the chosen symbol of Cholot Verdim."

"An' who's he?"

"A caravan trader baron," the man in black answered. "It is Cholot Verdim's opinion that halfers with red-gold hair are the best groomsmen for his proud horses."

A groomsman for a caravan trader's horses? Even while Wick was trying to absorb the answer, wondering if any of it was the truth, the goblin with the pliers quickly grabbed the little librarian, yanked him over, and tagged his other ear. He cried out in pain and felt fresh blood trickling down the side of his face.

The man in black leaned down, grabbed Wick's wrist manacles, and yanked him to his feet. "Come along, halfer. That didn't hurt that much." He glanced back at Boolian Toadas. "May fortune favor you, good sir."

Half-blind with pain, the whole side of his head throbbing, Wick stumbled after the man in black. The manacles pinched his wrists. He followed the man in black through the crowd, then into one of the side streets leading from the courtyard. The street was filled with people and wagons, all busy converging on the marketplaces down near the harbor.

———

"Why did you do that?" Wick asked a few minutes later as he followed the man in black down the winding streets of Hanged Elf's Point.

The man in black glanced down at him. "Do what?"

"Buy me."

"Why, to save your life, of course." The man in black headed down the street with purpose. "And, might I say, I find a truly startling lack of appreciation on your part."

"I don't think I have anything to be thankful for," Wick said. He pulled his hands back, but the man in black kept the chain tight. He glanced around, looking for some place to dispose of the journal if he could. That thought pained him, though, because he had put so much work into it and there were so many things that needed to be remembered. He wasn't sure if he could remember it all, or find the right words the second time through.

"True. Probably you don't. I should imagine that a resourceful fellow like yourself should be able to defeat any number of wild pigs in battle in the arena. You could probably even have worked your way into becoming a champion, maybe even winning your own freedom."

Sarcasm, Wick thought, *is not appreciated.* "What do you want from me?"

"You're an artist. I may have need for an artist."

"For what?"

"A special project. Something I can't do for myself."

"What special project?"

"My, my," the man in black said. "You're remarkably curious, aren't you? When the time is right, I'll let you know."

Wick struggled to keep up with the man in black's long stride. Still, even in his frustration and anxiety, the little librarian couldn't help but glance around the city. The stories of Dream and the peoples who had lived there were infuriatingly lacking in detail. Yet, here he was—walking the same streets those legends barely spoke of. If he could learn anything at all of Dream, he knew he could write a book that would sit in the Vault of All Known Knowledge. And it would be a treasured work, too, something seldom seen. Librarians these days usually only wrote books that were compilations of other books, or educated guesses from other sources to fill in holes in histories or biographies.

His mind filled with images of what the city must have looked like when everything was new. But he remained on the lookout for someplace to lose the journal as well. He really couldn't afford to leave it where it would be found.

He was so intent on finding a place that he didn't see the man in black's sudden turn around a corner into an alley. Before he knew it, the little librarian hit the end of his manacle chains and was yanked into the alley after the man in black, stumbling into the man and falling to the ground.

As he got to his feet and dusted himself off, Wick happened to notice two goblins duck back into an alley further up the street. Both of them looked like guards that had been with Boolian Toadas. The little librarian acted as though he hadn't seen anything.

"Well, come along now," the man in black said, tugging gently yet firmly on the manacle chains. "For an artist, you're not particularly attentive, are you?"

Wick followed the man in black into the alley. *Should I tell him about the goblins?*

The man in black kept going down the alley and avoided the debris strewn between the two buildings. Empty windows stared into vacant rooms on either side of them.

"You may call me Brant," the man in black announced.

"Brant?" Wick blinked in confusion, wondering where that had come from.

"Brant," the man in black said. "You've probably been thinking of me as *the man in black* since you have no other reference for me. I find that appellation most distressing since it's based on my clothing and not me all. Should you happen to tell this story later, people will hear you call me Brant, which sounds rather friendly, I think, and not *the man in black,* which, I think, sounds rather off-putting."

"Off-putting?"

The man in black—Brant—frowned at Wick. "If I'd wanted a parrot, I would have bought one. Please don't repeat every last word I say while you take time to think. I find that habit most annoying. If you need time to think, just be silent and take it."

Wick glanced backward. There was no sign of the two goblinkin. *Did I imagine them?* His newly sore ear was paining him enough that he supposed it was possible.

"If you refer to me simply as the man in black," Brant said, "such choice will make me sound threatening, or perhaps—worst of all—a *caricature.*"

"Is your name Brant?" Wick asked.

"Do you not like it?"

"I think it's a fine name," the little librarian said. "I just don't think it's your name."

Brant smiled. "What is your name, little artist?"

Wick considered his answer. "Frazz."

"That's a lie," Brant replied without hesitation. "Give me your true name. I'm telling you, I'll know when you lie to me."

"Wick."

"Ah, there's a truth. Wick what?"

"Wick is enough," the little librarian said. "Just as Brant is enough for you."

Brant nodded. "Very well. Wick is a fine name. I think it suitably fits you."

Wick glanced back over his shoulder. The two goblins

stepped around the corner, acting painfully nonchalant.

"Wick," Brant whispered.

The little librarian turned back to face the man, wondering again if he should tell him they were being followed. "What?"

"Please don't stare at the goblins," Brant whispered. "I'd rather they didn't know that we know that they're there."

Wick swallowed hard.

"It would spoil the surprise," Brant went on.

"What surprise?"

Without warning, metal rang out dully, followed immediately by startled yelps. Drawn by the noise, Wick turned and peered over his shoulder. Two dwarves and two humans had stepped out of the vacant buildings on either side of the alley with small milk pails, evidently without being seen. Then the humans had upended the pails and covered the goblins' heads with them. While the goblins were stumbling around trying to yank the pails from their heads, the dwarves swung hammers into them. Hollow THONKs echoed in the alley and the goblins fell on their face on the ground. The humans and dwarves vanished once more into the vacant buildings.

"My associates," Brant said coolly, pulling on Wick's chains to get him moving again. "I really don't care to be followed."

"What are you doing?" Wick demanded. "If Boolian Toadas finds out his guards have been attacked, he'll have us killed."

"They won't know that I had anything to do with that."

"It wouldn't be that hard to figure out."

"Why should Boolian Toadas bother? You're just another slave to him."

"He sent those men."

"He was curious. Although, should I ever see that

goblin again, I'm sure he would remember me." Brant grimaced. "I really don't like being known. It's not good in my line of work."

"What are you up to?" Wick asked.

"Not now," Brant replied. "For the moment, we have to finish our escape."

"Escape?"

"I swear, I'd entertained real hopes that an artist such as yourself would be capable of carrying on a decent and lively conversation." Brant walked out of the alley and turned right.

A lean young human waited at the street's edge with three saddled horses. Only the lack of facial hair at her age led Wick to believe that she was feminine. She wore loose, dingy brown clothing, a traveling cloak pulled up over her head, and scarred boots that reached to her knees. Her blond hair was short-cropped, hanging level with her jawline. Wick doubted she was out of her teens, which was of a nearly adult age in humans, but she still looked young. "Did everything go according to plan?" she asked, reaching into a saddlebag.

"Well enough," Brant said. "Except that I think I'll have to be careful around Boolian Toadas for quite possibly the rest of my life."

"Brant, you're careful around everybody," the young girl said.

Wick stared at the young girl and felt terribly confused. Evidently Brant had planned on everything that had happened, but the little librarian still had no clue why anyone would go to such trouble for him.

The young girl walked to Wick carrying a dark green traveling cloak and a rolled-brim hat. "Hi," she said, smiling. Mischievous merriment glistened in her green eyes. A light dusting of freckles tracked across the bridge of her nose. "I'm Sonne."

"Hello, Sonne," Wick said, feeling awfully confused.

The girl seemed so open and friendly compared to Brant's arrogance. "I'm Edgewick Lamplighter, Third—" The little librarian stopped himself just in time to keep from giving away his position at the Library.

Already mounted on one of the horses, Brant grinned down at him smugly.

Angrily, Wick glanced away from Brant and looked back at Sonne.

The young girl held out the traveling cloak and hat. "Would you hold these?"

Wick accepted the garments after only a moment's hesitation, not really knowing what else to do.

Sonne took a hammer and punch from the other saddlebag. She waved the little librarian over to a broken window in the nearby building. "Let me get those manacles off you. It'll be hard to ride with them on."

Totally lost, Wick did as he was bid. With two swift strokes, Sonne knocked out the pins holding the manacles closed. Then she did the same for the ankle manacles. Finished, she returned the hammer and punch to the saddlebag. She left the chains lying at Wick's feet.

"Get dressed," she suggested. "It gets cold up in the mountains."

"The mountains?" Wick repeated.

Sonne looked at Brant.

"It could be," Brant told the girl, "that he's not as bright as I'd hoped."

"It's not like you to waste money," Sonne replied. She turned back to Wick. "Get dressed. Or we can leave you here with slave markers in your ears so that the first greedy goblins to come along can claim you as theirs."

Wick quickly pulled on the traveling cloak. He fit the hat more gingerly since it rode low enough to touch his sore ears.

Sonne held out a stirrup. "Get up on the horse."

Remembering his last riding experience in Greydawn

Moors, Wick said, "I'd really rather not. Horses and I just don't get along well."

"If we could walk there," Sonne said, "I wouldn't have brought the horses. Get up there."

Wick glanced around the street and wondered if he had a chance of running away.

As if by magic, a small slim blade appeared in Sonne's hand. "Don't," she warned coldly. "You wouldn't make it. Whether you lived or not, I'd take you down to the harbor and throw you in to the sharks myself."

Despite her youth and the slight smile on her lips, the coldness in her green eyes made Wick believe she meant what she said. Sighing, knowing he was still a prisoner just as surely as though he'd still been manacled, the little librarian pulled himself onto the saddle. He was still too weak from being underfed to make it on his own. Sonne helped with a shove that very nearly put him over the horse. He reached for the reins, but the young girl snatched them away.

"I'll be leading you," she told him. Effortlessly, she vaulted up onto her own mount. She kept the reins to Wick's horse clasped in one hand while controlling hers with her other hand. Without a word, she put her heels to the horse's flanks.

"Wait!" Wick protested, then grabbed for the saddle horn with both hands. The stirrups were close to the distance he needed them, but they were still a little too long. As he bounced on the saddle, he slid from side to side, touching first with one foot, then with the other, never quite balanced.

Sonne turned away from the harbor and headed east instead.

"Where are we going?" Wick asked, but his question might as well have been asked of a stone wall. His companions didn't answer. He stared at the tree-lined mountains up the path they traveled. At the other end lay the Forest of Fangs and Shadows, and the little librarian couldn't even guess what waited for him there.

15

The Den of Thieves

Let's rest here a moment."

Tired and aching from the past few days of hard manual labor, plus the last hour of riding the horse, Wick was grateful for the break. Sonne led his horse to the left side of the little-used trail they'd followed up into the mountains.

The lithe girl swung her leg over her own mount and dropped to the ground. She tied her horse's reins to a nearby branch and glanced over her shoulder at the little librarian. "Don't get any ideas just because the woods might tempt you. Even if you got away from me somehow, there are a lot of bad things in this forest that would eat you up in one gulp."

I don't think I can walk, let alone run, Wick thought ruefully. Moving carefully, wondering if any permanent damage had been done during the ride up the mountainside, he slid off the saddle, missed the stirrup on the way down, and landed on his posterior with a painful thump.

"Slow-witted and awkward," Sonne commented as she rummaged through her saddlebags. She gazed at Wick and shook her head disdainfully. "I still don't see what possessed you to risk so much to acquire this half-fer."

"When I saw him drawing in his sketchpad," Brant said, "he intrigued me."

Wick stood cautiously, his ill-treated knees protesting. They'd stopped at a wooded glen overlooking Hanged Elf's Point far below. From above, the city looked even worse, like a child's stack of toy buildings that had been cruelly smashed.

He scanned the harbor, counting twenty-two ships at anchor. Travel up and down the nine ledges fronting the sea was thick. The tree line around them was thick and verdant. Birds sang upon the leafy boughs. As they'd ridden into the mountains, the sun had finally burned through the clouds, bringing warmth and golden light.

"Was there anything interesting in the sketchbook?" Sonne asked.

"He is a good artist," Brant mused, "but I question his composition."

Startled by the announcement, Wick ran his hands along his shirt. *My journal!* It was gone. He'd been so frightened of the mountain travel on horseback that he hadn't even noticed. He turned and looked at Brant, who'd taken a seat beneath a spreading elm tree.

Brant casually flipped through the pages of the little librarian's homemade book.

"Hey," Wick cried, starting forward. "That isn't yours!" How much could Brant have already guessed from the things he'd seen? The little librarian brushed aside a branch, holding it back.

Sonne flicked her hand forward and a small silver knife thudded home in the branch the little librarian held out of his face. The knife quivered only inches from Wick's left eye.

"Not one more step, little man," the young girl ordered.

Brant didn't even look up from Wick's journal. "I believe she means it," he stated calmly.

Wick didn't say anything, and he didn't move. He stared nervously at the journal in Brant's hands. How had the man gotten hold of it? The little librarian had known for sure that he'd had the journal up until the time he'd mounted the horse. After that, he'd concentrated on holding on for dear life. He glanced at Sonne, suddenly understanding. "You!"

She smiled and batted her eyes.

"You picked my pocket," Wick protested. "You did it when you gave me the clothes."

"Yes."

"You're a *thief!*"

Sonne frowned in mock disappointment. "You say that as if it were a bad thing. I'll have you know there are many less honorable professions than thievery."

"And even more that are honorable," Wick replied.

She exhaled in rude disgust.

Brant closed the book and glanced at Wick. "You fascinate me, little artist. I've never known a dweller with talent such as yours."

The compliment, even coming under such strange and auspicious circumstances, embarrassed Wick. He felt his face burn, and it made his injured ears throb even worse.

"Of course," Brant continued, "I've not known very many dwellers. Why do you keep a sketchpad?" He rifled the pages. "And such a shoddy one at that. I'd think you'd want something far larger than this."

Sketchpad? Wick thought. *Doesn't he realize what he's holding? Or maybe I didn't write neatly enough for him to easily comprehend.* He hated thinking that the failing might be his handwriting, but if it was enough to keep his secrets secret, he resolved to be glad of it.

"I've seen the sketches you've done of Hanged Elf's Point," Brant went on. "Very true to life and easy to place. However, these other people and the ships at sea— and this." He held the journal open and showed Wick the picture of the Embyr. "I don't understand this at all."

Sonne stared at the pictured with vibrant interest. "She's pretty. But who burned her?"

"No one burned her," Wick said. "She's an Embyr."

Brant shook his head. "I don't know what an Embyr is except for small coals in a fire."

"She is one of the beings called Embyrs that Lord Kharrion created near the end of the Cataclysm," Wick explained, wanting to make sure they at least understood the picture.

"Lord Kharrion." Brant's attention returned to the journal and he flipped pages. "You believe that the Goblin Lord existed and that a war was fought that covered the world?"

"Yes," Wick replied.

Brant laughed and shook his head. "I can understand the goblinkin's interest in believing those legends. It makes them out as the near-conquerors of the world."

"They're not legends," Wick insisted. *Maybe if I can convince him how dangerous the knowledge contained in that book is he will give it back to me.* "Lord Kharrion existed. That city down there is proof of that."

"Hanged Elf's Point?"

"It was once called Dream. Haven't you heard of it?"

"No," Brant said.

"How can you live here on the Shattered Coast and not know of Dream?" Wick asked incredulously.

Brant's face hardened in warning. "I know of several other legends and myths, and I know when to separate fact from fiction. Therein, many times, lies the profit in a matter." He flipped through the journal's pages again. "You got here by sea, and presumably you traveled with dwarven pirates for a time. But where were you before that?"

Wick shook his head.

"I see this little house," Brant said, referring to the

picture Wick had drawn of his father's house. "I know
it has some significance to you. But it was drawn amidst
all the pictures of the pirates and the sea. So I think you
were thinking about some other place. A city you'd been
in before you joined the pirates. Where is this place?"

"I can't tell you."

"Why?"

"It's not my secret to give," Wick said.

Brant grinned. "Ah, little artist, you know how I am
about secrets."

Wick shrugged stubbornly.

"And what are these strange markings on these other
pages?" Brant asked. "I would think perhaps you'd gotten bored, except that the markings show rhythm and
measure, and a great deal of time and skill to get them
all right."

Markings? Wick looked at the page of script Brant
pointed to. Then the little librarian understood. "You
can't read," he whispered.

Color flooded into Brant's face and anger twisted his
features. "Are you trying to say that you can?"

Wick remained silent, not believing his good luck. He
already knew that not many humans bothered to learn to
read or write before the Cataclysm except those who
intended to become mages or historians. Even ships'
captains and merchantmen only learned the rudiments of
the written language of trade and navigation. Wick knew
his own writing was anything but common.

"I'm not stupid," Brant said angrily. "I know that only
mages can read. They have spell books, but I've never
seen any of them that looked like this."

Desperately seizing the idea that suddenly presented
itself to him, Wick stood up to his full height and lowered his voice. He tried to appear all-knowing and grave.
"Would you believe that I am a mage?"

Brant regarded the little librarian. "Perhaps. If you turned Sonne into a frog."

"I could—" Wick began, thinking maybe he could somehow gain the upper hand on his captors. Although, he had no clue what he would do then. He wasn't even sure in which direction Greydawn Moors lay after spending nine days chained in *Ill Wind*'s lower cargo hold.

Another knife magically appeared in Sonne's hand. "Don't even think about it."

Wick crossed his arms over his chest. "I have no desire to turn her into a frog."

Sonne smiled prettily at Brant. "See? He likes me."

Brant ignored her. "If you're a mage, how did you come to be captured by slavers?"

"I—uh—I—" Wick thought furiously. If there was a chance that Brant would believe him even for a little while, maybe he could turn it to his advantage in some way. "I was ambushed." He nodded, happy with his answer. "Yes, that's it, I was ambushed."

"Why didn't you turn into a puff of smoke and disappear from the slave pens in Hanged Elf's Point?"

"Because," Wick said, remembering Minniger's tale on the way up the mountain, "magic doesn't work in Hanged Elf's Point. Everyone knows that."

"True," Brant conceded. "Then why not turn the goblinkin slavers into frogs and take over their ship when you woke?"

"I didn't—uh—" Wick was stumped again, but only for a moment. Latheril Duonden had written a series of comical mage stories that were on the shelves in Hralbomm's Wing. "I lost my magic hat." Latheril's character had the habit of producing anything he needed from his enchanted hat.

"Pity," Brant said, "that you still don't have that hat. Otherwise, I'd find you dreadfully frightful."

Details, Wick thought sourly, remembering the admonishment he'd received from several First Level Librarians. *The work is always undone by sloppy attention to details.* He sighed. "All right. I'm not a mage."

"But you fancy yourself a writer?" Brant asked. "As well as an artist?"

"I do know how to write," Wick said. "And I know how to read."

The sound of horses' hooves striking the stony ground drew their attention. Sonne's hands seemed to fill with the small knives, and Brant put his hand upon his sword hilt as he stood.

Two dwarves and two humans on horses appeared at the top of the ridge, riding along the trail up the mountains. They called out greetings to Sonne and Brant, which were returned.

"Did anyone follow us, Cobner?" Brant asked as the dwarves and humans dismounted and tied their horses up as well.

"No one," one of the dwarves grimaced as if pained. His voice was gravelly and severe. He was almost as big as Hallekk had been, and may have even been a little broader across the shoulders. Blade scars showed on his face, disappearing under his sandy-gray beard. "Though Boolian Toadas was fit to be tied after hearing two of his goblins got knocked about."

Brant sheathed his sword. "You did rob them, didn't you?"

All four men nodded.

"Well?" Brant prompted.

Cobner dug in his traveling cloak and produced a small money purse. "They didn't have much. Evidently Boolian Toadas pays his help very little." He tossed the bag at Brant.

Brant caught the bag, briefly inspected the contents and frowned, then divided it up between himself and

Sonne. "Still, it's something. As long as we're still showing a profit, we're doing just fine."

Cobner nodded at Wick. "What's the story with the little halfer?"

Holding up Wick's journal, Brant said, "He says he can read."

Immediately the two dwarves and two humans stepped back and started drawing their weapons, swords for the humans and battle-axes for the dwarves.

Wick stepped back, letting go the branch he'd been holding. To his horror, he saw that the little silver blade embedded in the branch shot loose, flying directly at Sonne's face. The young girl didn't move at all except to snatch the twirling blade from the air as quickly as a frog flicking a fly. She smiled at Wick.

Brant held up his hands to stop the humans and dwarves. "He's not a mage. If he had been, do you think he would still be here?"

Still suspicious, the dwarves and humans put their weapons away.

"He forgot his magic hat," Sonne said.

"Make up your minds," Cobner growled irritably, keeping his hands on the haft of his great battle-axe. "I don't like your little jokes. I've told you that often enough before. I'd soon as lop a mage's head off as look at him. They're nothing but trouble in the end, you know."

Wick swallowed hard.

Amusement twinkling in his black eyes, Brant looked at the little librarian. "Go on and tell Cobner the truth. Are you a mage?"

Wick glanced at the fierce dwarf. Cobner didn't look as though he had a friendly bone in his body. "No," the little librarian said. "I'm not a mage. I only told Brant and Sonne that so they might let me go."

Cobner glowered at Wick and shook his head. "That's

mighty stupid, halfer. Orpho Kadar already don't allow mages into Hanged Elf's Point and will kill any that he finds. And Brant, why he'd tell you to change Sonne into a frog or somesuch to prove you were a mage." He spat. "You'd have been better off eating one of those sour green persimmons off those trees over there so that you'd foam at the mouth, then tell Brant that you were diseased or mad."

"Oh." Wick blinked, noticing the sour green persimmons on the small trees only a short distance away. *All those stories of brilliant escape plans and derring-do he'd read in Hralbomm's Wing,* the little librarian thought, *and the best I can do is,* I'm a mage!

"Don't judge him too harshly, Cobner," Brant commented. "I think he's totally new at being a slave. Which makes how he came to be here and what he really is terribly interesting."

"Faugh!" Cobner growled. "You and your secrets, Brant. They're going to be the death of you. And maybe us if we don't keep our wits about us. I say that anything—or *anyone,*" he fixed Wick with an icy stare, "that gets too mysterious ought to just get chopped on general principle. I don't like your little mysteries. I'm a good honest thief and know when I should be about my business and when I shouldn't."

"You're all thieves?" Wick blurted before he could think to make himself stop.

"Yeah," Cobner roared. "It's a fair trade for a man willing to risk his life. Better than fighting in some duke or lord's wars over land, which is only another kind of thievery. Or being an animal tender or a farmer having to fight off thieves. Everyone steals from each other in one way or another, halfer, and some of us are honest enough to admit it and be choosey about when and where we work."

Wick had to admit that the fierce dwarf had a point,

if a person was willing to accept his perspective. "Bah-barker voiced similar arguments in his book, *The Price Is Right: A Rogue's Tale,*" the little librarian said.

"He reads?" Cobner raised his eyebrows.

Brant shrugged. "So he says."

Cobner glanced back at Wick. "And where would you find books outside a mage's library, halfer? Them things are legends, myths poor people tell each other."

"No," Wick insisted. "Books did at one time exist outside of a mage's library. Every city had libraries."

"And everyone could go there?" Cobner asked. "Free?"

"No," Wick answered. "Most libraries and academies charged a small price for their use. And there were scribes who would copy books for a buyer if he or she had the price."

"I don't know anyone that would have a use for a book," Cobner said.

"The goblinkin search for them in Hanged Elf's Point," one of the humans said.

The others turned to look at him.

"I've heard them," the human said. He was tall and lanky, barely into his shaving years by the looks of him. His light brown hair swept down into his gray eyes.

"Where have you heard them talking about such things, Hamual?" Brant asked, suddenly interested.

"In a few of the taverns down near the docks," Hamual answered. "When the garrison guards search the slaver ships for disease, they always check for books as well. Orpho Kadar pays a bonus gold piece for any that are found."

Excitement flared through Wick and he couldn't still himself. "Have any books been found?"

Hamual swept hair from his face. "No. I overheard some of the goblinkin bemoaning the fact that no books had ever been found in the time that Orpho Kadar took over Hanged Elf's Point."

"Well," Brant said, "we have one." He flipped Wick's journal open again.

"Let me see that," Cobner growled. He caught the book when Brant tossed it to him and quickly flipped through the pages. He closed it. "Maybe you could claim it's a book, but I doubt you'd get a gold piece for it. There's no color in it. It's not very well done."

"Not very well done?" Wick exploded. "How can you say that? Why, you've never even seen a book before in your life. Who are you to judge my efforts?" Filled with fury and outrage, the little librarian stepped toward the dwarf. "I had to make those pages and bindings myself. I had no access to inks or colors. I used charcoal because that's all I had. And the work is very well done. I daresay I'm a very good writer. I make beautiful Qs. I've been told. And if you could read, you great oaf, you'd realize that my word choice is lyrical and—" Suddenly, he realized that he was standing on the dwarf's boots and staring squarely up at the bigger man.

Cobner glowered down at him. "You're standing on my toes."

"Oh." Wick was mortified and scared. He took a quick step back. "I'm sorry." He kept waiting for the dwarf to swing his great axe and lop his head from his shoulders.

"I believe you insulted him," Brant said calmly from behind Wick.

Cobner shook his bushy head and spat, making Wick dodge back quickly so the spittle wouldn't land on his bare feet. "One thing I do hate," the dwarf said, "is a halfer that don't know his place. Makes me all itchy inside. Maybe you ought to tell me again why I don't just whomp him and leave him here for the wolves to feed on."

"The puzzle," Brant replied. "He's an artist. I think maybe he can help us with the puzzle."

"And if he can't," Cobner asked hopefully, "then I get to whomp him?"

"Or maybe we can look into this book angle," Brant said. "Maybe we can put our new friend Wick to work producing books that we can sell to Orpho Kadar."

"You want me to write books for a goblin?" Wick asked. "Why, there's no way that I—"

Cobner ran a callused thumb along his axe blade. "Piping halfer voices get on my nerves."

Wick swallowed and quieted. He folded his arms across his chest. "I won't."

"Good," Cobner said, "because then I'll get to whomp you and that'll be the end of it."

"Oh, don't be so hard on him, Cobner," Hamual said. "He's just scared. Can't you see that?"

"I do," Cobner agreed. "And see, that's the last thing you want: a scared halfer is capable of doing darn near anything. Suddenly they think they're ten feet tall and invincible."

Hamual squatted before Wick and smiled. "Well, I like him. He makes me laugh." The young human reached into his traveling cloak and brought out an apple. "Are you hungry?"

Wick hesitated, but his growling stomach betrayed him at the sight and smell of food. The apple was deep red and smelled oh-so-sweet. "Yes."

Hamual gave the little librarian the apple and dug in his pockets again. "I think I have a bit of cheese in here, too." He produced it and handed it over.

"Thank you," Wick said. "I am in your debt."

"There's no debt between us," Hamual assured him. "It is my pleasure." He pulled his sleeves back, exposing scars on both wrists. "I've been a slave before myself. Until Brant rescued me."

"It's time to ride," Brant said. "It will be nearly dark by the time we reach the house."

Clutching the apple and cheese, Wick graciously accepted Hamual's offer to help him onto his horse. Once mounted, the little librarian turned his attention to his meal, enjoying the sweet juices from the apple and the tangy taste of the cheese. It was gone almost before he knew it. Hamual let him drink from the waterskin hanging from his saddle.

They rode deep into the Forest of Fangs and Shadows. The trees and brush were so thick that sunlight seldom penetrated the leafy canopies to touch the black loamy ground. Every now and then, a strange cry or a predatory growl came from the woods around them. Wick's skin prickled between his shoulder blades and he glanced nervously around.

His fellow travelers seldom conversed, their attention warily on the narrow game trail they followed. Cobner passed Wick's journal to the other dwarf, who looked through it for a time, then handed it to the other, older human man who didn't bother to look at it at all before passing it to Hamual beside him.

Hamual glanced at Wick and held up the journal. "May I?"

Wick hesitated only a moment. *They don't know how to read,* he reminded himself. The secrets of Greydawn Moors and the Vault of All Known Knowledge were safe from them. "Yes," he answered, and part of him hoped for some pleasant comments regarding his efforts. The Blood-Soaked Sea pirates aboard *One-Eyed Peggie* had liked his work. He couldn't see why the thieves wouldn't appreciate it. Although he was convinced that Cobner just didn't like anything.

After a time, with his balance better on the horse, a decent meal in his stomach for the first time in days, and fatigue catching up to him while he was warm in the traveling cloak, Wick slept.

"C'mon, Wick. Wake up. We're here."

The little librarian came awake with a start, feeling someone gently shaking his shoulder. He blinked and glanced at Hamual standing beside him, barely remembering the young man's name in his lethargy.

An owl screeched somewhere in the distance, followed by the keening howl of a stalking wolf. Night had fallen, filling the narrow cracks between the trees and brush till it looked like a wall of solid black around the clearing where the house was. Jhurjan the Swift and Bold sped across the star-filled sky.

The log house was old and gray from weathering the elements. It stood three stories tall and leaned against a tall cliff. Unless a rider was nearly upon it, Wick thought it would be all but invisible. Gray smoke furled from a crooked stone chimney but was quickly lost in the trees on the cliff above the house. A small lean-to built beside the house sheltered other horses.

"Where are we?" Wick asked as he eased from the saddle and dropped to the ground.

"Our house," Hamual answered.

"You live here?" As Wick watched, he saw three more men step from the house. They all had the rolling gait of dwarves and carried battle-axes and war hammers. One of them carried a lantern that barely cut through the darkness.

"Only for the time we are working in Hanged Elf's Point," Hamual replied. He held the reins of his horse and Wick's and led them into the lean-to.

"While you're working?" Wick repeated, his thoughts still foggy. He'd been dreaming of Greydawn Moors, but the dreams hadn't been happy ones. In those dreams, he'd been at the Library where he discovered he couldn't read, and in his father's shop where he discovered he could no longer put Ardamon's stubborn lantern together. He'd felt very alone and afraid in the dreams, and they had continued to spin inside his head until he'd been awakened.

"Sure." Hamual led the horses into stalls. "Thieves can only work an area so long before they are discovered and the work turns dangerous." He stripped the saddles and bridles from the horses.

Brant and the rest of the party saw to their own mounts.

"I thought all thieving was dangerous," Wick said.

"It is." Hamual closed the stall doors and tossed an armload of hay into each compartment. "But it gets even more so when the local Thieves' Guild discovers you. And the Thieves' Guild in Hanged Elf's Point pays tribute to Orpho Kadar." He handed Wick his journal back.

Wick nodded his thanks and quickly tucked the book back under his shirt. "You're not part of the local Thieves' Guild?"

"No." The young man's chest swelled proudly. "We're independents. The last of a dying breed, Brant says."

"Make sure that little halfer stays in your sight, Hamual," Cobner commanded gruffly as he tossed his battle-axe over one shoulder and walked toward the house. "If he gets loose in these woods, I don't want to be tripping over his guts in the morning after whatever might catch him in the night gets done with him."

Wick peered into the darkness surrounding the clearing. In truth, the idea of trying to escape had been immediately dismissed from his mind. If they had traveled most of the day to get to the house on horses, he had no chance of getting back to Hanged Elf's Point on foot, much less in the dark and his having slept nearly the whole trip. And what would there be in Hanged Elf's Point to return to? No, he was convinced that only death awaited him there.

"Before you bring him into the house," Brant said as he passed, "get him a bath and a change of clothes. I won't have that stink in the house when I'm trying to eat."

"I will," Hamual promised.

"Eat?" Wick's ears pricked up instantly. It had been so long since he'd been properly fed that he honestly couldn't remember what it felt like to have a full, button-bursting stomach.

"After the bath," Brant admonished. "Then we'll speak of what I bought you for, little artist. Though I have to admit that after seeing your so-called *book* I find myself somewhat enthusiastic about my decision to get you."

"If it doesn't work out," Cobner promised, "I'll whomp him good. Even the wolves out here won't find the body."

Now that, Wick thought, *is not a cheery thought.*

"You expect me to bathe in that?" Wick asked, gazing at the moon-kissed stream that wound down from the cliff overhanging the log house. Although the temperature was somewhat warmer in the mountains even after nightfall than Hanged Elf's Point fronting the sea, the little librarian was certain he'd freeze to death in the water.

"The creek is fed from a hot springs further up in the mountains," Hamual explained. "There's a volcano not far from here. And I've heard sailors in the harbor taverns talking about some not far to the south and east that belch islands up into the ocean from time to time."

Gingerly, Wick approached the creek. Then he spotted

the low gray fog that hugged the waterline and swirled within the cattails and brush on either side of the stream. Heartened, he took another step toward the water, creeping down the side of the creek. He shoved his fingers into the water and found it only the slightest bit chill. "It's not warm," he protested.

"It's not cold," Hamual promised. He carried soap, towels, and a change of clothes that looked like they belonged to one of the dwarves. "And they won't let you in to eat until you bathe. You do stink, even upwind."

Still unhappy about the whole process, Wick started taking his clothes off. "Are there any snakes in the water?"

"No. We bathe out here all the time."

"What about turtles?" Wick asked, hesitating. "Turtles can bite quite fiercely when they get hold of you, you know."

Hamual sniffed the air like a dog drawing a scent. "Do you smell it?"

"What?"

"The aroma of fresh-baked bread."

Wick sniffed, and this time he did smell the bread. The faint yeasty odor made his stomach growl. "Yes."

"Lago bakes it fresh every second or third day," Hamual said. "Today must have been one of his baking days. And only a month ago he found a beehive in the forest. He mixed the comb with butter till it's as sweet and creamy as you please." He smiled in anticipation.

"Honeyed butter?" Wick said. He stepped out into the stream and took the soap. He washed quickly. Even if the thieves killed him in the next hour, he would die with a full stomach. It was something at least. But even as he worked the soap into a lather, his curiosity remained aroused. "You said you were a slave and Brant rescued you?"

"Yes." Hamual stayed at the top of the ridge leading down to the stream, keeping watch over the forest. "My father got into debt with his gambling and sold me to goblinkin slavers. Brant freed me from that. He also took Sonne in. She was living on the streets as a cutpurse until the night she crossed a pair of elven merchants." His young face darkened. "They were despicable. Both were mercenaries filling Samarktintown with the bodies of the local population who rose up against their employer. We were barely able to get her away from them before the elves did for her. Brant chose all of us, and we all chose Brant when the time came. I'd never had a true family before, Wick, but I have one now."

Hamual's words, spoken with quiet and honest conviction, touched Wick. When he'd first met Brant, the man had scared him. It was nice to know that there was another side to him.

"He's a good man," Hamual said.

"For a thief?" Wick asked.

"We're all thieves," Hamual said. "It's the only trade we've found that supports us and allows us freedom from being under some lord's protection. You take a lord's protection, you also take his burdens and goals on as your own to die for. None of us have found a lord we'd be willing to die for."

"What about Brant?"

There was no hesitation in Hamual's answer. "I would die for him, and I know that he would die for me should the time come for it."

"How many of you are there?" Wick scrubbed soap through his hair and beard. Truth be known, it felt good to do so.

"Twelve, counting Brant himself. We lost two men to the Thieves' Guild swords less than a week ago. That's how we knew they were aware of us."

"Then isn't it time you were getting out of Hanged

Elf's Point?" Finished with his bath, Wick stepped from
the creek and took the towel the tall young human offered.

"We are," Hamual said. "But Brant is certain we can
pull off one more job before we go. Until he found you,
he was ready to give up on that. But now—" The young
man shrugged. "We'll see. Brant is a very careful man."

"Except when he gets obsessed with other people's
secrets," Wick said.

"Then," Hamual agreed, "Brant gets really, really dangerous. It's as if he doesn't even recognize risk any
more. That drives Cobner crazy."

Although the clothes he'd been given were dwarves',
Wick found they didn't fit well at all. He had to roll the
shirtsleeves and pants legs up, and the clothing still
bagged on him outrageously. He felt like, and was sure
he resembled, an orphan child. He sat at the long table
that filled one of the rooms in the log house and helped
himself to the wonderful dishes that had been prepared
and laid out.

At first, the little librarian had been timid about joining in, wondering if Brant would consider the food simply another torture he could use to get at the secrets
Wick wasn't willing to share. So he'd casually helped
himself to the buttercrunch sautéed turnips, braised wild
onions, the roasted cucumbers steeped in vinegar pepper,
the thin vanilla crepes rolled around generous dollops of
fresh-picked raspberries, and washed it all down with
huckleberry tea. When no one said anything, he went
back for more, adding spiced and smashed sweet potatoes covered in walnuts, yeast rolls two at a time, carrot
and garlic pudding, green beans, peas, and slices of
cantaloupe and sawtooth melon picked clean of the vicious barbed seeds that gave it the name.

Talk was sparse during the meal, and Wick enjoyed that as well. It was good to dine with people who knew that a meal was a meal and conversation was conversation, and that the two shouldn't needlessly be commingled. Dining with the band of thieves was almost like dining among dwellers. Except that dwellers wouldn't possibly kill a fellow diner once the meal was finished.

Gradually, Brant, Sonne, Hamual, and the others sat back in wonder as they watched the little librarian eat. Wick saw awe on all their faces and tried to ignore it. *If this is to be my last meal, then let me enjoy it.* Two weeks of starving at the hands of goblinkin slavers was too much to forget.

"I swear," Lago said in quiet wonderment, "the little halfer's going to burst himself before he gives up that plate, he is."

The other thieves laughed, and Wick pointedly ignored them.

Lago, the little librarian had discovered, was an interesting fellow. He was an elderly dwarf who'd grown old and bent, but he was an excellent cook. He liked to sing old drinking songs while he cooked and baked and served out. His voice boomed and filled the small log house.

Only Cobner was able to eat more than Wick, even though the grumpy dwarf had started before the little librarian. Wick was convinced that Cobner hadn't eaten all that he had out of hunger, but rather out of spite. And when he finally pushed his plate away as well, Cobner didn't look happy about having eaten.

Wick was in that nice area between being totally sated and on the verge of being miserable.

"Now this here's a story," Lago said as he and Hamual cleared the dishes from the table, "to tell your grandkids, it is. When have you ever seen such a little man eat so much at a single sitting?"

"Never," Sonne exclaimed, folding her hands together and staring at Wick in delight. "I don't know if he's going to be able to help you out much with your puzzle, Brant, but he's going to be entertaining."

"We don't need entertainment," Brant said, standing up from the table. "What we need is elucidation. Let's talk in the main room."

Sleeves and pants legs flopping loosely, having to keep one hand on the pants to keep them up because he had no belt, Wick followed the thieves into another room on the lowest floor of the log house.

The main room was large and spacious. Three long couches and several chairs filled the open area before the large fireplace where a well-laid fire burned merrily. Brant seated himself nearest the fire, then took a huge, fragrant pouch from a small chest at his feet. The chest also held several pipes.

"Do you smoke?" Brant asked.

"Yes," Wick said at once. He gratefully accepted the pipe, a filling, and then a light from his host-captor. The little librarian settled back into a couch between Hamual and one of the other big dwarves, feeling incredibly small and almost lost among them.

"As you know," Brant said, "we're thieves. But we're independent thieves, not owing allegiance to any king or any flag. The world is chaos these days, and finding a place to settle down where a man can feel safe from oppressors is all but impossible." He lit his pipe and puffed, showing great satisfaction. "So we have become a family in our own right. We came to Hanged Elf's Point three months ago, and we set about our business with professionalism and pride. Unfortunately, Orpho Kadar controls the local Thieves' Guild, which is incredibly large and successful. You see how this can be a problem?"

Wick puffed on his pipe contentedly, hanging on

every word. No one at the Library had ever known real thieves, and he knew if he survived and got back there the things he could learn could be fascinating and enlightening reading.

"Do you know how a Thieves' Guild works?" Brant asked.

Wick took the pipe from his mouth, watching how everyone in the room turned to look at him. Cobner scowled at him evilly, leading the little librarian to believe the big dwarf was only waiting for him to prove himself unworthy of Brant's attention. Wick cleared his throat. "Not so much how, but I think I understand why."

"Tell me what you know," Brant encouraged.

"Every king, lord, or ruler knows anytime they get a large group of people into an urban setting that this leads to the development and growth of an infrastructure of those who prey on that urban area," Wick expounded.

Cobner's scowl deepened.

"Exactly," Brant agreed, nodding to himself. "Go on."

"Once this criminal element becomes established inside the city," Wick said, recalling the structure of Forbish Hagladen's *Treatise on Merchant Cities and Purveyors of Opportunity; or Tales of the Shadow Prince,* "and such an occurrence can't be completely thwarted, the rulers have only two choices to make."

"And they are?" Brant asked.

"They can elect to take the strongest measures against these thieves and black market dealers," Wick said. "However, if they choose to do that, they will soon find themselves locking up a great many of their populace as well, because easy money is a great temptation. And work comes and goes inside the city, not always enough to feed a man and a large family. If the rules stays with that course long enough—"

"He eventually earns the enmity of the very people he wanted to protect," Brant finished. He smiled delightedly. "For an artist of no mean skills, you are a very astute person."

Wick blushed modestly, then realized how out of place that was seated in a room with people who would very likely kill him before morning if they decided they couldn't trust him.

"What, then," Brant asked, "is the other course?"

"To embrace the criminal element," Wick answered immediately. Although when he'd first started reading on the subject, he'd felt greatly confused. Grandmagister Ludaan had sat with him one afternoon and explained everything Hagladen had laid out. "At this point, the ruler must search for a man who is strong enough to take and hold the criminal element, who is willing to risk his own life, to hold the criminals to an accountable code of thievery."

"Fascinating," Brant said. He glanced around at the others as if proud of himself. "And what would that code be?"

"The ruler and the master thief," Wick said, "have to come to terms about who is to be robbed, in what manner, and what areas are off-limits. Those terms can be renegotiated at any time. In recompense, the master thief is given control of several legitimate businesses—"

"Such as warehouses and taverns along the docks," Brant said.

"So that the legitimate earnings will tide the master thief over during periods of the ruler's active efforts against these crimes must take place to soothe the citizens and allay their fears." Wick puffed on his pipe.

"And what does the ruler get out of this?" Brant asked.

"A—to a degree—controllable criminal element," Wick said. "As well as a percentage of criminal profits to shore up the treasury when new roads must be built and when the ruler has to appear magnanimous to his or her people."

"Splendid!" Brant said. "And the foremost job of any Thieves Guild is to—?"

"To keep out other thieves who don't obey the code or who take too much from the criminal profits."

"Exactly," Brant said. "Which would be us at this time." He relit his pipe. "You surprise me with your knowledge. Maybe you can read as you claim you can."

For a moment, there was silence in the room, then all the thieves laughed at the very notion.

Wick's face burned, but he said nothing.

"In these last few weeks," Brant said, "we've drawn the attention of not only the Thieves' Guild, but also of Orpho Kadar. Either of those would be dangerous. Together, venturing any longer in Hanged Elf's Point is decidedly foolhardy."

"Yet that is what you are hoping to do," Wick said.

"Precisely. I'll be right back." Brant got to his feet and left the room. He returned momentarily carrying a purple velvet bag. "We discovered this among the goods of one of our heists. While we've been in Hanged Elf's Point, we've targeted, isolated, and robbed various members of trading guilds within the city. No one really too big, and only those who would be worth the risk involved. We've been quite successful. But this bag," he shook it for emphasis and clacking echoed over the room, "was well hidden by one of Orpho Kadar's favorite goblinkin tradesmen. The man has been in Hanged Elf's Point almost as long as Orpho himself." He paused, shaking the bag. "Would you like to see what's in here?"

Wick regarded the bag with trepidation and curiosity. True to his dweller nature, any possible container not directly open to his sight intrigued him. But at the same time, if he couldn't make any sense of what was in the bag, he knew Cobner would deal mercilessly with him.

"Yes," the little librarian answered.

Without hesitation, Brant poured the contents of the bag into his hand.

16

The Mystery of the Keldian Mosaic

At first, Wick thought the bag in Brant's hand only contained jewels and he didn't know what had been so confusing to the man. They spilled out in a cavalcade of shiny, bright colors: emeralds, sapphires, rubies, diamonds, and amethysts.

It was, the little librarian knew, a small fortune in its own right.

"Do you see?" Brant asked quietly.

At first, Wick didn't. His inability to do so scared him. For a moment, all the little librarian could see was Cobner's malicious grin. Then his eyes, sharp little dweller eyes that never lost their allure for anything that sparkled and shined, saw what Brant had to be referring to.

"The gems fit together," Wick breathed raptly. Before he knew it, his hand was out, reaching for the pile that lay gleaming in Brant's palm.

"Yes," Brant said. "Do you know what this is?"

"It's Keldian," Wick said.

His reply made Brant a little nervous. The man drew the handful of jewels back. "What is Keldian?"

"Those jewels," Wick exclaimed excitedly. He pushed himself up and walked over to Brant. "They fit together to make a mosaic, a picture."

"A picture of what?"

"I don't know," Wick answered truthfully. "Whatever this particularly Keldian felt was important."

"I've never heard of Keldians," Brant said.

"Neither have I," Sonne agreed, coming closer herself. Bright interest shone in her eyes.

"If you ask me," Cobner said, "I think he's making up what he's saying on the spot to keep from getting whomped."

"No," Wick insisted. "The fact that you haven't heard of the Keldians only attests to how old this thing is that you found." He hesitated, almost not daring to ask his next question. Except that he had to. "Are you sure you have all of it?"

"I don't know," Brant answered. "We took all that was there."

"If you have all of it," Wick said, "you can't possibly imagine how much such a thing is worth."

"How much do you think?" Brant asked. "In gold pieces?"

Wick looked at the man and blinked in astonishment. "In gold pieces?"

"Yes. A nice, round, tidy figure will do quite nicely," Brant said. "Oh, and don't worry. I won't hold you to that figure. It really depends on whether you're desperate or the buyer is desperate when you try to sell something like this. Sometimes you can get more if you sell it, and sometimes you can get more when you break it up."

"Sell it?" Wick exclaimed, unable to believe his poor savaged ears that throbbed painfully in his excitement. "Break it up?" He stuttered for a moment, trying to regain his composure. "You can't do that!"

Brant frowned a little. "I think you're getting overly interested in these gems, little artist. These belong to us. Not you."

"They could be part of an important Keldian historical find," Wick said.

"History," Brant declared, "was yesterday. I'm not interested in yesterdays. Only how much I might be able to sell these for on some tomorrow."

"Please," Wick pleaded. "I would like very much to see these."

Brant hesitated. "And after seeing your reaction, I can see that you do. However, now I find myself not overly enthusiastic about letting you see them. I had thought with your artist's eye you might see something in these gems that I hadn't. With it so apparently true, I'll admit that I am somewhat discomfited."

Wick stood his ground, trembling slightly in his eagerness. He had read about the Keldian mosaics in the Library, but none of them had been shipped there that had been found so far. Of course, there were still numerous rooms to go through at the Vault. He breathed out and tried to be calm. "You brought me here to look at those gems," he stated plainly as he could. "You would be remiss in your risk if you didn't let me do it."

"How do you know about these . . . these Keldian mosaics?" Brant asked.

"I read about them," Wick answered.

No one laughed this time.

"Maybe I can put it together," the little librarian said. "At least let me try. If I can, then you'll better know what it is that you have." He couldn't bring himself to say *sell*.

"I will have someone watching you the whole time," Brant warned.

"That's fine." Wick held out his hands and felt the cool, delicious weight of the stones as Brant poured them into his palms. They were small, barely the size of his littlest fingernail. Human hands or dwarven hands would be hard-pressed to handle them properly to see to the fittings. "I'll need a table to work on. A good lantern.

And maybe some jeweler's tools if some of the fittings have been damaged."

"To the dining room, then," Lago said. "It has the biggest table in the house."

Wick walked carefully as he followed the old dwarf. His fear of his newfound associates melted away as he faced the mystery and possibilities he held in his hands. They needed him, true, but even greater than their need was his to find out what mystery the Keldian mosaic hid.

"The Keldian elves," Wick said as he nudged a small ruby into place next to the last one he had fitted, "lived far east of Dream. Or, rather, Hanged Elf's Point as you know it. So I don't know what one was doing there."

Brant, Sonne, Lago, Cobner, Hamual, and the other thieves sat around the dining table as the little librarian worked.

"But then again," Wick went on, thinking out loud, "these gems might not have belonged to a Keldian elf. They may have belonged to someone who'd ordered a mosaic made."

"And if it didn't belong to a Keldian elf?" Sonne asked.

"Then it's still an important find," Wick said, wanting them to be very clear about that.

"But if it did belong to a Keldian elf?" Brant pressed.

"Then it will be even more important." Wick sifted through the rubies and didn't find one the proper shape to fit to the last one he'd slipped into place. *A change of color then?* He started trying amethysts. Already his back and shoulders ached from the work he'd done. It was nearly morning. For the first few hours, the thieves hadn't talked at all, carefully watching what he was doing and not wanting to break his concentration. *Please let all the pieces be here.* The intrigue was killing him.

"Why?" Hamual asked.

"Because each master craftsman created his life's work, a piece that revealed something of great value to whomever was able to ferret it out."

"You're talking about treasure, aren't you?" Brant asked.

"I don't know," Wick said. "Sometimes the Keldian elves created mosaics that told their life stories."

"Oh," Brant said sarcastically, "and wouldn't that just be delightful? Long-dead Keldian elves probably have the best stories to tell."

"I think it would be delightful," Wick said honestly. "You wouldn't believe how much is unknown and speculated about regarding the Keldian elves. They were master craftsmen who worked for kings and queens throughout the world, but only if they chose to."

"And quite possibly," Brant said, "you couldn't even begin to comprehend how little I care. I don't know any Keldian elves, so they have no secrets that would interest me. Only the living have the best secrets to know, little artist. Especially if they want to keep those secrets hidden from others. They often pay handsomely for that."

Wick ignored the comment and played to his own mounting excitement. The seventeenth amethyst he tried that looked like it might fit slid smoothly into place. He reached for the amethysts again, certain that the next piece he was looking for was there.

"That's a skull," Sonne said, leaning over Wick's shoulder late the next afternoon.

Eyes burning, shoulders aching, Wick looked at the small skull made up of twelve amethysts and two dark sapphires that represented the eyesockets. The skull sat by itself on the table. "Yes."

Sonne placed a fresh mug of huckleberry tea on the table beside him.

"Thank you," he said as he searched for the next piece of the mosaic.

"Do you know what it is yet?" Sonne asked, taking a seat beside him.

"No," Wick admitted, and his impatience to know pushed at him incessantly. He'd gotten stumped a few times, so had searched out new stones and begun pieces again. At the moment, he had five different pieces of the mosaic going. Instead of coming faster, the gems seemed to fit into place even more slowly. "I don't even know if it's all here."

"Have you told that to Brant?"

"No." Wick grimaced. "I shouldn't have told you." He wiped perspiration from his face. He looked at the young girl hopefully. "Please don't let him make me stop until I find out if I can do this. I need to finish this, Sonne. Really I do." He searched for words to explain how he felt but none came easily. These people were thieves, not Librarians entrusted with keeping back the dark ignorance of the world that Lord Kharrion had tried to unleash.

"I know," she said. "Brant knows, too." She shook her head. "I don't know what drives you, halfer, and I don't know how many of the stories you tell are true, but I know that you will finish this—if it can be done."

"I will," Wick promised. And he could almost hear Grandmagister Frollo in his head, telling him that he was working far above his abilities as a Third Level Librarian, that he was doomed to failure. *I am more than a Third Level Librarian,* Wick thought forcefully.

"But Hamual and Karick saw goblin soldiers scouting the foothills this morning. Luckily, they skirted past the game trail that leads to this place and never saw Hamual and Karick."

"What are the goblinkin doing up here?" Wick sorted through the emeralds, searching for one that would fit the stone he was working on now. He knew from overhearing conversations between the thieves that the goblinkin laxly patrolled the main trade roads in and out of Hanged Elf's Point.

"Searching for us," Sonne replied. "What else could it be?"

Wick didn't know and couldn't even hazard a guess. He took a sip of huckleberry tea and refocused on his work. The emerald he picked up didn't work. Neither did the next ten. He sighed in exasperation.

"You should get some rest, halfer. We have extra beds in the house. Sleeping in the saddle the way you did yesterday did you no good at all."

"I know," Wick replied. "Just let me work a little while longer." He wasn't even aware of when Sonne left the room.

Wick woke with a start, hearing voices. He blinked his eyes open and discovered he was on one of the couches in the log house's main room, though he had no idea of how he had gotten there. The room was dark and the fire in the fireplace had burned low. He guessed that it was probably early morning. A heavy blanket covered him and a slight chill lay over the room.

Nightmares of Lord Kharrion and the battles Wick had read about had filled the little librarian's mind while he'd unwittingly slept. He was so fatigued that he hadn't even known he'd been dreaming till he woke. And he really wasn't sure that he wasn't dreaming now.

"The goblinkin patrol is camped only a few hours from here," Brant was saying. "I don't know how much longer we can hole up even here."

"We'd be better off if we could just pick up and go,"

Cobner growled. "If we wait too long, the goblinkin will cut off the Trade Roads and the North Road. We won't have any other choice except to cut through the Forest of Fangs and Shadows and strike out for the halfer villages at Blackgate Cove, and there's nothing to say that those really exist."

"So do we stay or go?" Brant asked.

Wick listened to the silence for a moment, his heart beating in his chest as he drifted in and out of sleep. Over the past few days of working so diligently at the puzzle, he'd talked with most of the thieves. Brant gave them all voice in what they were about to do, but when it came down to it, the master thief made the decisions for the group. He treated them like family, and from the things Hamual and Sonne said while they were visiting, the little librarian knew they all owed some part of their lives to Brant. Despite his gruff manner, he cared deeply for his people and they all knew it, but he would never allow his leadership to be questioned.

"I say we stay," Sonne said. "One more day. The little halfer has worked at this harder than anyone I've ever seen. He's earned that much."

"Enough to risk our necks?" Cobner protested. "We don't owe him anything. He's nothing to us. In fact, it could well be that his disappearance from Hanged Elf's Point is what renewed the goblinkin's interest in finding us."

"No," Brant said. "Wick was bound for the arena. If he'd stayed there, he'd be dead today. And he is something to us. I bought him, and I'll not see him so readily abandoned just because his presence causes a bit of a hardship on us."

"We're not talking about a hardship here," Cobner argued. "We're talking about getting outright killed by the goblinkin or Fohmyn Mhout's dratted Purple Cloaks.

They've been searching for us since we took those blasted gems."

"Cobner," Brant spoke sharply. "There's not been a person added to this group who's not caused a bit of a hardship at the time. Even yourself."

Silence filled the room for a time.

"Is that what you're talking about?" Cobner asked. "Adding that little halfer to our group?"

"He doesn't fit in with the other dwellers we've seen from these countries," Brant said. "We know that from the time that Hamual and Karick observed the slave pens and the work crews the little artist was assigned to."

Wick was surprised that he'd been watched and had had no clue. Of course, at the time he'd been concerned with how things were going between himself and the other dwellers. And with just simply surviving.

"We could let him go," Cobner said.

"And since when has that been our way?" Lago demanded.

"The little fellow wouldn't make it in the wild," Hamual said quietly. "I've watched him the night before. He's not used to being outside. Wherever he's from, he's lived a sheltered life."

"I'm telling you now," Cobner said, "adding that halfer to our group would be a mistake. It would mark us to anyone. If you're worried about him suffering, I could take him out into the woods, slit his throat, and leave him."

"Could you do that, Cobner?" Sonne demanded. "Truly?"

"If I thought the little halfer was going to be responsible for the deaths of me or any of you," Cobner said, "I'd slit his throat and sing 'The Engagement of Tokner Dweet' at the same time."

"The Engagement of Tokner Dweet," Wick knew, was a particularly humorous dwarven tale told in taverns when the audience was deeply into their cups. The little librarian shuddered. *I will never again think of that song in the same fashion.*

"Enough," Brant said with quiet authority. "I took responsibility for the little artist the day I purchased him from Boolian Toadas. I had a feeling about those gems and the way they appeared to fit together. Look at this table, the little man has done more than any of us have been able to."

"It's not our way to take in strays," Cobner growled.

"Cobner," the master thief said pointedly, "were it not for strays, I'd have no family at all. I've lost one family to an axe of a headsman ordered by a tyrant who saw fit to proclaim himself king. I'll not lose another one to dissent within our ranks."

"And should it come time that the little halfer proves dangerous to us?" Cobner demanded.

"Then I'll do what needs to be done," Brant answered. "As I have ever done. But if this mosaic can lead us to other riches, need I remind you that we need it? We've lived well enough while we've plied our trade in Hanged Elf's Point, but it takes time—and *coin*—to set up an operation in another village where we are not known. If the little artist can help us do that, can help me take care of this family, then I'm going to wait."

"One more day," Cobner said.

"One more day," Brant said.

Tired and chilled from the talk of who was going to slit his throat should the time come, head swimming from fatigue, Wick forced himself from the couch. He stumbled into the dining room without a word, watching as the thieves slowly moved away from the table.

"Wick," Brant said, smiling uncertainly. "I didn't know you were awake. I hope we didn't wake you with our banter."

"No," Wick lied. Momentary thoughts of trying to escape through the woods flitted through his mind. But where would he go? He didn't know anything about the geography of the surrounding countryside, and all the dwellers in these lands seemed to be the property of one group or another.

"Good. We were just concerned about your progress. It seems you've done a lot with these gems, but maybe we need to face the possibility that not all of them are here."

The little librarian faced the master thief. "I can finish the mosaic. I almost have it now." He swept his gaze over the table where the five clumps of jewels sat in the loose debris of at least a hundred more jewels to go. "I realize my mistake now."

"Time is against us, my little artist."

Wick sat in the chair where he'd sat for nearly thirty hours straight before he'd passed out and evidently been carried to the couch. He reached for the piece with the amethyst skull on it, then swiftly slid an emerald into place. He'd awoke with most of the design in his head; a gift from his unresting subconscious mind. "This isn't a Keldian mosaic master's swan song," the little librarian declared. His fingers started to come awake now and his eyesight sharpened. His excitement increased despite the uncertainty of his future with the thieves.

"Then what is it?" Brant asked.

"It's a map," Wick declared. Six more emeralds flew through his fingers, then he reached for one of the other clumps, fitting it easily now. His fingers moved more confidently, and he could feel the excitement suddenly infusing the thieves gathered around him.

"A map of what?" Brant asked softly.

"I don't know," Wick admitted. He put another twenty gems together, then added another piece of the mosaic. Only two of the big chunks remained, and less than fifty gems. "But it's three-dimensional, see?" He held the three assembled pieces together in his hand and showed them.

"It's a room," Hamual said.

"A room with a skull in it," Sonne added, biting her lower lip excitedly.

"You see," Wick said, "I'd been thinking of the mosaic as two-dimensional, and I guess my preconception kept my fingers from knowing what to do. Two-dimensional means that the mosaic would only have height and width. The third dimension added is depth." In minutes, he had the pieces all together. And in the same breath, he knew what the mosaic represented.

Brant took the mosaic from Wick and placed it in the center of the table. It glittered and sparked under the lantern light. Scarcely as large as Brant's hand, the mosaic stood three inches deep. It gave the illusion of walls around the rectangle that resembled a bed where the skull sat.

"What is it?" Lago asked.

"It's a crypt," Wick answered, suddenly feeling colder.

"And what would be so special about a crypt?" Brant asked.

"This." Wick flicked a finger against the back of the skull. Neatly attached by a clever linchpin created by two emeralds, the skull flipped forward and stayed there. Beneath the skull was one of the two black opals that had been in the bag of gems Brant had given him.

"What is it?" Cobner asked.

"A key," Sonne answered in a hoarse whisper, her quick eyes flashing confidently.

"A key to what?" Hamual asked.

Wick moved his finger again, moving aside a clever arrangement of gems that formed what looked like a portrait on the wall behind the skull. There, made of the second chipped black opal, was the outline of a keyhole.

The little librarian traced the rectangle created only in relief by the placement of the gems. "This door," Wick said.

"What does it go to?" Brant asked.

"I don't know," Wick replied.

"This could be someone's idea of a joke," Cobner pointed out. "A fool's errand with only death waiting at the other end."

"But it could be treasure," Brant said, black eyes afire. "Who would go to this kind of trouble without what lies on the other side of that door being worth a fortune?" He shook his head. "No. I'm willing to take the risk. Who's in it with me?"

All of the other thieves agreed, with Cobner waiting till the very last.

"Good," Brant said enthusiastically, "it's settled." He reached out and tousled Wick's hair. "And you, my little artist, you have turned out to be one fine investment. Now, what can you tell me about where to find this crypt?"

Wick turned the mosaic over in his hands, revealing the small symbol made up of emeralds and rubies that had been created by joining two of the five pieces he had assembled. "Only that it will bear this—the symbol of a crowing cock." He tapped the symbol with a finger.

A ruby comb and ruby spots on his wing topped the emerald rooster. Dark blue sapphires made up the cock's tail feathers. The animal symbol was set inside an amethyst banner created by the joining of the pieces at the top.

"A crypt should be easy enough to find," Brant said, "even in Hanged Elf's Point. If we leave first thing this morning—only a few hours from now by the looks of the sky—we could make the city again a couple hours before sunset."

Despite the fact that Hanged Elf's Point no longer dealt with graveyards, and that the only gravediggers were slaves used to dig mass graves for arena victims in too many pieces to properly dispose of to the sharks in the harbor, there were still a number of graveyards. After they'd arrived in the city shortly before sundown, Brant had divided everyone into six two-man groups, keeping Wick with Sonne and him.

The little librarian had managed to sleep again in the saddle during the trip even though he'd been highly nervous about the trip back into the city. That ability to sleep had astounded all of the thieves, but they'd never tried to sleep in a dweller house with younger children scampering everywhere. During the trip, they'd only had one close encounter with a goblin patrol that had missed their hiding place.

Wick sat astride the horse Brant had assigned to him, the reins actually in his hands now, and stared at the wrought iron gates of Serene Haven Cemetery leaning haphazardly in their moorings. Trees and brush had overgrown the cemetery, and several of the crypts had been damaged beyond repair by the spell Lord Kharrion had used to reshape the Shattered Coast.

Brant took the lead, a shadow barely limned against the darkness crouching in the cemetery by Jhurjan the Swift and Bold's passing overhead. The horse's hooves clopped through the silence overlying the cemetery. The sounds of the city taverns still open this late at night seemed far away.

Wick rode after Brant, his eyes roving constantly. Sonne rode behind him, and from the way she glanced around, Wick was certain she wasn't any happier about the location than he was.

As Wick studied the graves, he noticed that several of

them were open. Ornate caskets stripped of their gold inlays and accessories lay crushed and broken on the ground. Thieves hadn't stopped at stealing from their victims when they'd been alive; they'd also stolen from the ones long dead as well.

Am I any different from them? Wick asked himself unhappily. Surely what they proposed to do was no different than the pilferers that had left skeletons scattered in their wave on the ground. But someone had left the mosaic behind, a map for someone clever and knowledgeable enough to find and decipher. *Why leave a map behind if someone didn't intend for whatever it was that had been hidden to be found?* Whatever it was, it had to be important. *But what would someone possibly hide in a crypt?*

Fog drifted in from the sea, rolling up over the harbor and the nine ledges leading to the city proper. Clumps of fog drifted like twisting ghosts through the cemetery. Wick strove to reconcile himself with what they were about to do.

Voices echoed faintly across the cemetery grounds, coming from the city proper on the other side of the broken gate. Wagon wheels clattered across the cobblestone streets. In the fog and the darkness, Wick barely made out the dim lanterns that glowed through the windows of businesses still plying the late night trade. Goblinkin night patrols under Orpho Kadar's command passed through the streets as well, their faces grim and hard beneath the wavering light of the flaming street torches and the lanterns they carried.

Twice, the little librarian spotted lean wolf-shapes dragging bones through the tangle of grave markers in the cemetery. His horse had shied from the strong smell of the wolf, but luckily it hadn't bolted.

Sonne lifted the crossbow that hung from her saddle pommel and readied it. The arming click echoed hollowly in the cemetery. The presence of the weapon made Wick feel a little better, but was offset by the fact that it was behind him.

Brant explored the cemetery systematically. His attention shifted from crypt to crypt as the breeze blew over him. He seemed not to even notice the chill that made Wick shiver.

Less than twenty minutes later—twenty *long* minutes by Wick's estimation—the master thief reined in his horse. Brant lifted his lantern, shoving the bull's-eye cover out of the way. The cone of yellow light pierced the foggy darkness and lit up the broken remnants of a stained glass window at the back of a crypt.

If we hadn't known to look for a crowing cock, Wick thought, staring at the scattered pieces of stained glass lying on the ground and remaining in the crypt's small, inset window, *we wouldn't have found it.*

All that remained of the rooster in the inset window was the red and green head, which could have easily been mistaken for a red flower. The white banner around it had been created from bleached limestone that had long since turned black with stain. Weeds and brush covered most of the broken shards that had fallen to the ground, but Brant's careful eye, then the little librarian's, caught sight of them.

"Hold my horse," Brant whispered to Wick as he closed the lantern's bull's-eye again. "Keep it at the ready." The master thief raised his leg over the saddle pommel and slid lithely to the ground. He handed the reins of his horse to the little librarian.

Dressed in black as he was, Brant melted into the shadows. Only his movement and Wick's certain knowledge of where he was revealed him to the little librarian. The master thief kept one hand on his sword. Wick's horse snorted and stamped its feet, shifting under him. Wick kept hold of his saddle horn and watched the cemetery grounds fence, thinking that some of the roving guards were going to catch them at any moment.

Sonne urged her own horse into motion, guiding it into a flanking position next to Wick's so she had a clear field of fire.

Brant stepped around to the front of the crypt and peered inside. The wrought-iron doors hung ajar, draped in shadows. A leg bone—whether elven or human, Wick couldn't tell—lay in the doorway. Drawing his sword, the master thief stepped on into the crypt.

Wick's breath caught in his throat. Although he had only spent a few days with the thieves, the little librarian had come to respect the way they conducted their lives with each other. Except for Cobner, all of them were open about their feelings for each other. Wick knew it was due largely to the example Brant set. Thievery wasn't a career the little librarian would ever choose for himself, but he respected the way Brant went about it. And he worried about the master thief now because without Brant around, Cobner might well make good his threat to slit the little librarian's throat in some quiet part of the woods.

A long minute went by, then another. Wick fidgeted, glancing back over his shoulder as another pair of goblinkin guards rode past the cemetery's entrance. He breathed a sigh of relief when neither of them even looked into the graveyard.

Another minute went by.

Wick watched the crypt entrance, starting to worry more. *Something could have gotten Brant and we wouldn't even know. The foul creature could be there in the darkness, waiting for its chance at us.* The little librarian scented the air for fetid breath and animal musk, then listened intently for the sound of claws or teeth scraping along bone. The darkness remained complete, uninterrupted. *We might not be alone. There could be a*

whole den of foul creatures camped out in that crypt.
He glanced at Sonne and whispered, "Maybe we
should—"

"Quiet!" she shot back. "We won't leave Brant." Her
eyes never left the crypt entrance.

Chastised, Wick fell silent. He glanced at the trees
overhead, making certain nothing was climbing through
the naked, dead branches overhead to get at them unexpectedly.

Then a shadow eased from the crypt.

Standing up in her stirrups, Sonne lifted the crossbow.

"Sonne," Brant called out softly, then stepped out into
the moonlight so he could be clearly seen for only an
instant. He didn't look happy. "Someone has been in the
crypt. The key isn't there." He crossed to his horse, taking the reins from Wick.

"Well, it was a long shot," Wick said, more to convince himself than the master thief. "There's no telling
how long ago the key was left in the crypt. Did you find
the keyhole?" He at least wanted affirmation that he'd
been right about the mosaic.

"I found it," Brant responded. "That's why I want you
to take a look in the crypt as well."

"Me?" That was surely the last thing Wick wanted to
do. "Surely you don't think that I could find something
when you—"

"Get off your horse," Sonne ordered. "We don't have
time to waste."

"I agree," Wick said. "That's why I thought it would
be better if we just—"

Brant pierced him with a black-eyed glance. "Now."

Wishing he were almost anywhere but in Serene Haven Cemetery, Wick stepped down from the horse's saddle. He had to drop the last couple feet to reach the
ground and very nearly fell on his rump. He joined Brant
at the crypt's entrance.

"I want another perspective, little artist," Brant confided in a soft voice. "Perhaps I am missing something." He swept aside the black silk sheet hanging over the door to the crypt and gestured the little librarian inside.

17

Skull-diggery!

Filled with dread, Wick stepped through the crypt entrance. He hadn't even seen Brant put the black silk sheet up, but now the little librarian understood why he hadn't seen a light inside the crypt.

Brant placed rocks on the tail of the sheet to keep it in place against the gentle wind that followed them inside. The master thief took a glass candle from inside his cloak. For the first time in weeks, Wick smelled the fragrant odor of lummin juice. The sudden sharp sweet scent of it made him immediately homesick. Brant lit the candle with a tinderbox, then held the light high in the room so the soft glow filled the crypt.

For one mad moment, Wick imagined that perhaps some mind-controlling beast had overcome Brant in the darkness and the master thief might even now be setting him up for another such creature to slither in through his ears the way the mind spiders had in Cathel Ool's *Cerebral Crawlers and Other Puppetmasters*. The little librarian glanced around the crypt fearfully, wondering if he would see the spiders swinging from their silken strands in the gloom.

A stone casket occupied the center of the room. Shelves lined two of the walls, but whatever had occupied them had long since been removed. Wick believed they had probably contained family histories and tokens of love or friendship. All of it was gone now. Stubs of wax candles stood on the shelves, and ashy remains of campfires offered mute testimony that others had occasionally used the crypt as a respite from the elements.

The casket's stone cover lay in three broken chunks on the floor. Some of the carved stones that made up the flooring had been pried free and used to make the campfires. No body remained inside the casket, and only scraps of stained, deep red material stood out from the edges. The casket didn't contain a key—or even a body.

"It's empty?" Wick said.

"Yes," Brant replied, sounding irritated.

"What about the body?" Wick asked. Now that his curiosity was aroused—and there were no mind spiders lurking about—the little librarian found himself caught up in the mystery.

"There are three. One is obviously fresh." Brant moved the lummin juice candle to the far corner of the crypt. Two skeletons and a dead man that had been there for months occupied the corner. All of them had been stripped of their clothing.

"Did you check the inside of the casket?" Wick asked.

"Thoroughly," Brant answered. "If there were any hidden or recessed areas, I would have found them."

Wick believed him. Brant had shown himself to be quite capable. "Show me the keyhole."

Brant moved the candle to the back of the room.

On one hand, the little librarian wanted nothing more than to quit the crypt. Fear slithered restlessly through him, staying barely under control. He followed the master thief to the back wall. The broken stained-glass window let in the wind and a cautious curl of curious fog.

"Those who've been in this crypt before have never found the keyhole," Brant said softly. "And it's not a painting that the keyhole is hidden behind." He brushed at the hammock webs he'd broken in his earlier exploration of the crypt.

Soot from the campfires and years of accumulated dirt and grit had caked over the picture of the elven profile rendered on the stone there in bas-relief. Brant pulled away the hammock webs, then caught the point of his dagger under one corner of the picture. Stone rasped against metal for a moment, then the picture pulled forward with a creak.

"Concealed hinges," Brant said. "Some of the finest work I've ever seen. If you hadn't told me about the existence of it I wouldn't have known it was here." He held the candle closer to the small door. "And look how thin this door is." He held it between his fingers. "Fantastic workmanship."

Wick ran his fingers along the small door. It was hardly as wide as a sheet of paper and looked like it had been crafted of a single sheet of slate dyed alabaster to match the crypt's interior. Rainwater had left rust stains over decades or even hundreds of years.

"Do you recognize the elf in the picture?" Brant asked.

Studying the stern features, Wick experienced a momentary feeling of recognition, but it quickly faded. The elf looked to be in his middle years, with the high cheekbones and pointed ears of his kind. His beardless cheeks gave him a more youthful appearance than his eyes gave him reason to claim. The elf had been a man used to getting his way, and the little librarian wondered how the elf had died. Had it been during the carnage wreaked by Lord Kharrion when the Goblin Lord had reshaped the Shattered Coast? Or had it been during the later sacking of Dream by the goblinkin hordes?

"No," the little librarian answered when he realized Brant still awaited an answer.

Brant nodded. "Pity. Maybe if you'd known who he was you might have remembered something else you'd read about him."

"I can read," Wick said automatically.

"I believe you, little artist," the master thief said. "I was only commenting, not disparaging. Now, have you a look at the locking mechanism."

Wick had to stand on tiptoe to peer better at the keyhole. The opening looked like it had only been made yesterday, completely clean and flawless. The keyhole was as big as two of his fingers together. Before he knew what he was doing, the little librarian reached up and thrust two fingers into the opening.

"That," Brant advised, "was not overly bright."

Wick, realizing then what his curiosity had made him do, yanked his fingers back from the keyhole. They'd fit very easily. Dark liquid coated the little librarian's fingers. *Poison!* his frantic mind insisted, and he awaited the sudden clench of nausea that he thought might cramp his stomach. *How did I manage to do such a thoughtless thing? Dwellers know better than to do something so foolish! My da taught me not to do something so foolish! I'm going to die!* He turned to Brant. "I've been poisoned!"

"That's grease," the master thief said, examining the liquid on the little librarian's fingers. "They packed the tumblers so they would stay in good shape. That was one of the heartening things I discovered."

"Oh. Grease." Wick wiped his fingers on his breeches in relief. "You'd know poison from grease, wouldn't you?"

"Yes," Brant replied. "Goblinkin are notorious for their use of poisons. Most of them are not very exotic or quick-acting, though, and I know how to concoct remedies for most of them." He moved closer, peering into the locking mechanism. "I've also seen them put blades inside locks. Usually, the blades are intended to snap lockpicks and jam the lock so that a thief is left with no recourse except to somehow pry a hiding place or vault door from the moorings. Of course, there are any number of less salacious thieves that have left fingers inside locks."

Fingers? Wick glanced at his own digits and almost felt sick. *How could I handle a quill at the Library if I lost my fingers?* The thought was absolutely horrifying. He put his hands in his pockets in case any other regressive dweller habits suddenly showed up in him. *I have been in uncivilized areas for far too long. Greydawn Moors is the only safe place for me.* He cleared his throat so Brant couldn't hear the fear and tension in it. "Surely you can pick the lock then."

"I've tried," Brant admitted. "Somehow, skilled as I am in locksmithing, this design has defeated my best efforts. I find that most curious." He moved the candle around, probing the locking mechanism with his eyesight and not his fingers.

"Then it's no use," Wick said.

"No," Brant replied. "I haven't yet given up on this exercise. There still remains the possibility of driving anchor bolts into the door and trying to tear it from the wall."

"But," Wick protested, "that's going to cause a lot of noise. The goblinkin patrols would come to investigate."

Brant glanced at him. "Perhaps not, little artist. Those goblinkin aren't quite as dedicated as you'd think, considering how bloodthirsty and unforgiving Orpho Kadar is. And a slight diversion isn't completely out of the realm of possibility."

"A diversion?"

"Yes." The master thief smiled. "Young Hamual is quite adept at diversions."

"But he would be risking discovery."

"As are we at this very moment."

Fear traipsed down Wick's spine on ice-cold mouse paws. He glanced around the crypt, wishing he were anywhere but there. Then the little librarian's eyes lit on the three bodies in the corner. "Brant."

"What?" the master thief asked, poking at the wall around the bas-relief door with his dagger.

"One of the skeletons in the corner belongs to an elf," Wick said. He could tell from the elongated shape of the skull. Torluud's *Elven Bodies and Physiography* and *Bumps or Knots, Krystark's Study of Elven Phrenology* were both excellent resources on the subject of elven craniums. Both tomes had been interesting reading, but Wick had never managed to get his hands on any elven skulls—and he would *not* have wanted to study the detached kind.

"So?"

"Do you think it could belong to the person who was in this casket?"

"Would it matter?"

Wick hesitated a moment before putting his thoughts into words. "What if the map didn't mean that the key was under the skull? Neither of us found a depression in the casket where the key could have been found."

"Then where do you think it might—" Brant turned to gaze at Wick, then at the two skeletons. A hesitant smile flickered to life on his face. "Of course. Hold this." He held the lummin juice candle out.

In a daze, his mind cringing from the possibility that he had suggested, Wick accepted the candle. "What are you going to do?"

"Have a look at those skulls." Brant crossed the room and pulled the corpse from the picked-clean skeletons. He dumped his disgusting burden unceremoniously into the casket. Then he knelt by the remaining skeletons. "Which of these is an elven skeleton?"

"The one on bottom," Wick said. "You can tell by the elongated skull, and by the canines, which in advanced years have a tendency—"

Brant grabbed the top skeleton and threw it into the corner by the door covered by the black silk sheet. "The one on the bottom is enough." The skeleton landed on the crypt floor with a rattle of bones.

"Brant!" Sonne whispered from outside.

"I'm fine," Brant called back. "Keep watch." He hauled the skeleton left in the corner out into better view. Seizing the skull in both hands, the master thief gave an experienced twist that popped the skull free of the spine with a splintering crack. He grinned as he held his prize up. "There! Easy as taking a grape from a vine."

Wick wretched before he could stop himself. The sour taste of bile burst at the back of his throat.

"Don't be sick," Brant warned. "I don't want anyone to know we've been here if we can help it."

"I'm sorry," Wick replied.

"It's just a skull, little artist." Brant held the skull up on one palm. Shadows filled the dark hollows of the eye sockets. "And I assure you, whoever this was no longer has need of it. Move the light over here a little closer."

Still fighting the gag reflex, Wick unwillingly stepped forward.

Brant turned the skull over slowly. A hollow click sounded. A smile twisted the master thief's lips. "You have proven invaluable, little artist."

Wick took some solace in that. At least Cobner might not be slitting his throat any time soon.

"There's something in there," Brant said. He shook the skull with the eye sockets turned down. "But something's holding it back." He glanced around, then picked up a rock chunk as large as a dinner plate. "How quick are you?"

"Wh-what?" Wick stammered.

Brant handed him the skull. "Hold this on the floor so I can hit it with the rock."

The little librarian's stomach recoiled. He'd read several books about physicians and healers during his years at the Library. For a time, Grandmagister Ludaan had assigned Wick to the medical books. The little librarian much preferred reading those works concerning magical healing and herbalists than those involving bone saws and surgical knives. But he'd never wanted to hold a dead man's skull. His skin crawled at the touch of the rough, cold surface of the skull.

"Well?" Brant prompted, holding his rock chunk in both hands above his head.

Wick placed the skull on the stone floor.

"Ready?" Brant asked.

"I think so," Wick replied.

Brant raised the rock higher. "Steady, then. Just remember to yank your hand back. Having you screaming in the graveyard isn't going to go unnoticed."

Wick nodded, wondering if a crunching skull would go unnoticed.

"Now!" Brant said.

The effort reminded Wick of games dweller children played back in Greydawn Moors to test their reflexes against each other. He held the skull steady for an instant after Brant started his swing.

The master thief didn't hesitate and held nothing back.

Wick yanked his hand back, then the rock smashed into the skull. The little librarian tried not to think about what the original owner of the skull would think about the use they showed his mortal remains.

Bone snapped and broken skull shards spilled out from under Brant's rock.

Surprisingly, the *crunch!* wasn't very loud inside the crypt. Wick had another nauseating moment when he realized the skull seemed to collapse more than shatter.

Brant moved his rock. "Bring the candle over here."

Controlling himself through what he considered a stupendous effort of will, Wick moved closer. Brant's fingers flew through the wreckage of the skull. Then a metallic sheen caught the little librarian's eye. "There!"

"Ah!" Brant gasped. He smiled as he plucked up the key. "Well, here's one individual who certainly had a lot on his mind at one time." He pushed himself to his feet. "Do you suppose he gave instruction to those who buried him that it was supposed to insert it after his death? Or do you believe he might have had some wizard magick it into his head?"

"I prefer not to think about that at all." Wick brushed his hands against his traveling cloak but couldn't rid himself of the sensation of the skull's rough exterior. Actually, he didn't think he would ever forget it.

"Do you know what would be ironic?" Brant asked as he faced the locking mechanism in the wall.

"What?" Wick asked, following the master thief.

"It would be very ironic if this were the *wrong* key."

Actually, Wick thought, *that would be terrible.* He could see Brant organizing a party to search all the skeletons lying out in the graveyard, ordering that all the skulls be smashed and searched.

Brant thrust the key into the locking mechanism and turned. A series of ratchets echoed faintly in the crypt. The sound of Brant's breathing sounded louder in Wick's ears.

Then the slightly recessed area on the wall fell into a million pieces, dropping away to reveal a wall less than a hand span deep.

"A wall?" Brant took the lummin juice candle from Wick's hand and played it over the recessed area.

The little librarian, his curiosity overcoming his nausea and fear, moved closer.

"What kind of insane joke is this?" Brant asked angrily. "Who would go to the trouble of building such a hidden area for no reason?"

Wick stared at the wall. Like the bas-relief hiding the keyhole—which didn't appear to exist anymore—the wall resembled a door and was created of a single sheet of slate, except that this was black. "It's not made of stones," the little librarian said.

"What?" Brant glanced at him irritably.

"The wall," Wick pointed out. "It's made of a piece of slate that overlays the stones that make up the crypt. I was just thinking that it was odd that it would be constructed in such a fashion."

"Unless there was another reason." Hope flared on Brant's handsome face. "My father had such hiding places in our home. I remember finding some of them when I was a young boy. He was sorely vexed at me. But at that age, my curiosity did little to endear me to him."

"My own da shares the same opinion of my own curiosity," Wick admitted.

"Your father is still alive?" Brant ran his dagger blade over the slate, and the rasp of metal on stone prickled the little librarian's neck.

"When I last saw him, he was," Wick said.

"Are you close to him?"

Wick hesitated. "It's—it's hard these days. Things are strained between us."

"Why?" Brant turned to face the little librarian, as if the answer to that question was more important than the conundrum before them.

Wick suddenly remembered that Brant's own family had been lost to a headsman's axe, although he still didn't know what those circumstances were. "Da didn't approve of what I chose to do with my life."

"And what would that be?"

Wick hesitated. "I can't tell you."

"Still carrying secrets, little artist?"

"It's nothing that would hurt you or anyone," Wick replied earnestly, "but it is someone else's secret, and I'm oathbound to keep it."

"Truly, you are an enigma. Where did you hail from?"

"I can't tell you that either."

Brant nodded, his eyes focused on Wick's. "I thank you for not trying to lie to me."

Wick's throat tightened. "I know you saved me from the arena, and I know you've stood up for me when Cobner would have slit my throat. I thank you for that."

"Don't think me altruistic, little artist." A grim cloud crossed Brant's face. "If I were out to save slaves from Hanged Elf's Point, there are hundreds who yet remain unsaved. And I have no plans to rescue them. I saved you for my own purposes."

"I know," Wick admitted, not holding the master thief's motivations against him. "Were I to paint you remiss in their salvation, I'd have to consider myself the same."

Brant eyed him. "Do you?"

Wick dropped his eyes, feeling suddenly guilty. "Yes. Today, when I realized that you weren't going to have Cobner simply kill me—or even do that job yourself— I suddenly thought of how I'm still alive when so many that I shared that slave pen with are now dead." He wondered briefly about Harran, and regretted that the other dwellers had ever found reason to ostracize him.

"And now you feel guilty because you're alive and they probably aren't?"

Wick took a shuddering breath, feeling the weight of all that responsibility and guilt washing over him, and nodded. "I'm glad I'm not dead, Brant. It shames me that I feel that so strongly."

Brant was silent for a moment, then reached out and tousled Wick's hair. "Only a man who has come so close to death can ever know the true joy of living. Such knowledge doesn't come without a price, and usually a price that should never have to be paid."

Wick nodded.

"But you have to keep in mind, little artist, that you *have* paid a price for your continued existence. Once you have lived when others have died, you feel you owe a debt to keep on living."

"How did you go on after you lost your family?" Wick asked before he thought such a question was wrong to ask.

"One day at a time," Brant replied grimly, his voice coldly neutral in the confines of the crypt. "I was little more than a boy when I lost them."

"I'm sorry."

Brant nodded and let out a deep breath. "Such talk is not a pleasant subject. We'd do better to save it for another time. Preferably a time when we were far from here and had our purses full."

Wick nodded.

"Your father didn't like the work you decided to take on," Brant said. "What did he want you to do?"

"Become a lamplighter in my town as he was."

"And you showed promise at being a lamplighter?"

"Yes."

"It's hard for a father to watch his son do something other than what he believes to be in his son's best interests. This other work that you took on, does it have anything to do with the sketchpad that you keep?"

"Book," Wick said. "It's a book. And yes, that calling has everything to do with that book. In a way."

"Are you any good at this other calling?"

Wick shook his head. "I am average. At the best I have ever been, I've only been average. I was even allowed into the field only because a good and kind man felt sorry for me." Thinking on it now, the little librarian didn't know if Grandmagister Ludaan's decision could be considered a kindness or not.

"Average?"

Wick took a long breath and let it out. "Yes."

"Little artist," Brant said in a soft voice, "I've seen you working at your—your *book* while you were making notes regarding the mosaic, and I'll tell you this: Nothing you can do in that calling is going to be average. There's a passion in you that I've seldom seen in others."

"Thank you," Wick whispered. *He doesn't know,* he told himself fiercely. *Despite his kind words, Brant has no idea of what goes into being a Librarian at the Vault of All Known Knowledge. He doesn't know the failure I've been.*

"Let's think of pleasanter things," Brant suggested. "Like whether or not this piece of slate really hides some kind of death trap, which would be the best joke on all of us." He smiled, then directed the candle's flame toward the slate inside the wall again.

"It's about the size of an elven or human door," Wick said.

"I see no hinges or knob." Brant pried at the edges of the slate. "And even should it open, where would it go? There's hardly enough room in here for it to be more than laid over the top of the outside wall. That's mortared together so that even that passage would not only be improbable but impossible."

"Perhaps," Wick said, "it was a door that was once considered then filled over."

"Then why build the mosaic?" Brant asked. "And why construct the locking mechanism and the false wall that fell away when I turned the key?"

"I don't know," Wick admitted.

"No, little artist," Brant said. "This door was meant to represent something. We just haven't the inclination set in our minds that we might fathom what it is. But there is no doubt there was purpose here."

"Brant." Cobner's voice came from outside.

Raising to his feet, the master thief crossed to the door. He blew out the candle, filling the crypt with darkness that left Wick terribly unsettled. "What is it?" Brant asked, peering through the black silk curtain.

"Tyrnen and I finished our searches of the graveyards you'd assigned me. So have Lago and Zalnar."

Tyrnen and Zalnar, Wick had come to know, were twin dwarven pickpockets. The other four dwarves—Baldarn, Volsk, Rithilin, and Charnir—completed the band of thieves. They'd been together for years.

"The others are all here as well," Cobner continued, "except for Hamual and Karick." Karick was the other human of the group.

"Have you heard from them?" Brant asked.

"No."

"Then we'll go look for them," the master thief declared. "They should have been back along the route I'd chosen for our group as you were." He turned and handed the lummin juice candle to Wick. "I want you to stay here for a time. See if you can divine the secret to that mysterious door while I'm gone."

Wick fretted about that as he accepted the candle. "Is it safe here?"

"Little artist," Brant said with a humorless grin, "I'd guess that it's as safe in this crypt as it is in all of Hanged Elf's Point for any of us."

"Oh," Wick said.

"Cobner," Brant said, "let's you and I and Sonne take a quick look for those two and make sure they haven't gone off and gotten into trouble they can't handle. Wick, keep your attention focused on our current problem. You've shown good judgment. Use it now. I trust you."

"Thank you," Wick said. He listened to the brief discussion the master thief had with his two compatriots, then heard the sound of horses' hooves going away from the crypt.

Lago pushed through the black silk curtain. "If you don't mind, little artist, I'll keep you company."

"That's fine," Wick said. "Please make sure that the curtain is in place while I light this candle again."

Lago bent to the task, replacing the stones Brant had chosen for the task.

A moment later, Wick had the candle lit once more and the fragrant scent of the burning lummin juice again filled the crypt.

"Well," Lago said, gazing at the skeletons, "I guess these haven't been much for conversation."

"No," Wick said, and a small smile touched his lips in spite of the fear that he felt. *Where is Hamual?* He worried briefly about the young human, but knew that Brant would do all that could be done. The little librarian turned his attention to the mystery of the wall and the door that wasn't there.

"Is that a door?" Lago asked.

"I don't know," Wick answered.

"So, have we found any treasure yet?"

"No." Wick placed the lummin-juice candle on the empty casket. The flickering light played over the recessed area in the wall. He pried and probed, but nothing more came to him. The slate wall refused to give up its secret.

He studied the bas-relief featuring the elven face. Taking his journal from his backpack, the little librarian turned to a blank page and took out a stick of charcoal. While working on the Keldian mosaic, he'd taken time to burn himself several sticks of charcoal as well as making a small pot of ink from sugar beets Lago had on hand. It was all very crude by Library standards, but his homemade tools had served him.

He placed the blank page over the bas-relief and

rubbed the charcoal stick over it. The face took shape. Unfortunately, none of the journal pages were large enough to cover the whole face so he had to do sections at a time.

"What are you doing?" Lago asked.

"Taking rubbings of this face," Wick answered.

"Why?"

"On the chance that I may be able to identify the face at some point."

"Oh, and you plan on seeing the man who owns that face?" Lago asked, glancing at the skeletons. "I'm telling you now, Wick, he probably doesn't look like he did for that picture."

Wick ignored the statement and let the old dwarf have his fun.

"Want a bite of bread?" Lago asked.

The little librarian accepted the offer kindly. Finding himself constrained by his backpack, he shrugged out of it and set it down next to the one Brant had left. With careful effort, he finished capturing the elf's face. *Of course,* he couldn't help thinking, *it's not going to do any good if this man isn't listed in one of the books at the Library or if this isn't him at all.* He closed the journal. *Or if I never get back to the Library.* He tried not to think about that. He was alive and he was free. After being in the slave pens with only the fate of certain death awaiting him in the arena of Hanged Elf's Point, being alive and free was nothing to sneeze at.

He leaned back against the casket, thoughtfully chewing the nut bread Lago had baked at the thieves' hideout in the Forest of Fangs and Shadows. Then he noticed a dulled glow streaming from Brant's backpack. His breath caught in the back of his throat. *Surely that means no good.*

"Lago," the little librarian croaked.

"Yes?" the old dwarf asked.

"Does Brant have anything in his backpack that would, um, *glow?*"

"No. Not that I'm aware of."

Curious despite the fear thrilling through him, Wick finished the nut bread and hunkered down to examine the master thief's backpack. He unfastened the strap holding it closed, then opened the flap. Inside was a cheesecloth bag. The dulled red glow was sharper inside the backpack, and the little librarian noticed dulled green, blue, and white as well.

The Keldian mosaic! Wick knew in an instant that nothing else could cause those glowing colors. Hypnotized by the glowing colors, the little librarian reached into the backpack. A faint itching sensation washed over his skin as he took the cheesecloth bag out.

"What is that?" Lago asked.

"The mosaic." Wick removed it from the cheesecloth bag. Exposed now, the gems glowed even more brightly. He held the mosaic in his hands, trembling a little with excitement. *What does it mean?* He shifted, turning toward Lago, and noticed that the glowing gems dimmed. He froze, suddenly afraid he'd broken something or a horrible event was about to occur.

"Why did they stop glowing so much?" Lago asked.

"I don't know," Wick assured the old dwarf. Slowly, he turned back the other way. *Maybe I only knocked it out of adjustment,* he thought, though he had no idea what had caused it to start glowing in the first place. As he continued turning, the gems glowed even more brightly.

"Look!" Lago said.

Wick glanced up and saw the reflection of the gems in the slate door shape inside the wall. Acting on a hunch, the little librarian moved toward the slate. Before he knew what was happening, the mosaic broke back into the individual gems. They hovered in midair like fireflies, then shot toward the slate.

The gems embedded in the slate with *plink-plink-plinking* sounds. They formed a series of looping designs that glowed star-bright, eclipsing the light from the lummin-juice candle.

I've never seen anything so beautiful, Wick couldn't help thinking. The gem whorls were so hypnotically entrancing that the fear that dawned within him was a distant thing.

In the next moment, the gems exploded in a bright flash of multicolored fire!

Oh no! Wick thought frantically. *What have I done? Brant is going to kill me! Or maybe he'll just have Cobner do it when no one is looking!* The little librarian blinked his eyes rapidly, amazed at all the spots that remained in his vision.

Volsk, the dwarven thief who spent most of his time with Cobner, whipped aside the black silk sheet and strode into the crypt room with his battle-axe in his fist. He cursed graphically, embarrassing Wick. "What is going on in here?" the dwarf asked. "Those lights could have been seen by the goblinkin patrol in the street in front of the graveyard. And you liked to have scared me out of ten years of my life, which I can ill afford to lose."

"I didn't do it," Wick said. "It was the mosaic." He pointed at the slate wall where the gems had lodged. "It was—" He blinked in consternation, his vision returning enough so that he saw the slate was no longer there as well.

In fact, nothing appeared to be there at all. Emptiness yawned out where once there had been a wall.

For an instant, Wick thought that the gems had somehow blown out the back wall of the crypt. Then he realized the view he saw was of a long, winding staircase that led away from him. It certainly wasn't the graveyard that should have been lying in back of the crypt.

"Magic," Volsk said hoarsely. He warded himself against evil, his free hand moving quickly while he raised the battle-axe with the other.

In disbelief, Wick peered down into the winding staircase. *That certainly isn't part of the crypt.* Tentatively, he bent down and picked up a small rock from the floor, thinking that maybe the winding staircase was only an illusion, somehow produced by the explosion of bright light. *Maybe the gems are even still embedded in the* slate. He hoped that was true. He could pry them out of the slate and, although it would take long hours of hard work, he could reassemble them. He tossed the rock at the opening in the wall, hoping that it would only bounce off and the illusion would be broken.

Instead, the rock bounced down the winding staircase, quickly disappearing.

Wick listened to the *klunk-klunk-klunking* for a long moment, then heard nothing at all. He blinked. Everything in him cried out for him to run and get out of the crypt. Only bad things could happen from this.

Instead, as if drawn by some arcane power, the little librarian seized the lummin-juice candle in one hand and walked toward the doorway that couldn't exist—yet did. Fearfully, he thrust his hand into the doorway.

The candlelight spilled down the long spiral of narrow stone steps.

Wick noted the masonry of the walls that made up the staircase. They'd been carefully fitted, expertly mortared.

"What is it?" Lago whispered hoarsely. The old man held his war hammer in front of him.

"A staircase," Wick replied.

"I can see that. Where did it come from?"

"I don't know." A dim shape on the wall caught

Wick's eye. He recognized it as a torch in a sconce—
and it was just out of reach. Summoning his courage,
drawn by curiosity that surely had to be a throwback to
earlier dweller days before such deadly interests had
been bred out of the race—or, at least, providentially
removed for the most part—he set a shaking foot on the
first stair step. He paused only long enough to grab his
backpack, not wanting to be separated from his journal.

The little librarian was really amazed that the step
held. He stretched up and took the torch from the sconce.
The oiled head caught flame easily. The bright yellow
light carved a long hollow from the spiral stairway's
throat.

"What are you doing?" Lago demanded.

"Seeing where these stairs lead," Wick answered.
"They can't start without going somewhere."

"That's what you think," Lago replied. "They came
from nowhere. It could well be that's exactly where they
lead."

"Stay or follow me," Wick tried to say bravely, and
hoped that the dwarves followed him. The thought of
descending into the darkness below alone and basically
unarmed—he did have the small knife at his waist, of
course—made his stomach churn.

"What if that wall seals up behind you?" Volsk asked.

"It won't." Wick hoped that he wasn't lying to them
or himself. Still, it stood to reason that the magic doorway had to lead somewhere. *But there is the fact that
the staircase may have been waiting for someone in particular.* He almost stopped when that thought hit him.
But he really liked less the idea of explaining to Brant
what had become of his fortune in gems. Maybe the
gems would never return. The thought of Cobner and his
sharp axe kept the little librarian moving when fear
would have otherwise paralyzed him.

"Hold up, Wick," Lago called. "I'm coming with you."

Only a little ahead, Wick found another torch in a sconce. He reached up and lit it with the torch he carried. "There's a light, Lago."

"I've got it, I've got it."

The shadows ahead of Wick suddenly shifted as the old dwarf plucked the torch from the sconce and trailed after him.

"Hold up," Volsk muttered angrily. "I'll get the others."

Although good sense told him he should wait on the other dwarves because they were trained fighters while he was only a Third Level Librarian, Wick found he had no choice but to keep going. He vaguely wondered about Brant's mission to find Hamual, but his thoughts centered more on what waited at the other end of the staircase.

The chill wind pursuing them from the crypt and the graveyard beyond finally dwindled away. The air filling the staircase became steadily warmer as they descended. The torchlight suddenly opened onto a room.

Wick paused on the final step and held the torch higher so the glow would better fill the room. Shelves filled the room, and wine bottles filled the shelves.

"Oogley Moogley," Lago gasped over the little librarian's shoulder. "A wine cellar! You've done went and found a wizard's wine cellar, little artist!"

Staring out at the shelves and the dust-covered bottles, Wick assumed that it had to be true. "But it's insane that a wizard would create some kind of magic doorway leading to his wine cellar."

"Ah, boy," Lago growled, pushing past him, "you've got a lot of learning to do about connoisseurs of fine spirits. Why, if you get men together who knows great grape squeezings from run-of-the-mill bottles of near-to-vinegar, you'd have yourself a fine education." The old dwarf scurried over to the wine shelves and selected a bottle. He bit the cork and pulled it from the bottleneck, then spat out the cork and took a healthy swig. He turned and offered the bottle to Wick. "Have yourself a pull."

Feeling slightly stunned, Wick took the bottle.

Lago moved down the wine racks, searching avariciously for another bottle. He wasn't long in making a choice, then biting out that cork as well.

In a daze, Wick moved around the room. Although the means of getting to the room were magical without doubt, the room seemed to be nothing more than a wine cellar. He sipped the wine cautiously. It had a nice bouquet and a good, sweet taste. He couldn't immediately identify what it had been pressed from.

A couple moments later, Volsk descended the magic stairway with the other dwarves. They quickly joined Lago in celebrating their good fortune. Their torches flooded the room, stripping away most of the shadows but leaving others hunkered down between the wine racks.

Wick wandered through the large room. *It doesn't make sense for a wizard to create a magic doorway that only leads to a wine cellar. Not from a* crypt! *And this place looks as though the owner just stepped out.* The little librarian paused at that thought. *Which means that he might step back in at any time.*

He recalled stories of wizards he'd read in Hralbomm's Wing. Mostly, all the taletellers had agreed that wizards and mages in general didn't care to involve themselves in the affairs of common people—unless it was to some benefit of the wizard. They wove their own weaves. But some of those tales told of a wizard's special places. They also told of the wizard's revenge when he'd returned there to find plunderers within his walls. None of those stories had ended in a particularly pleasant fashion. *Unless the reader was a fan of wizards,* Wick amended.

The little librarian considered putting the wine bottle back on a shelf, then thought better of that. Facing wizards, he decided, was much better with a little wine.

At the back of the wine room was a wall with another door.

Wick stood in front of the door. The sturdy wooden edifice held no markings. He took another drink of wine, then realized there was a label on the bottle. Incredulous, the little librarian raised the bottle and peered at the label. However, try as he might even as conversant as he was in so many different languages, this was one that he wasn't immediately intimate with. Still, he was excited to know that the wizard or wine-maker was able to write, which meant reading.

"Wick! Wick!" Lago called behind him. "You might not have found the treasure Brant was looking for, but you struck the mother lode according to this old dwarf! I don't know how many different kinds of wines are on these shelves, but I intend to sample them all!"

Wick felt a little glow already and decided the wine was more potent than he'd thought. Of course, it probably helped that he was nervous and scared. Wine always proved more intoxicating when he was exhausted in some fashion. He glanced down at the door and spotted the knob. There were no locks.

Cautiously, knowing that the wine cellar itself might be some kind of magical creation that could evaporate at any second, Wick reached for the doorknob. The lever twisted easily in his grip. A hollow click echoed through the room but was quickly lost in the dwarves' verbal celebration of their good fortune.

The door swung easily inward and Wick followed it in, heart hammering in his chest. He couldn't name what it was that drew him on, but he knew that it couldn't be denied. His torch invaded the next room.

A dead man lay on a small four-poster bed in the middle of the room.

18

Embattled!

Wick stopped and looked at the gauzy curtains blunting the view of the figure lying on the bed. The skeleton wore ornate robes decorated with sigils and symbols the little librarian wasn't immediately familiar with. He watched the skeleton for a time, till he was convinced that it wouldn't be getting up.

Filled with dread, wishing the compulsion that filled him would quickly evaporate so he could follow what he thought was his true nature and go screaming back up the spiral stairway, Wick turned slowly to survey the room. A great, freestanding chest of drawers filled one corner of the room. And, incredibly, a writing desk occupied another.

Wick's eyes were immediately drawn to the desk—*and to the books piled neatly on one corner!*

The little librarian crossed the room in disbelief. According to all the teachings of the grandmagisters, all the books that hadn't been shipped to Greydawn Moors had been destroyed by Lord Kharrion's goblin troops. Under the Goblin Lord's savage and unswerving instruction, all libraries and books had been sought out with brutal dedication and destroyed.

Yet Wick's eyes assured him that four existed here.

He stopped at the desk and took up the first book in his trembling hand. The book was thick and fat. Expensive red vellum covered the edges of the pages. Cautiously, afraid that the book might disintegrate, he brushed at the thick dust covering the gilt letters.

The raucous excitement of the dwarves plundering the wine stores served as a strange counterpoint to the discovery Wick had made.

As quickly as his excitement had escalated, a frenetic stupefaction filled the little librarian. Although the gilt letters were now brushed free of dust, he couldn't read them. Dismayed, hoping that it was only the title that escaped him, he quickly turned the cover and flipped page after page till he reached the first page of script.

I can't read any of it! Wick stared incomprehensibly at the writing that tracked across the page. It was written in a clean, unblemished hand that denoted authority and an organized mind. It was enough of a disappointment to make the little librarian want to cry. *I've discovered something new, an impossibility that shouldn't exist, in a place carefully hidden and protected by magic, and it is still beyond me.* Now more than ever, he felt like a Third Level Librarian. *Any First Level Librarians and probably most Second Level Librarians could read this book with ease.*

Despite his frustration, Wick gently closed the book. *There's more than one book! Surely there's one among them that I can read!* Instead of returning the book to the desk, he slipped it into his backpack. Then he turned his attention to the other three books. One, two, three; they went that easily. The books were comfortable weights in his hands, a sturdy, solid feel that he'd missed for weeks. And yet, because of the language barrier, they were still denied to him.

Wick held the last book he'd inspected and sat heavily in the finely crafted wooden chair in front of the writing desk. In the back of his mind, he heard his father's voice again, telling him that he had wasted his time becoming a Librarian, that he would have been better off taking up the family trade and becoming a lamplighter.

Here is irrefutable proof, Wick told himself. He stared at the pages of the final book. As with all the others, this one had elaborate illustrations. But they were illustrations of people and places and things that he couldn't know about. He was banned from knowing by his own lack of skill and talent.

Then a word caught his eye. He knew that word, he realized with a sudden exhilaration that lifted the despondency from his shoulders. He quickly scanned the page. And perhaps he knew a few others as well, now that he studied them more closely. The books were *definitely* written in the elven tongue. *But I've translated those before! There's not been an elven tongue that I couldn't decipher, given enough time and the proper resources.* His heart leapt at his discovery. *Why, when I get back to the Vault of All Known Knowledge, I can—*

Suddenly, Lago and the other dwarves stumbled into the room. Wick started in momentary confusion, having almost forgotten about the others while considering his own dim prospects.

"Lad," Lago yelled explosively, waving a wine bottle happily, "you've got to try this vintage! Why, I've never had the like before!"

The other dwarves crowded in behind Lago. Their eyes were immediately drawn to the skeleton on the bed.

"A ring!" Baldarn growled. He pointed at the figure on the bed. "That skeleton's got a ring on its finger, and I claim it as my own!"

"No!" Wick interrupted, thrusting the last book into his backpack. "That man was a wizard! You shouldn't—"

"One thing I learned," Charnir cried gleefully, "you

don't have to worry about dead wizards nearly as much as you have to worry about live ones!"

Like a flock of hungry crows, the dwarves descended on the room. They rifled the chest of drawers, crying out in delight as they found bits and pieces of jewelry and a hefty stash of gold and silver coins. Cheers went up as each dwarf showed off his purloined loot.

"No!" Wick argued. "You shouldn't disturb anything! There could be a curse on those things!"

"The only cursing to be done," overweight Rithilin declared, "will be done by Brant if he finds that we didn't properly loot this place as he would have had us do!"

"Yes," Tyrnen said, looking under the bed with his twin brother, Zalnar. They tore at the gauze surrounding the bed. "And it would be in your best interests, halfer, if you were able to give him something . . . *impressively* valued. Before you tell him you lost our gems."

"But I didn't lose them," Wick defended himself. "They were obviously part of the spell that led to this place."

"If we'd stayed away from here," Volsk grumbled, "the gems wouldn't be lost. We'd still have the first fortune we found and wouldn't be looking for a second."

"It wasn't my idea to come here," Wick protested.

Volsk brushed the little librarian aside and began searching the writing desk. "You're the one who put the puzzle together. If it had remained in pieces, we'd have been well on our way out of Hanged Elf's Point by now."

Disbelief flooded Wick. *How has everything now become my fault?* He peered anxiously around Volsk's massive shoulders as the dwarf quickly went through the drawers of the writing desk. While the dwarven thief avoided the writing utensils, although he did take one quill that looked like it was plumed with a solid gold feather, the little librarian snatched wax-sealed inkwells and quills. He also managed to take at least half a ream of the most exquisite writing paper he'd ever seen in his life.

"Don't blame him for everything bad that's gone on," Lago said, emerging from the chest of drawers with an armload of brocaded robes much too long for his stocky body. "If it hadn't been for Wick, we'd have never found the wizard's wine cellar."

"We're just lucky," Charnir said, "that the wizard wasn't around to complain."

"Oh, I'm going to complain," a crotchety sounding voice warned. "I'm going to turn you all into warty toads is what I'm going to do!" Bones rattled threateningly.

Startled, knowing for sure that the dead wizard had somehow returned to life long enough to wreak vengeance on those foolish enough to disturb his eternal rest—*and* dare to take his books!—Wick quickly ducked down to provide as small a target as possible. He glanced at the bed and watched the skeleton rise from the blankets.

"Warty toads!" the maniacal voice warned. "Each and everyone of you will be warty toads come morning! A breakfast of flies, that's what you'll be craving!" The skeleton appeared to dance a jig, one arm waving, obviously preparing to cast a spell.

"No!" Wick cried out. *Can toads read?* He couldn't remember reading anything on the subject. Here he was—with those four mysterious books in his backpack, books that he should be concerned with getting back to the Vault of All Known Knowledge—and he was going to be turned into a warty toad by a vengeful wizard before he even had the chance to see if he could decipher the books. *It isn't fair!* He groaned out loud.

All of the dwarves looked at him, then doubled over in laughter.

"Tyrnen," Volsk commanded, "leave that skeleton be before you scare the little halfer to death."

Peering up between his fingers, Wick saw Tyrnen standing behind the skeleton, one big hand wrapped around the back of its skull to lift it from the bed. The young dwarf nonchalantly dropped the skeleton back onto the bed amid the roaring gales of laughter from the dwarves.

Face red with embarrassment, Wick stood again and straightened his clothing with as much dignity as he could muster.

"What about you, halfer?" Volsk demanded. "You entered this room first. Was there something you absconded with before we followed you in here? Something pretty and precious that you're hiding from us now?"

"Wick wouldn't do that," Lago said. "Why, he's hardly a thief at all. He's an artist."

"Mayhap," Volsk argued, obviously not convinced. "But there's many a starving artist out there, and I've known some of them who learned well how to look out for their own welfare. Most of them could cut a man's coin purse and be gone long before he knew what hit him."

Wick shook his head. He felt sorry for interrupting the dead man's slumber, and thought of the disrespect the dwarven thieves were showing the man by stealing from him after he was dead—although, Wick had to admit, that was probably much safer than being robbed by them while still alive. Then he thought of the four books in his backpack, knowing he was no better than the dwarven thieves. *All in the interest of my work as a Librarian,* he told himself. *It isn't theft; I'm rescuing knowledge that otherwise might be lost or used wrongly. Especially if these books turn out to be spellbooks. These books belong in the Vault of All Known Knowledge and it's my duty to take them there—if I can.*

"Wick figured out the secret of the mosaic," Baldarn pointed out. "And here the secret of those gems was stumping Brant for nearly two months. Why he's as great a thief as ever lived is what he is. A regular prince of thieves. And I've got just the crown for him." He lifted his hand and showed the blue metal skullcap he'd obviously found in the chest of drawers that the others had ignored.

Since the skullcap wasn't gold or silver the thieves evidently considered it worthless.

Baldarn crossed the room and clapped the skullcap over the little librarian's head. "I crown thee," he declared in a sanctimonious voice that filled the room, "Wick the Quick, Prince of Thieves."

The other dwarves burst out laughing. Evidently the strength of the wine stores were more than any of them had expected.

Leading seven drunken dwarves on a stealing spree into what could be a dead wizard's magic hideout, Wick told himself, *is definitely not something I should repeat.* Yet even as he told himself that, he couldn't believe he'd done it in the first place. No dweller he'd known had ever done anything so outrageous, and only a few of those in legends told—to scare young dwellers—had ever been so foolhardy. He put a hand to his head, surprised at the fit the skullcap had. Why, the wizard must have had the same size head, although from looking at the skeleton on the bed, the little librarian would never have guessed—

Without warning, a tall man strode into the room. He carried a naked sword in his fist. His height and bulk instantly identified him as a human. He was too tall to be anything other than elven or human, and too heavy to be the former. He wore his thick black hair and beard cut short. A black chainmail shirt glinted in the torch-light, and old battle scars in the links shone more brightly. He was dressed all in black—except for the long purple cloak that hung from his broad shoulders.

"A Purple Cloak!" Lago screamed in warning.

Galvanized into action, Volsk stepped forward im-mediately, roaring out a battle cry as he swung his battle-axe. The human wearing the purple cloak lifted his hand and gestured. Something wavered in the air between the human's hand and the charging dwarf. Then Volsk was thrown backward, sailing across the room to smash into the wizard's four-poster bed amid the gaunt skeleton Tyrnen had discarded there. Wood splintered and shrieked.

"You don't know what you've done!" the Purple Cloak roared as he stepped into the room. "Put down those things that you've taken and we'll let you live!"

We'll? Wick didn't miss the pronoun use. He had no doubt that others accompanied Fohmyn Mhout's hench-man. The wizard's Purple Cloaks never traveled alone. The little librarian grew very afraid. He also knew from scuttlebutt in the dweller slave pens that Purple Cloaks seldom left any they had physical confrontations with live as a message to any others who might think of fight-ing them. Volsk's attack had signed their death warrants.

One of the twins—Wick was never sure later which one it was, and in the telling of the story later both claimed to be the one— threw a dagger that pierced the Purple Cloak's throat. The little librarian couldn't tell if the throw was a killing one or not, although the idea of getting knifed in the throat wasn't pleasant by any stretch of the imagination.

Charnir rushed forward then and caught the Purple Cloak in the midriff with the long haft of his battle-axe. Maybe the keen blade wouldn't have sliced through the chain mail, but it certainly took the wind from the wounded human and knocked him back out of the room. Charnir gave a lusty cry of triumph and sped through the door on his short legs.

"Come on, Wick," Lago cried, catching the little librarian's arm and yanking him toward the door.

Stunned and almost paralyzed with fear, realizing that somehow Fohmyn Mhout's fearsome Purple Cloaks had discovered the magical gateway in the crypt, Wick followed the old dwarf. He shifted his backpack across his shoulders, making sure both straps were secure. The four books had added considerable weight and he didn't want to chance losing them.

Two other Purple Cloaks waited in the outside room, both of them armed with swords and spellcraft as well. One of them gestured and shoved his open palm forward. Something disturbed the air like a roiling cloud, then slammed into the twin dwarven pickpockets. Tyrnen and Zalnar were bowled over as Charnir went flying back. All three dwarves tumbled head over heels into a wine rack, knocking the big shelves down in a thundering, clattering crash.

Still, Baldarn and Rithilin bravely charged forward, their weapons flashing as they took the battle to their opponent. The dwarves scored hits, knocking the lead Purple Cloak down. The second Purple Cloak leaped forward, engaging the two enraged dwarves with his sword before they could kill the man stretched before them. Metal rasped against metal and sparks leaped into the shadows.

Wick and Lago had the only two torches still held in the wine cellar. The six younger dwarves had abandoned theirs to the floor as soon as they rushed to combat the Purple Cloaks.

Baldarn and Rithilin separated quickly, showing long practice of handling themselves in battle. They circled the taller, heavier human like two wolves, nipping away constantly at the Purple Cloak's defenses, making the man fight attacks in front and back. Outflanked as he was, the Purple Cloak had no choice but to defend himself. The clangor of steel filled the wine cellar.

The Purple Cloak with the knife in his neck rose unsteadily from the doorway leading to the dead wizard's final resting place. He tried to speak, but his voice was a hoarse, unintelligible croak. He gestured with one hand, but before he could complete whatever spell he planned, Volsk rammed into him from behind, knocking his foe down.

Things happened very fast then, and Wick was looking out for his own skin, aided by Lago, who obviously had the same agenda. They crept around the room, staying behind the stacks of wine shelves. Still, when one of the Purple Cloaks was forced back by the axes of Tyrnen and Zalnar, Lago didn't hesitate about acting.

The old dwarf pulled Wick into the wine shelf near the Purple Cloak. "There!" Lago cried, pushing against the tall shelves. "Put your shoulder into it!"

Understanding what the old dwarf meant, although he was afraid such action would only draw the attention of the Purple Cloak—which Wick had been terribly thankful for not receiving so far—the little librarian threw himself against the wine shelf with Lago. At first, the wine shelves seemed disinclined to tip over. They creaked and shuddered, their shadows wavering across the room from the torches Lago and Wick held. Too late, the little librarian realized that holding the torch marked him easily for the Purple Cloaks.

Then, just as the Purple Cloak turned in their direction to face them, the wine shelving fell over on top of him. Shelves and falling bottles cascaded over the Purple Cloak, crashing against the stone floor and sending the man to the ground under the immense weight.

"Quickly!" Lago yelled, pulling at Wick's arm.

The little librarian followed immediately, streaking for the stairs. He glanced around the wine cellar and saw that the six other dwarves had managed to fend off the two Purple Cloaks remaining and outmaneuver them. All six, led by Volsk, ran for the stairway.

"Up!" Volsk cried. "Up quickly! Perhaps we can yet escape them!"

Remembering all the tales of the Purple Cloaks' superhuman strength and constitution, seeing the man with the knife in his throat starting forward yet again, Wick headed up the stairs. The other dwarves set up a perimeter around the stairway entrance, brandishing their weapons and calling out their battle cries.

The nearest Purple Cloak stopped less than ten feet away and his hand danced in the air.

Wick summoned his desperation, set himself, and threw the flaming torch in his hand like a spear. The flames wreathed the torch's head as it shot across the room like a comet. Then it crashed into the Purple Cloak's face. The sticky oil smeared the human's face with flaming patches, making it look like his beard and hair had suddenly caught fire.

The Purple Cloak shrieked in mortal agony and beat at his face with his hands.

Standing paralyzed with horror at the foot of the stairway, Wick gazed at what his unthinking and quick action had wrought. He'd never dealt someone such a grievous injury, and the realization that he'd done it now—coupled with the stench of burning hair and perhaps flesh as well—sickened him.

The six younger dwarves thundered up the stairs, calling for Lago and Wick to follow after them. Even with their superior numbers, the dwarven thieves were evidently convinced that they weren't enough to take on the Purple Cloaks.

"Come on!" Lago yelled, tugging at Wick's arm.

The little librarian followed the old dwarf, suddenly aware that the stairway passage was only wide enough for one of them at a time to run up. Lago went more slowly than Wick would have been able to. Still, the old dwarf fought valiantly to drag Wick after him as if he were saving the younger man instead of slowing him.

The howls of the burning Purple Cloak echoed up the staircase.

For the first time, Wick realized that the Purple Cloaks had been using their magic against the dwarven thieves. *Magic isn't supposed to work in Hanged Elf's Point,* the little librarian remembered. That line of reasoning left only two possibilities. Possibly, Minniger had been wrong and magic actually could be used inside the city. *Or we're not in Hanged Elf's Point anymore.* That scared Wick nearly out of his wits. It wasn't unheard of in the texts that he'd read for wizards to do all kinds of things with twisting and warping time and space. Perhaps they were no longer even near Hanged Elf's Point or on the Shattered Coast. How would he get home then?

The books in his backpack slapped against his back as Wick ran after Lago. The little librarian peered up anxiously, hoping to see around the twisting staircase to make sure the doorway still let out into the crypt. He couldn't see anything beyond the dwarves fleeing ahead of him. Then an enraged bellow drew his attention back down the stairs.

A sword flashed in the stairwell below, held by at least one Purple Cloak pursuing them.

"Hurry!" Wick yelled, wishing Lago was more fleet of foot. The little librarian resisted the impulse to push the old dwarf.

Then a blast of cold air swooped down over Wick, stirring the flames of Lago's torch overhead. Three more hard driving pushes against the stairs and the little librarian spotted the door opening into the crypt. The other dwarven thieves cleared the doorway in a rush.

Lago missed a step and fell heavily against the side of the stairway. For a moment, the old dwarf couldn't find his balance. He flailed his torch and his free arm, on the verge of falling back.

Desperately, Wick pushed his palms out and caught the old dwarf on the back, then shoved him forward. Lago fell forward, toppling into the crypt. Unfortunately, the little librarian's effort left him insecure in his own balance and footing. Before Wick could recover, the sword-wielding Purple Cloak behind him grabbed the tails of his traveling cloak.

"Yaaaaahhhhh!" Wick screamed as he scrambled to reach the next step. His boots slipped on the stairs and he fell, bruising both knees. The man behind the little librarian tightened his grip, pulling him in like a fisherman trying to take a fish.

A shadow, limned by Lago's torch behind it in the crypt, suddenly filled the stairwell in front of Wick as the little librarian fought for his life against the Purple Cloak. *I'm going to die!* He was certain at any moment that the Purple Cloak's sword was going to cleave his skull.

"Get down, little artist!" Brant commanded gruffly. The master thief paused in graceful haste on the stair step in front of Wick, then lashed out with a boot. The kick must have caught the Purple Cloak full in the face, judging from the meaty smack.

For a moment, Wick thought the Purple Cloak was going to drag him back down the stairs. He stuck his hands straight out and dug his fingers into the cracks between the stones. As carefully as they'd been put together, there wasn't much space between the stones. His fingers started slipping at once, and he didn't have the breath left in him to yell.

Brant bent forward and grabbed Wick's traveling

cloak. The master thief slipped on one step, but set himself by the time he hit the next. Brant pulled hard, and Wick's traveling cloak tore.

"Come on!" Brant yelled, pulling Wick up the stairs. Three long-legged steps later, the little librarian passed through the door with the master thief.

Wick's feet got tangled with Brant's and they both went down. Heart in the back of his throat, he glanced back over his shoulder at the opening in the crypt wall. The Purple Cloak charged up the steps, his lower face masked by blood and his sword in his fist. Even as he came level with Wick, the Purple Cloak brought his sword down, hacking at the little librarian's legs. Turning quickly, Brant brought his own blade up and expertly turned the Purple Cloak's cut.

The clang of metal filled the crypt, then the multicolored flash blinded Wick once again. When the little librarian's vision cleared, he saw that the slate door had reformed and the Keldian mosaic gems lay glistening on the floor.

Incredibly, the Purple Cloak's arm and sword extended through the slate, trapped in the slate's stony grip.

Wick stood on trembling legs, aided by the master thief. He stared at the frozen tableau of the man's arm caught in the slate. In the next instant, the sword fell from the Purple Cloak's nerveless fingers and the arm relaxed.

"What happened to him?" Lago asked quietly. "Is he trapped on the other side of that magical door, or is it only his arm hanging there?"

Wick didn't want to know the answer to the question, but his mind couldn't help considering the possibilities.

"It doesn't matter," Brant said. "For all we know, those weren't the only Purple Cloaks in the area. Grab those gems!"

The dwarves scrambled to follow his order.

Wick watched helplessly as gems skidded across the crypt floor. The dwarves and Hamual and Karick scrambled after them, stuffing their pockets with the ones they picked up.

"Goblin patrol," Sonne called from the doorway. She held her crossbow at the ready, peering around the black silk sheet. "Brant, they're coming this way."

The master thief crossed to the doorway. "After the confrontation Hamual and Karick had with them, I'm not surprised." He paused, then glanced at Lago. "Put out that torch."

Lago reached under his traveling cloak and brought out a thick towel. He wrapped the torch head quickly, extinguishing the flames and plunging the crypt into inky darkness.

"The only chance we've got," Brant said in the shadows, "are the horses outside. The goblinkin will spot them and maybe think about it. The best chance we'll have is if we can spook their horses and buy ourselves a little time."

"I knew this halfer would bring us ill luck," Cobner snarled. "Better you should have left him wherever those Purple Cloaks were left on the other side of that wizard's gate."

"Quiet, Cobner," Brant commanded. He set up on the other side of the crypt doorway opposite Sonne. "Ready." He lifted the edge of the black silk sheet and peered through. "There's only six of them. We have a chance." He let out his breath. "Set."

No, Wick thought feebly. *I'm not ready and I'm not set! I don't want to—*

"Go!" Brant threw the silk sheet to one side and charged out into the cemetery. Sonne followed him through the door next, trailed only a half step by Cobner. Tyrnen and Zalnar plunged through the doorway next.

Wick got caught up in the general melee that hurtled pell-mell through the crypt door.

Outside, Brant rushed the goblinkin's horses while screaming at the top of his lungs and waving his arms. The horses shied, some of them rearing, all of them moving back hurriedly, their eyes rolling white. Sonne lifted her crossbow to her shoulder and stood her ground. One of the goblins mastered his horse quicker than the others and lifted his mace. The goblin urged his horse forward, intending to cave in the back of Brant's skull. Sonne fired deliberately, putting the short quarrel through the goblin's head. He fell from his horse, one foot caught in the stirrup. The frightened horse charged blindly through the graveyard, dragging the dead goblin at its side.

Another goblin chopped at Brant with a morning star. Quick as lightning, the master thief whirled, using both hands to block the treacherous blow before it landed. "Get to the horses!" Brant yelled. He danced clear of the goblin and grabbed the bridle of another horse, yanking it into the horse behind him.

Wick didn't hesitate. He'd be no good fighting goblins; he wasn't a warrior. He swept the graveyard with his eyes, spotting the thieves' horses tethered beneath a dead tree beside a broken monument depicting a rearing unicorn. The little librarian ran hard as he could, feeling pain shooting through both his bruised knees. Surprisingly, he stayed even with the longer-legged dwarves.

"More riders!" one of the twins warned.

Glancing over his shoulder, Wick spotted the torches carried by more arriving goblinkin troops. Brant remained a fighting whirlwind amid the first goblins, using the horses' fear and the twisting night shadows thrown by their torches against them. The master thief's sword swept out suddenly, thrusting through an opponent's midriff. When he withdrew the blade, the goblinkin fell screaming from the saddle. Brant yelled again, sweeping his traveling cloak to scare the horses yet again.

Some of the goblinkin reinforcements carried cross-bows. Short, deadly quarrels filled the air around the running dwarves. Thankfully, the overhanging branches of the dead tree deflected some of the missiles and none of them hit the dwarven and human thieves running for the horses.

Cobner took a stand as the goblinkin rode toward them. The surly dwarf spun his battle-axe in his hands expertly, yelling in battle fury. "I'm Cobner, fiercest dwarf of Swift River Hollow, and I stand before you as the last warrior of my clan, my kin, and my home! Come at me and die, you ugly toadfaces! My axe is thirsty!"

The dwarf ran forward and thrust the haft of his axe through the legs of the lead horse, bracing it against the ground. Cobner set himself, then yelled in triumph as the horse tripped over the axe. The goblin rider yelled in fear as he sailed from his mount's saddle.

Cobner turned again, his grim face pulled tight in a fighting smile, the first sign of good humor Wick had seen the big dwarf show. Cobner drew his axe back and drove it into the chest of the next rider, knocking the goblin from horseback in a tumble of flailing arms and legs.

"Come on, then!" Cobner yelled to the other goblins. "Have at you then and let's see whose steel bites more deeply!"

Despite the panic filling him, Wick couldn't help pull up short for just an instant and watch the dwarf's lone stand against the goblinkin. The little librarian was convinced that he was about to see Cobner die in the next moment. But even as the goblinkin turned on the dwarf, bringing their arms to bear, Cobner ran at them again, waving his arms and screaming lustily, causing their horses to bolt.

Low-hanging branches knocked two of the goblinkin

from their saddles, leaving the riderless horses free to run.

Cobner laughed uproariously, gleefully cursing the confused goblinkin.

Wick's mind worked furiously despite the fear that vibrated within him, searching for words that could do the brave dwarf's efforts justice. Then the little librarian saw the first goblin Cobner had unhorsed stagger to his feet. The goblin was behind the dwarf, out of Cobner's sight, as he took a crossbow from his fallen mount's saddle before it could get its feet under it once more.

Cold fear drained through Wick as he watched the dwarf lift the crossbow to shoulder. Before the little librarian knew what he was doing, he was running, covering the ground swiftly as he raced for Cobner. *No!* He couldn't allow the brave dwarven thief to be killed so out-of-hand by such a cowardly attack. He didn't run for the goblin, knowing the foul creature would probably only turn and put the quarrel between his eyes. Instead, he ran for Cobner.

"Look out, Cobner!" Wick bellowed.

Cobner turned, the battle-axe held in both hands before him, but the move wasn't going to be in time and Wick knew the dwarf didn't see the goblin taking aim at him.

The little librarian threw himself forward, flying through the air, intending to knock Cobner back. However, Wick hadn't planned on how solidly the dwarf stood his ground. The little librarian smacked into Cobner's chainmail and stopped as though he'd run headlong into a stone wall.

Wick felt the breath leave his lungs at the impact and was thinking to himself that the action had surely been the stupidest thing he'd ever done—then a sharp pain took him in the lower back. *I've been shot! I'm going to die!* The impact knocked him against Cobner again, rebounding him from the big dwarf's chest.

19

Broken Forge Mountains

Halfer!" Cobner's eyes rounded in surprise, then he caught Wick in one beefy hand. "Has he gone and killed you, then?"

A cold flash flared through the little librarian. He was afraid to reply, but he knew there could be no other answer. He was in more pain than he'd been in his entire life. "I think so, Cobner."

Cobner threw the long-hafted battle-axe with one hand and from the abrupt end of the dying scream from behind Wick, he had no doubt that the weapon's unconventional attack had nevertheless taken down the goblin.

"And you gave your life to save me?" Cobner shook his broad head in disbelief. "I wouldn't have thought you'd have a brave bone in your whole body, halfer."

Wick felt on the verge of passing out, sickness twisting his stomach. "I didn't mean to," he gasped. "I thought I could knock you out of the way."

"Nobody knocks ol' Cobner about so easily, halfer." Tears filled the big dwarf's pale eyes as he wrapped his strong arms around Wick. "That foul goblin couldn't have hurt me. You should have known that. I've been taking care of myself for a lot more years than you've been around."

"The goblin had you," Wick gasped. *Please don't let*

me throw up through my dying speech! In all the great death scenes he'd read about heroes in the books in Hralbomm's Wing, he'd never read about one who had thrown up as his last dying expression. "Everything is going black, Cobner." The little librarian hovered on the edge of passing out.

"I got you, little man," Cobner promised as gently as his great, booming voice would allow. "I ain't going to let you go into that big night all alone. I'll stay with you till the end."

Thudding hoofbeats sounded behind Wick as he let the big dwarf hold him. The little librarian's knees lacked the strength to hold him. "You need to go, Cobner. Get away."

"I can't do it, little man," Cobner said sorrowfully. "I'll not leave any warrior brave enough to lay down his life for another."

"I'm no warrior," Wick said, gritting his teeth against the pain.

"You're warrior enough for the likes of me," Cobner stated grimly. "I'll not forget what you've done for me."

"Cobner," Brant called.

Weakly, Wick craned his head and stared at the master thief sitting astride his horse only a few feet away.

"Saddle up," Brant ordered. "We've beaten the goblinkin back for the moment, but they'll be back in even greater numbers."

Wick couldn't believe it. Here he lay, shot and dying, and Brant wasn't even going to give him time to die properly. *Or at least die not throwing up!*

"I can't leave Wick," Cobner said, holding Wick gently. "He done give his life to save me, and the goblins killed him."

"Killed him?" Brant stood up in his stirrups. "He's been shot, Cobner, but I've never heard of a man who died from being shot in the, uh, posterior."

Posterior? Still in great pain, but now recognizing that the pain was coming lower than he'd thought, too low, surely, to be shot in the heart, Wick looked over his shoulder. Cobner looked behind the little librarian as well.

The quarrel, fletched in black and white feathers, did in fact stand out from Wick's . . . *posterior.*

"Why," Cobner shouted happily, "you aren't going to die after all, halfer!" He reached down and took hold of the offending quarrel. "And lucky for you, I know the goblinkin here don't use poisoned broad-bladed quarrels in their crossbows. This won't take but just an instant to have out of there."

"No!" Wick shouted. Now that he knew he was going to live, he didn't want to hurt anymore.

But Cobner didn't hesitate and ripped the quarrel out.

Wick screamed again as the pain swept through him once more. Nausea rolled his stomach. Before he was ready, Cobner had him on his feet but he didn't have the strength to hold himself up.

"Get him on a horse," Brant ordered.

Limp and shaking, not believing the harsh treatment he was enduring at the hands of the dwarf he'd tried to save, Wick groaned in pain as Cobner threw him up onto the nearest horse.

"Can you sit a horse?" Cobner demanded.

Sitting anything at the moment didn't sound appealing, but Wick nodded.

"Take his reins, Cobner," Brant ordered. "Lead his horse." The master thief kicked his own mount in the sides and guided it toward the back of the cemetery. "We're going through the woods out back. There's a creek back that way from what I remember, then about a mile of rough country. We'll stay clear of the main roads for the time."

Rough country? With his posterior hurting, Wick

didn't like the sound of that at all. He liked what happened next even less. Baldarn and Rithilin took up their bows from their saddles and set themselves to take up the rearguard at Brant's urging.

The master thief took up the lead, whipping his horse and racing across the graveyard.

Wick clung to the saddle pommel with both hands and tried to find a position that wasn't agony. *Can't I still bleed to death?* He wasn't certain, but there was no denying that even now a fresh group of torches marked the advance of another goblinkin patrol. Staying was out of the question.

Cobner led the little librarian's horse across the ransacked cemetery grounds as if the holes didn't exist. Wick clung to the horse in white-knuckled terror, certain that at any instant his horse was going to plunge into an open grave and break both their necks. The horse's muscles bunched, then it leapt forward over a skeleton sprawled on the ground below them. Wick screamed in wild-eyed terror as he momentarily lifted clear of the saddle. Then his injured rump slammed back into the saddle and he screamed again.

Before he'd had time to take another tight breath, the little librarian saw the cemetery fence coming up quickly. The horse matched Cobner's mount perfectly, running as if they were old wagon mates.

"Hold onto yourself, little warrior!" Cobner warned.

Wick tried desperately not to pass out from the pain and sheer terror. *Dwellers are not meant for such things as this! We're a peaceful folk! A warm hearth, a good meal, and a pipe! That's as much adventure as I ever wanted!*

The horse stutter-stepped for just an instant, then gathered itself and vaulted over the high fence.

Wick lifted again from the saddle, then crashed back down. Forested and treacherous terrain took shape ahead of him. The little librarian leaned over the saddle so he wouldn't be knocked loose from the horse. Even hurting and dizzy-headed as he was, he had the presence of mind to reach back and make certain the backpack with the four books remained in place. If he lived—and he wasn't at all certain that was going to happen—he had to find a way back to Greydawn Moors. The books had to be saved if at all possible.

And what will Grandmagister Frollo think of them? the little librarian wondered. The existence of the books shook the Vault of All Known Knowledge's edicts down to their core. *If not all of the books are safely stored at the Library, what is Grandmagister Frollo going to do?* But even as he thought that, he wondered again about the package Grandmagister Frollo had given him to take to the Yondering Docks Customs House.

The ride became a wild mixture of shadows and splintered moonlight, thudding horses' hooves and vengeful shouts from the rear, horses' breaths that formed gray plumes in the darkness. They splashed through the small creek Brant had told them to expect, and wetness covered Wick's legs, followed instantly by the biting cold of the night.

The horse redoubled its efforts beneath him as it charged up the next hill. Cobner called back encouragement. Wick lowered his head to the horse's neck, his nostrils filling with the great animal's musk, and prayed fearfully that none of them died in the insane race through the woods that led out of Hanged Elf's Point.

Hours later, Brant called for a brief stop to rest the horses, which were near exhaustion as much as their riders. In only a moment, the master thief assigned lookouts to establish a perimeter guard. And, to Wick's eternal chagrin and mortification, fierce Cobner insisted on tending the little librarian's wound. To make matters worse, Cobner had to clean the wound and needed the light from the small campfire they'd started in the foothills of the mountains deep in the Forest of Fangs and Shadows.

Once he was properly bandaged, though comfort and dignity seemed out of the question, Wick sat gingerly on the fallen tree near the campfire. The tree branches over the hollow formed a canopy that blocked out the star-filled sky.

Lago warmed soup he'd hastily thrown together from water in their waterskins, some spices in his saddlebags, and wild onions and mushrooms he found growing near the hollow.

Wick's mouth watered in anticipation when the old dwarf pronounced the soup fit to eat. Lago even had two loaves of bread in his saddlebags. To the little librarian's way of thinking and how his stomach felt, they had the makings of a feast.

"Here," Cobner said, fetching a cup full of hot soup over to Wick, "let me get that for you, halfer. Wounded as severely as you are, you ought not strain yourself."

Embarrassment flamed Wick's cheeks as he took the cup of soup and the chunk of bread the big dwarf handed him. At this point, he was uncertain whether he preferred Cobner distrustful of him or nursing him. There seemed to be no happy medium. Wick sopped his bread in the soup and ate it gratefully as Brant joined him.

"All the gems were found," the master thief said. "So if we ever had occasion to visit that wizard's hole again, we could."

Wick considered that an option he never wanted to exercise, but he didn't say that.

"All things considered," Brant said, "all of you took a good haul off the dead wizard."

Wick shook his head. "We don't know that he was the wizard that created that place."

Brant spread his hands. "Who else could he be?"

"I don't know." Wick sipped his soup miserly, knowing that Lago's cauldron wasn't bottomless and that it could be a long time between meals.

An owl screeched in the distance. The little librarian fell silent with the thieves as they carefully listened.

"Frustrated," Baldarn said, "from the sound of him. Probably missed a fat mouse."

Wick sopped more bread, too conscious of Brant's eyes on him.

"I couldn't help but notice," the master thief said, "that your backpack seemed a little heavier."

"Urm," Wick said, striving desperately to think of something to say.

"Everyone else has shared their loot," Brant said.

Wick looked around the campfire as small orange cinders drifted up from the burning wood. All the thieves' eyes were on him, though Cobner looked somewhat uncomfortable.

"Attempting to save Cobner," Brant said, "was very commendable."

"A very brave thing to do," the big dwarf added, scratching his beard. "Why, if the little halfer hadn't sacrificed his backside the way he did, doubtless I'd have a sore foot at the very least."

Grins passed around the thieves' faces, and only Hamual had the good grace to attempt to hide his amusement behind a hand.

"If I hadn't heard Lago's version of the events in the crypt," Brant said, "you could see how I could suspect how easily you opened that wizard's gate once I left."

"I didn't know you were leaving," Wick protested.

"I know."

"And I didn't know how to open that door. It was an accident."

Brant nodded easily. "I believe that. But I still wonder about the backpack. Baldarn said you were the first to enter the wizard's—" The master thief caught himself. "—the dead man's bedroom."

"It might not have been his bedroom," Wick said. "It could have been someone else's."

"I don't care." Brant let out a short breath.

Warily, wishing he had another choice, Wick put his soup and bread down on the tree trunk beside him. "I did take some things."

"See?" Baldarn asked, crossing his arms over his broad chest smugly. "I told you the little halfer took something."

Even Sonne shot the little librarian a reproachful look that cut Wick to the bone.

Wick opened his backpack. He took out the books, feeling guilty again for taking them in the first place, and then for not telling Brant and the others. He handed the books to the master thief, then added the paper, ink-wells, and quills he'd taken as well. When he finished handing over his ill-gotten gain, Wick felt a little better. Now there were no real secrets between them.

Brant looked at the books and the writing supplies. "This is it? This is all you took?"

Wick nodded.

"Well, Baldarn," Brant said, "it appears that you were right about Wick taking things from the room. Would you care to trade your share of the gold and silver that was in that room for these books and things?"

"They could be wizard's papers," Baldarn replied haughtily.

"Right," Tyrnen said sarcastically. "And if they had been wizard's papers, the little halfer and Brant would have been warty toads by now after touching them."

"Books could be worth something," Baldarn insisted.

Brant held the books on one hand toward the dwarf. "Would you want them then? I hear you can get as much as a gold piece apiece from Orpho Kadar."

Wick held himself back from objecting only through the knowledge that nothing he said would matter.

"No," Baldarn answered. "They're bigger and bulkier than carrying a gold piece, and traipsing through these woods with them in my pack isn't something I'm wishful of doing."

"Good," Brant said. "I'm glad we've settled that." The master thief turned his attention back to Wick. "You set some store by these books?"

"Yes."

The master thief flipped open the cover of the first book. "What are they about?"

"I don't know," Wick admitted.

"You don't?" Brant looked surprised.

"I can't read them."

The master thief chuckled. "And here I was, thinking you were so proud of your reading ability."

"They're written in a language that I can't read," Wick said. He shifted on the rough bark of the fallen tree, trying in vain to find a comfortable spot.

"If you say so, little artist." Brant handed the books, paper, and writing utensils back.

"I really can read," Wick said, slightly affronted.

Despite the tension surrounding the campsite, everyone laughed, which only annoyed the little librarian greatly. He put the books, paper, and writing utensils back in his pack.

"Those books count as a gold piece apiece," Baldarn added. "And they count as part of his share of the loot."

"Fair enough," Brant declared. "Little artist?"

Wick nodded grudgingly, not caring anything at all about the treasure the thieves had taken from the magic room. If there was anything at all that he wanted, it was safe passage back to Greydawn Moors.

The dark night around them seemed impenetrable, though, and the little librarian had no false hopes at all. He turned his attention back to his soup and bread, trying again to find a comfortable position.

"I could teach you to fight, you know."

Still groggy from lack of sleep caused by the all-too-short night spent in the woods and the painful wound, Wick glanced up at Cobner. The big dwarf rode beside the little librarian as Brant led them through the Forest of Fangs and Shadows.

"I appreciate that," Wick replied tactfully. Morning was still pink and gold in the east, and Jhurjan the Swift and Bold could still be seen racing as a red ball streaking through the dark purple of the western skies. "But I don't think fighting is something I would be good at."

"Maybe you've just never had a good teacher," Cobner declared, pushing a low-hanging branch from their way, making it obvious he was removing it from Wick's face as well even though the branch would have passed inches above the little librarian's head. "You know, a good teacher makes a lot of difference."

"I know." And Wick couldn't help but think about his father and Grandmagister Ludaan. Both of them had taught him things that had stayed with him all his life. Amazingly, though, he also thought of Hallekk and the other pirates of *One-Eyed Peggie* that had taught him to ride the ocean swells and race the wind.

"I had a good teacher," Cobner said. "And although I've never taught anyone before, I think I could be a good teacher."

"I'm sure you could," Wick replied.

"It's just that I've never found someone I really

wanted to teach before," Cobner said. "Until you."

Wick shifted painfully on the saddle, trying to find a new way to position the folded blanket that padded the saddle for his backside.

"Would you like another blanket?" Cobner asked. "I could suggest one of the others give up theirs."

"No," Wick said. "Thank you."

"I think you should really give fighting training some thought," Cobner said. "After seeing you in action last night, I think you'd be a natural."

Wick's ears burned. *Maybe I'd have been better off letting the goblinkin shoot Cobner in the foot.* Still, the big dwarf's good intentions were touching, even though they were also exhausting. *At least it would have made fleeing from Hanged Elf's Point much more comfortable.*

The group of thieves had started the day almost an hour before dawn with a cold breakfast made up of cold ham and bread. Brant had decided to head the group east, through the Forest of Fangs and Shadows, and across the Broken Forge Mountains, hoping to reach Blackgate Cove where the dweller villages were supposed to be. From there, Brant said, they'd be able to secure passage aboard a merchant ship away from Hanged Elf's Point.

No one had offered a better idea, and going anywhere near Orpho Kadar's city was considered too risky by all concerned.

Hooves thudded against the ground, coming up fast behind them.

Twisting painfully in the saddle, Wick glanced over his shoulder and watched Tyrnen riding up swiftly from behind. He and his twin had been assigned as rearguards.

"What's going on?" Cobner demanded as the young dwarf got closer.

"We're being followed," Tyrnen answered as he rode past.

"By who? Goblinkin? It's not like them to venture so far from Hanged Elf's Point."

"Purple Cloaks," Tyrnen shouted over his shoulder.

"Purple Cloaks?" Cobner shook his head as if he couldn't believe it. "Why would Fohmyn Mhout's lackeys pursue us so hard and so far?"

Wick could only guess that the Purple Cloaks' zeal could only have something to do with the things they'd taken from the magically hidden room. The only things that he would guess would be the books he carried in his backpack. And if Brant reached that assumption too, what would the master thief insist be done with those books?

"Well, Wick," Cobner said, "it sounds as though you're going to get more experience at fighting before this little chase is over." The big dwarf grinned confidently. "Stick with me. I'll show you everything you need to know."

Although Brant carried no map of the Broken Forge Mountains and had never traveled there, the master thief nevertheless had a description of the area. During his time there, he'd gleaned details from conversations with several trade caravan masters in Hanged Elf's Point.

Brant called a brief halt at the edge of the mountain foothills leading up from the Forest of Fangs and Shadows. There, the group had a clear view of the valley they'd just ridden up from. The master thief climbed to the top of a nearby promontory, lay on his stomach, and surveyed the valley.

Hobbling a little, actually more sore from all the riding of the last few days then the wound in his backside, Wick looked out over the valley as well, trying to fathom what the master thief was thinking. The little librarian held his journal, a piece of charcoal in his hand as he blocked out the scene. During the ride, in between Cobner's continued attempts to interest him in learning to fight, Wick had captured several loose images of the forest and the thieves.

Activity, barely seen but for a moment, drew Wick's attention from the drawing. The long line of Purple Cloaks threaded through a bare spot of the forest at a canter, following the same little-traveled trail Brant had chosen.

"Well," Sonne said in exasperation, "there's no question that they're following us."

"No," Brant agreed quietly as he pushed himself up from the ground. "What remains to be seen is what we're going to be able to do about it."

"We could try to ambush them," Cobner suggested.

"They're Purple Cloaks," Hamual said. "Away from Hanged Elf's Point, their powers will be strong."

"We'd have surprise on our side," Cobner argued.

"Only for a short time," Brant said. He loosened the saddle cinch on his horse for a moment, then tightened it again. "Once the surprise is gone, they still have their powers. And perhaps Fohmyn Mhout has equipped them with magic weapons as well."

The little group was silent again for a time. Wick watched the progress of the Purple Cloaks, knowing if any kind of physical confrontation took place they would surely lose. The Purple Cloaks outnumbered them nearly two to one.

"Then we go over the mountains," Sonne said.

Brant looked doubtfully up the sheer sides of the mountains. "If we don't find the mountain passes that the caravan traders told me they'd heard went through here, we'll have no choice but to face them."

Without warning, a distant rumble of thunder sounded, then came closer and rolled over the group of thieves.

Wick looked up but saw only blue sky overhead. He'd heard the thunder earlier in the day, but it had never sounded this close. "Was that a storm?" he asked. "And if it is, where is it?"

"That's no storm," Brant responded. "That was the volcano."

"Volcano?" Lago asked. "You didn't say anything about a volcano when we talked about this little trip over the mountains."

Brant shrugged. "The traders I talked to thought the volcano might have gone dormant."

The thunder rolled again, sounding more powerful this time. The little librarian felt the fierce cannonade vibrate through his body. *A volcano?* Something worried at the back of his mind, some half-buried memory of a description he'd read at the Library. Although he'd never found a single detailed source describing Dream, the city mentored by the Changeling race, he'd still read several different accounts of the city—and the land and sea surrounding it.

Just as Wick knew of the Silver Sea sailors, he also knew of the Broken Forge Mountains. Only the mountain range hadn't been called the Broken Forge Mountains then any more than the Forest of Fangs and Shadows had been called the Forest of Fangs and Shadows.

The little librarian turned to the thieves. "There may be another way."

Brant's eyes narrowed. "What are you talking about?"

"Once, a long time ago," Wick said, growing more certain as he put the pieces together in his mind, "these mountains were called the Iron Hammer Peaks, named for the dwarven clans that mined them."

"Dwarves, you say?" Lago asked, rubbing at his face and thinking about it. "My memory goes back a long time, and that of my clan stretches even further, young halfer, and I've heard stories from sailors and warriors and traders in all these parts. But not one of those stories has ever mentioned the Iron Hammer Peaks."

Wick stepped closer, hobbling because of his injury. Somehow, he felt he had to convince the little band he'd fallen in with. He didn't want to see any of them die, and—to his way of thinking—the tunnels snaking through the mountains offered a surer, faster escape.

He summoned all his conviction and stood before the group of thieves, making himself forget that he was smaller than them, weaker than them, and to remember that he was a Librarian at the Vault of All Known Knowledge. Not only that, but he was an experienced *Third Level* Librarian, not some wet-behind-the-ears Novice. He made his voice stronger, trying not to think about the Purple Cloaks riding toward their position even now.

"They probably haven't been called the Iron Hammer Peaks," Wick began, "since a time before the Cataclysm, before Lord Kharrion summoned the arcane powers that sundered the land known as Teldane's Bounty and caused it to be renamed the Shattered Coast." He looked out over his audience, knowing his words had captured their attention if not their belief. He kept the desperation from his voice as Grandmagister Ludaan had trained him to do.

A Librarian's greatest tool is his mind, Edgewick, Grandmagister Ludaan used to say. *But his next greatest tool is the manner in which he uses the knowledge he spends all of his life seeking and finding.*

Focusing on his presentation, Wick ignored the dull, throbbing pain in his wound. "The Goblin Lord's hatred for Teldane's Bounty was immense. All the dwarven, elven, and human forces that had dared face his goblin hordes in those last dark days after the fall of the Western Empire had taken refuge there. The desperate warriors regrouped there, all of them driven from hearth and home, riven from kith and kin, with only the Gentlewind Sea at their backs and no way for all of them to cross. When Lord Kharrion had finished his preparations, he unleashed the greatest spells of the Cataclysm and destroyed Teldane's Bounty."

The volcano rumbled in the distance.

The thieves, including Brant and Cobner, jumped at the sound.

"The ravages of the earth sank much of the coastline into the Gentlewind Sea," Wick went on. "Whole villages dropped into the ocean and were never seen again. A fleet of ships, standing by in scattered harbors to continue the work the warriors had done to preserve what they could of their histories and lives, was reduced by huge waves to flotsam and detritus. And further south, Dream, the Changelings' city where all races lived in peace, barely stood against the volcanoes that belched death from the sea floor. The proud Black Shields, the mountains that had protected the Silver Sea and the daring sailors that had lived there, crumbled and were lost beneath the waves. In one violent surge, the Silver Sea burst its boundaries and drank down the sailors and their families that had made their homes there for generations. And the Silver Sea rose as the land shifted, till the waters lapped at the feet of Dream, drowning all the humans and dwarves that lived in the lower regions."

"I don't understand," Brant said. "How does this help us now?"

"Dream was the unification of the three greatest races in the world at that time," Wick said. "Before you stands the dangerous woods that you call the Forest of Fangs and Shadows. But then the forest was called Bliss Arobor, and it was one of the largest sylvan homelands of the elves. It was also one of the oldest areas."

In the distance, the Purple Cloaks broke free of the

wooded cover. They still followed the trail as surely as wolves tracking blood scent.

Wick shifted his pack, terribly aware of the books he carried, and that he couldn't allow them to fall into goblinkin hands. *Yet if it came to it and I had no choice but to destroy them in order to prevent that, would I have the strength?* He didn't know.

The little librarian gestured to the mountains behind them. "Here in the Iron Hammer Peaks, as they were called then, there lived the Iron Hammer dwarven clan." He eyed the dwarven thieves among Brant's group, and walked briefly up and down the line that they made like a general in front of his troops. "Anyone of dwarven blood that was born within five hundred miles of these mountains might well be of Iron Hammer blood stock."

Cobner drew himself up straighter. "I'm from the Swift River Hollow clan. Less than two hundred miles from these mountains. The goblinkin wiped out my clan, but as long as one of us yet lives, we can rebuild."

Wick nodded. "That's how the Iron Hammer clan thought. When they saw that Lord Kharrion could not be defeated that day, and everything they'd fought for and crafted in Dream could not be held any more than the humans could hold the Silver Sea or the elves could hold Bliss Arobor, they left the Iron Hammer Peaks and moved to other lands to regroup and rebuild as is the dwarven nature."

"You're not saying that they ran, are you?" Cobner asked.

"They didn't run," Wick assured the big dwarf. "The dwarven clans have never run from a battle, only positioned themselves at the ready to once more take up the fight. And they did at the Cataclysm. Iron Hammer Peaks clan members struck back at the end of the Cataclysm and helped end Lord Kharrion's threat. But by that time, many clans took on new names because the

Iron Hammer Peaks held only death and nearly emptied mines."

"What good does knowing this now do us?" Brant asked. "Assuming it's true."

"It's true," Wick said, meeting the master thief's unspoken challenge. "And it matters because I know the Iron Hammer Peaks clan cut tunnels through these mountains to allow trade between the eastern and western territories."

"Do you know where one of these tunnels is?" Brant asked.

"I think so."

Brant hesitated a moment, glancing back at the Forest of Fangs and Shadows. "Then let's get moving in that direction. Going through the mountains will be easier than going over them. Safer, too.

"And there's a chance the Purple Cloaks may not know of those tunnels."

Stepping into his horse's stirrup, the master thief pulled himself into the saddle. The beast fidgeted, stamping its hooves nervously, ready to be on the move as well. "Mount up."

Gamely, Wick tried to haul himself into his horse's saddle. Unfortunately, his wounded backside made it nearly impossible to get up. Cobner leaned down and grabbed him by his backpack straps, then pulled him into the saddle.

"Thank you," Wick said.

"Take the lead," Brant instructed.

Wick hesitated only a moment, then pulled his horse's head around and headed south. Librarians weren't meant to be actual expedition leaders. *I'll go in the direction of the noise of the volcano. If things haven't moved around too greatly, I'll find one of those tunnels there.* He hoped they still existed.

Sonne urged her horse beside the little librarian's,

matching his gait. She carried a crossbow at the ready in her free hand.

Wick gazed up the steep slope of the mountain. *Please let the tunnels still be there.*

20

Dragon Myths

If so much work had been done here," Sonne asked after the group had been under way for a few minutes through the wooded foothills of the Broken Forge Mountains, "why didn't the Iron Hammer Peaks dwarves return to these mountains after the Cataclysm?"

"They didn't return because death was here," Wick said quietly. His horse's hooves rattled against small rocks that had been mined from the area and spilled down the mountain. For a moment he was almost convinced that the horse was going to tumble over the side of the small trail they'd found that led slightly above the treeline to the right.

"You're talking about the dead men left here?" Sonne looked confused.

"No," Wick answered. "Death itself. After Lord Kharrion sundered Teldane's Bounty and created the Shattered Coast, he also made a bargain with Shengharck."

"Who is Shengharck?" Sonne asked.

"A great and fearsome dragon," Lago answered. "Surely you've heard of him."

Sonne shook her head. "Dragons don't exist."

Wick started to respond, but his horse stumbled on loose rock and slid sideways for just a moment. The animal's muscles bunched and surged beneath him. He grabbed onto the saddle pommel fretfully.

"Dragons do so exist," Lago replied fiercely as Wick managed to resume an even keel and a position that favored his wound. "Why, dwarves and dragons have been at war with one another longer than elves and humans even knew the critters were about. Shengharck is the reputed King of the Dragons."

"Faugh!" Cobner stated from just behind Wick. "I think that's a story embellishment. Dragons don't have anything resembling kings. They don't get along too well between themselves, always warring and arguing over rights to lands and hunting areas. I'm just glad there aren't many of them left."

"I've only heard of dragons in stories," Sonne said. "No one I know has ever really seen one."

"Most who do see dragons wind up dead," Lago said. "Why, it's lucky we are that we have any information about them foul beasties at all. Dragonkin aren't overly tolerant of those that intrude on their lands. Upon occasion, dragons have destroyed whole companies of the fiercest dwarven warriors you could ever hope to meet."

"But you've never seen one," Sonne protested.

"A sailor never sees the wind that pushes his vessel either," Cobner said. "Yet the wind is there and he uses it as he sees fit. The problem with you humans—and I offer no disrespect here, Sonne, because you know I think highly of you—is that your lives are too short to properly appreciate everything you see and hear and do. Why, a community of humans hardly has time to learn from their own mistakes before a whole new generation comes along and makes those same mistakes all over again like they'd just been smithed."

"You don't believe this Shengharck is King of the Dragons?" Sonne said.

"No," Cobner agreed. "But I do believe that dragons exist."

"And why not a Dragon King?" Sonne persisted.

"Because it is said that the Dragon King receives fealty from all the other dragons," Cobner said. "I know that dragons aren't civilized creatures; they're solitary monsters. They hunt and feed and demand tribute for their own pleasures. They're evil, with no thought but for themselves. No man may ever befriend one or conquer one."

"Evidently Lord Kharrion did," Sonne said. "Unless Wick's stories aren't true."

"Lord Kharrion didn't befriend Shengharck," Wick jumped in quickly, wanting to guide the conversation back to more pertinent ground and to get the story back around to the facts. *I didn't say Lord Kharrion befriended the Dragon King, did I?* He sighed. Sometimes talking to the thieves was like presenting material to a group of hardheaded Novices who only wanted to prove a teacher wrong so they could be quickly on to greatness. "The Goblin Lord made a *bargain* with Shengharck after Teldane's Bounty was destroyed."

"I thought you couldn't bargain with dragons," Sonne said.

"At times," Lago said, "it has been done. But only as a last resort. Dragons will not be used, and they are very treacherous. If there is any room to break a bargain to a dragon's advantage, the foul creatures will."

According to some of the books Wick had read, the dwarves knew first hand of a dragon's deceitful nature. There were some scholars of all races who contended that the dwarves had been allies of the dragons in the beginning, only to find themselves later betrayed. Of all the races, the dwarves had the least use for dragons.

"What was the nature of the bargain Shengharck

struck with Lord Kharrion?" Hamual asked from further
back.

"Shengharck lived in the north," Wick told them, remembering the stories he'd read about the fearsome
dragon. "King Amalryn united the Western Empire further up the coast. The unified armies there killed two
lesser dragons in that area. One of them was Shengharck's child."

"You've got to understand," Lago said, "dragons
don't really experience the love a father feels for a
child." The old dwarf blinked when Sonne gave him a
hard look. "Or a mother feels, neither. But they do have
their pride about such things. A dragon's life spans
thousands of years. There are some that claim the fierce
beasts are eternal, as ageless as the Old Ones themselves."

"And others who say that the dragons are kin to the
Old Ones," Cobner added. He spat, and the spittle flew
out over the trees below. "That's a particular view I
choose not to share. I can't imagine the dwarven deities
having anything to do with dragons."

"It's said," Brant put in, "that the first dwarves stole
the secret of forging steel from the dragons."

"True," Cobner said, and his thick chest swelled with
pride. "That I can believe. Only a dwarf would have a
need so great and bravery enough to do that."

The other dwarves quickly agreed.

"Anyway," Wick said, seizing an opportune moment
to leap back into the conversation, "Shengharck long
held enmity against the elven, dwarven, and human
races. Although Lord Kharrion had destroyed Teldane's
Bounty, there yet remained the threat of Dream, which
stood in the south."

"Hanged Elf's Point, you mean," Baldarn said.

"The city still stood as Dream then," Wick returned
with stern politeness. "Dream was the grandest city in

the south, just as Cloud Heights in Silverleaves Glen was the grandest city in the west, and people of all races loved the city and the lives it made possible. Despite the ravages of the Goblin Lord's arcane spells, Dream yet stood, and it drew an army to its walls."

The little librarian heard his voice echo against the tall wall of stone the mountain made to his left. Eagles left their aeries above, giving careful watch over the interlopers that had chosen to travel through their territory. The *clop-clop-clopping* of the horse's hooves served as a counterpoint to his words.

"Massacring the remnants of the Western Empire armies took time even for Lord Kharrion's goblin horde," Wick said. "While those men gave their lives along the Shattered Coast, Dream pulled another army to her walls, embracing all who would take up arms against the approaching goblinkin. A bloodbath washed over all the broken coastline, but it flowed relentlessly toward Dream."

"By the Old Ones," Hamual swore quietly, "how many goblins were there in Lord Kharrion's army?"

"More died in those last dark days than lived to tell of the victories they'd had," Wick said. His mind filled with the grim narratives he'd read of those forced marches and skirmishes. There had even been journals saved that had been written by generals who'd fallen on the front lines. "But the goblins left no enemy alive behind them, no village unburned, no farm or orchard left unblemished and unsalted. When they were finished, nothing lived again in those places for a hundred years and more."

"I've heard it said," Rithilin stated quietly, "that if a man knows where to look around Lottar's Crossing, the scars of that march can still be seen."

"I've been told that some of the beaches along those coasts were first started from the bodies of the men who fell there," Cobner said. "That if you go out far enough, dig down deeply enough, you will find the skeletons of goblins, dwarves, elves, and men that make up the foundations of those shoals."

"Yes," Wick said. "The remnants of the Western Empire's armies and those who'd taken up arms in Teldane's Bounty were forced back into the Gentlewind Sea as far as they could go. Then they were killed, without mercy, without quarter. For a time, the Gentlewind Sea was supposed to have run red with the blood of those who died there. By some accounts, the dwarven, human, and elven warriors took down two or three goblins each before falling themselves. They were trained troops and they battled with the desperation of warriors defending their families."

"Their families were there?" Sonne asked.

The thundering roll sounded closer when it filled the mountains again. Rocks tumbled from the higher reaches of the mountain, and Wick thought he could feel the ground shiver beneath them.

"The families of most of them were there," Wick said. "In the beginning, the Western Empire had arranged for ships that would take their families to safer lands."

"Where?" Brant asked.

Wick deftly avoided the question, though he had the feeling the master thief had asked it with the same skill he plied his trade with. "I don't remember." But the destination, he knew, had been Greydawn Moors. Wick's own ancestors had come across on those ships, joining the Builders and the mages who labored frantically to create the Vault of All Known Knowledge.

"I see." Brant's response let Wick know the lie would go unchallenged, but that the master thief wouldn't forget it either.

"The spells that destroyed the land created huge tidal waves that devastated most of the ships before they could be fully loaded. Many families of those warriors died in the Gentlewind Sea, in a harbor that became known—at least for a short time—as Innocents' Despair. The rest of the families," Wick's voice tightened for a moment and his words were strained, "stood helpless before the butchery of Lord Kharrion's goblin horde after the last of their warriors had fallen. Every last woman and child was cut down by the bloody axes and claws and fangs of the goblinkin."

The thunder rolled again in the distance, and this time Wick thought he could see a dark smudge along the mountain ridges to the south.

"The armies of Hanged Elf's—" Hamual stopped himself. "The armies of Dream knew the Western Empire army fell?"

"Yes," the little librarian went on grimly. "Although the goblinkin losses were substantial as well, their numbers were far greater than any might have guessed."

"Some of the tales I've heard," Brant said, "suggest that Lord Kharrion rested for a time after that battle, and that he used more spells to raise an undead army from the fallen goblins."

"The Boneblights," Wick replied. "Lord Kharrion did raise them then."

"Dead goblinkin?" Hamual asked incredulously. "They didn't quit serving him even in death?"

"By that time," Wick said, peering over the decline ahead that bridged an even more narrow ledge, "Lord Kharrion's mastery of whatever dark arts he'd won over to his side had grown much greater. Even death was no longer a barrier."

Seeing Wick's discomfort at going along the narrow ledge, Sonne urged her horse forward, then grabbed the bridle of the little librarian's horse. Her mount clattered down onto the ledge in a spray of loose rock that had Wick's stomach turning flips. The little librarian held onto the saddle pommel with both hands and tried not to let his words sound terribly strained.

"Lord Kharrion sacrificed the last of the women and children from his attacks then," Wick said. "He tortured his victims, and used his vile arcane knowledge to bind their pain and anger to the corpses of his goblin troops and marched them once more south along the coast. He also called in the Embyrs, the nine daughters of King Amalryn who the Goblin Lord had changed into conscienceless creatures who lived only to kill and destroy under his orders."

"The daughters of a king?" Sonne repeated.

"Yes," Wick said. "When Cloud Heights fell, which was the heart of the Western Empire, King Amalryn, his queen, and his sons were executed. But the daughters were transformed into another weapon in the Goblin Lord's arsenal."

"These were young women?" Sonne asked.

"Some of them," Wick replied, remembering the Embyr he'd confronted aboard *One-Eyed Peggie*. "Others were children, just babes."

Sonne cursed then, and Wick knew the deep-seated anger and revulsion she vented came from some part of her as well. "Children should never be used for evil ends."

"Lord Kharrion did it for that purpose," Wick said. "And the Goblin Lord let it be known how those fierce, burning Embyrs had come to be. Those warriors that fought them couldn't help remembering the precious faces of the great elven king's daughters. Even if those warriors had somehow found a way to destroy the Embyrs, no one would have harmed them."

"Dream knew this was the army they faced?" Cobner asked.

"Yes," Wick said. He leaned into the saddle as Sonne led him up the other side of the narrow ledge where the terrain seemed a little safer. His wound still ached.

"They didn't run, didn't falter?"

"No," Wick said.

"Well," Cobner said proudly, "there must have been some Iron Hammer Peaks dwarves among them."

"Yes," the little librarian replied. "Since the beginning of Dream there had always been Iron Hammer Peaks dwarves among the citizens of Dream. Who do you think built those once-great buildings that you've seen there?"

"I had no doubt that it couldn't be anything but dwarven-made."

"The dragon," Brant reminded. "You've talked for a very long time, little artist, and the Purple Cloaks haven't faltered from their pursuit either."

Wick glanced over his shoulder. However, at the moment he saw nothing of the Purple Cloaks, though he was certain the master thief had been watching for them and had probably marked their location. "Lord Kharrion assembled his new army, reinvigorated by the Boneblights he'd raised, and he marched on Dream. As he neared the great city, he realized that Dream had escaped the rising waters and yet held together. Still standing as it was, the city promised a possible grinding campaign that would wear away at even the number of goblinkin he commanded, and it would allow the few remaining areas that he hadn't yet attacked to further shore up their defenses. He contacted spies inside Dream."

"Who?" Cobner demanded.

"In all the books I have read," Wick admitted, "the men that betrayed Dream were never mentioned by name or in any fashion that might serve to identify them."

Cobner cursed them as only an incensed dwarf might, and his booming voice was swallowed up in the crash of thunder that sounded even closer.

Wick surveyed the southern horizon again, feeling

heartened by the forbidding, black smoky color staining the sky. "The leaders of Dream had a plan to flank Lord Kharrion's army as they came from the north along the Shattered Coast. As the goblin horde advanced, troops were sent out into Bliss Arobor. They were given orders to join the Iron Hammer Peaks dwarves in a flanking maneuver designed to turn Lord Kharrion's army in on itself. There in the forest of Bliss Arobor, confusion was believed to be the greatest weapon the humans, elves, and dwarves had. The commanders at Dream were convinced that the goblinkin would overreact in the shadows of the forest where all manner of creatures fought against them under the leadership of the elven warders. Given the ferocious and uncivilized nature of goblinkin, and the fact that they were from different tribes that had warred with each other in the past, it was believed that the horde would turn on itself in confusion and wreak havoc among its own forces before they knew it was each other they fought. When that happened, the forces of Dream would launch another attack from that direction. They believed that Lord Kharrion's goblin horde would break and stall there, and be unable to regain momentum."

"It was a good plan," Cobner declared. "Did it work?"

"It never had the chance," Wick said. "Before the goblin horde reached Bliss Arobor, Lord Kharrion contacted Shengharck and made a bargain with the dragon."

"What bargain?" Lago asked.

"Through his spies in Dream, Lord Kharrion had learned of the campaign that would be used against him. His bargain with Shengharck ceded the dragon rights to the Iron Hammer Peaks."

"Those rights weren't the Goblin Lord's to give," Sonne said.

"If he conquered Dream," Wick said, "they were Lord Kharrion's rights to give. And with Shengharck's help, the Goblin Lord destroyed the flanking move that had formed in the Iron Hammer Peaks. The Dragon King flew in from the north, catching unaware the dwarven, human, and elven warriors gathered there. Shengharck descended upon them, breathing flames and rending with his great and terrible claws. The human, elven, and dwarven ranks held only for a moment. Their arrows and spears broke against the great dragon's impenetrable scales. Even the powerful mages among them couldn't halt Shengharck. Then the line gave way as Shengharck continued his attacks. Before the warriors had a chance to save themselves, Lord Kharrion's troops deployed from the edge of Bliss Arobor and marched into the foothills. The goblinkin ambushed the warriors at Dharl's Pass and there they died to a man."

The last of the little librarian's words rang against the mountains for just a moment before the next roll of thunder swallowed them. A startling silence followed.

"The Iron Hammer Peaks dwarven clan didn't come back because of the dragon?" Cobner asked.

"Yes," Wick said, watching Sonne as she guided him toward the next incline. Loose rock tumbled from under her mount's hooves and rattled over the edge of the drop to their right. "Shengharck settled in the Iron Hammer Peaks during the rest of Lord Kharrion's assault on Dream. Every attempt made by the dwarves to return there ended only in death."

"What happened to Dream?" Hamual asked.

"It fell," Wick answered. "At least, that's what everyone agrees happened. You've seen the city for yourself. If the goblins are there, it had to have fallen. Either then or later."

"Who is *everyone*?" Brant asked. "The *everyone* that agrees with you?"

Wick hesitated, not certain how to answer the question. "Friends."

"Fellow *readers*?"

That's safe enough, Wick thought, *isn't it?* "Yes."

"What happened to Shengharck?" Sonne asked.

Rolling thunder filled the air around them again. This time the vibrations coursing through the ground were so strong a small avalanche of rock and debris started high up on the mountain and tumbled down around them. Stones and foggy dirt slithered through the horses' legs, then rose up in dry, choking clouds.

Wick put a hand over his mouth and coughed so hard he thought his head would explode. His eyes watered from the grit that filled them. He shifted to stay in the saddle as his horse shied in terror beneath him, stumbling dangerously close to the ledge and the long drop beyond. Gradually, the dust subsided and the sound of falling rock drifted away over the trees.

Carefully, Sonne started her horse forward again, pulling Wick's mount after hers. Loose stones clattered over the edge from the hooves.

"Shengharck remained within the Iron Hammer Peaks," Wick said. "According to the tales I've read, none of those who attempted to flee from Dream over the mountains ever made it to the other side. Armies that attempted to mass either within Bliss Arobor or along the foothills of the mountains met only disaster and death when Shengharck flew among them. Lord Kharrion's flank remained protected throughout Dream's Ending."

"What happened then?" Hamual said.

"No one knows for sure," Wick replied. He, like all the other librarians before him at the Vault, and some after, had combed references in reports Grandmagister Ludaan had sought out. Thinking back on the mysterious package that had taken him down to the Yondering Docks in Greydawn Moors now, Wick thought he might inquire further into the new Grandmagister's requirements for Novices. *If I ever return to the Library.* "But it was documented in several sources that Shengharck remained within the Iron Hammer Peaks even after Lord Kharrion's war was finally ended."

"The dragon lives within the mountains?" Karick asked.

"Yes," Wick said. He noticed the hesitation in the faces of his companions. "But it's a big mountain, and there are a number of mine shafts. I'd say our chances of actually meeting Shengharck are very remote."

"Where did the dragon choose to live?" Hamual asked.

"Near the center of the Iron Hammer Peaks." Wick gazed at the smoky ridge clinging to the skyline. "It was there that the Iron Hammer Peaks dwarven clan had punched tunnels through the mountain. Shengharck liked the location because he had a back exit from his new lair and could be in the sky and attacking within minutes without anyone being the wiser. He hunted on either side of the mountain range."

"You say there are dozens of mine shafts?" Lago asked.

Wick nodded.

"How will you know which mine shafts will lead through the mountain range and which are dead ends or collapsed tunnels?"

"The Iron Hammer Peaks dwarves kept very good records of their tunneling," Wick answered. *Awfully dry, straightforward reading, though.* "Each mine shaft was said to be marked."

"Marked in what way?"

"The dwarven miners wrote where each tunnel ended," Wick said.

"In the human language?" Baldarn asked, looking very suspicious of the whole story.

"No," Wick said. "In one of the dwarven languages prevalent in this area."

"The dwarves had a written language?" Lago asked quietly.

"Yes." Wick stood up in the stirrups as Sonne led his horse down a steep decline. "They had several, though many of the clans shared an abbreviated common language."

"And you read dwarven?" Baldarn asked with a sneer.

"Quite well," Wick said. "The Steelringer clan near Mardath Falls believed that making hard steel required song as well as heat and the unyielding strength of a blacksmith's arm."

"They sang while they worked the metal?" Cobner asked in fascination.

"Yes," Wick said. "Several of their songs still survive."

"I've been told I've got a fine singing voice," Cobner offered. "I'd like very much to learn some of these songs, little warrior."

For a moment, fear touched Wick's heart when he thought of teaching the big, fierce dwarf some of the Steelringer clan songs. *Is there anything in those songs that the Library is oathbound to protect?* He couldn't remember, but he didn't think so. Generally, the Steelringer songs were about the craft and the beauty of the things their ringing hammers had forged on fire-hardened anvils. "When the time presents itself, Cobner, I'd be very happy to teach you some of the songs that I know."

"How is it you come to know how to read dwarven languages?" Baldarn demanded.

"I was taught," Wick answered.

"By who? Dwarves?"

"No."

"Then who?"

Wick thought quickly, not believing that the questions posed by his companions had to come now, when Fohmyn Mhout's Purple Cloaks pursued them. *How much longer will it be before one of them realizes that the Purple Cloaks may be chasing us because of the books I took from the hidden room? And what will they do if they do realize that?* The little librarian glanced ahead, feeling the ground quiver again as another tremor shook the mountains. "My teachers."

"And they weren't dwarves?" Baldarn asked.

"No."

"Then why—"

"Enough," Brant called from the rear. "All this jabbering is giving me a headache, and the Purple Cloaks could be close enough soon to hear your voices carrying down the side of these mountains."

Feeling momentarily relieved, Wick glanced back at the master thief. Brant's cold black eyes regarded the little librarian flatly. A chill flooded Wick. *Brant knows I'm hiding something! That's why he stopped them from questioning me!* The relief faded at once. The little librarian knew how exacting the master thief could be when faced with a secret. Resolutely, Wick turned his attention back to the mountains ahead as Sonne continued leading his horse.

Little more than an hour later, Brant declared the terrain too treacherous to risk while riding. All of them climbed from their mounts and led their horses over the loose ground.

Wick peered behind them constantly, seeking some sign of the Purple Cloaks, convinced their relentless pursuers would appear at any moment. The pain of his wound increased for a time, then finally went nearly numb, only offering the occasional twinge. Maybe the herbs and mendicants Cobner had used during the night had finally proven effective, or perhaps it wasn't as bad as he'd first perceived.

Despite the fact that the walking became easier, the little librarian couldn't quite keep up with the longer, stronger strides of the others. In a short time, he was at the back of the fleeing group, and Brant was matching him stride for stride.

"There's a place I've heard of," the master thief stated quietly.

Wick walked with his head down, not wanting to make eye contact with the man.

"In nearly every town you visit," Brant said, "there's always talk of a mysterious Vault that was created during the Cataclysm."

Wick remained silent, his breath tearing raggedly at the back of his throat.

"Now I've always figured that the Vault was another myth," Brant went on. "There are plenty of myths regarding the Cataclysm about fantastic treasures that were hidden by humans, elves, and dwarves as the goblins razed their homelands. Every now and again, I hear the tale of some group or individual who claims to have found one of those lost treasures."

A rock slipped from under Wick's foot and he nearly fell. Before he lost his balance completely, Brant seized his arm and helped the little librarian keep upright.

"I've never believed those stories," the master thief said. "And when I had occasion to question some of those treasure hunters—"

"To rob them, you mean?" Wick asked pointedly, wishing he had some way to stem the questions he knew were coming.

Brant grinned mirthlessly. "You do judge a man harshly, don't you?"

Wick's face flamed and he felt shamed. "I apologize."

"There's no need to, little artist," Brant said after a moment. "I know what I am as surely as you do. Only I don't paint as bleak a picture of it as you do. Those men that I questioned, they weren't good men. They had no more right to that treasure than I did. And if I'd been able, and if they'd *really* had those treasures, I'd have taken them."

"Why did you become—" Wick hesitated.

"A thief?" Brant's amusement appeared honest.

The little librarian let out his breath, knowing there was no other way to answer the question other than honestly. "Yes."

"I had no other choice."

"There are always choices."

Brant took a deep breath. "You don't even know me, little artist."

"No," Wick admitted.

The master thief glanced around the terrain, sweeping the sky as another black streamer puffed from the mountain ahead. "My father was a baron, and the land he controlled was a small bit of farmland tucked into the Sweetgrass Valley."

"I've not heard of it," Wick said.

"I'm not surprised. It had been in my family's holdings for generations. Then Malodoc Tramm rose up from other lands and sought to build himself an empire. He took on humans, elves, dwarves, and goblins, anyone who didn't mind slitting a throat for a chance at a few silver coins. The only way he stayed in command of them was by being more sly and vicious than anyone among their number."

As the master thief spoke, Wick heard the pain in Brant's voice. As a librarian, Wick had been trained to listen to others, to know the emotions that colored the experiences they related even if they didn't want to part with them.

"Tramm and his men came to Sweetgrass Valley thirty years ago," Brant said. "I was hardly more than a boy. My father managed to get me away to safety by having Cobner look after me."

"Cobner?"

Brant nodded. "Cobner was one of my father's oldest friends." He grinned sadly. "I don't know if Cobner even knows that my father considered him as such. All of you have much longer lives than humans. For most of you, friendship with a human is probably much like becoming used to a guttering candle flame."

The master's thief's comparison hurt Wick. The little librarian looked back to his own friendship with Grandmagister Ludaan, remembering the way the Grandmagister had seemed to age from a young man to an old bent one in just a handful of years. *Did I take him for granted?* He remembered when he'd learned that Grandmagister Ludaan had passed away. It hadn't seemed like weeks since they'd talked. "My teacher was human."

"I thought as much," Brant said.

Wick looked up at the master thief.

"See?" Brant said gently. "Even your look tells me much at this moment."

"I can't speak to you of this matter. I'm sorry."

Brant laughed softly. "Fret not, little artist. I believe I have most of your secret figured out, but I won't be telling anyone of it. Although, I must admit, that accepting it means having to believe the Cataclysm was also real."

"It was," Wick said.

"So that means that a dragon will be waiting on us when we find those mines."

"Unless something has happened to it," Wick replied, "then yes, Shengharck will be there. What happened to your da and ma?"

Brant regarded the little librarian with his black eyes. "Why are you interested?"

"Because that event seems to have shaped you the most."

Brant walked around a boulder. "Tramm had my father and mother executed." He took a deep breath and looked away. "I'd fled with Cobner during the night, determined somehow to get back to my father and mother and help them." He shook his head. "I didn't know what I was going to do. Only that I had to do something. Cobner caught me before I reached the town. Cobner held his hand over my mouth, almost so tightly that I couldn't breathe, and together we watched as the headsman's axe fell. Then fell again."

"I'm sorry," Wick whispered hoarsely as the master thief's words faded away.

"Twelve long years later," Brant went on after a moment, "I returned to Sweetgrass Valley. I was a grown man then, and Cobner had taught me everything he could about fighting. For a time, we'd earned our keep as mercenaries in other people's wars. Young as I was, confident in the cruel seasoning I'd had from surviving countless horrors on battlefields, I was convinced that I could kill Malodoc Tramm."

"Did you?" Wick stared at the master thief's scarred face, trying to imagine the things that the man had seen. It was a miracle that he'd lived through such engagements.

Brant shook his head. "Tramm had built the empire that he'd sought. I stayed in the city that Tramm had chosen as his crown jewel for six months, till my gold ran out. Then I started to live by my wits. That's how I became a thief. Of course, I was already somewhat accomplished at it. You can't be a mercenary without picking up some skills at a craft like that: you draw a monthly wage, but you take what you can from your enemies and the other mercenaries as well. I discovered I had a natural proclivity for stealing."

"Then why didn't you stay?" Wick asked.

"Because," Brant answered in a voice that faltered for the first time since Wick had met the man, "because I soon felt that I was no better than Malodoc Tramm." He sighed. "I stole from everyone in that city that I could, telling myself that I deserved what I took, that I was better than they were. They were living in peace with the man who had murdered my father and mother, after all. Then one day I had to leave."

"Because you could no longer believe the lie?" Wick asked.

Brant shook his head and smiled. "No. Because my success as a thief hadn't escaped notice. Cobner and I were very nearly caught taking tribute from Malodoc Tramm's money collectors. The description of us, although no one knew for sure who were really were, was enough to identify us too well for us to maintain any kind of anonymity. I'd gone there quietly as the vengeful hero, and I left as a notorious outlaw one step ahead of Tramm's soldiers." He laughed bitterly. "So now you know my secret, little artist. What do you think about it?"

"You did what you could," Wick said, a new respect in him for the master thief.

"And your secret?" Brant asked. "Are you so willing to part with it?"

Wick looked down at his feet as he walked along, trailing distantly behind the rest of the group. "I can't." He felt horrible that he couldn't tell Brant after the man had shared his own story.

"So which is it, little artist?" Brant asked.

"What?"

"Is the Vault filled with incredible treasures as some claim, or is it something else?"

Wick gave his answer careful thought. "I suppose that depends," the little librarian stated cautiously, "on what your perception of what you found there was. If such a place exists."

Brant laughed, and this time there was good humor in the sound. "Touché, little artist."

Wick knelt by the quickly flowing little stream that splashed down the mountainside only a short distance further on. His feet, legs, and back ached from riding and walking. He filled his waterskin from the stream as his horse drank its fill.

Above them, the sun had begun its descent, shining onto the side of the Broken Forge Mountains that they were on.

Lago passed out another hunk of bread and they ate from the razalistynberry brambles growing wild around the stream. Bright orange and yellow butterflies flitted from the succulent berries as well, filling the air with vibrant confetti.

Once his waterskin was tied back onto his horse's saddle, Wick took out his journal and a sharp quill. With an agile mind, he quickly wrote out notes that he planned to expand on later. Then he sketched a brief picture of Cobner, who had climbed up the mountainside more than a hundred feet to act as their lookout.

A few minutes later, after the horses had a breather, Brant whistled, giving the signal to get ready to ride on. Cobner scrambled down the mountainside, scattering rocks and loose soil in his path.

"The Purple Cloaks are still back there," the big dwarf told Brant when he reached them. "Closer than they were before, but they're resting their horses, too."

Brant pulled up into his saddle. "They don't show any signs of turning back?"

"No." Cobner stepped into the stirrup and pulled himself up as well.

"The horses aren't going to hold up," Sonne said. "We've been pushing them hard for a day and a half now."

"I know," Brant replied, striking out into the lead. "We don't have a choice."

"I don't like to see them treated this way," Sonne objected. She frowned in displeasure and irritation.

"I know." Brant continued moving resolutely across the foothills.

Arms trembling with effort, Wick hauled himself into the saddle. He followed Brant and Cobner through the scrub brush. The little librarian really doubted he could outlast his horse. Surely he would falter before it did. He looked around at his companions, recognizing how fatigued and worn out they all were as well.

The thunder rolled across the blue sky again, and this time Wick saw the distinctive puff of smoke that drifted on the wind. The volcano—and the entrances to the Iron Hammer Peaks dwarven clan mines—couldn't be more than another hour's ride off. Somewhat heartened, he searched in vain for a more comfortable position.

Hamual guided his horse over to join Wick. "Do you think the dragon—Shengharck—still lives within the mountain?" the young warrior asked.

"I wouldn't know," Wick answered truthfully.

"But if the stories are true," Hamual pressed.

Wick saw the excitement gleaming in his young friend's eyes despite the tiredness. "If the stories are true," the little librarian said, "about dragons in general and Shengharck in particular, then it's possible."

"Wouldn't that be something? To take a great dragon's treasure?"

Wick thought about it only a moment, but it was enough to make his stomach nauseous. The prospect definitely didn't have the allure for him that it did for the young human. "It's not been done very often."

"You're going to hear more about that kind of thing in lies than for real," Lago commented. "You don't just go about stealing a dragon's treasure after it has spent hundreds and mayhap thousands of years accumulating its hoard."

"Yes," Hamual said, "but if we could, our reputations as thieves would spread everywhere. Bards would sing about us in songs."

"Being well known as a thief," Wick pointed out, "isn't exactly a good idea."

"Oh." Hamual's face turned red.

Lago, Baldarn, and Sonne laughed, but the young human joined them.

Wick marveled at his companions' ability to laugh at a time when they seemed up against such desperate measures. Still, his own sense of humor brought a quick smile to his lips. Hamual clapped the little librarian on the back, which unfortunately caused Wick's wound to ache again, necessitating a move to find comfort again, and made them all laugh.

Amid the nervous laughter, Wick wasn't sure if the first scream he heard was a scream at all. When the scream was repeated, however, there was no doubt.

21

The Woman in the Web

That's a woman!" Sonne pulled her horse up short, causing the tired animal to stumble on the uneven mountainside. Rocks skipped from the horse's hooves over the ledge hanging over the Forest of Fangs and Shadows below.

The scream rang out again, more strident this time, and fear mixed evenly with anger.

"Brant," Sonne called out.

"I heard it." The master thief pulled his horse to a stop at the head of the line. Cobner sat astride his own horse next to Brant.

"It could be a trick," Baldarn said.

Wick gripped the reins of his own horse and glanced fearfully at the forest below the ledge. Even with the echoing effect created by the mountainside to his left, he was certain the screams came from within the dark mass of trees below. *It could be a trick,* the little librarian thought. *But the Purple Cloaks are behind us. And why scream out a warning?*

The woman's scream pierced the air again, sounding more desperate.

Brant surveyed the forest from the ledge. His horse pranced nervously.

"It's not our problem," Cobner said gruffly. The big

dwarf held his fierce battle-axe across his saddle pommel.

"We're not leaving someone in that kind of trouble," Sonne declared. Without another word, the young girl cut her horse around to the left and raced along the ridge for a moment. She disappeared with alarming abruptness.

"Sonne!" the little librarian called fearfully, just knowing that she and her horse had accidentally plunged over the ledge to their doom.

Brant pulled his horse's head around and charged after the young girl. Cobner cursed fiercely, but took out in quick pursuit as well. In short order, the other thieves followed.

Am I the only one who remembers that we're being chased by the Purple Cloaks? Wick wondered. But he didn't want to stay on the mountainside by himself, either. And surely anyone who sounded that scared needed help. The little librarian urged his horse into motion, racing in the same direction as the others. By the time he got moving, the thieves had vanished. For a moment, he thought he was going to drop over the ledge, then he spotted the broken defile that led back down into the forest. He clung to the saddle pommel, letting the horse pick its own way down.

At the bottom of the defile, Wick pulled the reins around and guided the horse in the direction of the moving brush left in the wake of the other steeds. The scream rang out again, more hoarse this time.

The little librarian hung onto the saddle grimly, quickly catching up to the mounted thieves. The afternoon sunlight barely broke through the thick copse of trees and brush, leaving long, dark shadows that lay over everything.

Sonne was in the lead. Wick barely glimpsed her through the trees. In the next instant, her horse reared, nearly tossing her from the saddle. Then a fat, hairy shape seemed to materialize in the space between the trees in front of her.

That's a spider! Wick recognized the familiar shape even at the same time that his brain was telling him the creature was far larger than he'd ever seen.

The spider measured at least eight feet long from forefoot to hind foot, and the fat, heavy body took up at least half of that. The spider clambered across a fifty-foot web, jarring the silken strands with every move. The creature moved rapidly, closing in on Sonne and her horse.

Despite the surprise evident on her face, the young girl retained her wits. She brought up her crossbow and fired as soon as she had the weapon level. The quarrel leapt from the weapon just as the spider jumped from the web. The quarrel smacked deeply into the spider's head, throwing it off balance. It plopped onto the ground before Sonne.

The spider raised on its eight legs, swaying slightly, obviously seriously wounded. Sonne's horse backed into a tree as she hung the crossbow from her saddle pommel. A fistful of knives appeared in her hands as if by magic.

Brant attacked without warning, coming up on the spider from behind. He lashed out with his sword, cutting the spider across the back. Drawing in on itself, lowering its heavy body to the ground, the spider balanced itself and leaped at the master thief. Even as the spider cleared the ground, Cobner stood up in his stirrups beside Brant and swung the battle-axe with both hands. The big blade caught the huge arachnid in the midsection and cut it in half. Both halves landed in quivering piles in the brush.

"Help me!" a hoarse voice shouted from above.

Hypnotized and numbed by the horror of how quickly the savage arachnid had moved, Wick glanced up the web. Thirty feet above the forest floor, a woman hung amid the strands, securely tied in place by webbing. Only her dark hair and violet eyes remained free of webbing.

"There!" Lago cried, pointing.

Brant dropped from his horse and tossed the reins to Cobner. The master thief carried his sword naked in his fist. "Keep a sharp watch. The stories I've heard about the spiders in the Forest of Fangs and Shadows suggest that those things don't often lair alone."

Wick shuddered, surprising himself when he drew the knife at his belt. He felt the warm steel in his hand. He'd drawn a knife before on *One-Eyed Peggie,* but it had never been with the intention of fighting something. Then it had been to make the Blood-Soaked Sea pirates trust him. And he had used the knife to cut grappling lines thrown by the goblin slaver party. He didn't want to fight a giant spider now, but he knew he would defend himself. His horse shifted beneath him, and his wound throbbed, reminding him that he'd also thrown himself at Cobner in an effort to save the big dwarf only last night. The little librarian couldn't believe the changes that had taken place within him in the past weeks. But there had been so much that he'd seen, and he'd learned to hate the feeling of helplessness that had plagued those past weeks.

Brant grabbed hold of the spider web and attempted to crawl up. But the web trembled, bouncing the woman above, and the strand that the master thief had stepped on snapped. He gazed up at the woman. "I'm too heavy."

Sonne vaulted from her horse and tied the reins around a nearby branch. She tried to climb the web as well, but even her smaller weight caused the web strand to break.

"The spider must have carried her up there," Lago said. "Then bound her so that her weight wouldn't break the web. They must not usually trap something as big as a person."

"No," Brant agreed. "But the stories I listened to suggested that spiders in this forest don't stop at taking people if they're given the chance. Their poison causes paralysis, and they eat their prey alive."

Wick shuddered, vividly imagining what it must feel like to be trapped on a spider's web while one of those great creatures prepared for a meal later on.

"The web is suspended between these two trees," Cobner suggested. "We could chop down the trees."

"By the time we did that," Brant pointed out, "the Purple Cloaks would catch up with us."

"The woman could also be hurt," Sonne told them.

Wick look up at the trapped woman. *She's not trying to persuade them,* he realized in wonderment. *How can she lie there so quietly, waiting for them to decide her fate without saying anything to win them over?* Most people he knew—then he thought of Hallekk and many of the other pirates aboard *One-Eyed Peggie*—*some* of the people he knew, he amended silently, would have been yelling their heads off at that point. They would have demanded help or pleaded for it—or both.

Sonne glanced at Brant. "I'm not leaving her to this fate." The young girl's face appeared to be cut from stone. "I can't do it."

"Neither can I," the master thief admitted.

Cobner looked up at the woman strung high above them. A stray shaft of sunlight penetrated the gloom and made the web glisten with diamond brightness. "Then we'll give her a quick, clean death. A quarrel through the heart. It would be a mercy."

"No," Sonne argued.

"Or we could leave her here and let someone else come along to finish the job of saving her," the big dwarf said.

"We're wasting time," Baldarn called out from the rest of the group. "Every minute we spend here puts the Purple Cloaks one minute closer. If we're going to get away, the time is now."

"No!" Sonne turned to Baldarn as if daring the man to speak again.

The dwarf started to say something, but a quick look from Brant shut him up.

"I'll go." For a moment, Wick wondered where the voice had come from. Then, when everyone else turned to him, the little librarian realized to his horror that he had spoken. His heart was suddenly in his throat.

Cobner grinned. "Told you the little warrior had grit in him, didn't I?"

Wick didn't believe for even an instant that what had compelled him to speak had anything to do with courage or grit or anything like that. He only knew how terrible it had been to be kept in the goblin slave pens, and that being wrapped in a spider's webbing could only be so much worse. *I can't leave her like that, either.*

Brant focused on him. "We don't have much time."

"We don't have *any* time," Baldarn growled angrily. "I can practically hear those Purple Cloaks thundering up on us now."

Trembling slightly but hoping the others didn't notice, Wick stepped down from his horse. His foot slipped through the stirrup and he very nearly fell.

"Steady there, little warrior," Cobner encouraged. "And don't you have no worries about any other spiders clambering through them trees and that webbing after you. We've got your back."

Other spiders? The skin at the back of Wick's neck prickled. Wasn't one spider enough? He crossed the ground to the web on weak knees, then caught hold of the web strands. The web shook slightly at his contact, and the strands felt like they were covered with paste that was curiously dry to the touch and wet at the same time.

The little librarian gazed up the web. *It's no worse than the rigging aboard* One-Eyed Peggie, he told himself. *And there's not even the pitch and yaw of the ship and the sea to contend with.* He placed a foot on a strand and pushed up, thinking no one could blame him if the strand broke and he couldn't climb the web either.

However, the webbing seemed to easily support a dweller's weight.

Taking a fresh breath, thinking for a moment that contact with the spider's web had somehow paralyzed his lungs, Wick started up the web. He climbed hand-over-hand, shaking with each fresh hold.

"Little warrior," Cobner called. "Wait just a second."

I can't wait! Wick silently objected. *If I do, I'm going to start shaking so badly that I'll never get this done.* But he paused in the webbing.

Cobner tied a coil of rope at Wick's belt. "When you cut the woman loose," the big dwarf said, staring into his eyes, "the webbing might not support her climb back down. Her weight might even tear the web so much that you both fall. Throw a loop around one of those tree branches up there and use the rope to support her weight and yours. I want you back safe."

Wick swallowed hard. He hadn't even thought of the weight problem. *This is so stupid. I'm the last person that should volunteer to do something like this. I'm no hero.* He gazed up again and met the woman's violet-eyed gaze. *She's got less choice than I do. I can't leave her there.* He nodded to Cobner, not trusting his voice. Then he climbed.

He covered the distance surprisingly quickly. Wick was amazed at how quiet the forest was around him. When he was twenty feet up, he was grateful that the web strands were sticky because it made his footing and handholds more secure in spite of the quaking fear that filled him. However, each time he pulled a hand or a foot free of the strands, the whole web vibrated.

He drew level with the woman only a moment or two later. Her violet eyes searched his, but she said nothing. He opened his mouth to speak, but his throat betrayed him and no sounds came out.

"Don't worry," the woman told him. "You can do this."

Grimly, embarrassed that no heroic words of reassurance had come from his own lips after all the grand stories he'd read in Hralbomm's Wing, Wick only nodded. He shook out the rope that Cobner had given him, then tossed it over a thick, sturdy branch above him. He tied it in one of the knots the pirates had taught him, then made sure it was fast by pulling on it. Satisfied, he looped the rope around his own waist in a support rigging.

He turned his attention to the woman, trying desperately to forget how long the whole operation was taking and that the Purple Cloaks might burst upon them at any moment. She was elven. He saw that now from her slender build beneath the webbing, and from her pointed ears and features. And he wondered what an elven woman was doing out in the Forest of Fangs and Shadows.

"Wick," Brant called up.

Shaken from the mystery the woman presented, Wick cut through the webbing with the small knife Cobner had given him. The strands parted easily. He freed the woman's right hand first so that she could grip the rope.

"I have it," she told him.

"Are you strong enough to hold yourself, lady?" Wick asked. He wondered only a moment at his address of her, but somehow—as it must have with Cobner—the address seemed correct.

"Yes," she replied confidently.

Wick nodded, then cut away the rest of the webbing that bound her. The elven woman wore a warrior's scarred leathers, the little librarian discovered when he had her free, and she climbed down the rope as easily as a monkey. Wick slid down jerkily behind her once she'd reached the ground.

Standing on still-trembling legs, trying not to gasp in relief, the little librarian expertly shook out the rope, freeing the knot around the branch above. The rope fell down in coils around him with enough noise to make him jump in spite of himself.

Cobner grinned and clapped him on the shoulder. "You did good work up there, little warrior."

There were so many responses Wick could have made that would have made the effort seem like a trifle, just another small diversion in an ordinary day. He'd read hundreds of them in the books in Hralbomm's Wing. But all he could say was, "Thank you."

The elven woman approached Wick. "I would have your name, halfer."

"Wick," the little librarian stuttered. "I mean, Edgewick Lamplighter." He bowed, not as deeply as he'd hoped, though, because his wound pained him.

The elven woman's brows lifted, then she glanced at the other thieves surrounding her. When she looked back at Wick, she asked, "Do you know me somehow?"

"No, lady," the little librarian replied. "I've never seen you before today." He felt nervous, wondering if he had done anything wrong.

"Yet you offer me such respect." The violet eyes glittered.

"It—" Wick stammered, "it seemed only natural. Somehow."

After a moment, the elven woman nodded.

"Look," Baldarn complained, "we need to get moving, Brant. We've still got Purple Cloaks tailing us."

"Purple Cloaks?" The elven woman glanced at Brant, somehow sensing that he was in charge of the impromptu rescue group. "You've run afoul of Fohmyn Mhout's bully boys?"

"A minor misunderstanding," Brant assured her. "We've only lately come from Hanged Elf's Point."

"Brant, is it?" the elven woman inquired.

"Yes."

"Who are you?"

Brant regarded the elven woman with his black eyes. "No one of consequence."

The elven warrior stepped toward the master thief fearlessly. Her stride challenged him. "No one of consequence?"

"No." Brant glanced around the forest. "Were I of a cruder nature, my lady, I'd be tempted to ask you what you were doing in such a place all by yourself."

"Are you a suspicious man, then, Brant?"

"By nature," Brant replied evenly, "and by practice."

The elven warrior laughed then, and Wick marveled at her aplomb. *How many people,* he wondered, *could come so close to being eaten, yet handle themselves so assuredly?* The little librarian knew the dichotomy the woman offered would definitely pique Brant's curiosity.

"Suspicion is not a charming feature in a man," the elven woman said.

"Then again," Brant replied mockingly, "there is so much of the man yet to know and the suspicion is such a small part."

Cobner and the dwarves laughed at Brant's quick turn of words.

A hint of color touched the elven warrior's cheeks. She nodded. "Another time, perhaps, and we could find out who is the better conversationalist."

"It would be my pleasure," Brant said. "Would it be

uncouth of me to ask your name? You already have the use of mine."

Nervously, Wick glanced along the ridge above. How far behind them were the Purple Cloaks now? They'd spent several precious moments of their lead in the forest.

"I am Tseralyn," the elven woman replied, drawing herself up a little straighter.

"Tseralyn, you say?" Brant eyed the elven warrior with renewed interest. "I've heard tales of a mercenary queen roving these parts of late named Tseralyn. She's supposed to be near to ten feet tall from the stories, as quick with a blade as Saraymon Hitalh, who reportedly refined bladesmanship for the elves."

"A coincidence of names," Tseralyn said, holding her arms demurely at her sides. "As you can see, I'm surely not ten feet tall."

"No," Brant agreed easily. "But I've found that tales told in taverns are often exaggerated." He glanced at the spiderweb now hanging a bit more loosely between the trees. "However, I've met few people who could endure what you've just gone through with quite the same self-control."

"I was scared at the time," Tseralyn insisted. "You heard me screaming." The admission, though, seemed to embarrass her greatly.

"It's your recovery time that amazes me, my lady."

Tseralyn gestured at the two halves of the spider. "But the danger is past now."

Wick knew that the danger from the spider was over, but the Purple Cloaks could even now be closing in. Still, he knew the trembling in his knees and his hands wasn't just from the pursuit, but was partly from the climb up the web as well.

"There is still the matter of the imminent arrival of

the Purple Cloaks to consider," Brant reminded. "We've got to take our leave."

"I find myself in your debt," Tseralyn said. "I don't like being in anyone's debt."

Brant shook his head. "If I had been in the same dire straits, I'd like to think that you would do the same for me." He took the reins for his horse from Cobner and stepped into the saddle.

"I might not," Tseralyn warned the master thief.

Brant grinned at her. "I said I'd only like to think that, not hold you to it, my lady. And, perhaps, you may find yourself in a position to return the favor soon." He glanced meaningfully around at the dark forest. "Unless you plan on staying here."

A small smile twisted the elven warrior's face. "No. I don't."

"Were you out here alone, lady?" Lago asked.

Sadness filled the elven warrior's face. "Not at first. Those that were with me are dead."

"Wick," Brant said, "I'd like you to lend the lady the use of your horse if you would. You can ride double with Sonne."

The little librarian took his mount over to the elven warrior. "Lady," he offered.

Tseralyn took the reins without hesitation. "Thank you," she told Wick. She stepped into the saddle easily and glanced at Brant. "I suppose you have a plan for evading the Purple Cloaks?"

Brant nodded toward the plume of black smoke showing through the canopy of trees. "We're going through the mountains."

"A pass?" Tseralyn handled her horse with definite skill.

"No." Brant guided his mount back toward the incline that led up into the foothills. "Through mine shafts made by the Iron Hammer Peaks dwarven clan."

"I thought they were a myth," Tseralyn said.

Brant glanced at her. "I'm surprised that you've heard of them."

Riding behind Sonne, clinging desperately to the saddle, Wick was surprised as well. Tseralyn didn't look like a mercenary queen or a scholar.

"It was probably only a tavern tale I was told at one time," Tseralyn said. "And you know how those stories go."

"I don't know," Brant commented dryly. "You'd be surprised at how many of those old tales turn out to have some small speck of truth about them."

"Then, perhaps, we'll have the opportunity to find out if the myth about the dragon has some truth in it as well."

"Only if we stay ahead of the Purple Cloaks," Cobner growled.

Conversation fell by the wayside, and the only sounds Wick heard were the deep breathing of the horses, the thudding hooves, and the loud rumble of the volcano.

The volcano loomed high in the mountains, and the land quaked as it rumbled. Black smoke and cinders pooled at its mouth, belying the snow that covered it below the crown.

Wick's breath was almost taken away by the sight of the restless giant grumbling above the small band. Gray cinders landed in his eyes and made them water. The little librarian clung to the back of Sonne's saddle and nearly panicked every time the horse shifted beneath them. Sitting on the back end of the horse, he'd discovered, made every move the animal made seem somehow much bigger and more sudden.

"Rest the horses for a moment," Brant commanded, stepping from the saddle atop a wide spot in the ridge through the foothills they followed. "Let's find out for sure where we are."

Gratefully, certain he'd been crippled for sure this time by all the horseback riding, Wick slid from the horse, borrowing the stirrup Sonne took her foot from. She dropped lithely to the ground beside him.

Tseralyn joined Brant. The elven warrior wore an extra traveling cloak Cobner had packed in his saddlebags.

Wick drew his own traveling cloak more tightly about him. Despite the presence of the volcano overhead, cold air blew down from the high mountains, mixing with the occasional warm gust. Scraggly brush and trees clung to the volcano's slope, but here and there the little librarian spotted edifices that had been made of cooled volcanic rock, proof that the volcano had erupted before, though it had obviously been hundreds or thousands of years ago. Glittering streams also showed in a dozen different places, proof that the snow on top of the volcano made its way back into the Forest of Fangs and Shadows.

Brant sent Cobner above to investigate the pursuit of the Purple Cloaks, and sent Karick and Hamual ahead to scout for any entrances into the mountain.

Baldarn studied the broken terrain with a grimace, then glanced at Wick, scowled, and spat contemptuously. "If there's no entrance into any mines that lead through this mountain, the halfer has killed us all. These horses aren't going to go much further."

"Maybe the Purple Cloaks are already afoot," Lago said. "They pushed their animals hard to try to catch up with us."

Wick busied himself helping Sonne care for the horse they rode double on. Luckily, even together they didn't weigh as much as some of the dwarves, or probably Hamual either.

"The local people call the volcano the Broken Forge," Tseralyn said. She glanced along their backtrail as well, and Wick had noticed her tendency to do that. "They say that the Old Ones once dwelt here and hammered out the different birds, fish, and animals that roam these lands. Then one day the Old Ones got into an argument over the creation of a new creature. The Old Ones supposedly fought for days and months over the design. In the end, the mystic forge they'd raised from the earth to make their creatures was shattered, never to be made whole again, and the incomplete creatures they'd labored on became the first of the trolls."

"Trolls are goblinkin," Tyrnen stated, brushing down his own horse.

"Only a lot uglier," Zalnar added.

"Orpho Kadar doesn't believe that," Tseralyn said. "No trolls are allowed into Hanged Elf's Point at night. And the ones that have been caught have been kept locked up, tied in different poses till sunlight turns them to stone the next morning. I'm told that Orpho Kadar has quite a collection of them in gardens around his castle."

"A collection of trolls turned to stone?" Brant mused and shook his head.

"In all kinds of poses," Tseralyn said. "I'm told some of them are supposed to be quite amusing."

"There's no accounting for some tastes."

Although Wick didn't care much for trolls, the idea of having ones turned to stone on purpose then placed in gardens was horrifying.

Cobner returned from the upper reaches of the volcano as a particularly nasty bit of rumbling nearly knocked the little band from their feet. "The Purple Cloaks have slowed some," the big dwarf announced, "but they're still behind us."

While Wick and the others digested that bit of news, and the little librarian felt even more pressure about the gamble he'd seemingly made with all their lives because

Baldarn kept staring at him, Hamual returned.

The young human smiled broadly. "I found a tunnel a short distance ahead. I only entered it for a moment and didn't really travel deeply into it other than to make sure it was a deep one, but it's definitely a major entrance."

"That doesn't mean it goes all the way through," Baldarn growled. "And even if it does, it could lead right to that dragon."

Brant flashed the surly dwarf a white grin. "Oh, and now the little artist's stories have got you believing in dragons, do they, Baldarn?"

Baldarn spent his energy on clambering onto his horse again and didn't answer.

Long years and hard wear had all but eliminated the once-proud sign that had been carved on the right side of the mine entrance. Hypnotized by the writing, Wick slid from Sonne's horse as the band of thieves gathered in front of the mine by the remnants of the rusty iron tracks where ore carts had once rolled. The little librarian crossed to the wall by the mine entrance, then carefully dug debris and packed dirt from the letters. It was in a dwarven dialect close enough to one of the others he knew for the translation to come readily to mind.

Mine Shaft Number Six
Property of
IRON HAMMER PEAKS CLAN
No Trespassing
Plenty of Graves inside for Trespassers

"Can you read it?" Lago asked.

"Yes," Wick answered. Although he'd been expecting to see the mine marked in some manner, actually seeing legible writing outside of Greydawn Moors seemed somehow . . . *heretical.* "It's written in a dwarven language." *Written!* His astonishment kept rolling over him.

"Well," Brant prompted.

Wick swiftly read the information.

"Plenty of graves inside, eh?" Baldarn repeated doubtfully. "Not very inviting."

"I know," Lago said, laughing. "It sounds very much like a busy dwarf's greeting."

"Can you tell if the mine shaft goes through?" Brant asked.

Wick read the inscription again. "It doesn't say."

"Will it inside?"

"Very probably." Wick took his journal from inside his shirt, then took a piece of charcoal from his coin pouch. Working quickly, the little librarian made a rubbing of the inscription, having to use six sheets of paper to get it all.

Brant organized his band of thieves, sending them scurrying into the nearby brush at the mouth of the mine to get branches to make torches using the pitch pots Lago carried. For the first time, Wick realized how dark it was going to be inside the mineshaft. He shuddered, not liking the images that his mind summoned up in no time at all. When a dwarven mine was operational, no creatures—not even bears or ogres—dared lair there. But now, with the decrepit state of the mine, anything could have moved into the shelter provided by the stone walls.

Lago piled the oily black pitch onto the torches the thieves found during their scavenging. The old dwarf also managed to find yet another bread loaf in the pack he carried, but Wick knew they had to be getting dangerously low on supplies. Would the Purple Cloaks or starvation overtake them first?

"Somebody else has been here before us," Cobner said, gesturing at the ground.

Wick looked at the hard-packed earth and spotted the tracks of horses that marred the ground.

"How long ago?"

"Looks recent."

"Can you tell who it was?" Brant asked.

Cobner knelt and dug loose dirt from the tracks. "The horses were unshod." He glanced around at the ground. "And there were a lot of them. Fohmyn Mhout's Purple Cloaks all ride shod horses."

Tseralyn knelt down as well and examined the tracks the big dwarven warrior had dug out. "Goblinkin slavers," she announced. "They work through the Forest of Fangs and Shadows and the Broken Forge Mountains. Blackgate Cove lies on the other side of this mountain range. There's a dozen halfer villages scattered through those lands that fish and trade with ships." She looked up at Wick. "I'd thought at first that maybe you were from there, but you're not, are you?"

"No, lady," Wick answered.

"None of the halfers there knows how to read."

Wick looked away, realizing that he'd inadvertently let yet another person in on his secret.

Tseralyn glanced meaningfully at the little librarian's journal. "You know how to write, too, don't you?"

Wick closed his journal and put it away. "Yes."

The elven warrior stood, a small, curious smile on her face. "How is it that you know how to do those things? Only wizards know how to read and write."

"I'm not a wizard," Wick said.

"Easy, my lady," Brant said. "The little artist's secrets are his own. For his own reasons."

Tseralyn looked over at the master thief. "You don't seem like a man much inclined to let mysteries and secrets pass you by."

"I'm not. But I let your secrets stand, my lady." Brant regarded her, his black eyes flat and neutral. "And so I let his stand as well."

Tseralyn nodded. "I respect that."

"Good. I should hate for any problems to arise between us." Brant took one of the pitch torches from Lago. The master thief popped one of his hands and sparks jumped onto the torch. The flames quickly crowned the torch's head, burning brightly for a moment before settling down somewhat. With a deft move that hid the flint and steel he'd undoubtedly used to light the torch, he held his hand out for the elven warrior's inspection. "Cobner."

"Yes."

"Would you take the lead?"

"I'd be happy to. There's always more action at the front."

"And keep an eye out for any more writing on the walls that you may see."

Cobner took another torch and lit it from the one Brant held. The big dwarf hitched his battle-axe up onto his shoulder and fearlessly strode into the mine.

"Wick."

The little librarian looked up at the master thief.

"Stay with Cobner. Use those quick eyes of yours well. You might find something Cobner misses." Brant held out the reins to Cobner's horse.

Wick accepted the bridle reins and took a final look around the mineshaft. The rusty iron tracks ran out into the level ground ahead of the mine, disappearing into the scrub brush and trees. Somewhere around there, he felt certain, would be the remains of the dwarven village of Mattletown.

Cuperious Eltuth had written dozens of monographs in different books detailing the wondrous automatons the Iron Hammer Peaks dwarves had forged over hundreds of years. There was supposed to be a mechanical deer that actually walked and ate corn, and a metal duck so cunningly made that it flew as easily as the fowl that it had been modeled on. Finding those, or any of the other automatons the human historian had written about, would have been amazing.

Resolutely, Wick took one of the torches Lago had made, watching as Tyrnen and Zalnar bundled dozens more sticks and strapped them to their horses. The little librarian stepped into the mine shaft after Cobner. Broken stone and debris littered the way, occasionally joined by rusted mining tools.

"A dwarven miner would never have left all this behind willingly," Cobner said softly. The big dwarf's voice echoed inside the cavern.

"Shengharck was said to have struck suddenly." Wick lifted his torch and examined the wall next to him. Curiously, he scratched at the black color. It peeled free of the wall in crystallized flakes.

Cobner stood in front of Wick, gazing at the clean patch on the wall. "What is that?"

"Soot," Wick answered in a small voice that cracked. He lifted the torch higher, revealing a large expanse of the wall. Cobner's own torch showed that the devastation continued down the cavern, all of it marked in black soot scarring.

"From the dragon's breath?"

Wick nodded, feeling small and insignificant while surrounded by the old scars of the conflagration that had once filled the mine. "There was nothing else in here to burn." Glancing at the rusty tools in the debris at his feet, the little librarian saw that none of the wooden parts had survived. Even the wooden planks between the iron rails for the mine carts were gone. *Everything was burned!* He continued following Cobner, amazed at how big the cavern was—and how extensively the fire had damaged everything. Blackened timbers still framed the three mine shafts ahead where Cobner had stopped.

The sound of the horses' hooves striking stone echoed behind them, making the cavern sound even emptier to Wick. The little librarian couldn't help wondering how many dwarves had died in the mines after Shengharck's arrival. *There couldn't possibly have been many survivors!*

Cobner turned and faced him. The torchlight fell only partially into the three dark-throated tunnels that split off the main cavern. "Which way?" the big dwarf asked. Although he kept his voice neutral, pain showed in his eyes.

Wick stepped forward, dropping the bridle reins. The horse snorted tiredly behind him and stamped its feet while munching on the bridle bit. The little librarian rubbed his hand across the stone on the right side of each shaft, clearing the soot and debris from the writing carved there. Plankless mine car tracks ran down each shaft, vanishing at the end of the flickering torchlight.

The shafts were marked in order from left to right.

Mine Shaft Six, Tunnel One
Mine Shaft Six, Tunnel Two
Mine Shaft Six, Tunnel Three

Smaller writing under the first tunnel indicated that the tunnel had been abandoned and had collapsed. A list of seven names followed the declaration, all of them noted as dwarves that had died in the cave-in.

Wick took out his journal and quickly copied the names off, thinking he might be able to cross-reference them back at the Vault of All Known Knowledge if he got the chance. At least the names might provide another linchpin bridging the information of the pre-Cataclysmic times and what historians believed to be true now.

"Is this the tunnel we need to take?" Brant asked.

"No," Wick answered. "This one collapsed a long time ago." He put the journal away.

"What about the other two?"

"They're both open according to the information there, and they lead to the other side of the mountain."

The volcano rumbled again, and the warbling growl trapped inside the cavern seemed to boil up from the bowels of the mountains. Debris and a cloud of dust shivered free of the cavern ceiling and rained down over Wick and the others.

"The way that sounds," Baldarn griped, "all these tunnels could come down at any time. We might be better off taking our chances with the Purple Cloaks."

"No," Brant said, wiping dust from his traveling cloak. "These tunnels have been here for decades—" He glanced at Wick and lifted his eyebrows.

"Hundreds of years, actually," Wick said. "Possibly as much as two thousand."

"There you go," Brant said. "If they've stood like this for hundreds or thousands of years, they'll surely stand for another few hours while we make our way through them." He paused. "Which tunnel, little artist?"

Wick didn't know how best to answer. The information carved beside the tunnels indicated that they went through to the other side of the mountains, but there was no way of knowing if that was true any longer. Shengharck could have caused damage that could have closed any of them down. "Either the center tunnel or the one on the right should be fine."

"Okay," Brant said. "We'll take the center tunnel. Cobner, lead on."

Without a word, the big dwarf stepped into the tunnel and moved forward. Wick watched for a moment, not really wanting to step into the waiting darkness. Then Cobner's light got far enough away that it created a bubble of illumination that no longer touched the little librarian's. Wick took a final glance back at the open mouth of the mine shaft on the other side of the large cavern. The dimming day had already cast a shadow over the outside world.

Heaving a quiet sigh, trying to convince himself that stepping into the unknown dangers of the mine shaft was preferable to facing Fohmyn Mhout's Purple Cloaks, Wick grabbed the reins of Cobner's horse and trudged into the mine tunnel.

Thoughts of Blackgate Cove kept the little librarian's mind busy. Brant and his group had talked about the area uncertainly, but Tseralyn spoke of it as if she'd been there. *Can there be villages of dwellers living on the other side of this mountain in safety?* After seeing everything that was happening to dwellers in Hanged Elf's Point only a couple days' ride away, it was hard to imagine.

Even should it exist, Wick told himself, *those people there may not know anything about Greydawn Moors.* He would be just as lost then as he was now.

22

Under and Through the Mountain

It's getting colder," Cobner said quietly as he led the way down the tunnel's incline.

"We're going deeper into the mountain." Wick pulled his own traveling cloak more tightly around him, hoping to stave off some of the chill. "There must be underground streams nearby," Wick replied. "There's supposed to be an entrance to an underground lake beneath the Iron Hammer Peaks as well. I've been told that people once lived on the islands there."

"Do you believe it?"

Wick shook his head. "I think that part of the stories is a myth. It was never confirmed, only mentioned in rumors. But I believe there could be an underground lake." Frost glistened on the tunnel sides now, proof of the water that ran through the land underground.

Probably, the little librarian guessed, remembering Ruital's *Basics of Ground Water*, rain occurred on both sides of the mountain range and fed the lands on either side. Dream had been located on a peninsula of land, and the Shattered Coast probably hadn't changed that much. Rain would sweep in from the oceans on three sides. Some of the Iron Hammer Peaks dwarven clan historical writings had included notes on underground rivers in the area that created the Dankmire Swamps further south. They hadn't mentioned the underground lake so big that it had an island in the center of it. Only the humans had written of that.

"With the volcano sounding so near," Cobner said, "you'd think it would be a lot warmer."

"In other places it is," Wick said. "The writings I read talked of the hardships the Iron Hammer Peaks clan faced in digging the mines here. In some of the shafts they dug, the dwarven miners broke through walls that flooded whole tunnels before all of them could get clear. Other tunnels gave way suddenly to bottomless pits. And still other tunnels led only to steam vents from the volcano that boiled the flesh from the miners' bodies in the space of a drawn breath."

Cobner walked silently for a few moments, gazing at the blackened walls of the tunnel. "I never did like mining that much. I like building things just fine, but the only time I want to go into a hole in the ground is when I really don't care about living anymore."

Wick silently agreed. He held his torch high and made sure he stayed far enough in front of Cobner's horse that he wouldn't get stepped on. The horse's hooves thudded against the tunnel's stone floor, echoing with the hooves of the other horses that followed them. The mine car tracks wound through the center of the tunnel, but there still weren't any planks between the twin rails. Only a little further on, Cobner stepped around a set of rusting wheels and iron brackets, remnants of at least one mine car that had burned at that point.

Cobner raised his fading torch. "There's another tunnel ahead."

"I see it," the little librarian said, peering through the darkness to see the mine shaft barely limned in the torchlight ahead.

A number of smaller tunnels branched off the one they followed. All of those tunnels followed veins the dwarven miners had discovered in the mountains, and all were clearly labeled and numbered. None of them led to the land on the eastern side of the Broken Forge Mountains. The miners had followed the ore veins until they'd played out, then marked the tunnel as closed, concentrating on the sections that offered the fastest return on their labors.

Wick handed his torch to Cobner, who called out to Lago that he needed a fresh torch for himself. The little librarian concentrated on scraping the writing out with his dagger point. His eyes burned from spending hours trudging through the darkness, and from the smoke and dust that filled the tunnels every time the volcano grumbled.

Cobner stepped closer with his fresh torch. "What does it say?"

"It's another closed tunnel," Wick replied. He took out his journal and flipped it open to the loose map he was making based on their progress. He jotted the notation on the new tunnel and started to move away when a flash caught his eye.

"Come on," Cobner said. "Do you think we're halfway through these mountains yet?"

"I don't know." Wick took his torch back and shoved it into the new tunnel. The access shaft was only a few inches taller than Cobner. The flickering flame triggered a flashing reflection from something deep inside the tunnel.

"What did you find?" Brant asked, joining Wick.

"I don't know. There's something shiny further down the tunnel." The little librarian peered intently, his dweller's covetous instincts combining with his librarian's curiosity. Before he knew it, he'd taken three strides into the tunnel, leaving his companions behind, hypnotized by the gleaming blue flash.

"Little warrior," Cobner called. "Give caution there.

You could find all manner of hostile creatures in that tunnel." The dwarf's hobnailed boots crunched in pursuit of Wick.

Although fear thrilled inside him, Wick didn't stop till he reached the blue gleam. Only as he knelt did he realize that whatever it was lay ensnared in a broad, bony ribcage that had once belonged to a dwarven miner. Soot covered the bared skeleton, as it covered four others huddled there beside it.

"None of them had a chance," Cobner whispered behind Wick. "That foul dragon burned them down where they lay." He paused in silent reverence. "At least it couldn't eat them the way it evidently ate all the others it found."

Wick played his torch over the skeletons, noticing for the first time that they'd fallen forward. "They were running from the dragon when it breathed on them. They died instantly."

"What was it that caught your eye, little artist?" Brant asked.

Hand trembling, Wick reached into the skeleton's chest. He tried to think that the dust and debris that he reached through was just that, and that it wasn't the ash of flesh that had once been part of the dwarf. He closed his fist about his prize and pulled it free. Unfortunately, his closed fist was too wide to fit back through the chest cavity.

The skeleton's brittle bones snapped with hollow pops.

The object was longer than Wick had at first thought. He handed his torch to Cobner, who took it automatically.

"Looks like you found yourself a knife, little warrior," the big dwarf growled in approval.

Wick studied the object in his fist. It *was* a knife. Not even an elegant piece or memorable in any way except the manner in which he'd discovered it. The double-edged blade seemed worn but well cared for, with a simple cross hilt handle. A small, irregular sapphire set in the handle had caught the torchlight. Overall, the little librarian felt disappointed by his find. He hadn't known what he was going to find, and he certainly wasn't expecting some bit of treasure, but a knife hadn't even entered his mind.

Brant thrust his own torch out, beating the darkness in the tunnel back but revealing nothing else of interest. "Maybe that old knife isn't worth much, little artist, but it's a wonder that you saw it at all."

"It's because he has halfer's eyes," Cobner said. "They catch a lot of things most eyes don't. Some have even told me halfers can even see around corners if you put something bright and shiny there."

Wick knew that wasn't true, but he also knew he had seen the flash when no one else did. He placed the knife back on the floor by the skeletons.

"What are you doing?" Brant asked.

"Leaving it," Wick said. "The knife doesn't belong to me."

"It's not going to do those men any good," Cobner said. "You should keep it. That's a good knife from the looks of it. Good steel and solid craftsmanship. And those men were warriors. All dwarves are. They wouldn't want it to be left lying here and getting no use. Not when it could serve someone."

"I'm no warrior," Wick reminded.

"You could be," Cobner said. "All it would take is a little training."

"You should keep the knife, little artist," Brant said. "Perhaps it's offered as a good luck piece. At the very least, the knife can be a memento."

"I've heard great stories told about much less than a knife that looks like it's been carried through a number of wars," Cobner agreed. "If you want, I can help you make up your first magnificent lie."

Reluctantly, Wick reached down and took up the old knife again. He thrust it through his belt. The blade was so long that it fit him like a sword. He followed the master thief and the dwarven warrior back into the main mine shaft.

After two more hours of walking, the mine shaft ended in a massive cave-in.

Cobner cursed when he saw the avalanche of rock that blocked the way, then he spent long minutes prying at the rocks, shifting some of them and starting spills that sent dust flying in choking clouds. All of the thieves stayed back from the frenzy. The mine car tracks continued under the blockage.

Wick pulled his traveling cloak over his lower face in an effort to block the dust from his nose and mouth so he wouldn't breathe it in. Grit still filled his eyes, making them tear and leave dirt tracks down his cheeks that crusted and felt tight against his skin.

"Cobner," Brant called gently. "Give it up. There's no way you're going to move enough of that rock to allow us passage."

Cobner yelled in angry frustration and hurled a small boulder at the massive blockage. Stone cracked and impacted with sharp retorts. "This isn't fair, Brant. We've got to be over halfway through the mountain. We should have been able to see ourselves clear in a few more hours. There's no other way around this."

"Not without going back," Brant agreed. "But that's what we're going to do, Cobner." The master thief turned and faced the whole group. "It's what we have to do, and we can still do it. There's another tunnel that we didn't take back in the main cavern."

Wick heard the exhaustion in both men's voices. He blinked at the mass of rock and felt defeated himself. His wound throbbed dully now from all the riding and walking, but surprisingly it wasn't anything crippling.

"It's well past nightfall outside this mountain," Brant said. "We'll rest here tonight."

"I don't like the idea of sleeping here," Baldarn stated. "There's no telling what else might be in these caves just waiting to catch someone sleeping."

"We haven't see anything so far," Brant reasoned. "I think we're safer resting here and getting a fresh start after a few hours of sleep than in trying to press on now."

"Brant is right," Tseralyn added. "A warrior is always at his best when he's had adequate rest and a full stomach."

Despite Baldarn's misgivings, the rest of the group voted to follow Brant's advice. They unsaddled the horses and fed them from small grain pouches they all carried. Once the feeding was done, the thieves hobbled the horses over on one side of the large mine shaft. The animals were given water from the waterskins, and they drank from one of Lago's pots in turn. Only then did Brant allow any of his group to spread out bedrolls. Wick was again amazed at the master thief's leadership skills. The little librarian had helped Tseralyn take care of the mount she'd been riding.

Tyrnen and Zalnar broke some of the torch sticks they'd gathered to make a small campfire. However, the campfire also reminded everyone there that they had only the meager scraps from Lago's once seemingly endless larder to eat. The heat barely cut the chill filling the mine shaft, but it was more than enough to be welcome and appreciated. The thick gray smoke pooled against the stone cavern ceiling. Nearly half the thieves were asleep within minutes after Brant had given them the watch rotation.

Wick stretched out on his stomach on his own bedroll and flipped through the pages of his journal. He took out one of the quills he'd found in the hidden room in the Hanged Elf's Point graveyard and elaborated on the notes he'd managed to take during the day, wanting to get everything down while it was fresh in his mind.

On the other side of the campfire, Tseralyn had set up her borrowed bedroll near Brant's. The two of them were involved in an animated discussion that Wick was unable to overhear despite the little librarian's best attempts to do so. He satisfied himself with flipping to a fresh page in the journal and capturing Tseralyn's likeness with a detailed rendering as she sat talking to Brant, her arms wrapped around her knees. Her hands stayed busy, grouping and regrouping the rocks near her as if she was filled with nervous energy.

The little librarian added quick drawings of the web and the scene in the Forest of Fangs and Shadows. *Is it a coincidence that Brant says he's heard of a mercenary queen with her same name? Most people wouldn't be as comfortable as she appears to be among this group—especially after what she experienced today.* Wick considered that for a moment. *However, she didn't have much choice, did she?* Still, the mystery that the elven woman presented was captivating. And the little librarian was certain the master thief was feeling the effects of it.

He capped the inkwell and pushed it aside, taking a moment to organize his thoughts. He'd thought to work at least an hour or so more, but his eyelids closed before he knew it. He fell asleep between breaths.

Later, although he had no idea of how much later, Wick awoke from a nightmare. His heart slammed against the sides of his chest and he gasped for air. The shadows wriggling amid the smoke pooled against the cavern ceiling didn't help ease his mind. For a moment he believed the foul creatures that had chased him in his dream were still after him. Then he realized it was the campfire casting the twisting shadows and most of the panic left him.

After closing his eyes and learning that sleep wouldn't so readily return to him, the little librarian tossed the thin blanket aside and crept out into the full chill of the mine shaft. He shivered, then his teeth chattered.

Rithilin sat near the campfire feeding small pieces of wood to the flames. "You should sleep, halfer," the dwarf whispered. "Brant has us all on short watches so that we won't get overtired after being up most of the night running from Hanged Elf's Point, but I also wager he's planning on having us up and about early."

"I will," Wick replied. "My throat is parched."

"It's all this smoke trapped in this mine shaft with us," Rithilin replied. "It dries a man out quickly. I'd thought perhaps it would rise up and follow the mine shaft back the way we'd come and clear out of these parts, but it seems insistent on staying."

As he drank from the waterskin, Wick glanced up at the stone ceiling. The smoke eddied against the ceiling that angled up in the direction they'd come down the mine shaft. By rights, the smoke should have drifted back up the mine shaft. Wisps of it did, but still more of it stayed in one mass.

Something is holding it here, Wick told himself. He secured the waterskin again, then stood and watched the smoke.

"It's drifting toward the caved-in section of the mine shaft," Sonne said.

Wick glanced over at the young girl. She sat up on

her own bedroll, her blanket draping her shoulders. "Where?" the little librarian asked.

"There." Sonne pointed.

Wick peered through the morass of slowly revolving smoke that seemed only to roll constantly into itself. He tasted the acrid burn of the smoke against his sinus passages and the back of his throat now. Watching carefully, he managed to spot the two thin tendrils that wormed into the caved-in section. They poked delicately at the jumbled rocks and vanished somewhere between them.

"If the smoke is being pulled through the rocks," the little librarian whispered, "it can only mean that—"

"That an opening exists on the other side of those rocks," Sonne finished. She pushed herself up from her bedroll slowly, as if afraid to get too excited about the possibility.

Wick followed her, wanting to know as well. So far, the Purple Cloaks hadn't put in an appearance, but that didn't mean that couldn't change at any moment. The little librarian had fled from those frightening men as well as gigantic spiders all night in his dreams. The thought of getting trapped in the caved-in mine shaft tunnel was nerve-wracking.

With athletic ease, Sonne climbed to the top of the rock hill. Wick hesitated below for a moment, then crawled up the rocks as well. His backside still pained him as he pushed himself up, but it wasn't agony. The smoke was thicker against the cavern roof when he reached it, and it burned his nose and throat like tiny, hooked claws.

Sonne coughed as she dug her fingers between the rocks near the cavern roof. She scraped out loose stones easily, and it had an immediate effect on the smoke flow. A steady stream of the gray cloud from the campfire curled into the opening she made, then disappeared.

Wick helped her dig but was quickly overcome by the wracking coughs. "We need wet cloths," the little librarian croaked. "Climb down a moment and catch your breath while I get them."

Nodding, Sonne climbed back down after him. "That last time," she gasped, "I think I put my hand . . . my hand through to the other . . . other side. The mine shaft continues on the other side." She sat on the rocks and hung her head between her knees as she continued to cough.

"Maybe," Wick cautioned, not wanting the young girl to get her hopes up too high, while at the same time desperately wanting to believe what she was saying was true. "But it could only be a narrow chimney of space that goes for a hundred feet before another cave-in. We wouldn't be able to shift that much rock very quickly."

Sonne coughed and wheezed a moment more. "I want to know." She looked at the little librarian desperately. "I've got a bad feeling about staying here, halfer, I really do."

Wick nodded, remembering how the young girl had stood by him and kept up his own hopes while he'd worked on the Keldian mosaic. "All right, then. We'll find out about this, Sonne." He crossed over to Lago's pack and took out two of the cheesecloth scarves the old dwarf used to wrap bread loaves in. The little librarian soaked the cheesecloth with water from his waterskin, then returned to the young girl. "There. Soaking the cloth will help filter the smoke out. We should be able to breathe better."

Together, they returned to the top of the pile of rock blocking the mine shaft. They worked in tandem, scooping out rock and letting it clatter down the side of the pile. Wick used his newfound knife to lever some of the bigger stones out of the way. After only a few minutes, they had a hole to the other side and both of them were soaked from the sweat of their exertions.

Sonne thrust her flaming torch into the narrow hole, following it with her head. Wick waited impatiently for his turn to peer through.

"The mine shaft *does* continue on the other side," Sonne said excitedly when she pulled her head and shoulders back from the hole. Dust and grit stained her features, darkening up some spots so that she looked bruised.

"The opening isn't very wide," Wick pointed out. Under the loose scrabble of rock and dirt they'd dug through, they'd found a huge, squared-off rock that looked as though it had split off from the section of cavern roof they'd dug under. The space they'd managed to clear resembled the upper and lower jaws of a cow's teeth, as if they could slam closed in the same flat, grinding manner.

The volcano rumbled again, filling the cavern with chaotic, booming thunder. Dirt and rock tumbled down from the cavern roof, littering the lower rock again. For a moment, Wick feared that the two rocks might slam closed without the other rocks and debris to help them stay apart. They yawned only a little more than inches apart, not even enough for a grown human or dwarf to slither through.

"Did you hear that?" Sonne asked after her coughing fit passed. Dust stained the front of the wet cheesecloth draping her lower face.

Grit crunched against Wick's teeth as he tried to find enough spit to clear the dust from his mouth. The cheesecloth helped, but it didn't keep all the dust out. "What?"

"The echoing on the other side of this hole." Sonne thrust her torch forward again, lighting the flat edges of the upper and lower shelves of rock.

Wick peered at the two rocks carefully. The ceiling section was huge, and the flat rock they worked on was larger than one of *One-Eyed Peggie*'s johnboats. *Have they gotten any closer?* He wasn't certain, but in the wavering torchlight it was easy to imagine that the two rocks had ground an inch or two nearer together. "No," he answered. "I only heard the echo here."

"The chamber on the other side of this blockage must be huge." Sonne grabbed a small rock and clambered between the two stone shelves. "Come over here and listen."

Wick joined her, feeling painfully sharp rocks gouging his stomach, chest, knees and elbows.

"Closer," Sonne ordered.

Reluctantly, Wick crept closer, finally sticking his head under the overhang of rock because he realized she wouldn't be satisfied until he did. The two shelves of stone were so close that he could scarcely turn his head without bumping his chin or his crown.

"Listen." Sonne pitched her rock along the bottom stone. The rock bumped and rattled across the stone shelf, catching the flickering light of the torch struggling in the cloud of dust that still hadn't settled from the volcano's last rumbling. Then it disappeared, falling over the side.

Wick listened intently as the stone struck once, then twice very quickly, sounding very clearly.

"Do you hear it?" Sonne whispered.

For a moment, the little librarian was going to say no, then he did hear the other sounds. At first Wick thought the sounds were just additional impact noises of the stone falling. Only the same pattern—*tap, tap-tap,* followed by the final *thud*—repeated.

"Echoes," Sonne whispered.

Wick started to respond, but the young girl held up a hand, grinning excitedly. More faintly this time, the tapping pattern of the falling rock sounded yet again.

"You heard it?" Sonne asked.

"Yes."

"The cavern on the other side of this landslide is big."

Wick nodded, trying to remember Chulinbok's *The-ories and Mathematical Progressions.* Somewhere in that reading—and Chulinbok's very humorous sidebars about past students—the little librarian had read about how to figure volumes based on echo patterns. However, Chulinbok's complicated equations evaded Wick at the moment. He glanced at Sonne, feeling the mud caked onto the wet cheesecloth plastered against his face. The accumulation was so heavy he tasted the mud. "Very big," the little librarian agreed, giving his best profes-sional opinion.

Sonne grabbed another rock and threw again. They listened to the quick *tap, tap-tap,* and final *thud* together. "The drop-off on the other side of this rock pile isn't too steep. We could make it."

"We?" Panic seized Wick in its icy claws, aided by the wet cloth across his face and the chill in the mine shaft. He rose up suddenly and bumped the back of his head hard enough to trigger blinding pain. "Ow!"

"Yes," Sonne insisted. "You and I could make it through this gap." She tested the rock shelves above and below them. "We're small enough to get through."

Wick shook his head. Crawling around on the other side of an immense rock pile that could keep the others from helping him when he needed it most was very probably one of the last things he wanted to do. "I don't think that's a good idea."

"We've got to do something." Sonne sounded exas-perated.

"We are doing something," Wick replied. "When everyone gets up, we're going back to try the tunnel we didn't take."

"That will take hours that we can cut off if there's a way through here." Sonne looked into his eyes. "Besides the Purple Cloaks, there are also goblinkin slavers in the area. I'd really rather not run into them."

Neither would I, Wick thought. But the idea of crawling into the darkness ahead was almost as frightening. "The others will never be able to get through this rock. They're all too big." *Surely she can see the common sense in that.*

"Cobner and the dwarves might be able to cut through it."

"In less time than it would take to walk back to the main cavern and take the other tunnel?" Wick raised his eyebrows in doubtful speculation.

"There are tools here—"

"Broken ones."

"—tools that we can repair," Sonne went on stubbornly.

"Sonne. Wick."

The little librarian gazed back down the rock pile and saw Brant standing there, a curious expression on his face.

"What are you doing up there?" Brant asked.

Beyond the master thief in the shadows, Wick saw Tseralyn watching them with interest.

Quickly, and with much more enthusiastic description and hope than Wick would have offered, Sonne laid out her thoughts about the cavern on the other side of the rock pile.

Brant crawled up to join them, stirring up even more dust to join the smoke already plaguing the area. The master thief shoved his torch into the space Sonne and Wick had cleared between the two massive stone surfaces. Brant struggled to ease through the gap but couldn't. He sat back and watched the smoke being pulled through the gap more readily.

"I want to try it," Sonne said.

"It does offer promise," Brant agreed. He stroked his beard and glanced at Wick. "Well, little artist?"

I think it's a bad idea. Wick wanted so very much to say that but couldn't. It was just possible that the other end of the mine shaft lay only a short distance away. "Maybe we can have a look."

Minutes later, armed with a fresh torch, Sonne started the climb through the tight gap between the stone shelves. By that time, word had gotten around to the rest of the camp and no one was sleeping anymore. All the thieves gathered at the foot of the rock pile and watched hopefully. Cobner had already rounded up a few picks, hammers, and chisels, and was busy cutting some of the torch staff into serviceable handles to fit the hammers and picks.

Halfway through the climb, Sonne got stuck, caught between the tight surfaces. Wick heard the young girl breathe out, then she wriggled free and continued on without taking another breath. Cold fear touched the little librarian when he feared that she might get caught between the rocks out of their reach and suffocate simply because she couldn't draw a breath. Then she was through, waving encouragement from the other side and saying that the mineshaft did indeed continue.

More nervous now that it was his turn even though he was more slightly built than Sonne, Wick wiped the perspiration from his palms, tied a fresh knot in the cheesecloth around his lower face, and tried not to hyperventilate. Here he was, about to do one of the really heroic things that he'd read about in so many of the volumes in Hralbomm's Wing, and he was on the verge of throwing up. Sour bubbles popped at the back of his throat.

"Are you all right?" Brant asked.

Wick nodded, not trusting his voice.

"Of course he's all right," Cobner growled. "Why, he's braver than any other ten halfers I've ever seen in my life." He winked at Wick. "You and Sonne come back when you know that tunnel goes on out of the mountain. I'll be sizing this rock up and seeing about where I can do the most damage."

"I thought you didn't like mining," Wick replied.

"Just because I don't like it doesn't mean I don't know how it's done," Cobner said gruffly. "My ol' da was a fierce quarryman in his day, and he trained me to help him." He hammered a big fist down on the stone slab. "I've taken on bigger chunks of rock than this and won." He offered his hand.

Wick took the dwarf's hand and hoped Cobner didn't break anything important in his zeal. His fingers were only slightly numb when Cobner returned them to him. The little librarian took one final breath before starting to squeeze into the gap. Halfway through, he thought and carefully turned his head to look at Brant. "I'm leaving the books I found in my bag."

Brant squatted before the gap, a torch in his hand. "I'll take care of them myself, little artist. Just make sure that you take care of Sonne and yourself."

Pride puffed up Wick's chest somewhat, which made it hard to shove through the gap, but he nodded and kept working his way through. When he got to the tight spot, he didn't have to hold his breath, but his stomach was pressed uncomfortably till he got on the other side of it.

Sonne waited for him on the other side of the gap.

Gingerly, Wick peered down at the steep descent over the loose rock. Evidently the mine shaft continued to angle downward under the mountain. He held his torch up and surveyed the wide cavern before them.

"There are four other tunnels branching off from this

one," Sonne said as they made their way carefully down the rock pile. "If you look on the other side of this cavern, you can see them."

Wick spotted the hollows carved into the opposite cavern wall. They were too perfectly made to be anything other than tunnel mouths. At the bottom of the rock pile, he gazed back up at the gap. The angle was too sharp to see Brant or anyone else who might be standing on the other side of it, but torchlight filled the hole.

It took only a few moments to scratch the legends on the wall by the tunnel mouths free of dirt and debris so that Wick could read them. Two of the tunnels were blocked by cave-ins and a third was a dead end because the miners had tapped out the ore vein they'd followed with picks and shovels.

But the fourth tunnel, actually the third one from the left, promised a path to the other side of the mountain. That tunnel was also the one most generously made and looked to be the same size as the one the group of thieves had followed in from the Forest of Fangs and Shadows.

"Let's see where this one takes us," Sonne suggested, stepping into the tunnel.

"Couldn't we just go back and tell the others that the mine shaft does continue?" Wick asked.

Sonne fixed him with a glance. "You're the one who brought up the fact that this tunnel might be caved in at some point as well. It wouldn't do any good for them to break through the rock pile up there if the way was completely blocked ahead."

"No," Wick had to admit, "I suppose it wouldn't." But he wasn't happy at just the two of them entering the tunnel. He took a fresh hold on his torch and followed her.

The mine shaft continued for over an hour without any kind of mishap. Rock and debris littered the stone floor in places, and every section of the tunnel Wick looked at resembled the last. He could no longer honestly say if he was coming or going judging by the surroundings. Every now and again, the volcano boomed and rolled thunder down through the tunnel, peppering them with small rocks and dirt clouds. The chill remained within the tunnel and Wick kept his traveling cloak pulled close.

As the last ringing echoes of the rumbling volcano died away, Wick heard another sound. It was gentle and purring, like a kitten that had struck one gurgling note.

Sonne stopped in the middle of the tunnel, holding her torch high. The flames burned orange color into her blond hair. "What is that?"

"Water," Wick answered. "That's the sound of a lot of water. Possibly a stream or even a small river." He studied the tunnel walls around them.

For the past half hour, the walls had gleamed, reflecting the torches they carried. Upon closer inspection now, he saw that they actually sweated water. The accumulation of water for hundreds or thousands of years had cut small channels through the rock that, upon further investigation, ran several inches deep. It was also almost ice-cold to the touch, and Wick was certain that the only thing that kept the water liquid was the fact that it was in motion. Even then it was probably a very near thing.

The water flowed down the incline of the tunnel. Sonne walked beside the channel on the right, her torch reflected in the running stream. "Do you think there's a chance that the mine shaft is flooded further on?"

"No," Wick said in an effort to convince himself as well. "This water hasn't been accumulating for the last few years. It's been spilling down this way for a very long time. Even as far as there must be to go in order to get through to the other side of the mountain, this mine shaft would probably be full by now." *Wouldn't it?* He wished he knew. He couldn't help feeling responsible for the present predicament they were all in. *How had Mettarin Lamplighter always seemed to be so sure of himself when his children and things that had gone wrong in his life challenged him?*

And how, Wick wondered in seemingly ever-growing amazement, *could I have ever been convinced that I knew so much about the world and my place in it?*

They continued down the mine shaft, neither of them talking. Sonne paused only once to light a fresh torch from the dying one she carried. Wick was uneasy with the knowledge that they'd used almost half of the spare torches they'd brought with them. If they continued on much further, they'd be returning in the dark.

If we return at all. The thought struck the little librarian suddenly and made him shiver. Thinking of being able to return seemed somehow overly optimistic given their present circumstances. His eyelids felt heavy and dragged across his eyes, blurring his vision. He felt as tired as he had back in Hanged Elf's Point when he'd been assigned to work crews cleaning up the city.

"Hey," Sonne whispered excitedly, "I think the mine shaft is getting lighter up ahead."

Wick glanced blearily ahead, almost certain that the young girl was imagining things. Only he saw it too. The stone sides and floor of the mine shaft were lighter, as if touched by some source of illumination other than their torches.

Sonne stepped up the pace to a near-jog, a surprise that caught the little librarian nearly flat-footed.

"Wait!" Wick cried.

"I can smell it," Sonne said. "I can smell clean air and flowers from the outside. Can't you?"

Still running, desperately trying to keep up to the

young girl, Wick noticed that he could smell hints of air that wasn't tainted by the cloying stink of dirt and metal. He reached up and pulled his mud-caked cheesecloth scarf down and drank in the fragrance of ripe blossoms and sweet grass.

He guessed that they ran another hundred yards along the mine shaft. The tunnel grew gradually lighter until the torches no longer created shadows on the walls. At the end, the mine shaft curved slightly, and the sound of moving water grew steadily louder.

The tunnel let out onto a short, stony beach that only had a thin crust of dirt covering it. The beach fronted a huge lake that looked like it was over three hundred yards across. The water was the deep, true blue of a polished agate. The twin rails of the mine car track ran out to the water's edge where rusted skeletons of iron poles jutted up from the stone. From the shape they presented, the little librarian guessed that the poles had once framed a small dock.

Wick gazed upward in awe, realizing that even as large as the lake was, they were still underground. However, eighty yards up the side of the wall on the left, at the very top of a series of steps cut into the stone wall, was the mouth of a cave. From the angle he stood at, Wick could only see puffy white clouds against a bright blue sky. To the right, a large stream poured down into the lake, falling fifty feet or more to gurgle into the lake. That rush of water had been the source of the noise Wick had heard.

"Come on," Sonne said, taking off to the left. She ran along the narrow stone beach toward the steps cut into the wall.

Though his legs were fatigued and he bordered on exhaustion, Wick followed. He wanted to protest Sonne's reckless choice of action, but he knew it wouldn't do any good. And he wanted to see the outside world again himself, just to make certain it still existed.

Sonne made it up the stone steps much more easily than Wick, but she waited on him in the mouth of the cave. Breathing harshly from his exertions and his excitement, the little librarian joined her. The bright sunlight hurt his tired eyes, but it was a welcome sight all the same.

A winding trail led down from the cave mouth and into a lush, green valley below. Though the trail had all but disappeared, it remained like a scar in a hairline, seeming both visible and invisible at the same time. In times past, Wick judged, the trail had been used by the Iron Hammer Peaks dwarven clan to take the iron ore into a base camp in the foothills of the mountains.

Very probably there had been a small city there in the foothills where the miners lived with their families. Bits and pieces of stone buildings stood up in ragged heaps in the foothills, and the little librarian knew something had razed the buildings to bits over the years. Soot clung to some of the building remnants and left him with evidence that Shengharck's tyranny hadn't ended within the mountain.

Beyond the forest and the valley, past the hills that Wick could see over from their position on the mountainside, green water glinted like diamonds under the bright sun. The horizon was distinct there, neatly divided between the blue sky and the ocean.

"Do you see it?" Sonne asked excitedly.

"Yes," Wick assured her. "Yes, I do." His stomach rumbled threateningly as the scent of wild heezle plums reached him. He scanned the forest below them, thinking that if the plums weren't too far off perhaps he could go fetch a dozen—or two—for their breakfast.

Then a discordant sound—the harsh clangor of steel ringing on stone—reached the little librarian's ears. He turned to Sonne only to find her frantically reaching for him. She fisted his traveling cloak, pulling him back and down inside the mine shaft entrance.

"Goblinkin!" Sonne hissed in disgust as she continued holding Wick and peering over his shoulder.

23

Shengharck, the Dragon King

Wick slowly turned and stared out the mine entrance in the direction Sonne was looking. The little librarian's heart thudded in his chest. For a moment, he thought the goblinkin were upon them and he tried to make himself as small as possible. Then he spotted the movement further down the mountainside.

At least twenty goblins rode horses along the narrow trail the dwarven miners had forged all those years ago. Nearly twice that many dwellers walked in slave chains in their midst.

Wick watched in growing horror as the group came on up the mountainside. Almost all of the dwellers were men, as they had been on board *Ill Wind*.

"Slavers," Sonne whispered. "Tseralyn was right about them working in the area. They must be using the tunnels through the mountains to get to Hanged Elf's Point as well."

"We've got to do something," Wick said. His heart went out to the dwellers in chains.

"What?" Sonne stared at him in disbelief. "You and I should charge twenty goblinkin and free those halfers?"

Wick looked back at the stumbling, ragtag line of slaves and didn't say anything. Rescuing the slaves from the goblinkin *was* out of the question at present, but he hated to see them go. He personally knew what fate awaited them upon their arrival in Hanged Elf's Point.

Sonne tugged at the little librarian. "We've got to go. They're coming this way."

Reluctantly, Wick followed the young girl back down the stone steps and across the narrow beach to the tunnel that led back to the mine shaft where they'd left Brant and the others. The gurgle of water pouring from the stream filled his ears again.

Sonne kept going down the tunnel, obviously headed back along the path they'd come.

Feeling guilty, unwilling to turn his back on the dwellers enslaved by the goblinkin without knowing something of their fate, Wick hunkered down by the tunnel entrance behind a rock spill that provided plenty of cover for him to hide behind. He watched the mine shaft entrance leading to the outside world expectantly.

"Wick!"

The little librarian glanced over at his shoulder and saw Sonne taking cover around the next bend.

"Come on," the young girl said.

"I can't," Wick replied.

"You can't help them. If we stay here, they may find us."

"I want to know where they're going. If there's another path through this mountain we should know about it." *There. That sounds reasonable, doesn't it?*

Sonne looked exasperated, but she crept back through the tunnel and slid in beside him to keep watch. "If we get spotted, I may brain you myself."

"You don't have to stay," Wick offered. "I can catch up." He said that like the idea of walking back through the desolate tunnel alone held no fear at all for him.

"We're going to stay together," Sonne said, "and we're going to go together."

"Thank you." Wick peered furtively over the top of the rocks at the mine shaft entrance.

"Don't thank me," Sonne replied tersely. "I'm not exactly happy about it."

Long minutes later, so long that Wick was beginning to think that the goblinkin weren't going to enter the cavern after all, the first goblin slaver rode his horse through the entrance. He clutched a bow in his fist, an arrow already nocked to the string. He gazed around fiercely—probably allowing his eyes to adjust to the dimness of the cave, Wick reasoned—then sniffed the air. Satisfied that no threat was forthcoming, the goblin stepped down from his saddle.

A handful of goblinkin marched down the stone steps to the beach by the underground lake. The dweller slaves followed meekly, backs bowed and chains rattling against the stone. The goblins left the horses at the mine shaft entrance. Two of their number stayed with the horses and rode them away. The rest of the goblins gathered around the dwellers and stared up at the cavern ceiling expectantly.

Wick stared up at the cavern ceiling as well. Even with the light from outside and the reflection of the same coming from the lake, shadows obscured many details about the cavern roof. Stalactites hung down in varying lengths like snake fangs.

The chief goblin reached for one of the packs the slaves carried and took a silver flute from it. Even though he showed practice with the flute, he seemed hesitant to use it. After he'd cleaned it and fussed with it, he strode to the lake's edge less than forty feet from Wick.

The flute sounded clear and true, an elven instrument if the little librarian was any judge at all, but the goblin's playing was clumsy and forced. Still, the strong notes reverberated around the cavern.

At first, Wick thought that nothing would come of the impromptu presentation. Then a thunderous flapping filled the cavern. Wind whipped down over the underground lake, rippling the water and blowing hot, fetid air over the little librarian. He hastily raised his mud-caked cheesecloth over his mouth and nose to alleviate some of the sharp stench. He'd never smelled anything so foul in all his life, not even when he'd found moldy, month-old clutterbeans under his bed.

The goblins drew back from the lake. Cries of fear rang out from the dwellers as they hunkered down onto the ground and covered their heads with their arms.

The dragon exploded from the ceiling, dropping down in a manner that suggested the presence of a tunnel or fissure leading down into the cavern from above. The foul creature was a hundred feet long from nose to tail. The batlike wings spread at least half again that distance as they flared out in a gliding swoop that carried it to the wall on the other side of the lake. The powerful creature perched on a large outcrop of rock jutting from the wall. The dragon caught the outcropping with its large hind feet and settled itself, wrapping the batlike wings tightly around its body. The wind died away, but the fetid stench remained, stronger than ever.

Its dinnerplate-sized scales glittered like jewels, flashing gold and green and black in the sunlight, picking up a smattering of blue highlights from the lake. Hoary white and pink growth sprouted from the dragon's long, gleaming black muzzle, and four twisted ivory horns jutted from the top of its head. The forelegs were half the size of the hind legs.

Without warning, the dragon opened its jaws in a wide snarl, then breathed flames that nearly reached across the lake. The dwellers bolted, crawling and rolling fearfully from the green and yellow flames. Although they tried to maintain their fierce demeanor, the goblinkin stepped

back as well. The stink of singed hair and sulfur mixed
with the fetid odor of the dragon.

The dragon spoke, and its harsh words thundered and
rolled inside even the great cavern. "I am Shengharck,
Dragon King. You will fear me, vermin, and cower before me or you will die!"

Immediately, the goblinkin prostrated themselves before the mighty dragon. They stretched their arms out
before them and shoved their faces against the stone
wall.

"We hear you, O Mighty Shengharck," the goblin
chief cried in a loud voice that quavered, "and we fear
you with all our hearts. But we would beg a boon of
you before you destroy us."

The dragon gazed out over the cowering goblinkin
and dwellers. The great creature fluttered its wings, and
the batlike appendages sounded like swords parrying. It
scratched its long chin with one of its forelegs and the
rough sound echoed over the lake.

Wick realized then that the dragon had chosen its spot
carefully. Sound traveled faster, stronger, and surer over
water, and the huge cavern served to magnify its voice
like an orator's stand in front of a Telludian speaking
shell used to speak from ship to ship out on the ocean.

"A boon?" The dragon laughed mirthlessly. "Well, I
am feeling generous today. What boon is it that you
would seek?"

Slowly, Wick took his journal from his traveling cloak
and fished out a bit of charcoal. He opened the book to
a fresh page and began sketching the dragon. His sense
of duty as a librarian, to capture information and bring
it back so that others might learn from it, overcame his
fear. He was amazed at how steadily he laid out the lines
and shapes that made up the foul creature.

"We would seek passage through your mountain,
Dragon King," the goblin chieftain said, "and in return

we offer you a gold piece per head on every slave that we transport through your mountain."

"A gold piece?" Shengharck mused. "Are slaves not selling so well these days in Hanged Elf's Point?"

"Orpho Kadar buys all that we have captured, O Mighty Wyrm. But a gold piece a head is the price we have always agreed upon in the past."

"True, but I count only forty dwellers in your catch," the dragon said. "The use of my mountain passages is surely worth more than a paltry forty gold coins. Perhaps you should consider sweetening the dish you set before me, Master Slaver."

Shengharck's greedy, Wick realized as the charcoal flew. The knowledge was hardly surprising. Every story the little librarian had ever read that dealt with dragons always talked about their irrepressible greed. Dragons were forged in flames, the myths and educated guesses said, but their hearts were hammered out of purest larceny. What was surprising, though, was that the dragon was adding to its hoard through the slave trade in dwellers.

"How could I do that, O Gracious Shengharck?" the goblin chieftain asked.

"By not showing up with less than fifty or sixty dweller slaves the next time you come through. Use of the passageway through my mountain should never be worth less than fifty gold pieces."

Sonne cursed quietly beside Wick. "How many slave caravans pass through here?" the young girl asked in a whisper. "No wonder Shengharck isn't known for pillaging and looting these days. At least not along the Shattered Coast. He's making a fortune off Orpho Kadar and Hanged Elf's Point."

Wick knew her statement was very probably true and it sickened him. Still, mercy was a trait that had never been found in a dragon.

"O Magnificent and Wise Dragon," the goblin chieftain replied after a moment of frenzied thinking, "I have the forty slaves now. Returning to Blackgate Cove to raid the dweller villages there would only delay payment of the forty gold coins I have for you now." The goblin held up a leather pouch that clinked musically. "And keeping watch over forty slaves while attempting to capture ten more would be hard. Maybe harder than climbing over the mountain instead of walking through it."

The gentle tinkling rolled across the underground lake. The dragon's head cocked and Shengharck's blood-red eyes glowed with avaricious interest. "Are you trying to debate with me, foolish goblin?"

"No, Dragon King. I would never do that."

Shengharck breathed flames that sent glimmering reflections streaking across the still, blue lake. "If you did, I would burn you down where you stand, then blow your ashes into the winds that your brutish kith and kin might know of your fate for generations to come." The dragon growled and flicked its long tail irritably.

The goblin chieftain is right, Wick thought as he watched the terrifying creature eye the pouch in the goblin's hand. *Shengharck wants the gold the goblin has now, not later.*

"I'll let you pass," Shengharck said, "with the slaves that you have now. But never again."

"Thank you, O Fierce and Mighty Dragon. Your generosity and wisdom—"

Before the goblin could utter another word, the dragon breathed flames that coiled around him. He died screaming, running and trying to flee from the mystic fire that held fast to him while the other goblins and the enslaved dwellers fled before him. In the space of a drawn breath, the goblin chieftain collapsed to the ground. The flames burned brightly one last time, then winked out, leaving only the goblin's blackened bones behind.

"I will not be known for my generosity," Shengharck roared. "*Never* my generosity. I am not generous. I am a dragon. I am sure and certain death on silent wings and ripping talons, with fiery breath and a cold heart."

All the goblinkin and the huddled dwellers quickly agreed with Shengharck.

Wick's nose wrinkled in disgust at the smell of cooked goblin flesh. He thought for a moment he was going to throw up, but quickly clapped a hand over his mouth and regained control of himself as Sonne glared at him wordlessly.

"The price for the passage of forty slaves," the huge dragon announced, "is the sum of forty gold pieces *and* the life of the goblin who foolishly thought to undermine my decision. As long as I rule these mountains, no one may make use of the passageway through without paying tribute to me."

The goblinkin quickly agreed in loud, supportive voices. Then they all praised the dragon for its show of ferocity and cruel nature.

Shengharck glared at the goblinkin. "I want the forty gold pieces and I want three fat sheep brought to me on your return to further appease my wrath."

The goblinkin readily agreed.

"And have a care not to run the fat off the animals on the way back," Shengharck continued. The dragon launched itself from its perch and swooped gracefully across the lake.

For a moment, Wick thought the foul wyrm might flatten against the stone wall of the cavern. Instead, it swerved at the last minute but plucked the singed pouch of gold pieces with the talons of its hind leg. It beat its wings fiercely, stirring up waves on the lake surface again, then flew back up into the entrance in the cavern ceiling.

The volcano rumbled almost immediately afterward.

Debris and a few stalactites dropped from the ceiling into the lake, making a few scattered splashes. Thick dust marred the sunlight for a moment.

"Let's go," Sonne whispered.

"Wait," Wick replied.

"No waiting." Sonne pulled at his arm. "We were lucky the dragon didn't scent us then."

"I thought you didn't believe in dragons," Wick said, "but now you believe they have all the powers you've heard about?" A dragon's sense of smell was supposed to be second to none. Reports said they could sniff out prey ten miles away and more once they had the scent.

"Dragons exist," Sonne said. "So I'm not taking a chance on their powers."

Wick watched as the goblinkin gathered their wits and their courage again. "Just a moment longer."

"There are still nineteen goblinkin," Sonne told him.

"I want to see where they go."

The goblins immediately took out their frustration and fear on the chained dwellers. Many goblins flayed the slaves' backs and arms with their cruel whips before one of their number finally got control of them.

"Stop beating the halfers," the goblin raged above the painful cries of the dwellers. The goblin walked through the ranks and slapped the heads of those who didn't heed him quickly enough. "A dead slave isn't worth anything in Hanged Elf's Point, and the arena won't buy slaves that have been beaten so badly that they're no longer afraid to die. We've already paid for their passage, and there are plenty of other dangers waiting for us in the Forest of Fangs and Shadows."

Grumbling angrily, the goblinkin nevertheless saw the wisdom of their new leader's words. They rounded the dwellers up and marched them past the tunnel where Wick and Sonne hid.

For a moment the little librarian was afraid that he'd

been wrong about the goblinkin using the passageway where they were. But the slaves and slavers kept walking. When he could no longer see them, Wick slipped away from Sonne before she could stop him and made his way to the front of the tunnel. He peered around the corner to the right and watched the goblins ascend a stone ladder cut into the side of the cavern wall where the large stream poured into the lake.

At the top of the stone ladder, the goblins walked into the channel from which the stream flowed, and Wick saw that the stream was much larger than he'd thought. With no proper reference point in the cave, there'd been no way to properly guess. The stream was at least twenty feet across and spanned perhaps two-thirds of the passageway. It wasn't the underground river he'd heard in several spots along the other passageway, but he guessed that the stream fed off the underground river.

The little librarian glanced back at the lake, thinking about it now. There weren't any demarcations on the wall that suggested it was ever higher than it was now. *So where does all the water go?*

"Wick." Sonne touched his shoulder.

"A moment more," the little librarian pleaded. The last of the goblins and dwellers had made it up the stone ladder and had disappeared. "We should take a look at that passageway, Sonne. Knowing where it goes might help." He couldn't believe he was saying that and was willing to risk the dragon's fury. Running, now that would have been more help.

"We've been gone overlong," Sonne countered. "Brant is going to be worried, perhaps even thinking us dead."

"Brant will wait," Wick said confidently, "or he will come to make certain something bad has happened to us. If Cobner has gotten impatient and broken through the rock slide blocking the mine shaft, then they're already on their way out of the mountain and we'll meet them on the way back." He looked into her eyes, reasoning the best and simplest that he could, knowing himself how risky what he was suggesting was. "But if Cobner hasn't gotten through that rock, then maybe taking the other tunnel back in Mine Shaft Number Six would be the thing to do." He pointed at the passageway with the stream. "That is dwarven-made, Sonne. And that's the passage the goblins take through the mountain."

Sonne hesitated, clearly not comfortable with the choice laid before her. "We need to look."

Wick nodded, feeling even more nervous because he knew that Sonne wouldn't walk away now without looking. "The only thing that bothers me," the little librarian said as he crept back out into the cavern containing the underground lake, "is what we're going to do if Shengharck happens to return."

"We die," Sonne said flatly.

Wick swallowed hard, then screwed up his courage as best he could. *I'm a Third Level Librarian at the Vault of All Known Knowledge. I can do this.* He felt the weight of his journal against his chest. *There is so much I have to return to the Library with, and this can be one more piece of the puzzle.*

Together, they crept across the cavern floor to the stone ladder cut into the wall. Sonne carried throwing knives in her hands.

Trembling in fear, almost missing the stone ladder rungs twice because he kept glancing over his shoulder at the section of ceiling where the dragon had appeared, Wick slowly made his way to the passageway. He remained just below the level for a moment, listening intently. *If I can hear goblins, then I can probably see goblins. And if I can see goblins, they can see me.*

"Now," Sonne demanded, clinging to the ladder below him.

Cautiously, heart hammering at the back of his throat, Wick peered over the top of the passageway lip. The rushing water spilled down the side of the cavern and into the lake less than five feet from him. But he couldn't see anyone in the passageway.

However, there were small boat docks on either side of the stream.

Curious now, Wick pulled himself up to the ledge and studied the boat docks. Two wooden boats remained tied up at one of the docks on the other side of the stream. Both boats had shallow drafts and looked nearly flat-bottomed, designed solely for traversing shallow water. Hooks on both of the passageway walls held a dozen battered lanterns.

"Boats?" Sonne glanced at the small vessels in puzzled fascination.

Wick pointed to the coiled lines in the center of the boats that were made fast to the prow. "The goblins walk along the sides of the stream." The ledges on either side of the water were six feet wide, plenty of room to march a group of slaves along. "They pull the boats with them, or may even have the slaves pull them. They probably tie them back up at the other end of the river, then take boats back down to this end of the passageway."

"The dwarves built this?"

Wick lit one of the lanterns, adjusted the flame, then held it up to the wall just inside the passageway. Debris filled the carved lettering there as well. He flicked it out with the point of his long knife. Now that he had work to do with his hands, he wasn't so worried about the dragon unexpectedly reappearing. And there was the chance that Shengharck would never see them in the passageway. "Yes," he answered, "the dwarves built this. They probably used it as a supply ferry route. There are probably disbursement tunnels that feed off of this passageway. It looks remarkably efficient." He blew the final bit of dust from the lettering.

Mine Shaft Six, Tunnel Three
Supply Route

"I guess the goblinkin thought it was remarkably efficient, too," Sonne remarked.

Wick had no reply for that. Thinking about how many dwellers might have been marched through the passageway to the other end and on to Hanged Elf's Point made him shudder. Very probably not all of those captured dwellers made it from one end of the passageway to the other. *How many skeletons must lie at the bottom of the lake?* he wondered.

"Where does the water come from?" Sonne asked.

Wick held the lantern over the stream. "See the straight sides of the channel?"

"Yes."

"The dwarves carved that as well. This whole passageway was carefully designed and built." Wick looked deeper into the passageway, but it quickly grew dark and there wasn't much he could see. "We already know there's an underground river that flows through the mountain. And the lake has to drain somewhere. The underground water that runs through the two valleys on either side of the mountain range probably feeds the lake. Maybe it even feeds the underground river." He shrugged. "I can only guess."

They looked around a moment longer, having a hard time talking over the loud gurgle of the flowing stream. Neither of them was willing to talk too loudly for fear of being heard by the dragon. Sonne took one more lantern from the collection hanging on the walls.

Tired and sore, but more intrigued and fearful than

ever, Wick led the way back down the stone ladder and
to the passageway where they'd left the rest of their
party. Once they reached Brant and the others, maybe
Cobner could find a way to break the big stone that
blocked the passageway. If that was possible, it felt good
knowing that escape was only an hour's walk away.

*Provided we don't run into the dragon on our way
out,* Wick fretted.

"They're gone!"

Sonne's startled announcement made Wick lift his
head as he slithered through the narrow jaws of the two
stones blocking the mine shaft. Sharp pain stuttered
through his skull when he hit the stone above. "Who's
gone?"

"Brant. Cobner. Lago. All of them."

The little librarian stared through the gap. He'd been
so tired and had his mind so full of imponderabilities
about what his next move was going to be that he hadn't
really been paying attention to Sonne or their arrival
back at the blocked area. He supposed he might have
had a vague thought about why Cobner hadn't been
hammering away at the massive stone block, but that
had quickly gone by the wayside.

Although the experience had been dreadfully frightening, seeing Shengharck had been a remarkable event
in his life. After all, how many other Librarians—even
first and second level ones and grandmagisters—could
say they'd seen a dragon?

Now he stared into the darkened chamber where
they'd left their friends only a few hours ago and realized that the campfire no longer burned. It was still dark
in the chamber, as well as cold. Brant would have kept
the campfire going if everything had been all right, and
there had been plenty of wood.

Slowly, Wick crawled through the space, his senses alive and his mind fixed on the latest conundrum facing them. Brant wouldn't have willingly left them. Maybe the master thief didn't feel so beholden to Wick, but the little librarian felt certain the man wouldn't have left Sonne without knowing her fate. So what had happened?

Sonne walked around the area with her lantern held high. The yellow light skated across the pick-scarred walls and chased the shadows away. She knelt by the fire and put her hand in the ashes. "It's still warm," she said. "They haven't been gone long."

"Brant wouldn't have left you," Wick stated.

"No," Sonne replied. The lantern light played over the hard planes on her face. "Something happened."

Wick scoured the stone floor. Enough dirt had fallen onto the cavern floor that impressions of footwear could be seen, but it was a jumbled mess. A dark stain covered the rock in front of him. He leaned down and played the lantern beam over it.

"That's blood," Sonne said from behind him.

Wick's lantern light glinted dully against the drying stain.

"Not enough to kill someone," Sonne added, "but it was a terrible wound all the same."

A faint, smudged impression above the bloodstain caught Wick's eye. He focused on it, turning the lantern so that the greatest amount of light shone on it. The impression of five ugly toes glared up from the loose soil.

"What did you find?" Sonne asked, moving over to see.

"A footprint," Wick answered worriedly. "A bare footprint." *Goblinkin don't wear shoes.*

Sonne's face paled as she surveyed the telltale print. "Goblins took them."

They moved outward. Now that they had found the

first goblinkin footprint, the others became easier to find. Dozens littered the floor.

"Come on," Sonne said tensely. "There's only one way they could have gone out of this mine shaft."

"What are you planning to do?" Wick asked.

Sonne whirled on the little librarian. "Do? What am I going to do?"

The way that the young girl re-asked the question Wick had just asked her was a clear indication to the little dweller as to how much trouble he was in for asking it in the first place. *It's bad enough when someone repeats an answer you've given him or her. But when they repeat the question you asked so that you'll more completely understand how stupid or foolish you've shown yourself to be, it's really bad.*

When Wick didn't answer right away, Sonne said, "I'm going after them."

"If there were enough goblinkin to take Brant and Cobner and the others," Wick pointed out, "what real good are we going to do?"

"I don't know."

"We'll just get ourselves killed or captured."

"So you think we should just make our escape and leave them to their own devices?"

Wick really didn't like the way the option sounded when she said it. "That would be the wisest thing we could do."

"No, it isn't!" the young girl exploded. "There's no guarantee that we'll get any kind of warm welcome from those dweller communities in Blackgate Cove. If goblinkin slavers have raided them for years, they probably don't take well to strangers. We'd be better off with Brant there to talk for us. He knows how to talk to everyone to smooth things over and make things work out."

Wick couldn't fault her logic. Still it chafed at him that she was asking him to do what she wanted him to

do now, but had forbidden it when the goblinkin had
arrived in the outer chamber with the dwellers in chains.
"There's only the two of us. Hardly a rescue squad."

"We won't know," Sonne argued, "until we see what
it is we're facing. Stay or go, halfer. The decision is
yours." With that, she turned to go.

Wick hesitated only a moment. He didn't like the idea
of Brant and the others in the hands of goblinkin slavers,
but he didn't know what they were going to do about it.
But he did know that no matter how afraid he was, he
couldn't let the girl go alone. "Sonne," he called.

She turned to look at him, unshed tears glinting in her
eyes. "What?"

"I'll go with you."

"Good." Sonne wiped her face and continued forward.

Wick glanced around, moving the lantern to and fro,
studying the ground. Then he noticed an odd assortment
of stones collected into a half-moon shape. His mind
wrestled with that puzzle, then he remembered how
Tseralyn had played with the nearby stones while she'd
visited with Brant earlier. Was this her work? And if it
was, why had she done it?

Before he had time to ferret out an answer, Sonne was
already striding down the mine shaft. Wick abandoned
the puzzle and hurried after her, dreadfully certain they
were chasing their doom.

Much to Wick's surprise, they reached the main chamber
of Mine Shaft Number Six without any further mishap.
Several times footprints Sonne followed so diligently
with her lantern faded out across patches of bare stone
floor, but they had only to walk a little further on to find
them again.

The little librarian's mind raced, fed by the fear that
filled him. *We're walking around in a dragon's lair*

that's filled with goblinkin slavers! The thought kept hammering away at him. Every now and then his knees almost buckled.

He lifted his lantern high as he and Sonne searched the main chamber floor. Along the way, he'd found a few more small rock piles placed in the same half-moon shape. As he recalled, those had been resting places where Brant had called for a break, or the pace had been slow enough that the markers—for that was what Wick was certain they were—could be laid. *But markers for whom?* That question made Wick uneasy. How had the goblinkin slavers found Brant and the others so easily?

"The tracks are confusing," Sonne whispered in hoarse frustration. "I don't know if the goblinkin took Brant and the others into the third tunnel or if they went outside with them."

Wick nodded, figuring it was best to speak as infrequently as possible while Sonne was in the emotional state she was in. The main chamber of Mineshaft Number Six was filled with footprints of goblins. Those prints were so easily seen now by lantern light. The torches they'd carried in had flickered a lot, and they hadn't been looking too much for goblinkin footprints. They'd already known the goblinkin walked through the passageways.

"Did they get caught by goblinkin coming out of the passageway through the mountains?" Sonne asked. "Or goblinkin going into the passageway?"

"I don't know," Wick answered. At first, he'd been afraid that they would overtake and encounter the goblinkin slaving party they'd seen at the underground lake, but that hadn't happened. Evidently the goblin slavers had made good time through the passageway.

"It doesn't make sense that they would take Brant and the others through the passageway, does it?" Sonne asked. "Shengharck would charge them for bringing slaves through, and they'd only have to turn around and take them back out to sell them in Hanged Elf's Point."

Wick refrained from stating the possibility that Brant and the others might have been captured solely for torturing. He preferred to believe the goblinkin in the mountains were greedy enough to get every gold piece they could. "We could check outside for them," the little librarian pointed out. "If we climb up the mountain, we should be able to look across the foothills and spot them."

Sonne glanced at the third tunnel. "And if we're wrong?"

"Then we'll come back here and search again," Wick said. "Sometimes you have to be willing to do the wrong thing in order to learn the right thing to do. Standing here, looking at footprints that we already know we can't make sense of isn't going to help us. Or the others."

Sonne nodded. Without another word, she headed for the main entrance to Mine Shaft Number Six.

Wick followed her, blinking his eyes against the harsh brilliance of the sun after being in the cave for so long again. He'd hardly taken two steps outside when he heard brush rustle behind him. Panic set in, making him turn quickly, a hand going up in front of his face when he thought of the giant spider he'd seen in the Forest of Fangs and Shadows. There were no guarantees the monstrous arachnids only hunted within the forest. Too late, he remembered the long knife at his side.

A heavy body crashed into the little librarian, driving him to the stony ground. Even as the breath left his lungs and his wounded backside screamed in agony from the impact, he felt relieved that whatever had attacked him wasn't a giant spider.

However, the grim visage of the man sitting astride him stripped away most of that happy moment. The man was human, dressed in scarred warrior's leathers. There

was no adorning insignia that identified the man or to
whom he belonged. His black hair hung loose about his
shoulders, falling out of place like a raven's dropped
wing as it sat cooling in summer heat. His gray eyes
were like ice, cold and merciless. Pockmarks scored his
cheeks and neck, mixing with the scars from blades.

Coolly and professionally, with no evident passion at
all, the man clapped a hand over Wick's mouth and pulled
a short skinning knife from the scabbard attached to his
leather chest armor. The little librarian breathed through
his nose frantically. The man's legs pinned Wick's arms
to his sides against the ground.

The warrior pressed the sharp blade against the little
librarian's throat. Wick felt the stinging bite of the knife,
then the warmth of blood running from the small cut.
"Move," the man warned in a raspy voice as he glanced
up toward Sonne, "and your little friend here dies first.
Trust me when I say that you'll die next."

Rolling his eyes, Wick was just able to see Sonne
standing ahead of him. Knives filled both her hands and
the lantern lay overturned and leaking oil at her feet.

Quiet as shadows, other men dressed as the big warrior was in unadorned warrior's leathers stood from the
surrounding brush. All of them were humans. Most of
them carried swords and battle-axes, but four archers
among them trained their weapons on Sonne.

Wick wanted to speak, but the big man didn't remove
his hand from the little librarian's mouth. He lay there
feeling helpless, the stone ground digging into his back.

"Do you understand?" the big warrior asked.

"Yes," Sonne replied dully.

"Drop your weapons."

Sonne let her knives clatter to the stone at her feet.
"What do you want with us?"

The warrior's gray eyes narrowed. "I want to know
what happened to Lady Tseralyn."

"I don't know," Sonne said.

"You lie," the warrior accused. "I saw the footprints around the spider's web, and some of them belonged to this halfer."

Sonne's face hardened. "If you saw the halfer's footprints around the spider's web in the Forest of Fangs and Shadows, then you also saw that we rescued her."

"Where is she?"

"I don't know." Quickly Sonne explained about the blocked passageway and how she and Wick had gone scouting ahead only to return and find their party—and Lady Tseralyn—missing.

Evidently the big warrior believed her because he took the knife from Wick's throat and stood up.

Wick coughed and gagged, thinking he was going to be sick. The big warrior grabbed the little librarian by the front of his traveling cloak and pulled him to his feet.

"My name is Dahvee," the big warrior said, sheathing the small knife on his leather armor. "I'm captain in Tseralyn's squad."

"What squad?" Sonne asked.

"We're mercenaries." Dahvee signaled with his hands.

Wick watched as three of the men melted back into the forest and three others raced up the foothills.

"We had an engagement deep within the Forest of Fangs and Shadows," Dahvee said. "Our group was sold out by a traitor and the goblinkin slavers had set up a trap with some of Orpho Kadar's troops. During our withdrawal, we were separated from Lady Tseralyn."

Wick blinked at the man. *A battle in the forest?* Images came to him of the warriors fighting the goblinkin amid the thick clusters of trees and brush, with giant spiders and other fierce creatures waiting on the sidelines for the dead and wounded.

"Where are you from?" Sonne asked.

Dahvee shook his head. "That's for the lady to tell you. If she decides that it's any of your business. We've tracked her through the forest and to the spider's web. Then we tracked her here."

"She's been leaving you the markers," Wick said.

"That's right." Dahvee scanned the foothills, searching for the men he'd sent up there. "She knew if any of us survived that we would come for her. Just as she would have come for us once she had a way and the manpower to do it. Evidently she chose to come with you."

"Why?" Sonne asked.

"My guess would be to find out about the passageways through the Broken Forge Mountains. We hadn't known about them. So far, we'd only been hitting the slave caravans and freeing the halfers. Lady Tseralyn probably thought if we could deny passage through the mountains to the goblinkin that we could better disrupt the slave caravans going into Hanged Elf's Point."

"Shengharck probably wouldn't like that much," Wick said.

"Shengharck?" Dahvee repeated.

"The dragon who lairs in the mountain."

Dahvee glanced at the mountain and nodded, showing no sign of concern at all. "I thought Shengharck was a myth."

"No," the little librarian replied. "We've seen him."

"Interesting," the mercenary captain mused. "I've fought hundreds of men and beasts, but I've never fought a dragon."

It wouldn't, Wick thought and barely refrained from saying, *be a very prudent thing to do.*

"Why would you be interested in disrupting the slave trade?" Sonne asked.

Dahvee eyed the young girl levelly. "Because Lady Tseralyn is."

A whistle echoed through the foothills.

The mercenary captain glanced up at the surrounding mountainside. "My men haven't found anything outside. That means that Lady Tseralyn—and your friends—are still inside the mountain somewhere." He gestured and the mercenary troops came from the forest and joined him at the mine shaft entrance.

"What are you going to do?" Wick asked.

Dahvee looked at the little librarian with a blank expression. "I'm going after her."

"Our friends are most likely with her," Sonne said.

"That's not my problem," Dahvee replied coldly.

"We saved Tseralyn's life. We want to go with you," Sonne said.

Wick, however, was perfectly content to wait outside the mine shaft entrance and let Brant and the others join them after the mercenary troops freed them—although he didn't care at all for the idea of sitting in the forest waiting for spiders or wolves or bats to come along and feast on him.

"No," Dahvee said bluntly. He crossed to the lantern Sonne had dropped and picked it up. He examined it quickly to make sure it was still in working order, then lit it.

Sonne picked her knives up from the ground. "We could help you."

"A girl who's not yet grown and a halfer?" The mercenary captain shook his head. "I've got battle-hardened troops I'm leading. That kind of help I don't need."

"But we've already been inside the mountain," Sonne argued. "We could guide you."

"By your own admission, you haven't been down that other tunnel," Dahvee said.

Wick breathed a sigh of relief. He felt badly about not going after Brant and the others during the rescue attempt, but the mercenary captain was right. At least, right about him. Dahvee didn't know how deadly Sonne could be with her blades or in a fight.

Dahvee started forward, leading the mercenary group toward the mine shaft entrance.

"There is something you can't do," Sonne challenged.

Dahvee didn't respond as he held the lantern up and stepped into the main chamber.

"The dwarves wrote descriptions and names of the passageways in there," Sonne said. "You can't read, can you, Dahvee?"

There was no response.

"Wick *can* read," Sonne yelled. "He's written a book and everything."

Aaarrrggghhh! Wick slapped his hands over his face. *Is there anyone I can keep a secret from?* If he ever got back to Greydawn Moors and Grandmagister Frollo found out how much he'd accidentally let other people know—*I don't even want to think about that.*

As the mercenaries continued to enter the mine shaft's main chamber, Dahvee stuck his head back out and looked at Wick. "Is he a wizard?" the mercenary captain asked.

Sonne hesitated, then crossed her arms. "Not exactly."

"Not exactly?" Dahvee repeated.

"No," Wick answered. "I'm not a wizard."

"Good," Dahvee growled, "because I don't much care for wizards."

Wick got the distinct impression that those Dahvee didn't care for didn't fare well around the mercenary captain.

"But you can read?" Dahvee asked.

Wick hesitated, but there was no denying the directness of the mercenary captain's question. "Yes."

"Then you can come with us."

"I would probably only be in the way," Wick said, not believing that Dahvee had changed his mind.

"More than likely," Dahvee agreed. "However, if there is a chance that you can be of any use at all to Lady Tseralyn's rescue, I'm willing to risk it."

Reluctantly, Wick walked forward.

"He's not going anywhere without me," Sonne spoke up.

Dahvee hesitated a moment, then released a long breath and nodded. "Fine." He withdrew into the main chamber.

Wick stepped into the darkness again just as the volcano rumbled and shook debris over them. He covered his head as small rocks and dirt rained down over his head and shoulders. The rolling thunder echoed inside the mine shaft's main chamber and made the little librarian think about Shengharck's bellowing roar and the flame-breath that had torched the goblin chieftain. It was absolutely not, he decided, the best thing he could be thinking about while they were setting about going on a rescue mission.

24

Rescue Mission

Inside the main chamber, Dahvee made Wick demonstrate his reading skills on all three mine tunnels. The mercenary captain even traced the letters as Wick called them out, but no emotion showed on the big man's face.

When one of the men found the marker Tseralyn had left at the entrance to Tunnel Two—and Wick was amazed again at how skillful Tseralyn had been about the placement of the markers, especially without Brant noticing it—Dahvee hesitated.

"That's the blocked passageway we told you about," Wick said.

Dahvee nodded. He turned to his troops and signaled. Two men fell out at once and moved into Tunnel Three. The volcano rumbled again during the long minutes they were gone.

Wick fidgeted and rubbed his sore backside, trying to work the pain from it. Dahvee's crushing landing on him had nearly crippled him again for a short time, and it was beginning to seem to the little librarian that he couldn't remember a time when he hadn't been tired and hurting.

"What do you know about dragons?" Dahvee asked quietly.

"Dragons?" Wick echoed.

Dahvee regarded the little librarian as if he were a simpleton.

"Oh," Wick said. "I've read lots of things about dragons."

"Read? Where?"

"Uh, here and there."

Dahvee didn't say anything, but his gray eyes bored into Wick's.

"I can't tell you," Wick finally admitted.

"Then tell me about dragons."

"In the beginning," Wick began, drawing a deep breath, "dragons were thought to be related to the Old Ones, possibly even a rejected clan of the Old Ones themselves, which is how they get to be immortal and have so many powers. But others say that the Old Ones made the dragons just as they did every other race. It's just that the dragons were the first and the Old Ones infused in them many gifts. Of course, dragons being dragons, the dragons took those gifts for granted. Also, they have malicious and greedy natures that—"

Dahvee waved a hand irritably. "Not that. I don't need to know how dragons got here. They are here. You say you've seen one here, so I'll accept that they exist. What I want to know is how to kill one."

"Kill one?"

"If I have to."

"If you have to?"

Dahvee sighed. "You're not much of a conversationalist, are you?"

Coming from the tight-lipped mercenary captain, the comment was almost hilarious. Or, at least, it would have been if Wick had been in a jocular mood. Talking about killing dragons, or even facing one again, didn't lend itself very well to jocularity.

"Dragons are very hard to kill," Wick said. "Usually

there's an army involved, several days of fighting—"

Dahvee waved his arm at his men. "This is all the army we've got. Seasoned men, each and every one of them, but they're not an army. And we're not going to have several days, either."

The volcano rumbled and boomed. Everyone in the main chamber took cover automatically.

"Okay, well then," Wick said, thinking furiously. "Usually dragons are armor-plated. Their scales are as tough as any steel ever smithed on a dwarven anvil. Swords and spears and even ballistae are pretty much useless against them."

"That's a good thing," Dahvee said sarcastically, "because I'm all out of ballistae."

Wick glanced around at the anxious faces of the mercenaries standing nearby. *Why are they looking to me for answers? I read. I'm a librarian. I don't have the answer to every question out there. Usually, I only turn up more questions that I can't answer by seeking to answer even one.*

"Isn't there one story of a man, a single man," Dahvee asked, "killing a dragon?"

Wick thought. "No." *There are numerous accounts of single dragons killing lots of men, though.* "It hasn't been done. No single man in his right mind would fight a dragon."

"He might," Dahvee said, "if he had to."

"But his best choice," Wick felt he had to point out, "would be not to fight a dragon at all."

The men Dahvee had ordered into Tunnel Three returned. Dahvee looked at them. "We found one of Lady Tseralyn's markers, sir," one of the men said. "It was quite a distance away."

"What about the passageway?" Dahvee asked.

"It's been used lately."

"And the stream the halfer described?"

"We didn't see it, sir."

Dahvee quickly marshaled his troops, placing them in four-man units with two units across. "Hendrell, you have the point."

"Yes sir." The man walked briskly into Tunnel Three carrying a torch and a sword naked in his fist.

Dahvee waved at Wick to accompany him. "What about weaknesses? Surely dragons have weaknesses."

"Their underbellies," Wick said at once. "Usually the armor over their bellies is weak. That's where the new scales form. Dragons lose scales through shedding, accident, and sometimes while battling other dragons. When a new scale is ready, a dragon will pluck it from his underbelly and place it over his body. Part of the inherent magic in dragons makes the new scale seal into place."

"A good archer could get an arrow in there?" Dahvee asked, stepping into Tunnel Three.

Wick glanced around the passageway, disheartened at once by the enclosed space presented and the darkening gloom ahead that already threatened to swallow the light from the torches. "Perhaps," the little librarian admitted. "But it would take much more than one arrow to kill a dragon."

"What if the archer shot it in the heart?"

"A dragon's heart is very small for its size." Wick made a fist and showed it to the mercenary captain. "Even on the largest, and Shengharck is probably the largest, they're no bigger than this."

"It's not an impossible shot," Dahvee said.

"No," Wick answered. *But it might as well be! Who's going to face a raging dragon, breathing fire and slashing everything in sight with its fierce claws, and still have the presence of mind to hit a target that small? Before getting burned up by dragon breath?* "However, dragons know their weaknesses as well and they take pains to see that they're protected. A dragon rarely presents its underbelly in a battle."

Dahvee shined the lantern he carried down onto a small group of dweller skeletons. Most of them had crushed skulls. Rusted manacles that were no longer serviceable and a few sections of broken chain were draped over the pile of bones.

"In fact," Wick went on, "some of the older dragons don't even keep their hearts in their bodies any more."

That caught Dahvee's interest. "What do you mean?"

"Dragons can work magic," Wick said. "At least, that's what I've read."

"Like wizards?" Dahvee scowled, showing his disgust with those people.

"Not like wizards," Wick said. "A dragon's magic is very limited. They can create a few special items during their lifetimes, weapons or jewelry with special powers, and enthrall a human or even a group of humans with their gaze occasionally. They can also heal themselves. And they can place their hearts outside their bodies, making them almost impervious to harm."

"What do they do with their hearts?"

"They turn them into jewels." Wick searched back through his memory of Jorgt's *Apothecary of Dragons*. "Wizards who get their hands on a Dragonheart jewel are said to be able to control that dragon and be safe from other dragons. They're also able to make more powerful spells by tapping into the mystical energy of the Dragonheart."

"Shengharck is the Dragon King, right?"

"Perhaps," Wick said.

"Would it stand to reason that Shengharck could have transferred its heart from its body?"

"If Shengharck was really able to do that and the story of the Dragonhearts isn't just a myth."

"Where do dragons keep their hearts outside their bodies?"

"Usually with their hoard. Which is usually as well hidden as they can make it."

Dahvee nodded, deep in concentration.

Quite frankly, all the talk of dragons had sent renewed fear screaming through Wick. The little librarian peered anxiously into the dark as they continued down Tunnel Three.

Less than an hour, and many volcano rumbles later, the point man, Hendrell, returned to the mercenary group. He signaled frantically with his hands, no longer carrying his torch. Instantly, the mercenary company doused their torches and Dahvee dimmed the lantern he carried. Only a pale yellow glow flickered over the group, barely separating them from the darkness surrounding them.

"I found Lady Tseralyn," Hendrell said as he squatted down in front of the mercenary captain.

Wick's heart climbed to the back of his throat.

"Is the lady well?" Dahvee asked.

"Yes sir. She appears to be."

"What about the others?" Sonne asked.

"There are eleven other people with her," Hendrell answered. "The ones that I clearly saw fit the descriptions you gave of them."

Wick's heart leapt for joy. Although they'd only been together a short time, he'd been deeply concerned over Brant and his band of thieves. And fierce old Cobner. "Were they all well?"

"There's one dwarf they've got tied up pretty securely," Hendrell said. "Looks like he's been banged around a bit, but he's tough enough." A grin lighted the mercenary's face. "*And* men. I've never heard the kind of language he's using on those goblinkin. Every now and again, one of the goblins gives the old dwarf a good whack for bellowing at them, but I think he's beaten them into the ground with it."

"That could provide a distraction for us," Dahvee mused. "But no one should speak that way in front of Lady Tseralyn."

The mercenaries around Wick quickly lost their grins at Cobner's rebellion.

"No, sir," Hendrell agreed. "I just hated listening to it myself." He looked away.

"How many goblins are there?" the mercenary captain asked.

"Twenty-two."

"What are they doing?"

"They appear to be waiting for someone to come up the stream."

"Stream?"

"Yes, sir. The stream's there just like the little halfer said it would be."

"Where does the water come from?" Dahvee asked.

"The wall. It appears the dwarves did construct the stream. Probably as a source of fresh water and for the supply line like we were told."

"What about their guards?"

"Three of them. All of them posted at this end. None of them are especially alert. And they're posted beyond the torchlight the other goblins carry. Probably to protect their night vision. If we move quietly and quickly enough, we can take down all three before the goblinkin know we're among them."

Dahvee nodded. "Fine. This is how we're going to do that."

Wick sat with the reinforcements ten minutes later, his heart solidly lodged in the back of his throat. No matter what he did, there didn't seem to be enough air in the passageway and he couldn't swallow his heart back down to where it belonged.

The men around him smelled of sour leather. The books in Hralbomm's Wing had always described the rescue cavalry as clean-cut and fierce fighting men. Wick had imagined steely-thewed warriors with daring smiles on their faces. Instead, the rescue party the little librarian crouched with behind boulders and rocks were all average-looking in build. Most of them were already wounded from their earlier battle or battles in the Forest of Fangs and Shadows, and they hadn't bathed in days.

The most shocking thing to Wick, though, was the fact that the men didn't look heroic. They looked afraid. Fear had tightened their faces and made lines around their eyes and mouths.

Their emotions touched the little librarian in ways he hadn't imagined. He'd seen the pirates aboard *One-Eyed Peggie* face dangers as well, but they'd done it with more confidence. As he ruminated about the difference in the two groups of men, he wondered if the difference might spring from the fact that the pirates had fought from aboard the ship, which was more or less their home territory, while the mercenaries had to invade land that they'd never seen before. When he got back to Greydawn Moors, he intended to research the subject to satisfy his own curiosity and reconcile his experiences.

Tunnel Three continued down a steeper grade than Tunnel Two had. Less than a hundred feet away, wrapped in the comfortable yellow bubble of light created by the torches the goblinkin carried as well as the bonfire they'd started, the captives and their captors sat along the edge of the stream.

The water gurgled from the left side of the passageway, pouring out into the carved streambed from a halfdozen holes cut into the wall. Judging from the pressure and the amount of water cascading into the stream, Wick knew that the underground river they'd heard earlier had been tapped by the Iron Hammer Peaks dwarven clan when they'd set up their mines.

Brant, Lady Tseralyn, and the others sat in shackles and chains in the center of the large boat dock. Fourteen boats were already tied up at the iron piers jutting up from the water.

The goblinkin sat around them, eating from three pigs slowly roasting over the bonfire on spits. The pigs had been gutted but otherwise left intact. Large tusks curved out of the pigs' mouths, giving clear indication what vicious opponents they must have been. The raucous voices of the goblinkin were louder even than that of the rushing stream and water gurgling from the wall. But Cobner kept up an incessant barrage of taunts of curses that interrupted their conversations.

Even with his excellent night vision, Wick only saw Dahvee's mercenaries as flitting shadows that descended upon the three goblin sentries. All of them died—a mercenary's hand over their mouth to prevent a final scream, and a blade through their hearts—in the space of a drawn breath.

Dahvee, crouched behind a large boulder, was sixty feet nearer the goblinkin. The bonfire and torches barely limned him in the darkness for Wick to see, and the little librarian had no doubt that the goblinkin wouldn't have been able to see the mercenary captain at all. Dahvee raised his right hand and dropped it.

Immediately, arrows flew from the bows of the mercenary archers. The gurgling sound of the stream covered the humming bowstrings. The shafts took the goblinkin without warning, piercing hearts and throats almost at the same time. By the time the first shafts hit, the archers had a second arrow on the way. The archers fired a third volley, just as Dahvee had instructed, as the goblinkin came to their feet. The shafts cut down the goblin slavers that thought to run toward their prisoners.

"Charge!" Dahvee shouted, rising up from behind his boulder with his sword naked in his fist. He ran toward the goblins, followed by his men.

Wick watched in mixed horror and admiration as the two groups closed on each other with hoarse shouts and curses. Steel rang against steel and sparks sprayed from the blades. Cobner and the other dwarves roared out their approval and encouragement, partaking of the fight even while tied down.

The goblins tried to present a unified front, but their line quickly collapsed and broke. At least two of them that Wick saw threw themselves into the stream in an effort to get away.

In seconds, the bloody battle was over. Dead goblins and pieces of dead goblins lay strewn at the feet of the mercenaries.

Dahvee gave quick, succinct instructions, setting up a perimeter guard and letting the men standing rearguard around Wick know that they were supposed to hold their positions in case a retreat was necessary. He checked the goblins as he spoke, quickly locating a key to the prisoners' manacles.

Wick left the rearguard and ran forward with Sonne. The little librarian knew he wore a foolish, excited smile but he didn't mind.

Dahvee freed Lady Tseralyn, then handed the key to one of his mercenaries while he helped the elven woman to her feet.

"Thank you, Captain Dahvee," Lady Tseralyn said. "Your rescue was very well planned out, and your timing is impeccable."

"My Lady," Dahvee said, blushing uncomfortably, "I only wish we'd not lost you in the forest."

"Nonsense," the elven woman said. "You survived after we were betrayed, and you came for me when you could. That's all anyone could have asked."

"So this is what you were waiting for," Cobner roared, clapping Brant on the back. "And here I was thinking we were all bound for the Hanged Elf's Point slave pens for sure this time."

"Of course I was waiting on this," the master thief said. "I'd noticed Lady Tseralyn laying her markers since we left the Forest of Fangs and Shadows. I took a chance that she really was what she said she was and left them intact. Didn't you notice them, you old brute?"

"No." Cobner looked sour for a moment, then he reached down amid the pile of goblin bodies and brought out his battle-axe with a grin. "Ah. Much better." He turned and saw Wick then, and his grin became even bigger. "There you are, little warrior. We were all wondering what had become of you and Sonne."

"We found a way out," Sonne replied. "Two, actually."

"Where?" Brant demanded, focusing his attention on her.

"This stream is one of them," Sonne answered. "It lets out into a big cavern at the end, but there's a way out there that puts you on the other side of the mountains."

Wick reached down and helped old Lago to his feet, who thanked the little librarian profusely. The old dwarf had worn worse for the wear during his captivity as well.

"So you're still alive?" Hamual greeted Wick.

"For the moment. There's still the matter of the dragon." Wick helped Hamual push a goblin body from his sword.

"What dragon?" Brant asked.

"What dragon?" Lady Tseralyn asked.

"Shengharck," Wick responded.

"So the legends are true?" Brant asked.

"Yes." Wick quickly sketched out the meeting between the goblins and the dragon that he and Sonne had witnessed.

"You know," Cobner said, brushing blood from his eye, "if we could find that blasted wyrm's hoard I bet we could all walk away from here rich men."

"If the dragon found us," Wick pointed out, "it's more probable that we wouldn't walk away at all."

"Perhaps another time, little artist," Brant said. "Even as strapped as we are for gold, I'm going to count this as a good day if we can simply walk away from here."

Wick searched through the goblins and finally found his backpack amid the gear they had taken from Brant and the others. He opened the pack briefly and checked inside for the four books he'd found. They were still there. Despite the wetness from the stream that had soaked the outside of the pack, the oilskin he'd wrapped them in had kept them dry and protected.

"We'll take the boats downstream," Brant declared.

Lady Tseralyn joined the master thief, a small smile on her beautiful lips. "The dragon lies in that direction."

Brant nodded. "So does the other side of these infernal mountains."

"And what would you find on the other side of these mountains that you couldn't find on the west side?"

"Lady," Brant said easily, "there are far too many of Orpho Kadar's goblin troops searching for my friends and me to entertain any ideas of staying here."

"I could use a few more men," Tseralyn offered.

Brant smiled. "A tempting offer, Lady, I assure you. But I'm not a man of premeditated violence."

"You've been a mercenary before. I've felt the calluses on your hands, and I've seen the way you move and think."

"I've had my fill."

"So it's better to be a thief?" Tseralyn challenged.

Brant didn't take the bait and remained respectful. "It is for now."

"There is much that can be done against Orpho Kadar here," the elven mercenary commander stated.

"By attacking the slave caravans?" Brant shook his head. "No, I'm all for a trip to the nearest port in Blackgate Cove, then a ship bound for somewhere far from here. At least for awhile."

"Then I guess this is goodbye."

Brant swept her hand up in his and lightly kissed it as he bowed. "For now, my lady. Only for now. Had I not somehow raised the ire of Fohmyn Mhout, I might consider your generous offer of potentially dying on some goblin's blade deep in the Forest of Fangs and Shadows. And I'll even admit to a certain curiosity as to who your present employer is, as well as how someone like you came to be in these circumstances. But there are those pesky Purple Cloaks to consider that I thought would have surely—"

"Purple Cloaks! Purple Cloaks are here!"

Wick turned back toward the rearguard as Brant drew his sword in a twinkling.

"Purple Clo—" *The warning cry broke off painfully.*

Wick watched the shadows further back in the tunnel suddenly break. Mercenaries flew back toward the dock like catapult-launched missiles. A dot of orange and yellow color swiftly grew on the palm of one of the arriving Purple Cloaks' hands. The Purple Cloak threw the burning orb and it rapidly expanded into a three-foot-wide fireball as it streaked toward the group.

"Down!" Dahvee roared, taking Lady Tseralyn to ground within his arms only a half step ahead of Brant's own reaction.

Wick stood, transfixed, unable to move, watching as the fireball streaked straight at him.

Then Cobner reached up and snared the little librarian's traveling cloak and yanked him down. "You can't stand up there and take a fireball in the teeth like that," the dwarven warrior growled. "Why, you'll crisp up in no time."

Wick swallowed hard and tried to find his voice. "Thanks."

"Archers!" Dahvee roared.

The mercenary archers rose to one knee and smoothly put arrows to strings.

The Purple Cloaks charged down the tunnel, their faces grim beneath the hoods, brought out of the shadows by the light of the bonfire. One of the Purple Cloaks staggered as an arrow took him deep in the chest. The rest of the fletched missiles were deflected away by their spells. Then the archers flew backward, twisting like rag dolls.

"To the boats!" Brant ordered. "Get to the boats! We're going downstream!"

Wick glanced over his shoulder and saw the hard look on Dahvee's face. *He's not going to retreat!*

"Dahvee," Tseralyn said at the mercenary captain's side, "we're going to retreat. That's an order."

"Yes, Lady Tseralyn." Dahvee raised his voice. "Retreat! To the boats!"

"Come with me," Cobner said, yanking Wick up from the ground.

Another fireball sped by and landed in the stream. The fireball extinguished in a roaring hiss that filled the tunnel with heated white fog.

Wick didn't think that any of them would have time to board the boats before the Purple Cloaks were among them. The little librarian dropped into the near-freezing water beside Cobner and discovered that it was deep enough to come up to his chest. He tramped after Cobner, half-dragged by the big dwarven warrior.

The volcano rumbled threateningly again and debris

splashed down into the stream. Then, even as the thundering echoes died away, another din took its place.

Wick whipped his head around to look downstream, gazing in disbelief at the small army of goblinkin that raced up from the tunnel in that direction. There had to have been at least a hundred of them, all of them screaming ferociously and waving their weapons. Some of them plunged into the water after the thieves and mercenaries, but a greater number of them ran past the water to challenge the Purple Cloaks.

The little librarian looked on, totally amazed. Maybe in the confusion of sound, rumbling, and white fog from the extinguished fireball most of the goblins thought that the Purple Cloaks were the real invaders, not knowing that the slaver group had already died at the hands of the mercenaries. Whatever it was, for the moment it worked out in their favor. The Purple Cloaks were kept too busy dealing with the goblins to offer any more threat to the escaping thieves and mercenaries.

Wick grabbed the nearest boat and was about to haul himself aboard when Shengharck's angry bellow filled the tunnel. He gazed back downstream and watched, terrified, as the great dragon raced through the tunnel toward the battle.

The tunnel was only half as tall as Shengharck. The dragon had to keep its wings folded tight against its body to make it through, but it moved as quickly as a cat along the narrow confines.

"Interlopers!" Shengharck roared. "Defilers! You've managed your own deaths this day!" The mighty jaws opened and flames roiled in its throat.

"Get underwater!" Wick yelled. "Dive or you're going to be cooked!" He heard Brant, Dahvee, Cobner, and Tseralyn take up the cry as he shoved himself beneath the water. Hypnotized by the incomprehensible events, the little librarian gazed up through the freezing water so cold it made his teeth chatter.

In the next moment, flame blasted from the dragon's jaws, spewing out to fill the tunnel. The water around Wick lightened so much that he could see the streambed clearly. When the flame breath ended, it left dozens of burning goblins in its wake. The little librarian wasn't sure if they'd lost anyone themselves.

Shengharck continued running, racing past them. The tunnel shook with the thunder of the great dragon's passing. The rending talons cut through dead and dying goblins that lay in smoldering heaps along the edges of the stream.

Mind racing, Wick surfaced, pulling himself up beside the boat. He shook the water from his eyes and watched as the dragon battled the Purple Cloaks. Fohmyn Mhout's minions had enough power to stand against the dragon even after surviving the flame-breath attack. Shengharck rocked slightly from their attacks, but its great maw flashed and gobbled down a Purple Cloak whole.

"The boats!" Brant called. "Climb in and cut them loose!"

Wick scrambled over the side of the boat and hauled himself in. His backside throbbed painfully, but thankfully was partially numbed by immersion in the freezing water. He grabbed one of the short, fat paddles in the bottom of the boat and watched as some of the thieves and mercenaries cut their vessels free. *They're too slow!* the little librarian realized at once, as the boats started downstream. *Shengharck will overtake us easily!*

He glanced around quickly, looking at the holes cut into the wall that filled the stream. "Cobner!"

"What?" Cobner asked, about to chop the boat free with his axe.

"The stream's too slow. We won't reach the other end of it before Shengharck gets us."

Cobner nodded in agreement. "There's nothing we can do about that except hope for the best. Some of us will make it."

Maybe. Wick wasn't convinced. "We can do something about it."

"What?"

The dragon roared again, then belched more flames at the Purple Cloaks. Even they weren't going to stand against Shengharck's wrath for long.

"If we can break those holes bigger, more water will pour into the stream. The stream will move faster."

Cobner glanced at the funnels sluicing water into the stream. He nodded and grabbed his battle-axe, heading for the funnels.

Wick glanced back downstream, watching as more of the boats drifted away. Brant, Lago, Hamual, and Sonne yelled at them to hurry. The little librarian gazed back at the dragon still battling the Purple Cloaks. Although the Purple Cloaks didn't have a chance, they couldn't break off the fight either because Shengharck was totally focused on them. *Will that last long enough?*

Shivering from fear and the wet clothing, feeling the sodden lump of the backpack on his shoulders, Wick drew the long knife he'd found. He stared at it, then at the leather strap binding the boat to the pole thrusting up from the stream. *All I have to do to get away from here is cut the leather strap.* Then he looked at Cobner, already hoisting himself up over the stream's edge. There were no other boats left tied up. *And if I do, Cobner will be stranded here.*

Reaching his decision, terrified of how things might work out for him, Wick stepped from the boat again and landed in the water. He pulled on the boat, moving it to the side, keeping it even against the stream's current with difficulty. *I can do this. I'm a Third Level Librarian—the* most *experienced Third Level Librarian at the Vault of All Known Knowledge.* He slashed through the leather strap with his knife, holding the boat with one hand long enough to sheath the knife again. Then he started backing it toward the stream's edge where Cobner was taking his first blow at the funnel system.

Rock chips and sparks flew from Cobner's strong blade. He drew back and swung again and again and again. Fist-sized pieces of rock fell from the funnels, and the flow into the stream started to get a little stronger.

Wick discovered the increased flow also meant greater work and risk for him. The greater buoyancy he experienced had him walking on his tiptoes at times, skidding downstream inches at a time, getting further away from Cobner and almost losing the boat. *Please! Please let me be strong enough!*

Cobner's axe fell as relentlessly as an executioner's, chopping larger pieces of stone from the wall now.

Wick continued pushing through the water, occasionally shoving burned goblin corpses from his path. Then he was at the stream's edge. The coarse rock rubbed against his shoulder, chafing him. He lacked the strength to crawl back into the boat and hold it in position at the same time. Fearfully, he glanced back at the mighty dragon, watching as Shengharck managed to trap the last Purple Cloak. The huge jaws gaped, then the dragon's head shot forward. Even as he was being bitten in two, the Purple Cloak never uttered a word. Twisting its head over its shoulder, Shengharck gazed downstream.

No! Horror filled Wick with such mind-numbing intensity that he almost lost his hold on the boat tugging forcefully at his grip.

"A halfer," Shengharck roared. "What are you doing out of chains?" Suspicion narrowed the dragon's eyes. Then it shifted its attention to Cobner, still hammering at the shattering funnels. The dragon turned and started forward.

"Cobner!" Wick yelled in warning.

The big dwarven warrior took one final swing. When the axe blade connected, a two-foot section erupted from the wall. A huge stream of icy cold water shot from the wall at Shengharck's feet.

Startled, the dragon swallowed the fiery breath it had been about to disgorge, then backpedaled almost comically from the water.

The dragon can't stand the cold, Wick thought. In the next moment, the surging deluge poured over him, lifting the water level well above his head and lifting the boat up as well. The boat reached the end of his arm and kept going, dragging him up. The little librarian reached out frantically with one hand, managing to snare the stream's edge barely within his reach. He held onto the boat stubbornly, afraid at any moment he was going to lose it and whatever chance he and Cobner had of escape.

Through the water, he watched Cobner step into the water with him. The dwarf threw his battle-axe into the boat, then grabbed the boat with one hand and Wick's wrist with the other.

"Get in the boat!" Cobner ordered.

Wick had no chance at a response. Cobner lifted him bodily from the water and flung him into the boat. Stunned, Wick struggled to get to his knees, intending to help Cobner board the boat. The dwarf had both hands on the boat as it sped along the increased stream current. Wick seized one of Cobner's arms and started pulling, desperately aware that the dwarf's weight pulled the boat over so that water slopped into it.

Without warning, another tremor shivered through the mountain from the volcano. Suddenly, the wall where the water poured in from broke asunder. Cracks spread out from the funnel section Cobner had destroyed. In the next heartbeat, the water pressure from the underground river on the other side of the wall cast aside immense stone blocks and a torrent filled the tunnel.

25

The Dragon King's Hoard

The area of devastation spread from the funnels that had poured the controlled flow of river water into the dwarven-made streambed. Cracks spread across the wall from top to bottom in the tunnel. More sections broke free of the wall, raising the water level in the tunnel drastically.

Wick, hanging desperately onto Cobner's wrist, rose and fell with the boat as it floated higher and higher. "Come on, Cobner! Get in the boat!"

The dragon roared behind them. Wick looked back just as the foul creature unleashed a gout of fiery flames directly at them.

We're dead! Wick thought miserably, but he couldn't let go of Cobner.

Before the flames could reach them, the tunnel wall split even more, cracking along the stream now, still reaching from top to bottom in the passageway. Water shot out, dousing the flames less than ten feet away.

Wick felt the blast of blistering heat slam into his face even after the water quenched the flames. His knees thudded painfully against the bottom of the boat as the little vessel bobbed like a cork on the current. Half the time, Cobner's face was underwater.

"Let go of me," the big dwarf bellowed. "I can't make it into the boat."

"Yes, you can," Wick argued, tears stinging his eyes along with the acrid stench of the dragon's breath. "If you let go, Cobner, I swear I'll jump in after you."

The dwarf gawped at him.

"Now stop your bellyaching and·help me help you into this boat!" Wick pulled harder, ignoring the throbbing wound in his backside, determined not to lose the dwarf.

"Well, since you're not going to quit griping at me . . ." Cobner grabbed the boat's side with renewed vigor and managed to haul his upper body over the side.

Wick seized the dwarf's belt and rolled him into the boat, falling in beside him. They lay there for a moment, struggling to recover, gasping for breath. Without warning, the boat surged up dramatically, bringing them within inches of the ceiling. The boat's prow slammed against a stalactite, jarring them.

"Paddles," Cobner croaked hoarsely, pushing himself into a sitting position when the boat dropped back down a few feet. "If we don't control this boat, we're liable to crack up on the sides of the tunnel."

Wick nodded and pushed himself up as well. Three paddles remained within the boat. They each took one.

"Take the right side," Cobner said.

"The starboard side," Wick automatically yelled over the roaring current. He'd been too long on *One-Eyed Peggie* to let that layman's mistake go by.

Cobner ignored him, however and set himself on the port side of the boat. He paddled furiously, digging into the water with just enough force to barely let them clear the wall.

Wick paddled as well, sometimes pulling backward to realign the boat, and sometimes paddling backward to help Cobner's efforts. His arms and back and hands ached, but he stubbornly held on. *I am a Third Level Librarian. I have accepted the responsibility of protecting the world's knowledge in spite of Lord Kharrion's savagery. I will get those books that I found back to the Library.*

For the first time, Wick noticed that the volcano hadn't ceased its rumblings. In fact, the rumblings were growing louder and longer. Stalactites tore from the roof and dropped into the water, providing danger from above as well as the raging torrent they rode.

"Do you hear the volcano?" Cobner shouted above the detonations.

"Yes." Wick spluttered as a wave splashed across his face. "The dwarves had carefully set up the stream system, including the lake at the other end of this tunnel. When that balance was destroyed, there's no telling what else was affected."

Cobner shoved away a dead goblin that suddenly washed up on the boat's prow. "Do you think it's going to blow?"

"I don't know," Wick replied.

Another wave swept over them, twisting the little boat sideways for a moment.

"Duck!" Cobner growled in warning as the boat rose as well.

Wick pressed himself flat to the boat. The crossboards hammered the side of his face unmercifully as two stalactites scraped alongside the boat. *How much further is it to the end?* He had no way of knowing, and couldn't even guess how far they'd come now. But they hadn't passed any of the other boats. But then, if the boats had cracked up and sunk to the bottom with everyone aboard, he wouldn't have known if they'd passed them either.

When the water level dropped again, Wick peered over the boat's stern, searching for the dragon. However, all the torches and the bonfire had been drowned in the rising water. Only the lantern attached to the side of the boat allowed them to see anything at all, and even that was extremely limited. Had the dragon given up? Or was it going around another way? Would they find it up ahead?

"I see the exit!" Cobner crowed.

Wick looked forward, spotting the patch of light as well. Despite the fear that flooded him, he still felt a small surge of anxiety.

"You said the stream empties out into an underground lake?" Cobner asked.

"Yes," Wick replied.

"We're going to make it easily." Cobner paddled furiously for a moment, pulling them away from the tunnel's side again.

"There's one problem," Wick yelled back.

"What?"

"At the end of the tunnel, the water drops off into the lake."

Cobner's face tightened. "How far?"

"Fifty feet," Wick said. And he was surprised that he could actually talk calmly about something as horrifying as that.

"That," Cobner said unhappily, "that is something you might have mentioned before now."

"I don't think it would have helped," Wick said in his own defense.

"No, and you probably wouldn't have found it as easy to get me into this boat if I'd have known."

The boat rode the fierce current, shooting forward as fast as a bird on the wing. Wick was completely drenched, shivering spasmodically from the cold. *At least the wall seems to have stopped giving way.* But he couldn't be sure about that. It might have only been lagging behind them. Or maybe it stopped where the underground river went up or down, out of reach of the tumultuous effects wreaking havoc along the passageway.

Once they got nearer the passageway opening—now filled up more than halfway by Wick's estimation—it was light enough to see. The little librarian stared into the underground chamber ahead that held the lake, wondering anxiously what all the extra water flooding into the lake had done. Maybe the water level was high enough now that they could simply paddle over to the door. That would mean that the fifty-foot drop was probably not a fifty-foot drop anymore, wouldn't it? That thought made him feel just a bit better. He was about to tell that to Cobner when he heard the dragon's roar behind him.

In disbelief, Wick glanced behind them, thinking perhaps it was only some trick of the volcano rumbling that had thrown off his hearing. And he had a lot of water in his ears as well at the moment.

At first, the little librarian saw nothing. Then a shadow far larger than any he'd been looking for exploded forward, lunging into the light.

"Dragon!" Wick yelped.

"What?" Cobner spun around, no longer quite as worried about the coming drop-off.

Shengharck ran through the water. Maybe the huge dragon didn't like the icy water, but it wasn't afraid of it after all. With its considerable bulk, the dragon nearly filled the tunnel, and it came on inexorably, catching up with the little boat with every stride while pushing a wall of water in front of it.

"Paddle!" Cobner yelled, turning and bending to the task.

Wick swiftly joined his friend. Before, they'd both been reluctant about approaching the drop-off at the end of the passageway. Now they rowed for it like their lives depended on it. They stroked for the center of the current, trying to stay with the greatest area of speed.

Shengharck continued running behind them, pushing the water wall before it. The dragon breathed fire just as they reached the drop-off.

"Down!" Wick yelled, throwing his paddle from the boat. He felt the mass of roiling flame approaching, growing steadily hotter and hotter. Just as he was nearly convinced that the flames were going to get them, the boat shot out over the drop-off.

Senses swirling and time suddenly moving so slowly he could see everything that was happening instead of it passing him by in a blur, Wick went deaf, only able to hear the pounding of his heart above the muted thunder of the volcano and the stream.

The burst of dragon's breath missed him, Cobner, and the boat with only inches to spare, coiling out and striking the wall on the opposite side of the cavern. The feeling of free fall twisted the little librarian's stomach into sick knots even worse than *One-Eyed Peggie* riding out swells during a storm.

Wick kicked free of the boat, aware that his backpack was still securely in place. He turned his head down, looking at the lake below, knowing that Cobner was screaming in wild-eyed terror.

It wasn't a stream that fed into the underground lake anymore; it was a raging river of white foam, dead goblins, loose rock, and debris.

And it wasn't an underground lake anymore, Wick saw; it was a huge lake now only thirty feet below. At the center of the lake was a whirlpool that danced to and fro across the surface.

It's emptying the overflow, Wick realized. *There must be another cavern system below.* He already knew from the dragon's arrival in the cavern earlier that there were caves above.

Boats and swimmers littered the lake's surface, all of them safe from the pull of the whirlpool. But they'd gotten through the passageway before the water had filled it and swelled to even faster speed. And before Shengharck had decided to charge through the passageway as well, creating the tidal wave of water that shot Wick and Cobner so far out over the lake.

Gravity seized Wick again then, bringing him down in a plummet. Flailing and on the verge of total and complete panic, the little librarian glanced back up toward the cavern's roof in time to see Shengharck charge from the passageway.

The dragon resembled a long, incredibly huge arrow as it left the passageway. Between heartbeats, Shengharck unfurled the huge batlike wings and flew.

Wick hit the water and it felt like he'd slammed against a stone wall. His breath left his lungs in a rush, and for a moment his vision blacked out, leaving him stunned. When he came to again, he spotted Cobner next to him. From the loose way the dwarf floated, Wick feared Cobner was dead. Still, he paddled over to the dwarf, grabbed his traveling cloak, and swam for the surface. He had to fight against the drag of Cobner's body as well as the suction of the whirlpool.

When he surfaced, Wick held Cobner before him, keeping the dwarf's head up out of the water. With the backpack weighing him down as well, he had a hard time keeping everything afloat. After a moment, though, Cobner came to his senses and floated on his own.

"Wick!"

"Cobner!"

The voices barely carried across the growling whirlpool and the cannonade of the volcano.

The little librarian looked back at his friends, having to turn in the water as the whirlpool swept him around in increasingly tighter circles. Most of the mercenaries and thieves seemed to have gained the ledge by the mineshaft entrance leading out into the valley on the other side of the mountain. *At least they made it,* he thought.

Wick fought and kicked harder against the swirling current, but it was no use. Despite his best efforts, the whirlpool sucked him in. Before he knew it, before he had one last chance to grab a fresh breath, the whirlpool took him under.

Amazingly, enough light penetrated from above that he could see the sides of the funnel that had been carved into the rock between the lake cavern and the one below. His lungs hurt, begging for air, and he knew all he had to do was take one deep breath of the icy water and it would be all over.

But he couldn't. So much fight remained within him. A rebellious streak that he hadn't even known existed had been fanned by the incredible journey he'd been on since getting shanghaied in Greydawn Moors. He held his breath till black spots filled his vision, and then he held it some more. The whirlpool—*I am Edgewick Lamplighter*—would have to destroy him—*Third Level Librarian at the Vault of All Known Knowledge*—because he wasn't going to surrender to it.

The light threading through the swirling water changed colors, becoming a rosy pink shot through with gold. The curiosity that filled the little librarian probably saved his life, allowing him to forget about breathing for a little longer when he thought he was on the verge of being beaten.

He shot through the other end of the whirlpool unexpectedly, falling through air as well as water as he plummeted to the shallow pool below. He went underwater again for just a moment, but knowing that it was only a body of water and not the whirlpool, he kicked out and paddled to the top.

He gulped down two quick breaths, noticing immediately that the water in the pool was much warmer than the deluge continuing to pour down from the whirlpool above. Then Cobner plummeted into the water as well.

Partially recovered, Wick swam over to the dwarf, hoping his friend wasn't dead. Instead, Cobner swam to the surface as well, spitting water and coughing as he took deep draughts.

"Where are we?" Cobner gasped, treading water.

"I don't know," Wick admitted.

"Smells like a cesspool."

Eyes and nose burning from the acrid stench of sulfur, Wick silently agreed. He turned to look at the cavern, listening to the roar of water whipping down through the whirlpool from above. The Iron Hammer Peaks dwarven clan had obviously taken advantage of the natural cavern below the underwater lake area as well. The funnel the whirlpool poured through could have been natural or dwarven-made, or a cunning combination of both. However, when the stream had been created, probably along with the lake to provide a constant supply of drinkable water, the dwarven miners had used this cavern in turn.

They swam in what was normally a natural cistern made of limestone. Limestone, Wick knew from reading *Bockner's Guide to the Study of the Earth and the Guessable Heavens (Concerning Certainly Heavenly Bodies That Have Unfortunately Plummeted From the Skies for Possible Examination)*, was a natural filtration system that made tainted water potable again.

However, at the moment the cistern was swelling past its normal boundaries. Twenty feet to Wick's right, great white clouds of steam billowed up from a crack in the earth. The crack was at least thirty feet wide and ran the width of the huge chamber. The rosy glow streamed from the crack, filling the chamber with light and mixing in with the water streaming through the funnel from the whirlpool above. The rumbling trapped inside the cavern was deafening, a growling roar of angry pain.

Curious, and needing to find another way out of the cavern if there was one, Wick paddled to the cistern's edge and stood in the shallow water. Cobner followed him, cursing the water and the fetid heat that filled the chamber.

The little librarian walked to the edge of the crack in the earth and peered down. Hundreds of feet below, red and golden molten lava surged, slapping up the sides of the crevice in turmoil. Every now and again, huge bubbles rose to the top of the lava and burst, sending a spray of molten rock almost to the top of the crevice. Each spray brought a fresh wave of heat and steaming clouds.

"We're on top of the volcano," Cobner said.

"No," Wick said. "That's just one of the arteries that feeds it. Maybe even the main one."

"If the volcano blows, is it going to blow here?"

"Not that far down," Wick said, and wished he felt more confident about his answer. "We should be safe here." *Trapped, maybe, but safe.* He turned to survey the rest of the room. *There has to be another way out. The dwarves surely didn't climb down that funnel mouth even before the lake was created to work on this room. All I have to do is—*

The little librarian's thoughts froze as he spotted what lay at the top of the rise from the cistern.

Glittering gold and silver, precious gems all the colors of a rainbow, and beautiful works of art lay in heaped piles at the top of the ridge. Wick stumbled toward the huge masses of wealth like a sleepwalker. Even though he'd read about the tremendous amounts of loot dragons demanded in tribute or took from the bodies of vanquished foes, even though he'd seen sketches of dragons' hoards in books, he would have *never*—on his most imaginative day—ever thought it could be something like this.

The volcano rumbled again, and wheelbarrow loads of gems and coins slid down the heaped piles in gleaming cascades.

"By the beards of the Old Ones," Cobner whispered hoarsely. "I've never seen the like. Nor even heard tell of the like."

"Neither have I," Wick responded. Together, they walked up to what had to be Shengharck's fabled treasure. According to legend, kings had paid all that they had so kidnapped family members would be returned to them unharmed. "The wily wyrm hid his hoard beneath the lake. He makes his appearances coming from the top of the cavern, no doubt to mislead the goblinkin who visit him there. But he hides it here."

"The blasted dragon," Cobner bent down and plucked a fat ruby from the ground, managing to scrape up a few gold coins as well, "is smart enough. Why," the dwarf said, as he picked up three emeralds and stuffed those in his pockets as well, "if a man could but get out of here with a bag or two of what lies here just scattered on the ground—" He added more gold coins, a ruby, and a fat black opal. "—he'd probably have more than enough to live out his days as a wealthy man."

"It's not about wealth," Wick said in a dazed voice.

"Says you," Cobner retorted. "If Brant was down here now, he'd tell you what's more important."

Wick bent and picked up a silver vase. He ran a gentle hand along the bas-relief done in small precious gems and gold that depicted a tartbird sitting in a tree. "Think of all the history that a trained scholar could find out from these things Shengharck has here."

"You're thinking way over this old dwarf's head, little warrior," Cobner said.

Wick stopped at the foot of the tallest mound of gold coins and precious gems. It towered several feet over his head. Another volcano rumble shook the chamber, mak-

ing him realize that if the gold coins toppled, the avalanche would smash him. He still held the silver vase.
"There's a lot of history here, Cobner," the little librarian
said reverently. "Kingdoms fell while Shengharck was
out gathering his ill-gotten gain. Kingdoms and people
history may never know of except through these pieces
in this chamber."

Cobner clapped the little librarian on the shoulder
good-naturedly. "Little warrior, I swear I wouldn't have
thought you'd have a greedy bone in your body, but it
sounds to me like you'd grab up all the dragon's hoard
and tote it off yourself if you could."

"Not the coins," Wick answered truthfully. "I'd only
need a few of those. I could research who made them
and when." He glanced at the dwarf and felt embarrassed
to see Cobner smiling hugely at him. "It's important to
know. Really, it is."

"Not to me," Cobner admitted. "Me, I'd rather see
how long I could spend as much as I could carry out of
here." He cast a judicious eye on heaps of jewelry lying
in an open chest nearby. Finally, decision made, he
scooped out a double handful and worked on putting his
loot in his already overflowing belt pouch. "I've got to
get a bigger pouch. Take a look around. Maybe there's
some bags made out of silk or silverweave or mithril
that I can fill. Those bags would probably be worth a
month's worth of hard drinking. Wouldn't that be a kick
in the pants to walk in carrying a bag worth as much as
the man serving you?"

Suddenly, Wick snapped out of his daze. He carefully
placed the silver vase on the ground. "We need to see
if we can help the others. The dragon probably thinks
we're dead, but it will be stalking Brant and the others."

"How are we supposed to help them?" Cobner
growled.

Wick started to shake his head, but his eyes fell on

the gems scattered throughout the dragon's wealth. "There may be a way. Look for a gem." The little librarian walked along the outer perimeter of the heaped treasure.

"There are lots of gems," Cobner complained. "Too many to go searching for any particular one."

Wick recalled the descriptions of Dragonhearts he'd read about. All of them shared traits. "The gem will be very distinctive in design or shape. Everyone that has ever written of dragons has always said that they're too vain and proud for their own good."

"Goes along with them being so powerful and nearly unkillable," Cobner complained. "Give me a magic weapon that could cut a dragon and I'd stand there toe-to-toe, bellybutton-to-bellybutton with one of them blasted wyrms."

Wick didn't doubt the fierce dwarf at all, but surely defeating the dragon could be less risky than that. "Dragons, the old dragons at least, have a habit of taking their hearts out of their bodies so they can't be harmed. When they do, they have to turn their hearts into gems. Dragonhearts." He spotted a particularly interesting ruby with a carved owl on it, but decided even that was too ordinary for a dragon like Shengharck.

"How much would one of them sell for?" Cobner asked with renewed interest.

"I don't know," Wick admitted. "But I do know that wizards go to extreme lengths to get them."

"Don't know that I would be all that interested in finding one," Cobner said. "There's an old saying: Wizards sometimes pay in pain and death those that they can't pay in gold and gratitude. I don't know how true it is, but I've heard it all my life."

"We're not going to sell it to a wizard," Wick said.

"And why not?"

"Because we're going to use it to control the dragon."

Wick knelt and sifted through a basket of gems each as large as his fist and all incredibly beautiful.

"A wizard's spell?" Cobner asked suspiciously.

"No. I don't know any wizard's spells. But I do know that if the Dragonheart is destroyed—which isn't an easy thing to do either—then the dragon will die."

Cobner rattled through gold coins more enthusiastically. "So you're going to get the Dragonheart and threaten to break it if Shengharck doesn't leave us alone."

"Yes."

"Ah, extortion," Cobner said. "Not a favorite of mine, but I do like the simple way it works. And the fact that it works nearly every time."

Putting it that baldly made Wick feel somewhat uncomfortably ashamed, which was also ludicrous because he had no doubt the great dragon would eat them all if it got the chance. It also made the plan sound too good to be true. Was it really possible to menace a dragon with a gem that was supposed to be its heart? Or was that just a myth started by the dragons themselves as a means of finding out who would try to control them? Or possibly even to lure brave warriors to their deaths? The little librarian didn't know and he wished that he did.

The volcano rumbled and the chamber shivered again, sending a deluge of coins and gems spilling down the tall mounds. Wick surveyed the shifting treasure with heart-sinking dread. *How am I ever going to find one gem among all this—*

He froze, afraid that if he shifted perspectives at all that he would lose sight of the gem he'd just spotted. The gem—a ball of dark sapphire around a starburst of black pearl trimmed in goldweave—sat at the top of the tall mound of gold and gems and jewelry. It glowed with an incandescence that was purer than the pink and gold light spewing from the lava-filled crack that lit the room.

Breath caught in the back of his throat, Wick moved forward and started cautiously climbing the hill of gold coins. Gems and coins slid from beneath his waterlogged boots, but he made his way up the stacked treasure inch by inch. Then, just as he was about to reach out and gently take the gem, the volcano boomed again, filling the chamber with ear-splitting thunder.

The entire chamber shuddered as the ground rocked from the force of the explosions. A thick, steam fog-bank rolled into the chamber from the crack in the floor. Without warning, the treasure mounds quivered and shifted, flattening out.

Afraid that he was going to lose the gem in the collapsing treasure, Wick lunged for it. His fingers closed around the hard edges of coins and he couldn't tell if he'd gotten the gem at all until he opened his hands. There, amid a dozen gold and silver coins of different shapes and sizes, lay the curious-looking gem.

Wick plucked the coins away, dropping them at his feet like peels from a fruit. The gem felt icy cold to the touch, but threw off heat in strong, measured beats. *Like a beating heart,* he realized in wonderment. The beat was so strong, so sure in his hand that he knew nothing dwarven, elven, human, dweller, or goblinkin could ever hope to hold it. *This is it!* A wave of triumph washed over him, pushing all his uncertainty into the back of his mind. He turned to Cobner. "Cobner!"

"Yeah?"

"I've got it! I found—"

Suddenly, the funnel that drained water into the chamber from the whirlpool and the lake exploded in a silvery spray.

Wick turned to face the cistern as Shengharck spread its massive batlike wings and rose from the shallow water.

"Put that back!" the dragon commanded in a thun-

dering voice that echoed dizzyingly in the confined space of the chamber. *"Put it back now, halfer!"*

Frightened out of his wits to be staring into the dragon's fearsome eyes, Wick dropped the gem.

Shengharck launched into the air and flapped its great wings, streaking toward the little librarian.

"Move, little warrior!" Cobner bellowed. Suddenly, the dwarven warrior was there, shoving Wick out of the way with one hand while raising an ornate full shield in front of him.

The dragon struck the shield a solid blow that rang like a gong.

Cobner fell back a dozen feet and smashed up against a pile of treasure that cascaded down over him. "It held!" the dwarf howled. He thumped the shield proudly. "Did you see that, little halfer? Why now, that's a shield a fighting man would be proud to carry!"

Cobner might have deflected Shengharck's attack, but the gem had been lost in the encounter.

"He's coming around again," Cobner yelled, pushing himself to his feet.

Wick glanced at Shengharck, watching as the dragon flew expertly through the tangle of stalactites and stalagmites.

"Stupid dwarf!" the dragon roared. "I'll slash your head off this time and eat it whole before your eyes have time to go blind."

"You come ahead on, you great flying lizard," Cobner challenged, moving away from Wick. "Why, if I had a proper weapon, I'd put a few knots on that ugly skull of yours for pestering me so."

Wick couldn't believe Cobner was talking to the dragon so demeaningly. Didn't the dwarf know that the dragon could kill him without scarcely blinking an eye?

"Come on, little warrior," Cobner whispered. "I can't bait that wyrm for long before he ups and eats me like

I was a fly being eaten by a long-tongued frog. Find that gem and let's move on into the blackmail."

Frantically, Wick scattered the coins at his feet, hoping the gem would turn up.

The dragon straightened itself in flight, turning tightly back toward Cobner. Malevolent evil glinted in its eyes. Then it opened its jaws and breathed flames.

Cobner cursed and tucked himself behind the shield. For the first time, Wick saw that a layer of pearl-blue dragon scales had covered it. *No!* the little librarian thought as the flames lunged forward.

The flames struck Cobner's borrowed shield and blazed into an inferno that was almost blinding. Wick felt certain the brave dwarf was dead this time. Then the flames died away and Cobner stuck his head out. "Ha! Take that! And the shield's fireproof, too!"

It made sense, Wick realized, that Shengharck would have among his treasure weapons that could be used against dragons as well. How long had the shield laid among the hoard, taken from the hands of a hero who'd fallen in battle or traded it for the life of a loved one?

Even as the flames had died away, a flash of blue and black and gold caught Wick's eyes. He grabbed immediately, coming up with the gem again.

Shengharck lashed out with a hind talon, chasing Cobner back into hiding. This time the dread beast also struck with its tail, slapping the dwarven warrior aside as if it were an afterthought.

Lifted from the ground by the blow, Cobner flew through the air and landed nearly twenty feet away with a resounding thump. The shield spun out of his grasp, flying another twenty feet past him. The impact obviously left the dwarven warrior dazed, but he still struggled to get to his feet.

"Now," Shengharck cried, "you will pay for your impertinence, dwarf. I'll eat you in bites, only taking off

enough that you have a lot of life left in you for awhile."
The dragon flapped its huge wings and streaked toward
Cobner.

"No!" Wick shouted. He tried to ignore the fact that
his voice had cracked and broken and squeaked while
he tried to sound so commanding. "If you touch him,
I'll—" *What,* he wondered, stealing a quick look at the
gem in his fist, *exactly will I do?* He watched the dragon
swooping down on Cobner, knowing if he'd guessed
wrong he was about to see his friend eaten alive before
his very eyes.

Shengharck seemed determined not to break off the
attack. Then, at the last moment, the dragon turned aside.
Gracefully, Shengharck dropped to the top of the treasure trove in front of Wick. The dragon cocked its head
to one side. "And what, little halfer, exactly is it that
you will do?"

"I'll—I'll break this gem," Wick threatened.

Shengharck ran talons through the treasure at its feet.
"So? As you can see, I have plenty of other gems."

"Not like this one," Wick replied, his voice quavering
uncontrollably. Even his hand holding the cool, pulsing
gem shook like a leaf in a gale wind.

"Pray tell me what you think makes that one so special?"

"It's a Dragonheart," Wick said.

"Is it, now?" the dragon asked. It scratched at the
bottom of its massive jaw with a tentative foreleg. The
scratching of claws against dragon scales sounded rough
and harsh and made Wick's teeth hurt.

"Yes."

The dragon regarded Wick silently for a moment, then
flicked its wings out to emphasize its size. "You are such
a little thing, halfer. Surely hardly big enough to have a
brain. Yet you claim to know things that are well beyond
your ken."

"I know about Dragonhearts," Wick replied. "I know that dragons sometimes remove their own hearts to make themselves more invincible in battle."

"You," the dragon said with slow deliberation, "remind me of a mouse. A small, pathetic little mouse. Hardly worth the trouble at all to eat." The dragon cocked its head the other way. "But I will eat you, little mouse."

Slowly, Wick backed away from the dragon. The lava-filled crack was only forty feet away.

"Where are you going, little mouse?" Shengharck curled up his tail like a cat and stretched luxuriously. Gold coins spilled from beneath him with musical tinkling.

"Y-y-your b-b-breath," Wick stammered, "is t-t-terrible."

"Really?" Shengharck didn't appear offended in the slightest. "It's probably from eating too many dwellers. The goblinkin bring me the sick ones and the old ones that they capture in their slaving raids. And sometimes I demand a few young ones. Just because I like to annoy the goblins and because I've found young dwellers are much sweeter. Especially when they're flame-breath roasted to a crackly, scream-till-they-die crunch."

Sickened, Wick said nothing and kept backing away.

"Let's say you were right about that being a Dragonheart," Shengharck said. "How do you know it's even mine?"

"Whom else would it belong to?" Wick demanded.

"Another dragon, perhaps. You are aware that I control other dragons, aren't you?"

"Yes."

"Then what makes you so sure you have the right Dragonheart— assuming, of course, that what you're holding is a Dragonheart?"

Wick's voice betrayed him twice, coming out as a

whistling gurgle before he could speak. "B-b-because you'd h-h-have b-b-burned me up or eaten me by now if I'd been w-w-wrong." He kept backing away, almost to the edge now. He felt the heat from the lava warming him from behind.

"Would I?" The dragon did its best to appear innocent.

To Wick, the look bordered on the obscene. The little librarian stood at the edge of the crack. Cobner was slowly making his way toward the shield, trying to remain invisible to the dragon.

"You don't know me very well, little mouse," the dragon said. "I *do* like to play with my food before I eat it." It uncoiled from the pile of treasure and walked across the chamber toward Wick. "Now give me that gem before I make even your death miserable."

Wick wanted to demand why fiercely, to put the dragon on notice, but he couldn't get his throat or tongue to work. He just raised his eyebrows and looked the question at the great creature while his jaws quivered. Hopefully he looked more challenging than goofy.

"That gem is a particular favorite of mine," Shengharck said. "I detest the thought of something happening to it."

"S-something w-w-will happen to it," Wick stuttered, "if y-y-you keep coming t-t-toward m-m-me."

"W-w-what?" the dragon mocked, then burst out laughing. "Oh, little mouse, you do so amuse me." The dragon's feature hardened. "Now give me the gem!"

"No," Wick replied. "If I do, you'll kill m-m-me." *This would sound so much more convincing if I weren't stuttering.*

"I'm going to kill you anyway," Shengharck promised. "What makes you so sure you know anything about dragons at all?"

"I'm a Librarian," Wick declared proudly. "It's my job to know something about everything."

"Really?" Shengharck grinned. "A Librarian? Lord Kharrion hated your ilk. Hated books. And he got rid of them."

"Not all of them," Wick said.

"That's interesting to know. Some dragons know how to read."

Wick swallowed. *The dragon's lying! It's got to be lying!* He'd never heard anything about dragons knowing how to read.

"I take it you didn't know that, little mouse."

Wick swallowed again, suddenly aware of how close the dragon was to him. He should have never let the foul creature get that close.

"Do you trust your skills as a Librarian that much, little mouse?" Shengharck asked in a harsh voice. "Are you willing to risk your life on those skills?"

"I'm a Third Level Librarian," Wick stated. "I'm good at what I do."

"What? Not even a First or Second Librarian?" The dragon shook its head as if in disbelief.

"I am extremely well read," Wick continued, ignoring the dragon as best as he could. "I love my work."

"You're afraid," the dragon accused.

"I am easy to work with," Wick said, going over the list of positive things he'd thought up about himself all those weeks ago in Greydawn Moors when he was going to face Grandmagister Frollo and thinking that he was about to be dismissed *from* the Library. "I stayed dedicated and made it into the Library even after being passed over during the Novice Librarian selection for three years running."

"So you're a working failure," the dragon taunted.

Wick thought furiously, trying to find one more thing to feel good about. "I-I-I make beautiful Qs."

At that, the dragon laughed uproariously. "Beautiful Qs? Oh and now there's a skill that will save your life in the next moment, little mouse. Beautiful Qs, indeed." The foul creature paused. "In all this reading you've done, have you ever read about a dragon's speed?"

Wick nodded. Dragons were fast. He'd seen it for himself.

"I think," Shengharck said, "that I can bite the hand from your arm, maybe even take the whole body, before you can throw that gem into the lava. What do you think?"

Wick trembled and his stomach turned sour. *Is a dragon that fast?* He thought about everything he'd read, then wished he'd read more, and still didn't know for sure.

"I also look into your eyes," the dragon went on, "and I don't see the eyes of a predator. You've never killed even so much as a butterfly before, have you, little mouse?"

Without warning, the volcano rumbled again, so fiercely this time even Shengharck trembled and shifted.

Wick, however, thought the dragon was lunging at him.

The little librarian stepped back, forgetting how close he was to the ledge. Suddenly, there was nothing but thin air beneath his left foot and he fell. "Yaaaaahhhhh!" He dropped the gem as he clawed for the edge of the ledge. After everything he'd been through, he barely had the strength to catch himself and hold on. When he pulled his head up past the ledge, he found himself almost nose-to-nose with the dragon.

"Now," Shengharck roared, touching Wick's face with one blade-sharp talon, "where is that gem?"

Regretfully, knowing the dragon was probably going to bite his head off then and there, Wick glanced sorrowfully over his shoulder. "I-I-I d-d—" Down below, still falling toward the lava, the gem glinted blue and black with a hint of gold.

"What?" the dragon thundered.

Wick tried again. "I-d-d-"

"*WHAT*?" the dragon demanded.

"I dropped it!" Wick screamed. "I swear I didn't mean to! You scared me! It just slid right through my fingers!"

"What?"

Instinctively, Wick drew his head back down, dropping to hang by his arms. Shengharck's great maw closed over the little librarian's head, then the great dragon launched himself into the lava-filled crack, beating the batlike wings inhumanly fast as it streaked down to try and catch the gem.

Wick watched in absolute fear as the dragon got within inches of the falling gem. Shengharck snapped at the glittering jewel spinning through the air—and *missed!*

In the next moment, the gem disappeared into the red-hot lava.

"*NO!*" Shengharck's cry of despair filled the chamber. The dragon spread its wings and flapped them, rising again. Its furious and unbelieving gaze riveted upon the little librarian hanging at the end of his arms from the crack's edge. "*Do you know what you have done?*"

Wick was so scared as he watched the dragon flying toward him that he couldn't even think straight. Cobner reached down and grabbed Wick's wrists in a grip like iron. With a growl of effort, the dwarven warrior yanked the little librarian back to solid ground.

Wham! The dragon collided with the rock wall where Wick had been hanging only a moment before.

Sprawled on the ground beside Cobner, Wick watched as the dragon's forelegs slid over the crack's edge. Slowly, straining with effort, Shengharck raised his head above the crack, staring straight at the little librarian. "You've killed me."

Despite the fact that he knew the dragon would have killed him and not thought twice about it, Wick felt sorry for the creature. Dragons were meant to be hated and feared, and he had no problem with that. They were even meant to be killed. *But not by me!*

The dragon's maw was mottled with huge blisters and singed flesh. Life was leaving its eyes even as it glared at the little librarian. "I am the Dragon King," Shengharck said. "Do you know what that means?"

Slowly, cautiously, Wick got to his feet. He didn't think this could be some final ploy on the part of the dragon, but he didn't know for sure. "All the other dragons have to show you fealty."

"Yes," Shengharck agreed. "And with that position among the dragons comes special powers and privileges that no one outside Dragonkin knows about. When a Dragon King is killed, those powers pass on to another dragon. And do you know what the first duty a fledgling Dragon King must fulfill, little mouse?"

Not trusting his voice, Wick shook his head.

"Why," Shengharck said, "to track down the one who killed the last Dragon King, that's what."

Cold fear filled Wick and it must have showed on his face because Shengharck, despite the agony the dragon was evidently in, laughed in great bellowing gusts. The dragon continued laughing so hard and so cruelly that it shook itself from the perch on the crack and disappeared.

Wick ran to the edge and peered down, watching the dragon fall a little more slowly because of the outspread wings. Shengharck laughed the entire way, till the molten lava took the great dragon into its embrace and so that the foul creature would never again be seen.

"You killed him, little warrior!" Cobner shouted with glee. "See? I told you that you had the heart of a warrior! Why, if I'd had time to give you a few more lessons in fighting, I bet you'd have killed him in half the time!"

The little librarian watched the molten lava bubble. Somehow, the unexpected victory seemed hollower to him than it did to the dwarven warrior. The dragon, even for all its savage ferocity, was a part of that forgotten knowledge that Librarians sought after with so much dedication. What stories had Shengharck known of the times before the Cataclysm and Lord Kharrion? *Now*, Wick thought sadly, *they will never be known.*

Wick glanced up at Cobner, who was guiding him back toward the piles of treasure. "Do you think it's true?" the little librarian asked.

"Do I think what is true?" Cobner asked.

"The story about the Dragon King? That the new Dragon King will seek out and destroy the person who killed the last Dragon King?"

Cobner grabbed the little librarian in a fierce hug. "I don't know, little warrior, but I'll guarantee you this: Should another dragon come calling for you, why you've already got the experience of killing one dragon. That new dragon is the one that should be afraid. Not you."

Somehow, Wick didn't find that guarantee very reassuring. Shengharck's final laughter kept ringing in his ears.

"And I'll make you another guarantee," Cobner went on, lifting Wick's hands in his and scooping gold coins and gems into them till they were overflowing. "With this bit of treasure we've found, I'll bet you never have to be bored while you're waiting on your next dragon! Even better, think of all the new stories you have for that book of yours!"

The volcano rumbled again, and the effect was stronger, knocking Wick and Cobner from their feet.

"Wick! Cobner! You're alive!"

The little librarian glanced back toward the cistern. The water had finally stopped cascading through the funnel and Brant hung from a rope, one foot thrust through a loop.

Wick pushed himself up and swiftly asked about the others. All of them, it seemed, had survived the goblin attack and getting dumped into the whirlpool. They'd waited until the lake had drained after seeing the dragon fly down into it, then climbed down to see what had become of the dwarven warrior and little librarian.

The volcano kept grumbling, and each wave got worse and worse.

"It's going to blow," Brant declared, looking morosely at the pile of treasure. "Let's get what we can get now and get out of here before the mountain comes down on top of us."

Less than thirty minutes later, the thieves and the mercenaries retreated down the eastern side of the Broken Forge Mountains. Their bags and pouches and every conceivable thing they could find that could be used to transport gold and gems and jewelry were quickly filled and hauled up the rope to the lake area.

Wick carried his backpack. Although Cobner had complained, the little librarian had kept the books inside instead of replacing them with gold.

The sky was dark with thick black smoke as they worked their way down the mountain. They went as fast as they were able, considering the fatigue from everything they'd been through and all the treasure they carried. Before they reached the foothills, the Broken Forge Mountains blew in a long series of explosions that filled the sky with cinders and ash and spilled lava down the sides.

In less than two minutes, the mountain range had reformed itself, crumbling and caving in, creating rubble where once proud dwarven mines had been.

Maybe it was just time for the volcano to explode and relieve the underground pressure.

Or maybe the underground river emptying into it triggered the explosive release.

Or maybe, Wick mused as he surveyed the incredible damage that had been done, Shengharck's death and fall into the lava caused the eruption when the dragon's mystical energy was unleashed.

Cobner summed it up best after they'd all stood there in silence for a while. "Well," the dwarven warrior sighed, "I hope you all got enough treasure to last you for awhile, because we aren't going to be going back there any time too soon."

Epilogue
Home Again, Home Again

W hat are you doing there, halfer?"

Wick looked up from his new journal and saw a dwarven sailor standing before him. For the last three weeks, ever since they'd reached Imadayo's Pilings, the largest of the port cities on Blackgate Cove, he'd started coming to the little tavern down by the docks to work.

"Only passing the time," Wick replied, politely closing his book.

He'd rested for the first few days after reaching the port, but the urge in him to write—to record everything that had happened in the Broken Forge Mountains; he'd decided to use the modern name for them, at least for now—had been too strong to ignore. So he'd bought supplies from the local mercantile with a very small part of the gold he'd taken from Shengharck's Lair—which was what he was calling that chamber in his narrative—and made paper very nearly the way it was made at the Vault of All Known Knowledge.

He'd cut and trimmed the pages, fitting them proudly and tightly to the binder he'd made of plain pine slats because he didn't want thieves to mistake the book as being worth something. That last bit of advice had come from Cobner, who generally started his mornings in a

tavern somewhere telling stories that only got grander
and larger as the evening wore on.

The little librarian worked most of every day in spite
of invitations from Brant and the thieves, and even a few
tendered meal invitations from grateful mercenaries who
wanted to spend time with the famed Scourge of Dragons, as Cobner was fond of calling him in the stories he
told. Thankfully, most of the dwellers living in Imadayo's Pilings didn't believe Cobner's stories; they just
took his gold and kept his mug full.

"Aye," the dwarven sailor replied, hooking a chair
with his foot and pulling it out to sit without being in-
vited, "I can see for meself that yer a-workin' really hard
at passin' the time." He blew the froth off his ale, but
turned his head so that none of it flew toward Wick or
the new journal, then drained half the contents. "But I
was curious about them marks ye was a-makin' in that
book."

"I'm an artist," Wick said. That answer covered most
of the questions the local population asked of him. When
they offered to look at his work and pass judgment on
it, the little librarian always politely declined.

"Aye, an' I thought that's what ye might be. But it
seems like to me that ye might be more, too."

Wick waited, his heart thumping a little quicker now.
He hadn't stopped looking over his shoulder for the new
Dragon King either.

"Ye see," the pirate said, "there's a place I've heard
of, a place I've been to upon occasion, and a place my
cap'n is a-shippin' out for this evenin' where there's lots
of halfers with an unnatural predilection for . . . art. If ye
know what I mean."

Wick gazed into the sailor's eyes. He'd been coming
to the tavern and asking questions of every ship's crew
that pulled up at anchorage for all of the past three
weeks, seeking someone who might know where Grey-

dawn Moors was. Only that task was almost impossible without naming the city and the island.

"If you're a Blood-Soaked Sea pirate by trade instead of a sailor," the little librarian whispered so that only the two of them could hear, "then you'll know the name of the place."

The sailor leaned in conspiratorially and grinned. "So how did a Librarian get so far from Greydawn Moors in the first place?"

Wick smiled, feeling excited and sad all at the same time. He was going home, but that meant telling all his new friends goodbye. "That," the little librarian said, "is a very long story."

"Well, the sea's the place for them," the sailor replied.

That evening, while the sun sank over the blasted remains of Dwarven Forge Mountains, Wick stood on the docks and watched as the crew of *Kov's Heartache* finished loading the cargo the captain had taken on. He'd packed all his belongings in a new travel case he'd bought two weeks ago—in which Cobner had cleverly installed a hidden bottom where Wick could hide his share of the treasure—and told his friends that he was leaving.

All of them had decided to see him off. Cobner stood there with his arm around Wick, and the big dwarf had a smile on his face that advertised the fact that he was already heavily into his cups. Sonne and Hamual were there, as well as Baldarn, Rithlin, old Lago—who'd brought two loaves of fresh-baked bread—Kerick, Volsk, Charnir, and the twins Tyrnen and Zalnar. Even Lady Tseralyn and Captain Dahvee had come to see him off.

When the last crate had been loaded aboard the pirate ship, the quartermaster called the final boarding.

"Are you sure this is what you want to do, little artist?" the master thief asked. "You're still welcome as part of my family."

"Thank you," Wick said, "but no. I've got another family that I haven't seen in far too long." *Even while I was there,* he thought sadly. "And I've still got a job to do."

Brant nodded. "I guessed that you would feel that way, but I wanted you to know how we felt." He sighed. "If I have your secret straight, my friend, and I'm sure that I do—" Brant grinned. "—I know that you have a higher calling than being a thief. Still, you were a pretty good one."

Heart heavy and light all at the same time, Wick said his final goodbyes and hugged and shook hands as the fierce dwarves preferred. Even grumpy Baldarn shook Wick's hand and offered his best wishes for a safe trip. Despite his best intentions, Wick got misty-eyed when he told Cobner goodbye. The fierce dwarf had a lot of pain in him, and Wick could feel it.

"Should you ever get out this way again," Brant said, "know that you'll always have friends here."

"I will," Wick promised, then he turned and boarded the ship.

"Well, that's quite a tale you've told," Grandmagister Frollo said.

"Yes, Grandmagister," Wick replied contritely. The ship's voyage across the Blood-Soaked Sea had taken two months. The little librarian had enjoyed his time aboardship despite the ever-present threat of sea monsters and fierce pirates. He'd even taken the time to sketch and write about some of them. While he'd sat on the deck or in the rigging, he'd worked on his journal, putting all the pieces together in a final document that he'd presented to Grandmagister Frollo upon his arrival at Greydawn Moors.

That had been two days ago. Now they sat in the grandmagister's office—and Wick waited to see what the man had to say. After he'd disappeared so abruptly immediately following the Boneblight attack, rumors had run rampant through Greydawn Moors that Edgewick Lamplighter, Third Level Librarian at the Vault of All Known Knowledge, was dead.

Even Wick's room with Erkim had been filled. Upon his return to the Library, Wick had had to stay with the Novices until Grandmagister Frollo decided what to do with him.

"Your writing lacks polish, Librarian Lamplighter," Grandmagister Frollo said. He pushed across the journal Wick had given him to read. "Oh, in places there is a cunning phrase or two, or a description that really catches the mind's eye. And most of the dialogue rings true. However—"

Even after facing pirates and goblinkin slavers and thieves and Purple Cloaks and even a dragon that had died by Wick's own hand, the little librarian waited in breathless anxiety.

"However," Grandmagister Frollo said, "you can tell that you spend far too much time reading that drivel you find in Hralbomm's Wing."

"Yes, Grandmagister." Wick glumly guessed that whatever salvageable material was in his journal would be rewritten by more experienced Librarians. He tried not to sigh aloud.

"I'll expect much better effort from a Second Level Librarian," Grandmagister Frollo said.

Wick blinked, wondering if he'd really heard what he thought he heard. Was it a trick? No, Grandmagister Frollo really had no sense of humor. A mistake? Grandmagister Frollo wouldn't have made that kind of mistake. "*Second* Level Librarian, Grandmagister Frollo?"

Grandmagister Frollo gave Wick a curt nod and pointed a quill at the four books the little librarian had brought back with him. "I've shown those books to all the present First and Second Level Librarians. None of them know the language. Someone has to decipher it."

"I can do it, Grandmagister," Wick promised, trying to keep the excitement from his voice.

"I hope so. Your new position is only temporary, dependent upon whether or not you can decipher those books."

For a moment, Wick wondered if the grandmagister was setting him up for failure, fully expecting him to fail at the translations. He kept the doubts closed up inside him. "I can do this, grandmagister."

"We'll see." Grandmagister Frollo gestured toward the four books with his quill. "Get your work off my desk, Second Level Librarian Lamplighter. I've enough work of my own to do."

Struggling to keep the smile from his face, Wick grabbed the books, added his own journal, and backed away. "Thank you, Grandmagister Frollo. You won't regret this." Suddenly, the little librarian stepped on the hem of his robe. The robe tightened at the neck and choked him, causing him to stumble and fall heavily on his rump.

Grandmagister Frollo stared at Wick solemnly. "I certainly hope I don't regret this."

Blushing, Wick gathered himself and stood, quickly retreating from the room.

"Dragon-Killer," Grandmagister Frollo muttered to himself loud enough for Wick's keen ears to hear. "Dragon-Killer, indeed."

As Wick made his way down the steps to the nearest reference room, he spotted an envelope sticking out of one of the books. He took it out and found only WICK written across the face of it. Opening it, the little librarian read:

> *Well, have you been off to see the world, then? I trust this letter finds you hale and hearty. If not and it's left among your effects to be tossed out after your funeral, then my scrying mirror isn't what it used to be regarding foretelling the future.*
>
> *By now you'll also have the four books you found in the cemetery at Hanged Elf's Point. When you get those translated, we'll need to talk again.*
>
> *In the meantime, would you like to play chess? Grandmagister Ludaan and I used to play all the time. I think we could both learn a lot. If you'd like to play, simply drop off your letter at the Yondering Docks Customs House. They'll know how to reach me.*
>
> *Or I could amuse myself by turning people into frogs.*
>
> > *Best,*
> > *Craugh*

Wick closed the note and put it back in the book. Craugh was a wizard and had been Grandmagister Ludaan's closest friend. He didn't know why Craugh would get in touch with him or how the man had known about the four books from Hanged Elf's Point. Craugh was another mystery that he'd have to explore when he had time. For now, he wanted to have lunch with Nayghal, work on the books, then help his father with Ardamon's lanterns that evening. After that, though, he planned a trip to Hralbomm's Wing.

A Second Level Librarian, Wick mused, would probably be better off cutting back on the things he read from

Hralbomm's Wing, but he wasn't ready to completely give them up.

After all, now that he'd had adventures of his own, he might have a deeper appreciation for a tale told well!